Harmattan

Gavin Weston

MYRMIDON

Myrmidon
Rotterdam House
116 Quayside
Newcastle upon Tyne
NE1 3DY

www.myrmidonbooks.com

First published by Myrmidon 2012
This edition published 2013

A catalogue record for this book is available from the British Library.

ISBN 978-1-905802-75-3

Set in 10.5/12.5 pt Sabon by Falcon Oast Graphic Art Limited,
East Hoathly, East Sussex

Printed and bound in the UK by
CPI Group (UK) Ltd, Croydon, CR0 4YY

1 3 5 7 9 10 8 6 4 2

HARMATTAN

Harmattan *n*. A dry, dusty wind that blows from the Sahara across West Africa. (Probably from the Arabic *haram*, a forbidden or accursed thing.)

For Ramatou Hassane

Glossary

ar: Arabic   fr: French   ng: Nigerien (Djerma, Hausa, other)

A ban (ng)	Departed
Adhan (ar)	Call to prayer
Algaiita (ng)	Musical instrument (wind)
Alsilamo (ar)	Believer
Anasara (ng)	Foreigner/white person
Bani samay walla (ng)	I'm fine
Barka (ng)	Congratulations
Barkarko (ng)	Beggar
Beignets (fr)	Doughnuts
Boori arwasu (ng)	Fine fellow
Boro dungurio (ng)	Unimportant, stupid, nobody
Boule (ng)	Porridge/thin gruel
Ça marche? (fr)	Are things going well?
Camion (fr)	Desert lorry/truck
Capitaine (fr)	Type of fish
CFA (ng)	Nigerien currency (pronounced 'seefa')
Cheche (ng)	Desert head wrap/scarf
Cure Salée (fr)	Festival of the Nomads
Djembe (ng)	Drum
Djerma (ng)	Tribe name (pronounced 'Zarma')
Egerou n-igereou (ng)	'River of rivers'
Eghale (ng)	Beverage
Eid al-Adha (ar)	Festival of Sacrifice
Eid ul-Fitr (ar)	Holiday marking the end of Ramadan
Fofo! (ng)	Greetings!
Foyaney (ng)	Hello
Fulani (ng)	Tribe name

Gerewol (ng)	Annual courtship ritual among the Wodaabe Fula people
Gurumi (ng)	Musical instrument (stringed)
Harmattan (ar)	Wind that blows from the Sahara across West Africa
Hausa (ng)	Tribe name
Imzhad (ng)	Musical instrument (stringed)
Inshallah (ar)	God willing
Ira ma hoi bani (ng)	Good afternoon
Ira ma wichira bani (ng)	Good morning
Jellaba (ar/ng)	Unisex robe
Jingar ceeri (ng)	Menstruation
Kaaba (ar)	Most sacred site at Mecca
Kala a tonton (ng)	Until the next time
Kanuri (ng)	Tribe name
Langa-langa (ng)	Children's hopping game
Marabout (ar)	Spiritual leader
Marcanda (ng)	Meeting of women before marriage
Mate fu? (ng)	Are you okay?
Mate ni go? (ng)	Are things going well?
Mate ni kani? (ng)	Did you sleep well?
Mgunga (ng)	Acacia
Muadhdin (ar)	Caller to prayer
Nagana (ng)	Disease
O jo-jo (ng)	Spicy meat
Pagne (fr)	Wraparound garment
Peulh (ng)	Tribe name
Pique (ng)	Prick/inject
Piste (fr)	Track
Sahel (ng)	Semiarid region of Africa between the Sahara and the savannas
Samaria (ng)	Youth organisation/community group
Solani (ng)	Branded dairy product
Songhai (ng)	Ancient empire of West Africa
Surah (ar)	Any chapter of the Koran

Tamashek (ng)	Touareg language
Tassinack (ng)	Musical instrument (wind)
Tendi (ng)	Wooden drum
Tiddas (ng)	Board game
Toh (ng)	Okay, fine
Touareg (ng)	Tribe
Walayi! (ng)	Oath/expression of exasperation
Waykuru (ng)	Prostitute
Wiki (ng)	House
Wodaabe (ng)	Tribe name
Zaneem (ng)	Scoundrel

Prologue

Niamey
January 2000

The floor feels cool against my hands. It is how I want my face to feel. Instead, my cheeks burn and my hot tears, splattering on the ground, form tiny craters and are sucked into the dust; lost forever.

Like a giant, I crouch above the little landscape my tears have made. Cradling my throbbing left ear now, I rock backwards, forwards, backwards, forwards. I tilt my head to one side and then, cupping my ear, I swoop and sway above the tiny dunes and gorges, again and again, like a great, shiny aeroplane.

I think of the walks I used to take with Fatima and my mother – before I came to this house, this city. We would walk out into the bush, far from Wadata, and climb to the plateau where our ancestors lie. Sometimes my mother would weep. Often, on the way home, Fatima would be tired; we would take turns at carrying her on our backs. She was almost as heavy as me, but I didn't mind. My mother would fix my *pagne* and make sure that Fatima could not slip.

'You are a good girl, Haoua,' she would say, and it made me feel so proud. Beyond the plateau, the dust is swept into a rolling sea of red by the strong Sahelian winds. If you struggle to the crest of one of these great waves of sand, and look north, all that you will see is range after range of glowing red dunes, taller even than the baobab trees. The desert is very beautiful, but one day I would like to see the ocean. My father used to tell me that there was, truly, a Red Sea. I no longer believe my father.

I had been looking at my treasures when Doodi hit me. I had my back to the doorway and did not hear her come in. I had sensed that she hated me from the very first moment Moussa had introduced me to her and Yola. Yola does not hate me, I am sure, but Doodi has eyes like stagnant wells.

My beautiful pictures lie torn and crumpled around the room. Most of them are so badly damaged that it would be impossible to tell what they had depicted without first gathering together many fragments. Over near the window I can just make out the shape of the prow of a boat on a piece of shredded postcard. Nearby, the mangled remnant of a snapshot of my beloved brother, Abdelkrim, in his military uniform lies forlornly by the door: the head has been severed and is nowhere to be seen. Tiny pieces of photographic paper lie scattered over the chair, the bed, the woven mat. It had been a gift from my mother.

I place one hand cautiously on the seat of Moussa's chair and, holding my ribs with the other, I slowly straighten my back. A narrow shaft of sunlight cuts across my face and, as I pull my head back with a jolt to shield my eyes, a searing pain shoots through my body.

Yola enters. She is older than me – in her twenties I think – but much younger than Doodi. 'Doodi has sent me to clean up in here,' she says. Her eyes belie the coldness of her words and I know that she wishes she could help me. She stoops uneasily to pick up the debris and it is only then – although I have been here for some three months – that I realise she is bearing Moussa's child. As she works, she makes a small pile of the torn paper on the bed. When she has finished, she glances at me, momentarily, with something close to a smile. She scoops the fragments up, turns to leave the room, then pauses, handing me several larger pieces of the postcard and the twisted torso of my brother. I open my mouth to thank her for this small kindness, but it is so dry that no sound comes out. As I watch Yola go, it occurs to me that she too has felt the wrath of Doodi. When all is still again, I move my left knee and ease my most precious surviving picture from the earthen floor. This, together with the torn postcard pieces, the headless image of my brother and the one which I keep hidden, is all that is left of my collection. I raise the battered photograph to my mouth, to blow the dust away from the image. The faces of the two *anasara* children smiling before me somehow give me strength, and I push myself up into the seat. With my bare foot, I sift frantically through the dust in the vain hope that it might yield the face of my brother. But Yola has carried out her duty thoroughly; not a single shred of paper has been overlooked.

When I have caught my breath, I place the crumpled pictures and the fragments carefully onto my lap and begin to smooth them out. The familiar, pinkish faces are like old friends, although I have never actually seen or spoken to these children – Katie and Hope. In the photograph they are standing in some sort of compound. Locks of their strange, almost golden hair stick out from beneath their bright, knitted hats, and the ghostly vapour of their breath in the cold air frames their happy faces. One of them (Katie, I think) holds a gloved hand out towards the person who has taken the photograph. In it she holds a ball of snow! (I have seen pictures of snow before – in Monsieur Boubacar's beautiful books in my school – shrouding the mountains of places far away, cool and clean and whiter than Solani.) Behind the children lies more snow, caught in thick pockets on a tall, dense hedge and beyond that again, on top of a hill, stands a huge, grey stone building with a tower. Near the building, spindly trees are silhouetted against an almost white sky. In the top right-hand corner, a black bird flies high above it all.

The building reminds me a little of the great mosques at Niamey and Agadez, which are also in Monsieur Boubacar's books. I am not supposed to think of my school, of my teacher Monsieur Boubacar, or of my friend Miriam. Moussa has told me I must put all of that behind me now that I am a woman. When I have smoothed out the photograph of Katie and Hope as much as I can, I set to work on the postcard. It was a beautiful picture before Doodi's rage. In their letters, my *anasara* friends said that the place in this picture is called Portaferry and that it is the village nearest to their home. When I start to piece it together, I realise that more than a quarter of the image is missing now. Still, I can make out a cluster of brightly painted wooden boats on a dark blue sea. It must be quite a small sea rather than a great ocean because, beyond it, I can see the mountains of another country: blue-green mountains nestling under fat white clouds, in a sky much bluer than that in my photograph of Katie and Hope.

Monsieur Boubacar once showed me a wonderful book with a map of Ireland, where they live. It looked so tiny I could hardly believe that anyone could live there. On another page, Africa looked so big – and Niger so far from its shores – that I doubted if I would ever see the ocean. But Monsieur Boubacar said that anything was possible. He had travelled – to Benin, Burkina Faso, Ivory Coast and Liberia – so I had no reason to doubt his words.

That was before my twelfth birthday.

1

Mr N Boyd
Member No. 515820
Ballygowrie
Co. Down
N. Ireland
BT22 1AW

Haoua Boureima
Child Ref. NER2726651832
Vision Corps International
Tera Area Development Programme
C/O BP 11504
Niamey
Republic of Niger
West Africa

10th April, 1995

Dear Sponsor,
Good morning! Your sponsored daughter is very happy to be
your new child and my parents greet you a lot for this. They
are very happy. I am very happy to receive your letter and
your beautiful photograph. Thank you very much, you
and your family.

May God bless you.

We live in a village called Wadata – in a house made with
bricks. The weather is so warm in our country. I have a sister
called Fatima who is two years old, a brother called Adamou
ten years old and a grown up brother called Abdelkrim. My
father grows millet and sorghum and my mother is a house
keeper and grows okra and ground nuts.

I am schooling now, but I am in primary one. Friends make
the world go round.

Some of my friends help me to draw our country map (Niger Republic). I like so much to draw. I and my family are greeting you. It is my supervisor Richard Houeto that helps me to write this letter.

Affectionately yours,
Your child Haoua (8 years)

I first heard about Katie and Hope when Sushie, an *anasara* nurse, came to visit my parents one day. I had just turned eight and had never seen an *anasara* before. Sushie was strong and tall and elegant, with large white teeth and brown, wavy hair – not braided, but bunched together, untidily, in one gathering at the back of her head. The oddness of her pale face unsettled me at first, but soon I grew to think of her as beautiful. I was pounding millet in front of our little house when she called out to me. '*Ira ma wichira bani,*' she greeted me, in Djerma. 'Is your mother here?'

I stared at her without answering. It was not fear that kept me fixed to where I stood, but the strangeness of this creature before me.

She smiled at me, her great white teeth flashing in the sunlight, then made the hand gesture which my people do whenever they want to say, 'Well, what?' without actually saying anything: the right hand is swept, lazily, to the left, then flipped and dropped, palm outwards, under its own weight. It can be used as a question, as Sushie had done, or as an insult, in which case it is usually accompanied by air being sucked in noisily through the teeth. I dropped my pestle and went to fetch my mother.

Later, when my father came home, he and my mother went inside and talked for what seemed like a very long time while I bathed Fatima in the red plastic basin outside. I will always remember how happy my mother looked when she came back outside to tell us that our family was to join the Seed

14

Loan and Education Programme run by Vision Corps International.

'God has smiled upon us,' she said. 'In time, they may even give us a sewing machine!' Not long after that, I started to attend Wadata's school. Soon, letters and packages began to arrive from Katie and Hope together with the photographs and postcards which gave me glimpses of their lives. The first package contained gifts for my entire family – candies, brightly coloured trumpets and whistles, picture books, a little doll for Fatima, a rubber ball for my brother Adamou, and watches for my father and mother. Even my older brother Abdelkrim – who had joined the Nigerien Guard – received a gift. Some weeks later he sent a note from his barracks in Niamey, asking me to thank Katie and Hope's parents for his tiny transistor radio. I felt proud to be able to read a few of his words myself. (He had learned to read and write in the army.) I think it was then, really, that I began to understand how lucky I was to be at school, while many of my friends would continue to spend all their days pounding millet, washing clothes, fetching water from the river, herding animals, cooking, gathering firewood and tilling the dry ground.

My father immediately took his watch to the market and sold it. A few days later my mother was unable to find hers.

My most treasured of these gifts were a small, soft bear with bright orange glass eyes and the photographs and postcards which our new friends sent to us. I usually kept the bear hidden in my *pagne*, but at night time I wrapped him carefully in a piece of fabric and placed it under my bean hay mattress, along with Katie and Hope's letters and pictures. One morning, not long after I had begun going to school, I discovered that the bear was missing. I was sure that Adamou had taken it, to sell or swap for something else. I went outside into the cool morning air. My mother was cooking sorghum and beignets and preparing tea for my father.

'Adamou has taken my bear!' I said.

'You do not know that, child.' she replied. 'It is wrong to accuse others without just cause.'

'But he has taken it from me before, Mother!' I protested.

After school, my friend Miriam Kantao and I went down to the river and found Adamou and a handful of his no-good cronies, up to mischief, as usual. We all knew that we were not supposed to go there without an adult, but it was a favourite pastime for the boys of my village to taunt crocodiles with sticks and stones from the safety of the river bank.

'Give me back my bear, Adamou,' I pleaded.

'I don't have it, stupid girl!' he said, looking to his friends for confirmation.

They grinned at each other. As far as these boys were concerned, Miriam and I existed – like the crocodiles – only for the pleasure of tormenting.

'Fawako enjoyed it very much!' one of the boys called out, pointing to the river. Fawako, 'butcher', was the name we had given to the largest of the male crocodiles. There were stories of how he had devoured many people over the years, and of how two children from the neighbouring village of Goteye had gone missing and only their water pitchers had been found. But there was only one incident which we knew to be factual. It had happened the previous year when a government surveyor, while preparing a report for a pro-posed water tower and borehole for the Wadata region, had lost a leg. We also knew that crocodiles do not actually devour their prey instantly but, having drowned it, lodge the carcass underwater, on a submerged tree trunk or the like, where it can rot and be picked at according to the creature's urge.

I looked out over the lazy, fetid water and knew that I would never see my little bear again. As we turned to go back to the village, one of the boys fired a stone at us from a slingshot which he'd fashioned from a twig and an old piece of inner tube. It struck me just above my right buttock, stinging sharply.

'I will tell Father!' I promised, through my tears. My threat was greeted only with wild cackling.

The walk from the river to Wadata takes thirty minutes – twice that if carrying water. When we got back, my father and three or four of the other village elders and griots were sitting on palm-leaf mats in the shade of a woven reed canopy, playing dominoes and drinking mint tea. I was fearful that he would be angry with me for being home late, and that he would guess that Miriam and I had been to the river. I greeted him and his friends respectfully, all of whom remained engrossed in their game.

My father patted my back, barely pausing from his game to even look at me. 'Help your mother now, Haoua,' he said. 'There's a good girl.'

I decided not to mention the bear.

Mademoiselle Sushie visited our house quite often, sometimes bringing with her other *anasara* workers – doctors, photographers, teachers and interpreters. One of our visitors – Richard – had grown up in Goteye, studied in Niamey and Washington D.C. and now worked for Vision Corps International, the same organisation that had brought Sushie into my life. Richard opened up my world further still. Through him, the strange words which Katie and Hope and their father wrote to me became real, mine. Richard translated their letters from English to French, and, when necessary – which was often at first – from French to Djerma. At first I had nothing much to say to my new friends in Ireland. Monsieur Boubacar showed me how to make a thumb print, in ink, at the bottom of a little drawing, but it did not occur to me that they might actually reply: I did not think that they could really be interested in my life in

Wadata. But Katie and Hope wrote often, asking me questions about my family, my school, my village. They enquired about my father, my mother, my sister and brothers – even Abdelkrim – and I began to want to tell them more.

Mr. N. Boyd
Member No. 515820
Ballygowrie
Co. Down
N. Ireland
BT22 1AW

Haoua Boureima
Child Ref. NER2726651832
Vision Corps International
Tera Area Development Programme
C/O BP 11504
Niamey
Republic of Niger West Africa

3rd July, 1995

Dear Noel Boyd,
Thank you very much about the gifts that you sent me. Every one of us have received gifts from you. My mother got one perfume and one watch, my father one watch and all my brothers and sister they got gifts. Thank you very much, you and your family. May God bless you always and your Mrs Boyd and your daughters.

I don't have dog, but we possess goats, sheeps and hens. It is quite cold now because of the rainy season. My family is greeting you. My supervisor Monsieur Richard Houeto helped me to write this letter.

Kindly your daughter,
Haoua

Not everything that the foreigners brought to Wadata was pleasant. Before Sushie's arrival, the old folk in the village had revelled in teasing children with stories about monstrous, pale-skinned *anasaras*, and how they would come and *pique* us with their needles if we misbehaved.

Every child in Niger, whether at school or not, was

familiar with the story of Capitaine Paul Voulet, the French officer who, a century ago, had ravaged our country; destroying whole villages and ordering his troops to slaughter men, rape women and throw children down wells! Now, here was one of these monsters, flesh and bone, in our midst!

To we older children (Miriam and I were eight when Sushie first arrived) the promise of health and protection through Sushie's medicines and injections, and the fact that both our teachers and mothers actively encouraged such practices, seemed reason enough to grin through our tears and fears: Wadata had seen many infants die – of mal-nutrition, dehydration, dysentery, malaria and AIDS. Before Adamou was born, my own parents had lost two children. Both were boys, little more than babies. My mother rarely talked about them.

In one of Katie's letters she had told me that her great grandfather was still living. He was ninety-five! That in itself seemed good enough reason to take the *anasara*'s medicine. I had never known my father's parents, or my mother's father. My grandmother, however, continued to treat Sushie and her 'potions' with the deepest suspicion, right up until her death. Bunchie, as we called her, was equally wary of Monsieur Boubacar, Richard and anything to do with my school. She would shake her head and click her almost tooth-less gums. 'These ways will do you no good, Little One,' she used to tell me when my mother was not nearby.

It seemed to me to be the only subject on which my father and grandmother agreed: 'Educated girls argue with their parents more!' my father would say. Bunchie was fifty-two when she died; her skin hard and leathery and wrinkled as a dry date. She had been a widow for over three decades and had never even visited Niamey. Perhaps, looking back, she was right to warn me, but back then my greatest wish was to see more of the world, and slowly I had begun to believe that, one day, I might do so.

Little Fatima had just turned two when Sushie came into

our lives. At first, my sister became hysterical each time she set eyes on the kindly white nurse. My father and his friends took great delight in Fatima's terror. Whenever they saw Sushie or one of her colleagues approaching, they would call out, '*Attends! Attends!*' before disappearing into our compound and reappearing with Fatima, or one of the other babies from our part of Wadata. The child would then be held up, in front of Sushie's face, whereupon it inevitably began to squeal – much to the delight of my father and his cronies. Sushie would make great play at being angry with the men, swearing wildly in Djerma, much to their amusement, while at the same time trying to pacify my sister or whatever unfortunate child had been seized from its mother.

One day, when I had been attending school for nearly three years, my family received a letter from Abdelkrim. Although it was still necessary for me to carry out many chores at home, I had also worked hard at my studies and so took great pleasure in being able to read my brother's news to my mother and father, Adamou and Fatima. The letters from Ireland had also continued, and I enjoyed replying to Katie and Hope. Richard or Monsieur Boubacar were never far away if I got stuck with either reading or writing, so that the process now felt like a natural and important part of my life.

Abdelkrim wrote that he had some leave to take and that an army vehicle, en route to the military base at Tera, was going to drop him off at Wadata for a short stay. We children were overjoyed, as was my hard-working mother: she had grieved for a full year since the death of my grandmother and had not seen her eldest son for four years.

With each day, my father grew more agitated by my mother's sadness and inability to pay attention to his needs; indeed, he made no secret of his dissatisfaction, and Miriam's brother Dendi had heard talk in the village that Father planned to take another wife.

2

Katie and Hope Boyd
Member No. 515820
Ballygowrie
Co. Down
N. Ireland
BT22 1AW

Haoua Boureima
Child Ref. NER2726651832
Vision Corps International
Tera Area Development Programme
C/O BP 11504
Niamey
Republic of Niger
West Africa
21st June, 1998

Dear Katie and Hope Boyd,

I have received happily your new letter with the little gifts and photos (ten coloured pencils, two notebooks, four pencils, twenty-five balloons, two erasers, a pen, three pencil sharpeners, some candies, three photos, three postcards of your country). For these gifts thank you.

My father is working and my mother is working. Soon we will see my brother. I am fetching water. I have a friend called Miriam (also eleven years old). We like to play in groups. My father and mother wish you God's blessing. Also to your father and mother we wish you God's blessing. Peace be with you.

I am liking school very much. My teacher Monsieur Boubacar shows me where is your country. I am liking the photos and the postcards. It's my supervisor Richard Houeto who helps me with writing to you.

Lovely,
From Haoua

It was early September. The sun continued to beat down relentlessly and the air was humid and alive with mosquitoes at dusk and dawn. The rains had been good and the hard, baked ground around Wadata was covered in a thin fuzz of greenery. There was a feeling of well-being in the village but, not long before Abdelkrim returned home, a fierce and unexpected harmattan blew in from the north, whipping up the desert and coating everything in a thick blanket of red dust. Darkness enveloped Wadata. The storm lasted three days, during which time it was difficult even to venture outside. Tempers flared in our little house. Meals consisted mostly of dried dates and *boule* without sugar. On the afternoon of the first day, my father abandoned his basket-making, wrapped his *cheche* around his head and made himself scarce, leaving my mother to cope with the problem of how to keep Adamou, Fatima and me from squabbling. While the wind howled and beat our wattle fences flat and the sand worried and bombarded our walls and stripped away what little hardpan topsoil there had been to nurture our crops, she sang to us and proudly told us stories about Abdelkrim's childhood. She made plans to make a hard, goat dung floor. She told us about her visits to Niamey, of my grandmother, Bunchie, of her hopes for all of us. I missed school desperately and, when I wasn't helping Mother to prepare food or repair clothing, spent most of my time reading to Fatima and writing to Katie and Hope.

It was a great relief to everyone in Wadata when, finally, the battering ceased and a strange silence filled the air. I eagerly bundled my books together and skipped most of the way to school, across unmarked sands. I could not wait to hand my letter over to Richard. I had also made a little drawing of our chickens for Katie and Hope because Hope had written that their father also kept some animals.

Later that day, when I returned from school, I was surprised to see what appeared to be a civilian truck parked near our compound. Very few vehicles passed through

Wadata. Aid workers visited, of course, and, very occasionally, a bush taxi or a party of lost *anasaras* would turn up on the outskirts of the village. Yet any vehicle that did make it here was still an object of wonder. Even the trans-Saharan *camions* would not venture this far off-piste, so that anyone returning to Wadata, having already endured a long, arduous journey onboard one of these massive, over-laden trucks, still faced a three hour walk after drop-off.

Although we had been expecting Abdelkrim, we had not known exactly when he might arrive, and it did not occur to me that the figure sitting on the bonnet of the white Land Rover might be my brother. When I drew nearer I could see that he was dressed in army fatigues and a maroon-coloured beret. He wore expensive-looking sunglasses. A cigarette hung from his lip. Another soldier, somewhat older and scruffier, stood beside the vehicle, talking to my father, who pointed towards me as I approached.

'Aiee! It's the scholar,' my father said.

The soldier on the bonnet inhaled deeply on his cigarette, then tossed it into the dust. '*Fofo*! Look at you, Little One,' he said. 'How you've grown!' He jumped nimbly down from the vehicle and removed his sunglasses.

'Abdelkrim? *Mate fu*?' I said, uncertainly. The handsome, athletic-looking young man standing before me bore little resemblance to the gangly youth I'd last seen some four years earlier.

Abdelkrim grinned and held out his arms. '*Bani samay walla.*' When his lips parted in that cheeky, lop-sided way, I knew that this was, truly, my brother. Pressed close to him, I found his garments and military accessories alien, their scents unfamiliar, and yet somehow I felt safe in his arms. It was a feeling I had also experienced when Bunchie used to rock me, singing, 'Haoua-Haoua-Haoua, Haoua-Haoua-Hoo,' over and over again, until sleep took me. My father often teased me with my gentle grandmother's lilt but, although he was not always a cold-hearted man, I had no

23

memory of him holding me like my brother did now: Abdelkrim held me like he knew not to let go until I'd had enough. The only other person who could make me feel that way was my mother.

We went into the compound where my mother was talking excitedly to another of Abdelkrim's comrades. Fatima clung to Mother's *pagne*, clearly using her as a shield.

'Haoua,' my mother said, tapping the soldier's forearm lightly, 'this is Sergeant Bouleb.'

I nodded, a little shyly. Sergeant Bouleb was a massive man: taller even than Abdelkrim, with broad, square shoulders and piercing eyes. His cheeks were marked with small, regular scars and, when he smiled, his teeth seemed even more perfect than Sushie's. He transferred a fat cigar from his right to his left hand, before greeting me with a little wave.

'*Foyaney. Ça va*, Haoua?' His accent was not local; his voice deep, almost musical but slightly intimidating. Scarification was not something we saw often in these parts, but I guessed that he was Hausa nevertheless. I could not stop myself from staring at the gold ring on his finger; valuable, unclean, forbidden. Towering above the slight figures of my mother and sister, he looked odd here in the bush; like he did not belong here, like someone who had never before left the city perhaps – like a hippo who has strayed too far from the river.

'Abdelkrim's friends will eat with your father,' my mother said. 'Fetch some wood now, while I make some tea for the sergeant. That's a good girl.'

I could tell that she was nervous and keen to impress my brother's superior.

I had just gone a few yards when I met Adamou, coming back towards the compound with a freshly slaughtered chicken. He flapped his elbows and made a silly squawking sound in the back of his throat, then held the bird up by its legs and shook it, dripping, close to my face.

'We're having chicken!' he exclaimed. A slick of blood on the bridge of his sandaled foot was peppered with dust.

'I know,' I said, dodging past him. Meat of any kind was for special occasions only. I followed the trail of blood spots back out to the little animal enclosure my father had made, and gathered up some twigs and branches under the watchful eyes of our few scraggy sheep and goats.

I had not realised that I had missed Abdelkrim quite so much until I began to think of him leaving again. Fatima had been too young to remember our brother when he had left to join the army but, as I watched her watching him that evening, I could tell that she had already begun to feel a strong family bond towards him. Adamou, too, was clearly pleased to have Abdelkrim home. He took great delight in showing off his soccer and wrestling skills to our big brother, and to Mohammed – the soldier who had been talking to my father earlier that day.

As we served the men their supper, Sergeant Bouleb told us that he had had to 'pull some strings' in order to be able to visit Wadata; our village was something of a detour from the route to Tera. The vehicle in which the soldiers were travelling had been specially built and imported via the Togolese port of Lomé for the use of the Presidential Guard. It was to be taken to the military base for 'specialisation' and a paint job. He described his experience of sheltering in the Land Rover with two other grown men during the sand storm in such precise detail that I could almost smell their bodies and feet. His strange, clipped pronunciation of our language mesmerised me and I listened, fascinated, as he told us how, at the age of seven, his parents had sold him as a slave. He had been taken to Sierra Leone and worked in the diamond mines. Then he served as a child soldier. He eventually converted to Christianity and, many years later, returned to Niger to live with his uncle, finding happiness in the form of both the army and what he called 'a modern approach to spiritual life.' It was impossible for me to imagine such hardship.

I was about to join my mother and sister so that we too might eat, when my father called me back to his guests. 'Be sure to drink plenty of goat's milk, Haoua,' he said, hooking a ball of rice and meat from the dish. He smiled, slyly, at Sergeant Bouleb. 'We must fatten this girl up!'

We ate quickly, leaving the dishes to steep in a basin, so that we could rejoin the men without further ado. Abdelkrim amused us with his story of the soldiers' ferry crossing that morning. It seemed that they had arrived at Bac Farie around mid-morning and had had to bide their time for an hour or so before the ferry arrived back at shore. A huge, African-American woman – a C.A.R.E. worker, my brother thought – was also waiting with a small party of colleagues and another vehicle.

'She was very loud; very irritating,' Abdelkrim said. 'She kept yakking on and on – I think she had an eye for Mohammed here!'

'Aiee! It was you she was after, you fool!' Mohammed pushed Abdelkrim, playfully.

'*Walayi*! Not me, my friend. Although why any woman would pursue a Peulh farmer like you is beyond me. She'd have been better going for Bouleb here.' Abdelkrim nodded towards the sergeant, 'At least he has some money!'

Sergeant Bouleb said nothing. Instead, he shrugged and held out his huge, clean palms towards my mother, as if to say, 'And why not?'

My mother rocked forward, grinning, and slapped her thigh.

'There was an incredibly tall, thin mulatto with them,' Abdelkrim continued, 'I think he's something to do with the clinic at Goteye. He had a camera with him, and the old girl kept plaguing him to take pictures of us.'

'It was my uniform she liked!' Mohammed said.

We all laughed. Mohammed's uniform was identical to

Abdelkrim's, yet somehow it seemed to hang on him like a *jellaba*.

'Of course photographing military personnel is not legal,' Sergeant Bouleb reminded us, 'but this was no ordinary camera, my friends. . .'

'No, indeed!' Abdelkrim interrupted. He drew a small, almost square picture from his jerkin pocket. 'Look, Mother,' he said, handing it to her.

'I told the American woman and her friend that I would turn a blind eye,' the sergeant continued, 'on the understanding that she gave each of us one of these instant photographs.'

Mohammed and Bouleb passed their own images around our gathering also. All of the pictures were quite similar: the three soldiers were on the ferry, standing proudly and sternly beside their Land Rover.

'She kept telling us to smile,' Abdelkrim said.

When my father had looked, briefly, at Abdelkrim's photograph, he handed it back to my brother, without a word.

Abdelkrim passed it to Mother again. 'It's for you,' he said.

'*Toh*,' my mother said, nodding. 'Thank you.'

Then Mohammed intrigued us with his account of sharing an evening with a group of nomads – *Wodaabe*, who were slowly making their way to Ingal, near Agadez, for their *Gerewol* at the festival of *Cure Salée* – a celebration of the fattening of the cattle after the summer migration. Their Fulani traditions, beliefs and rituals are so very different to ours and Mohammed's descriptions of their elegance, finery and wide-eyed dancing were so vivid that, when sleep took me later that night, I dreamed of a vibrant city, alive with laughter, music and colour, and awoke the next morning feeling as if, somehow, I had really been there.

As we sat around our dying cooking fire that evening, listening to the soldiers' stories and jokes, it became clear to all of us that Abdelkrim was as popular away from home as he always had been here in Wadata. The sky was clear, the moon a mere sliver, so that the stars glittered like the gemstones I'd seen in Mademoiselle Sushie's magazines. Fireflies danced around thin plumes of smoke rising lazily from the fading embers and broken-hearted cicadas sang like an invisible Samaria troop. I looked around the compound at my family and friends and suddenly everything seemed close to perfect. I felt safe and warm and thankful. Mother is right, I thought: God has smiled upon us.

At last, Sergeant Bouleb and Mohammed thanked my father for his hospitality. They would not, they said, join us to watch television but would instead retire early to their Land Rover, as they needed to be underway before first light. They wished us goodnight and, taking a plastic kettle filled with water for their ablutions, disappeared into the darkness to pray.

Abdelkrim remained seated and took a packet of cigarettes from his shirt pocket.

'Aren't you going to pray with your comrades?' my father enquired.

Abdelkrim lit a cigarette and shook his head. 'You go, Father,' he said, through a cloud of blue smoke.

My father sucked his teeth, then followed our guests. Through the darkness, I could hear him spitting. When he had gone, Abdelkrim rummaged through his kitbag and presented all of us with gifts: candies and delicious guavas for we three children; a beautiful Agadez Cross on a black leather string for my mother; and a yellow, nylon toothbrush for my father. Abdelkrim handed the cardboard package to Mother. 'It's from the French *supermarché* in Niamey – very expensive!' he explained.

'Don't you want to give it to him yourself, Abdel?' my mother asked.

'You give it to him, Mother,' he said, sternly, pressing a roll of CFA into her other hand. 'Now hide this well.' He had been sending money home whenever he could, but I had overheard my mother telling one of our neighbours that my father often gambled it away.

My mother gently touched his face. 'My Abdel,' she said, softly.

In the flickering light, I realised that she looked tired, frail even.

'Hush now,' my brother said, lifting his bag as he stood up. He paused then, looking sadly at Mother. 'I'm sorry I wasn't here when Bunchie died. . .'

My mother nodded silently. It was no secret that Abdelkrim had been our grandmother's favourite and that he had been equally fond of her.

After we had finished clearing up, we walked across the village to Monsieur Letouye's house, where a fairly large and excited group of villagers had already gathered outside. Monsieur Letouye was not, he often reminded us, a rich man, but his brother – who had made a pilgrimage to Mecca and was, therefore, an *El Hadj* – traded in minerals and lived in a large, concrete house in the French quarter of Niamey. Monsieur Letouye's brother was keen that both his family and the people he had grown up with would know just how well he was doing, and so he had set Monsieur Letouye up in business with Wadata's only 'shop'. In truth the shop was little more than a market stall, but Monsieur Letouye's brother had supplied enough building blocks, tin and timber to enable Monsieur Letouye to construct a small but sturdy lean-to, and so ensure that his few products would be protected from the sun by day and from pilferers at night. Many of the villagers whispered that it was sinful to see such things better housed than they themselves were, but none would complain to Monsieur Letouye's face; to do so would have risked the privileges that we enjoyed.

The shop sold kola nuts, peri-peri, peanut butter, Solani, ginger water, kerosene, thread and other bits and pieces. Occasionally Monsieur Letouye also acquired coffee, teabags, candies, first-aid kits and the like, but there was an understanding among the villagers that one did not enquire as to how he had done so. Above the hatch, which Monsieur Letouye opened faithfully every morning (except Fridays) at ten o'clock, a Coca-Cola sign had been nailed, upside down. Monsieur Letouye did not actually sell Coca-Cola – few of the villagers had ever actually tasted such a product – but he knew what the sign meant and, until I had learned to read, I too had considered it a very handsome thing.

It was in the hope of watching television that the growing crowd had gathered. This was a treat that Monsieur Letouye permitted on special occasions. If, however, he was in a bad mood, or it was widely known that he had not done much business at his shop for some time, we knew not to expect so much as a glimpse of either Monsieur Letouye or his television set. Occasionally he would try to charge for the privilege, and there would be great arguments between the adults before the set would be turned on.

Everyone in Wadata knew that Abdelkrim had returned home and everyone who saw him greeted him warmly (even Monsieur Letouye), so it was naturally presumed that this evening was a special occasion.

My brother helped Monsieur Letouye carry the large black television from his house to the centre of his compound, where they placed it on a table in the hope that everyone could at least get a glimpse of the screen from time to time. Two of Monsieur Letouye's neighbours followed them outside with a heavy car battery to which the cables of the television set were attached with metal clips.

In all there must have been sixty or so of us present that evening, representing some ten different families. Some people had brought their own plastic chairs. Others sat on crates or logs, while we children mostly squatted on palm-leaf mats nearer to the set. Even Sushie and Richard stopped by Monsieur Letouye's compound to introduce themselves to my famous brother. Miriam and I became quite giddy when Abdelkrim came and joined us on our mat, but when the

Kung Fu movie started we settled down and watched in silence – even though the picture rolled and the sound crackled and hissed like a snake.

The movie was followed by a weather report and news broadcast. The presenter – wearing thick, black glasses and a grey suit and tie, and seated in front of a swirling, flowery backdrop highlighting his ochre-coloured shirt – announced that there had been some unrest in the south-eastern town of Diffa. By now, though, most of us children were so tired and fidgety and the din of squabbling infants was so loud that little attention was paid to either the dandy or his story.

It was time to go home. As we filtered out of Monsieur Letouye's compound, each of us thanking him and wishing him God's blessing, our national anthem boomed out majestically from the television's speaker, while the images of President Bare Mainassara and the Nigerien flag flickered in the darkness behind us. We headed home, tired but happy, Adamou and his friends high kicking, whooping and karate-chopping their way across the village in the cool night air. I linked arms with my mother and my best friend Miriam while Abdelkrim carried Fatima, who was already asleep. A few metres from our compound, my father, who had been following behind, bid us goodnight and turned off in the direction of my school.

'Where are you going, Salim?' my mother called after him. 'It is so late!'

'I have business with the elders,' he said, disappearing into the night.

'Where do you *think* he goes, Mother?' Abdelkrim said under his breath as we approached the house.

My mother sucked her teeth and went inside.

3

Haoua Boureima   Hope Boyd
Child Ref. NER2726651832   Member No. 515820
Vision Corps International   Ballygowrie
Tera Area Development Programme   Co. Down
C/O BP 11504   N. Ireland
Niamey   BT22 1AW
Republic of Niger
West Africa

3rd August, 1998

Dear Haoua,
Thank you for your last letter and the drawing of your chickens!
We love hearing from you so much!
  We are feeling very sad today because our pet guinea pig
(Miles) died a few days ago. (We told you about Miles before, I
think.) Katie and I decided to have a little funeral ceremony for
him, and on Saturday, after swimmers, we invited our friends
Roisin and Anna and our cousin Charlotte over to our house. We
had found a little box in my dad's workshop and used it as a
coffin. Katie put it in our freezer in the garage, but I took it out
again because I knew if my mum found it she'd go mad! We
buried the coffin in our back garden, down near the duck pond. It
was very sad. We had had him for almost three years. Roisin
(whose uncle is a priest) said a prayer for Miles. I couldn't stop
crying for ages.
  Some good news: we are going to visit our friends in Dublin

for Christmas. There are lots of shops there and really cool things to do. We can't wait!

Katie is at the dentist now but she sends her love and will write again soon.

I hope you are all well there.

Lots of love,

Hope
XXX

I could not get Abdelkrim's story of the 'magic' camera out of my mind the next morning. My Irish friends had continued to send photographs of themselves, their family, their home, their animals, and I was keen for them to hear – and see – that I too was growing, learning and proud of my family, friends and country.

When we had first encountered Sushie, she and her Vision Corps International people had given me a number and photographed me for their files and records, but I did not like this photograph; it showed me wearing a grubby, striped blouse and looking confused and sad. I did not feel sad then.

When I had finished my millet gruel and cleared up our dishes, I discussed my plan with Mother before putting on my best *pagne* and setting off happily for school.

'Remember, child; your father will not be happy if you are very late,' Mother called after me. 'And stay away from the river!' she added.

'Don't worry, Mother,' I called back. 'I will be fine. Be sure to tell Madame Kantao that Miriam is with me.'

She shook her head in an exaggerated and exasperated manner, and went back into the house. Somehow, it struck me that it was not just concern for me that she was expressing, but a genuine desire for my father to be as happy as possible – even though he now seemed incapable of recognising this fact and seldom seemed to care.

At first, Miriam was not keen on my idea because she was not wearing her best clothes – although I thought she looked fine.

'If you had suggested this last night, I would have known, Haoua!' she complained.

'Please, Miriam,' I said. 'My mother has forbidden me to go alone. Besides, you will be able to send a picture to your sponsor too.'

She seemed unconvinced. 'I haven't heard from my sponsor in over a year!'

'But perhaps a photograph will encourage him to write more often.'

'And perhaps he's just a lazy oaf – like so many men,' she said.

'Well, you can give it to your mother then.'

She tutted. 'My mother won't even know where I am!'

'I've asked Azara to tell her,' I said. 'Come on. You look very pretty.'

She was wearing a dark blue *pagne*, with a repeating pattern of azure flowers. Although it had been repaired in several places, it was quite pretty, but I had to agree that it was not her best. Mine, however, was a deep orange and cinnamon, with a wonderfully drawn aeroplane design, repeated in rust red. With the money that Abdelkrim had been sending home, my mother had ordered a bolt of the cloth from Monsieur Letouye when I had first started school. Richard had told me that the name of the aeroplane was Concorde, and that such a machine carried rich westerners from one side of the world to the other in minutes. I was sure that he was teasing me, but still I loved this design. I had covered my head with a matching piece of fabric, and around my neck I wore a string of blue and yellow and white beads which I had made at school with the help of Monsieur Boubacar.

That afternoon, as soon as class ended, we set off from Wadata at a brisk pace. The sun was still high in the sky and the sands still soft underfoot, but we marched on with determination, knowing that the sixteen kilometre journey to Goteye would take us quite some time. Halfway there, we came to a great bend in the river, where we stopped for a short rest and Miriam helped me to dig a thorn out of the sole of my foot. We drank a little of the water which we carried in small gourds strung around our waists, chatted for a while – about school, the previous evening's movie, Abdelkrim, my father's rumoured desire to take a second wife – and then resumed our journey.

The remainder of our route ran close to the river and I enjoyed being near the hulking, listless water with its less familiar sounds and smells. I was mindful of my mother's warning, but equally aware that, as a child, she too had experienced its allure. In spite of its stagnant shallows, dried up wadi tributaries and shores littered with man-made debris of every kind, it still filled me with awe.

The Touaregs gave the River Niger its name: *Egerou n-igereou* – they called it: river of rivers. For centuries their camel trains have carried heavy tablets of salt across the Sahara, through the Ténéré Desert and the Sahel, until finally they reach the mighty river – the third largest in all of Africa, Monsieur Boubacar had told us. The tribes of my country – Djerma, Hausa, Kanuri, Touareg and Fulani – had shared its wonders since the beginning of time, when, it was said, giant crocodiles, ten times as large as Fawako, had hunted in its waters and even pursued fishermen overland, through the thick forests which once covered the Sahel. It was said that there were bones of such creatures preserved in a museum in Niamey.

Happily, there was no sign of such a monster – or indeed Fawako – but, just about two kilometres from Goteye, we came across a group of vultures, furiously picking at a carcass of some kind. Miriam and I armed ourselves with sticks and threw stones at the birds to frighten them away. With a chorus of indignant screeches from their gory beaks, they scattered reluctantly, their sinister silhouettes hovering above us all the while we investigated. When we drew closer we realised that their find was a baby giraffe, although there was very little of it left to inform us of the fact. Why we wanted to gape, I do not know; we already knew what death looked like. It was not a pleasant sight, of course: several torn remnants of the animal's once beautiful hide hung, like bloody rags, from its ribcage. I wondered what had happened here: where the creature's mother had gone. Giraffes are a rare sight in the Sahel.

Half a kilometre away from the village, we encountered two fishermen who were preparing their lift nets for the evening's trawl. Their pirogue had ploughed a deep furrow in the mud as it had been dragged out of the water, and all around it the shore was strewn with buckets, bits of timber, lengths of twine, plastic sacks and strange-looking tools.

'Ira ma hoi bani! Mate fu?' one of them greeted us. 'Where are you off to, little sisters?' He was an elderly man – fifty, at least – with a kindly face and a thick, white beard.

We addressed the fisherman and his younger colleague respectfully, and enquired if they knew where we might find the mulatto or the American woman who had photographed my brother and his colleagues on the ferry the previous day.

They laughed, heartily. 'Ah! You mean Monsieur Longueur,' the younger man said – fondly, I thought.

'Monsieur Longueur?' Miriam repeated.

'Go to the *dispensaire*,' the older man said, with a smile that revealed his missing front teeth. 'There you'll see the tallest fellow in the world!'

'Ask for Ken,' the younger fisherman added. 'He's staying in the little house right beside the *dispensaire*.'

They returned to their work and we thanked them for their help and went on our way, continuing without stopping again until we came to the village.

It had been quite some time since I had visited Goteye; the last time had been with Abdelkrim when he had been visiting a friend who had also later joined the Nigerien Guard. It was much larger, wealthier and closer to the river than Wadata, and although, at times, there was some rivalry between the residents of the two villages, usually concerning rights of pasture and competition for firewood, this was good-natured, for the most part.

A wide, open space – known locally as the quadrangle – formed the centre of Goteye, and at one end of this area stood the village's own school, comprising not just one small, open-sided reed structure like the one at Wadata, but four sizeable mud-brick buildings, each with a tin roof. Hordes of rowdy boys were playing soccer in front of the school and eventually, after a great deal of taunting and name-calling from them, we received directions to the *dispensaire*. As we approached the building, I began to question my resolve to have the mulatto photograph Miriam and me for Katie and Hope. Miriam was clearly faltering too, but we goaded each other on nervously. We had come too far to give up now.

A girl no older than Fatima stopped pounding millet to stare at us as we passed; on her back a tiny baby slept soundly, despite the violent, jerking movement of the girl's work.

A smaller group of boys – each leading a thin, scruffy dog by a filthy scrap of twine – whistled at us, one of them calling out, 'Wadata witches!' I did my best to ignore the boys, but the dogs intrigued me. In Wadata there were very few dogs. Most of our older folk considered them vermin and, in an effort to despatch as many of them as possible, poisoned meat was regularly left out in our village. My parents discouraged any contact with such animals, but I had started to think of them somewhat differently ever since a little troop of strays had befriended Adamou and his mob. Furthermore, Katie and Hope had sent me a photograph of their own dogs. These animals were not scruffy nor were they thin. They had squat little bodies and long droopy ears and, with their large, round eyes set in baby-like faces, they were unlike any dog I had ever seen before.

Like its school, Goteye's *dispensaire* was considerably grander than Wadata's. Sushie had a small consultation room, but all of her treatments were administered from behind a rattan screen in her modest compound. It was a proper, covered veranda, serving not only to provide shelter from the sun, but as a waiting area for patients. Two screened windows looked out onto the veranda and beneath them were narrow window-boxes filled with sweet-smelling, unfamiliar yellow blooms. On either side of the entrance, a row of tatty, wooden chairs were occupied by women and girls of various ages.

'*Foyaney. Mate fu?* You're a long way from home, girlies,' one of the older women said as we climbed the concrete steps to the veranda. 'What brings you here? Have you fallen pregnant?'

'*Bani samay walla.* No, Mother,' I answered, respectfully but a little embarrassed too. 'We are looking for Monsieur Ken.'

'Monsieur Longueur!' a girl about my age exclaimed.

All of the women laughed, even though several of them looked so frail that the effort might cause them harm.

'Oui, Monsieur Longueur,' Miriam said.

'*Toh.* And what do you want with Monsieur Longueur, Missies?' the older woman asked.

'We heard that he had a magic camera – one that can make pictures instantly!' I said.

'He has a camera alright,' said another woman, scowling. 'It's never out of our faces. But magic? I don't know about. . .'

'Black magic, more like', the first woman interrupted. 'He's forever stealing souls with that damn thing!'

I guessed, from the look on her face, that she did not really believe these words.

'*Walayi!* I heard it's not the American's *camera* that's magic!' someone else chipped in.

A great deal of thigh slapping and sniggering followed.

'You'll find him round the back,' said the woman who had scowled, now with a mischievous look in her eye. She gestured with her thumb. 'He's staying with the Peace Corps nurse. . .'

A chorus of laughter erupted across the veranda as she continued to pump her thumb up and down suggestively.

We found Monsieur Longueur sitting at a plastic table in the compound behind the *dispensaire*. He was writing in a notebook and did not see or hear us approach. I immediately spied the camera, lying on its back, next to a half empty bottle of Bière Niger. We stood beside his table for what seemed like a very long time before he looked up, and when he finally did so he was clearly startled by our presence.

I had never before seen anyone who looked quite like this man. I had seen mulatto people before, of course, but this man's features were very fine, his skin almost gold in colour – lighter even than that of the Touaregs of the far north, who occasionally passed through Wadata. His hands were large, but elegant like a woman's, his fingernails scrupulously clean. He wore fine, metal-rimmed spectacles and a beautifully stitched khaki shirt with matching trousers. His shoes – jutting out from beneath the table, at the end of incredibly long legs – were also well made. Despite the fact that he was seated, it was obvious that he was, indeed, a very tall man.

When he had composed himself, he set down his pen, gave a little wave, then smiled, warmly, through a tightly cropped black beard. 'Hi,' he said.

We greeted him in Djerma but realised, almost immediately, that he was not at all familiar with our language. He shrugged – his kind, clear eyes indicating that he was willing to try to communicate with us. I tried Hausa, but the result was the same. When he spoke again, in English, I recognised occasional words from our sessions in front of Monsieur Letouye's television. Miriam then pointed at Monsieur Longueur's camera, but the response was not what we had expected.

'*Ne pazz doo cadeaux*,' he said, abandoning his mother tongue.

His French was not good, but I suddenly realised what he had presumed and felt disappointed and a little insulted that he should think of us as *barkarko*. Beggars indeed! I shook my head, vigorously, and mimed the action of looking through a camera, while Miriam pointed again.

'Do you think he only speaks one language?' I said.

Monsieur Longueur – Ken – mumbled and reached for the camera, then held it towards us, questioningly. Still his words meant nothing to us, but we knew, nevertheless, that they formed a question.

I tried again. 'We want a picture,' I said. 'A *magic* picture – like the one you took of my brother.' I racked my brain to remember some simple, English word that the stranger might usefully recognise. It was no good. '*La photo*,' I said, giving up on English, as Miriam once more pointed at the camera and then at herself.

Monsieur Longueur pushed his seat back and stood up. I had to stop myself from gasping out loud. Truly, he was the tallest man I had ever seen: taller than Abdelkrim, taller than Sergeant Bouleb, taller than any Touareg. He set the camera down and, nodding furiously, indicated that we should stand facing the cooling sun.

When he was satisfied with our positions, he picked up the camera and proceeded to fiddle with its various buttons and dials, before lifting it to his right eye and pointing it at us. There was a smart click, followed quickly by another. I looked at Miriam and giggled foolishly. To our surprise, Monsieur Longueur then placed the camera on the table again and sat back down in his chair.

We remained, uneasily, in our positions, wondering what might happen next. Monsieur Longueur rested his chin in one hand and looked at us, quizzically, then seemed to realise that we did not yet consider our business there concluded. He raised his eyebrows and shrugged.

Once more Miriam and I both gestured towards the camera. '*La photo*,' I repeated.

Monsieur Longueur gabbled something incomprehensible. Then – in a frustrated flurry of Djerma, French and English – we all gabbled together. I wished that Richard was there with us.

When at last the frenzy ceased, we heard a loud clatter of pots and pans from within the little *wiki* at the far end of the compound. Monsieur Longueur stood up and beckoned us to follow him towards the open door.

Inside the house, an ancient, gnarled old woman was preparing food on a gas stove. The room was small with a very low ceiling, but enough light seeped in from the doorway and a long, narrow window to the left to reveal a display of locally carved masks. On the opposite wall, a beautiful and complex tapestry hung above the rickety table at which the old woman toiled. Mosque-like motifs and diamond patterns, in the colours of my country's flag, had been worked onto a backdrop of thin orange cloth with painstaking care. Someone had obviously paid a great deal of money for this item. A sweet, unfamiliar scent lingered in the room, despite the heavier smells of cooking. Clearly, this was the home of the Peace Corps nurse.

Smiling, Monsieur Longueur spoke to the woman, falteringly, his head cocked to one side to accommodate the ceiling. 'Azara. . .', I heard – the same name as my mother. '. . .*les photos. . . cadeaux. . . comprendre*. . .' Everything else evaded me.

It was evident that Madame Azara, too, was struggling with Monsieur Longueur's use of French. Her reply was terse, slightly agitated, but I guessed that she was quite used to such clumsy exchanges.

At last she turned to us and addressed us in our own tongue. 'Wadata girls, eh?'

We nodded. 'Yes, Mother.'

'He took your pictures – our Monsieur Longueur, no?'

'Yes, Mother.'

'And what else do you want from him exactly? He's very busy, and so am I!' she said, not unkindly.

'Well,' I said, 'we were just hoping that he would give us the photographs now. Yesterday he photographed my brother and then gave him the picture straight away.'

'*Toh.*' She faced Monsieur Longueur again and explained what I had told her.

Monsieur Longueur put his hands up and, looking at us apologetically, shook his head. '*C'est different! C'est different!*' he said. The 'magic camera' belonged to Madame Garrison, the large African-American woman who had been on the ferry with Monsieur Longueur, Madame Azara told us. Both of them worked for an aid agency called Africare, which had its central office in Niamey. Madame Garrison had, it seemed, been delivering Monsieur Longueur to Goteye, to enable him to make a report on the needs of the village, but she had set off for the city again, earlier that day, taking her camera with her.

'A good, kind-hearted lady,' Madame Azara said, as if addressing herself, which was just as well, for by now I was only half listening. 'She took my daughter with her in her truck. My poor daughter is pregnant. She will visit the hospital, buy some goods and see her husband who is working in Niamey. They have not seen each other for six months! I pray to God that Madame Garrison will find some work there for my daughter too.' She motioned for us to wait and hobbled through another doorway. When she reappeared, she was proudly clutching a small, rectangular object in her leathery hand. 'Look,' she said, handing it to Miriam. 'I had my picture taken too!'

None of this helped Miriam or me, of course. Secretly, I was a little angry with all of these people, even though I knew that such feelings were not really fair. Monsieur Longueur assured us that he would send copies of our photographs when he had had them printed, but I was sceptical.

As we were making our farewells, Goteye's Peace Corps nurse appeared, introducing herself as Maggie. Like Sushie, she was pale-skinned and spoke perfect Djerma. Unlike Sushie, she was not tall and elegant; rather, she was short and breathless, with the kind of plump, round body that men like my father wished for their daughters. Her hair was yellow and thin, but she had a pretty face and deep, warm eyes.

'You must eat with us before you return to Wadata,' Maggie said.

The smell of Madame Azara's cooking wafted around us; I guessed they were having couscous and mouton, probably with chillies and peppers. Miriam looked hard at me, her eyes imploring. I knew what she was thinking.

'We should probably get going,' I said, ignoring both Miriam and the voice in my stomach. 'It's getting late.'

'It's a long way,' said Maggie. 'Eat with us and then I'll drive you back.'

It was tempting, but I felt uncomfortable, not to mention disappointed.

Suddenly I just wanted to get away from that place. 'Thank you,' I said, awkwardly, 'but no.'

Maggie shrugged. '*Toh. Kala a tonton.* Tell Sushie I said hi.'

The gangs we had seen earlier had now joined forces and were playing a rough game of *langa-langa*, each boy hopping on one leg while holding the ankle of the other. One of the dogs had pinned a weaker animal down and was tearing at its throat, while the others ran excitedly through their owners' legs, their leashes trailing behind them. As we passed the quadrangle, the barrage of abuse began all over again.

'Did you get your syphilis treated, girlies?' one of the boys called out.

We did our best to ignore such filthy remarks, but inside I was seething. I considered showing them just how furious

I felt: the gesture I had in mind was recognisable anywhere in the world – we had seen it used often on Monsieur Letouye's television – but instead we kept our dignity and did not so much as look at them.

A little further on, we met a group of women and girls returning from the river. They had been drawing water and each of them carried a large gourd or a plastic bucket on her head. In addition, some carried extra containers in their hands also. It was a chore which Miriam and I had to carry out many times each week in Wadata. We all prayed that the scheme for a water tower for Wadata would be approved. I was envious of these Goteye women and the short distance they had to travel from the river. I was envious of their smart *dispensaire*, their big school, their window-boxes, their quadrangle, their houses, their food, their Monsieur Longueur. I was also reminded that to make this journey we had shirked our own chores and that we might well have to answer to our fathers for doing so.

'I'm hungry!' Miriam said, as we left the village behind us. 'Why couldn't we eat with them? Why couldn't we have the *anasara* drive us home? What were you thinking, Haoua?'

'Just walk!' I snapped.

Back at the river, the two men with whom we had spoken earlier were busily hauling in their nets.

The older man noticed us on the shore and called out from his pirogue. 'Did you see that fellow, little sisters? Isn't he something?'

'We saw him, Father,' Miriam answered.

'But he does not have a magic camera,' I added.

'A wasted journey then, girls?' the younger man called across the water.

The older man tutted, then sucked his teeth. '*Walayi!* Not a wasted journey: see what a fine evening it is. God is good!' He lifted something shiny from the floor of his pirogue and threw it onto the shore. It landed in the mud, with a splash, a few metres from my feet.

I could see now that the object was a medium-sized capitaine, freshly caught. Its head poked skywards from the stinking mud which thwarted its dying efforts to protest.

'It's your supper, sisters,' the fisherman called. 'Take it home to your mother and have her cook it up with some peri-peri.'

I waded through the mud and, with a loud, sucking noise, extracted the fish by its tail, holding it up to let the fisherman know that I had retrieved his gift. The creature gave a final, weak wriggle as life left it. 'Thank you, Father!' I shouted. 'That is very kind of you.' I stooped down to brush a small area of the water's surface clear of its bubbly scum, and rinsed the capitaine off.

'Thank you, again!' we called. As we left the river bank we could hear the younger man complaining to the older man. Like the trees, the giraffes, the giant crocodiles, the water itself, *Egerou n-igereou*'s fish stocks were disappearing dangerously fast and the younger fisherman was evidently not so happy to share its bounty.

By the time we reached the great bend where we would turn off towards Wadata, an angry, orange sun was just beginning to kiss the river's surface.

The fish was slimy and had also begun to feel a little heavy in my hand. 'Will you carry this fellow for a while, please, Miriam?' I asked my friend.

But Miriam was still sulking. 'I'm not touching that!' she said. 'It stinks.'

'But you'll want your share, no doubt!' I said, angrily.

She continued walking and did not answer.

I untied my headpiece and used it to wrap the capitaine up in a bundle. This I then tied onto my waist, alongside my water gourd. 'Now my favourite *pagne* will stink too!' I called after Miriam, through the fading light.

* * *

We knew the route home from the bend in the river very well – even in the darkness which had enveloped everything rapidly – and continued on without trepidation, our sandals slapping a steady rhythm. I was more concerned about my father than any mythical monsters. We were tired and hungry and, each time we stopped to rest for a moment or two, we soon began to feel cold. The fishy ooze on my thigh did not help my spirits. Above us, in an immense, blue-black sky, more vast even than the desert, the stars flashed as usual, like a thousand jewels. We padded over the cool, firm sand, until at last we caught sight of Wadata's own twinkling array of wood fires and kerosene lamps in the distance.

Miriam's house was situated on the outskirts of our village and so we came to it first. Monsieur Kantao was sitting outside in his compound, spitting and chewing on kola nuts and waiting for his daughter. When he saw us at the entrance, he said nothing. Instead, he stood up, crossed the compound and took Miriam by the shoulders, staring at her all the while, as if to make sure that she really had returned home intact. Then he turned to me and simply pointed in the direction of my house.

I knew that his intention was for me to leave immediately; Monsieur Kantao was a gentle man but he was clearly angry. I made to go, but then remembered our capitaine.

Quickly, I unwrapped the bundle at my side, and held the fish up, proudly, for him to see by the light of his lamp. 'Half of this is for your household, Monsieur,' I said.

Without a word, he crossed the compound and disappeared behind the latrine, where a few scraps of kindling were stored. There was a brief rattling of metal implements, then Monsieur Kantao re-emerged, holding a machete in his right hand. As he walked back towards us, I was seized more by curiosity than fear.

'Father?' Miriam said, concern in her voice.

46

Monsieur Kantao took the capitaine from me and slapped it onto the rickety table at which he had been seated. Seconds later, the machete ripped through the creature's innards and hacked into the timber surface. Silently then, Monsieur Kantao scooped up the front portion of the fish and handed it, dripping, to me.

I took the bloody mess and ran the rest of the way home, where my mother was waiting, anxiously.

'You'd better get straight to bed, Haoua,' she whispered, as I wiped fish guts from my hands. 'Your father is in a foul mood. He and Abdel have quarrelled!'

4

Fatima and Adamou were already sound asleep when I rolled out my grass mattress and flopped down in the little room that our whole family shared. It was too cool during the night to sleep outside now. My belly ached with hunger and, despite the fact that I had made some attempt to wash, the pungent stench of fish still wafted from my body.

I lay awake for what seemed like a long time, thinking over the events of the day and worrying that I had caused more trouble than the trip had been worth. At least, I thought, tomorrow is not a school day. After my chores, I would go to Miriam's house, apologise to her parents and make up with my friend.

With that thought in my mind, I drifted off, but was woken some time later by the sound of voices. Through the darkness, I could just make out the sleeping form of my mother, on my parents' raised bed. I sat up and strained to listen, quickly realising that Abdelkrim and my father were outside. Both were attempting to subdue their voices, but the tone was hostile.

'. . . It makes one forgetful of Allah and prayer, Abdel!' I heard my father hiss. '*O ye who believe! Approach not prayers with a mind befogged*, the Holy Koran tells us!'

'Your ways are no longer my ways, Father,' Abdelkrim replied, his voice cold, like a stranger's.

'I forbid you to bring that vile potion to my house! It is an abomination of Satan's handiwork! The Devil wants to cast hatred and enmity amongst us by means of strong drink! See how he turns us against each other?'

'Doesn't the Koran mention games of chance also, Father? Have you forgotten that? Shall I set aside my alcohol and you your gambling with your cronies?'

'You will respect me and my house!'

'Like you respect my mother?' Abdelkrim slurred.

There was a scuffle and the sound of clay water pots breaking. I sat up, fearful, panic-stricken. Just then I felt something touch my shoulder, and I looked up to see the silhouetted form of my mother looming over me in the darkness.

'Lie down,' she said, stepping over my stirring siblings and leaving the room. 'Everything will be fine.'

The sound of quarrelling intensified as she opened the door of the house.

'Enough!' I heard her say, firmly. 'There will be no more of this tonight!'

5

I knew that there would be a lot of catching up to do the next day. I had woken even before the *Adhan* – the *Muadhdin*'s first call of the faithful to our tiny mud-brick mosque: *Allahu Akbar, Allahu Akbar*, Allah is the Greatest. *As-Salatu khairun min an-naum, as-Salatu khairun min an-naum*, Prayer is better than sleep. Having sensed an uneasy atmosphere while the others dressed for prayers in the gloomy morning light, I asked God to forgive me as I feigned the sleep of one still exhausted, pretending not to notice the competing clamour of cockerels and cattle outside. When I was sure that my father and brothers had left to tend our crops and graze our livestock, I faced the direction of the *Kaaba* and prayed quietly, then I rolled my bed up and went outside. My thoughts were still clouded by fragments of dreams and the morning sunlight hurt my eyes. My mother and Fatima were busy pounding millet, the musical rhythm of their work familiar and comforting.

My mother looked up as I approached, then, all at once, she doubled over and launched into a hacking cough. 'Here,' she spluttered, handing me her pestle. 'You finish this. I will get you some food.' She shot me a scolding look, as if to warn me that she was fine and wanted no fuss.

I was ravenous, and wanted nothing more than to eat immediately, but knew better than to challenge her. I stretched, then took the heavy pestle, worn smooth as young skin by years of toil, and began to pound.

'You're in big trouble!' Fatima whispered, without missing a beat, her huge pestle bouncing back into the grip of her tiny, expert hands as I began to ease into the rhythm.

We worked side by side for a few minutes, my fatigue and hunger forgotten for now, the labour hard but satisfying, and the familiar sounds of ancient wood on ancient wood reassuring, soothing, before my mother handed me a dish of rice with a little of the fish meat. The capitaine ought to have been a welcome change – most days began with sugarless *boule* or millet gruel – but in truth I would sooner have gone without it. The sight of the large, bloody head, lying in a pail nearby, made me feel slightly nauseous, but I knew better than to refuse food of any kind. A swarm of fat, black flies seemed to find it more appealing, until my mother swatted them away and draped a piece of cloth over the bucket. The head would be boiled up for a broth later and I would partake of that too, and be glad of it.

'Are you angry with me, Mother?' I asked.

'No, child,' she answered, 'but your father was worried last night.'

'But I told you where we were going,' I said.

'He is not angry with you. He is angry with me.'

Fatima's pounding ceased for a moment. 'Father is angry with everyone!' she said.

'Your father does not want you wandering off so far,' my mother continued. 'He fears that some ill fortune might befall you. We must respect his wishes.'

I made to protest. 'But. . .'

'You will apologise to him later. . .' she said, '. . . as I have done.'

I finished my food and then resumed my work. Afterwards, all three of us took calabashes and pails and made our first journey of the day to the river, stopping numerous times along the way to allow my mother to catch her breath. As we walked along, Fatima chattered away like a green monkey – about the upside-down trees, the happiness the proposed water tower would bring to Wadata, about my school, Adamou's mean friends, the candy which our friends in Ireland had sent, and the yarns with which Abdelkrim had teased her the previous day.

'*Walayi!*' My mother listened attentively, shaking her head proudly, casting kindly glances intended to draw me into the conversation; smiling or chuckling occasionally, while I sulked in silence. 'She is just like you were at that age, Haoua-hoo!' In truth, she knew that I longed to tell them all about my misadventure of the previous day.

By mid-morning I had cheered up considerably. We had carefully stored our water supply and were sorting clothes and tidying up when Abdelkrim appeared.

'Aren't you helping your father anymore?' my mother asked.

'I can't work with him, Mother!' Abdelkrim said. 'He forgets that I am a man!'

'Be patient with him, my son,' Mother said.

Abdelkrim shook his head. '*Walayi!*' He sighed. 'I'm not sure that I can.'

Mother had been sweeping a woven mat with a twig broom that had seen better days. She leaned the handle against the wall and wiped her hands on her *pagne*. 'We'll have some mint tea,' she said.

Fatima's tasks had been to fold clothes as I pressed them and to fetch me glowing embers from the fire for my irons.

'You two may take a break also,' Mother said. 'You girls have worked hard this morning.'

We thanked her, and Fatima ran off to find some of her little friends, while I took my exercise book and sat down on the floor near the door to write a letter to Katie and Hope. I wanted to tell them all about Abdelkrim, and about trying to have a magic picture taken for them. I decided that, to make up for the photograph, I would make a little drawing for them.

My mother continued to bustle about, and Abdelkrim leaned against the door frame, watching me chew the end of my pencil while I considered what picture my friends would find most interesting. I looked up and smiled at him, still scarcely able to believe that he was home with us. My mother filled a little blue pot with tea, sugar and mint leaves, took two glass beakers from a basin full of clean utensils and added boiling water from an old, enamelled saucepan. She stirred the infusion by agitating the mint stalks, then lifted the pot and poured the steaming liquid back into the pan. When she was satisfied with her brew, she took the utensils outside and summoned my brother to join her on the mat.

Abdelkrim winked at me. 'You can show me your photographs and letters later, ok?' he said.

I nodded. '*Toh, kala a tonton.*'

'*À bientôt.*'

As he went outside I heard my mother whisper, 'We can talk more freely out here.'

I went about my business and truly did not mean to eavesdrop. Evidently, however, my mother quickly forgot that I was sitting in our small living area, just inside the doorway.

'Are you alright, Mother?' I heard Abdelkrim say.

'Just a little breathless,' she replied.

'You must not do so much.'

'But there is so much to be done!'

'Mother. . .'

'Abdel. . .'

They both laughed.

They sat in silence for some time and then, at last, Abdelkrim spoke again. 'I'm sorry about last night.'

Mother sighed. 'You know that alcohol is forbidden anywhere near this house, my son. You are breaking your father's heart – and you will break mine too.'

'A soldier's life is hard, Mother. Sometimes it just helps me to forget.'

'It is not our way, Abdel.'

'I've been away from those ways for a long time,' Abdelkrim said, softly.

'You would do well to remember your upbringing, my son. Do not turn your back on the teachings of the Prophet Muhammad, peace be upon him. *Alsilamo*. A time may come when you will need your faith, and you will have call to reach out to Allah. I pray that He will always be there for you.'

There was a long silence, then Abdelkrim spoke again. 'Last night. . . I meant what I said about Father, you know?'

'I know you did,' my mother said, wearily. 'But what can I do? If he has decided it shall be, it shall be. And if God wills it. . . *Inshallah*.'

'Aiee! Look around you!' Abdelkrim snapped. 'He can't even support the four of you! How will he feed and clothe another wife? This is madness. You must not let him do this!'

'Abdel,' my mother said, sadly, 'do you think that I could stop him?'

'And how will he pay? He'll have no more of my money! I won't send it to you for him to squander!'

My mother did not answer.

'God will provide, I suppose? Yes? When will he provide, Mother?'

'My son, God will provide.'

There was the familiar sound of teeth being sucked, marking the end of their conversation. My mother came back into the house, bundled up a pile of soiled clothing and placed it on her head.

'Put your papers away now, Haoua, and bring the rest of the clothes down to the river, please.'

I groaned. Washing clothes was a chore that I did not like, and I had made a good start with my colouring pencils and had drawn a fine chicken for Katie and Hope.

'Just do it, child! You've had your rest!' she said, curtly. 'And remember, you had your fun yesterday.'

Abdelkrim wandered into the house after my mother had gone. He was smoking a very bad-smelling cigarette. I screwed my face up and smiled when he threw it outside, onto the dust, with a mutter.

'So,' he said, 'are you going to show me your treasures?'

It was the first time that my letters and pictures had been referred to as 'treasures', but the word suited perfectly: it was exactly how I had come to think of them. They were, to me, like little doorways to another world. I knew that I would probably never actually go there, but it somehow reassured me to know that this other world existed. I knew that my friends, far away in Ireland, were every bit as real as me and my family. At night, as the cicadas sang their lullaby under a majestic canopy of stars and I waited for sleep to take me, I wondered if Katie and Hope were sleeping under those very same stars too.

'Mother needs me to help her at the river. But I will show you quickly.' From beneath my bed roll, I eagerly took the large, tatty envelope that Monsieur Boubacar had given me, and spread its contents on the floor.

Abdelkrim squatted beside me and began sifting through my photographs and postcards. 'Phwooo!' he whistled. 'Quite a collection.'

'Yes,' I said, happy to share this secret world with my favourite brother.

'Everything looks so green!' He picked up a postcard showing a huge, rocky hill with an imposing stone tower on top. Dotted all around the base of the hill were tiny houses – as white as sun-bleached bone; while in fields plump with grass and divided by hedges as coiffeured as human hair, clusters of fat, strangely patterned cattle grazed themselves fatter still.

'And blue, too!' I said, pointing out the image of the sea at Katie and Hope's village.

'Beautiful. Reminds me, a little, of Tarqua.'

'Tarqua? Where is that?'

'Nigeria – on the coast,' Abdelkrim replied. 'We had to go there last year for training exercises.' He shook his head. 'I've seen the sun set over the ocean, my god!'

'You like the army, don't you, Abdel?' I said.

'I've met some very good people – Bouleb is one of them – and some very, very bad people. I've seen things, done things, been places I could never have imagined. I've shaken Mainassara's hand! . . . The toad. . .' he laughed. 'It's my life now, Little One.' He shook the postcard wistfully as he spoke.

'I'm not so little now!' I protested.

He smiled. 'No. Not so little. But when I left the village you were not much older than Fatima.'

'Seven,' I said. 'I was seven.'

He nodded. 'Anyway, yes, I like the army. Don't tell Mother though – she has enough to worry about – but things have been difficult recently.'

'How?'

'Well. . . you know. . . some of the barracks have not received their wages for quite some time now. There is a great deal of unrest across the country. Many people want our president to step down. There has been a lot of trouble – unpaid wages, protests, plots, rumours of another coup, that sort of thing – mostly in the provinces, but there is talk that it may reach us in Niamey too.'

'It's not serious though, is it?' I asked, somewhat alarmed by his tone. We were used to hearing frightening reports from neighbouring countries all the time on Monsieur Letouye's television or Sushie's wind-up radio. For the most part I was too busy to pay much attention, but I did not like the sound of Nigeria – *Hausaland*. Monsieur Boubacar had told my class about a letter he had read in a newspaper when he was visiting relatives in Lagos. It had haunted me. The writer had demanded that the authorities remove a body from the roadside which had been dumped there three weeks previously. I could not imagine a world which treated human life with such disrespect. It was a world apart from the Djerma ways in which I had been brought up. 'You won't be in any danger, Abdel?'

My brother shook his head. 'It's nothing, Little One. It will pass.' He set the postcard on the floor and raised his eyebrows quizzically as he leaned across to pick up a photograph of Katie and Hope.

I was keen to change the subject; I did not know or care much about the ways of our capital and government. 'That's Katie,' I said, pointing, 'and that's Hope. . . I think.'

'They're twins?'

'Yes.'

'They're very pretty. And they're from Ireland, you said?'

'Yes, Ireland. Have you been there?'

He laughed. 'No! The Nigerien Guard don't often have much call to be in Nigeria, never mind Ireland!' He tapped the photograph. 'And these twins are what age?'

'Eleven,' I said. 'Like me.'

'*Toh*' For a moment he seemed lost in thought. 'There are twins in Niamey,' he said. '*Dancing* twins – I see them almost every day at the corner near the barracks. At least I *think* they're twins. They are very alike.'

I was intrigued. There were no twins in Wadata. Once, Miriam's grandmother had told me about twins whose heads had been joined together. They had not lived long. Their mother had been cursed by a witch from Tillaberi, she said. In our own village Madame Monnou had given birth to twin girls, five years earlier, but one of them had died while Madame Monnou was in labour. The surviving girl – Amina – was a friend of Fatima's. I always imagined that Amina felt like half a person. We knew that twins were powerful yet dangerous, lucky, extraordinary. Bunchie told us that we should fear them, because they could kill offenders and see things which normal people could not see. Often she would repeat the story of Adamu and Hawa (after whom my brother and I had been named). They had been blessed with fifty sets of twins, and had hidden the more beautiful twin of each pair away from the Creator in a secret cave. The god saw that they had deceived him and made the hidden twins invisible for ever. Bunchie said that the spirits who plague people were the descendants of the beautiful twins.

'It is a strange and wonderful thing to watch these lads,' Abdelkrim continued. 'They have a big radio which they set on the sidewalk with the volume turned up really loud. They could be ten years old – they are very small, very skinny. They could be fifteen. . . I don't know. Victims of polio, I think. There are a lot of beggars in the city – and thieves. . . and other bastards! But these boys do not beg. Oh no! Instead, they dance! What a show they put on. Their legs may not work, but you should see them dance on their hands!'

'They have no legs?'

'They have legs, but they are wasted, thin, useless. They drape them over their shoulders like rags. Their feet wobble like a galloping *mouton*'s teats as they dance wildly to their music! They are excellent *artistes*. Every once in a while they will catapult themselves onto their feet. Their dead legs can hold them there – for just a second. Then they crumple. But as they do so they somersault themselves back onto their palms. It truly is an amazing sight!'

'*Walayi!* And people give them money?'

'People give them money. Lots of money. They stand around and watch these boys perform and they marvel! It is sad that they cannot walk, and yet they do not seem unhappy.'

'Where do they live?' I asked. 'Do they have a family?'

'I don't know,' said Abdelkrim. 'Perhaps. Perhaps not. A great many children in Niamey beg all day and receive only crusts from an adult for the privilege. I hope my twins get to keep their money.'

'*Bakarka*? But they are not beggars. They have earned this money. Why should they not keep it?'

He sighed. 'Because that is the way things are, Little One.'

I was spellbound by his stories.

Abdelkrim placed the photograph of Katie and Hope on

the floor again and tapped it with his forefinger. '*Toh*. Thank you for showing me.'

Keen to impress, I picked up another photograph and handed it to him. 'And these are their parents – and their dogs.' Katie and Hope were also in this picture, kneeling on a grassy surface behind the two dogs with babies' faces. The girls looked very happy. Katie was hugging one of the dogs, which was sitting upright and looking very proud to be there; as if it thought of itself as a human being, or at least an equal. The other dog was looking away from the camera and had its tongue hanging out. Hope was holding this one on a leash. The adults were also kneeling on the grass, behind their children and the dogs. The father – Noel Boyd – was leaning forward, protectively, towards the camera, a tight smile on his pale face. His hair was cropped very short and he wore small, round sunglasses which, I thought, were not as nice as my brother's. The girls' mother was wearing a cap which cast a heavy shadow over her face. This was the only picture of Katie and Hope's parents that I had, and it perplexed me a little that I was unable to see the eyes of either of them.

'Strange dogs,' Abdelkrim said.

I nodded. 'Like babies.'

'Hmm.'

'You can't really see their mother's face. . .'

'The sun has been high,' Abdelkrim said, 'and she is wearing a hat.'

'Yes.'

'It looks like they are somewhere very high – a mountain, perhaps?'

'I don't know.' I took the photograph from him and turned it over. '*Downhill, 1997*, it says on the back.'

'Uhuh. And where is that?'

I shrugged.

We sat in silence for a few moments, just looking over the postcards and photographs before us.

'It's nice that you have these friends,' Abdelkrim said.

'Yes.'

'And they write often?'

'Every few months,' I said. 'Sometimes their father writes too.'

'That's good,' he said. 'Doesn't the mother write?'

'No.'

'Perhaps she can't,' Abdelkrim said.

'Oh,' I said, 'everyone can read and write there.'

Abdelkrim nodded slowly. 'They must be very rich. What does the father do?'

'He's a teacher. I think their mother is too.'

'That's what you should do, Haoua,' my brother said. 'You should continue to study hard, get away from here. Travel. You'd make a good teacher. You are a bright girl.'

'Perhaps,' I said, 'but Wadata is my home. And what about our mother? How would she cope?'

'You could come back! Go to the USA. Or France. Learn all you can, then come back – and change things. Niger is a sick country! Make things better!'

'How, Abdel?'

'Somehow, Little One. We will find a way. I will help you, if I can.'

I knew that he meant it.

He smiled and put his hand in his pocket. 'Look. . . I still have the little radio your friends sent.'

I took the radio and fiddled with its switches and dials and Abdelkrim showed me how to wear the tiny earphones. A barrage of music bombarded my ears until I moved the dial again. Then, voices. News from the capital. Something about the Paris-Dakar rally. I took the earphones off and handed the radio to my brother. I was a little envious. 'I like it.'

'I will get you one, Haoua,' he promised. I knew that he meant that too.

I gathered up my belongings and put them back into the

envelope, then placed it safely under my bedroll again. 'Mother will be waiting for the rest of our washing,' I told Abdelkrim. 'I'll finish my drawing later.'

He nodded. 'Please give Katie and Hope and their family my greetings when you do.'

'I shall,' I said.

Abdelkrim stood up and stretched, then crossed the room to where his army issue kitbag was leaning against the wall. As he flipped it open to search for more cigarettes, I noticed the neck of a bottle protruding from one of its pockets.

'What's that?' I asked, as I tied the remaining clothing into a bundle in preparation for the journey to the river.

'Whiskey,' he said. 'Want some?'

'No!' I said, appalled.

He laughed and made to go outside.

'Abdel!' I called after him.

He stopped, turning to face me – an unlit cigarette in one hand, pink plastic lighter in the other. 'Hmm?'

'How long can you stay?'

'Not long, Little One. A few more days, perhaps. . .'

'Oh.'

'. . . If I don't murder Father first!' he added, with a grin.

I lifted my bundle and walked towards the door. 'Why do you squabble with Father?' I asked, pretending that I had not overheard his discussion with our mother. 'Is it because of the rumour?'

'He is opposed to alcohol. That's all. It's nothing for you to worry about,' he said, lighting his cigarette.

I searched his face, but it gave nothing away.

'*Kala a tonton*. I'll see you later, Little One,' he said, and we parted company.

6

The sun beat down intensely as I walked to the river. The load I carried on my head was not a particularly heavy one. Mother had taken the majority of our garments but I was still tired from the long trek of the previous day.

I wondered what Miriam was doing – how difficult things had been for her with her father. I was reminded that I had yet to face *my* father.

As I neared the river, I could hear singing and my spirits began to lift. In all, there were about thirty people there, mainly women and girls, most of whom were scrubbing garments in the shallows. Draped over bushes and low branches, articles of clothing of every size, type, pattern and colour dried in the sun. A group of infants were amusing themselves on the riverbank. Some of the women had younger babies tied onto their backs as they worked.

Souley, a girl Adamou's age, made a rude gesture at me when she was sure that no one else was paying much attention. Miriam and I had no time for Souley. She was a clever girl, but her parents did not send her to school and we were sure that she was jealous.

I sucked my teeth at her, set my bundle down on the dry ground and waded through the silted water to join my mother. She was stooped over, her hands moving furiously back and forth over my father's *jellaba*, as she sang the chorus of our working song.

Han kulu ay ga maa zanka jindey. Every day I hear children's voices.

Han kulu ay ga ba aran. Every day I love you.

At first, she did not hear me hail her.

'Mother!' I called again. 'Azara! Are you alright?' For a moment, when she looked at me with weary eyes, I almost thought that it was Bunchie, my late grandmother, standing before me.

'Haoua,' my mother said, breathlessly. She stood upright and coughed a little, banging her chest with the flat of her wet hand. She nodded, then, frowning, she turned her head away to clear her throat.

The realisation that she was getting old, and that one day I would lose her too, suddenly filled me with dread.

'*Toh*,' she said, returning to both her work and her song.

7

It was mid afternoon by the time we got back to the village. We found Abdelkrim in our compound sitting on a plastic crate and surrounded by Adamou and his friends.

As usual the boys were in a great state of excitement. Abdelkrim was busily working at something with a rusty pair of pliers – I could not make out what – while, all around him, the boys shouted and jostled and pushed each other playfully.

'We're each going to have our own rally car!' Adamou told us excitedly, as we approached them.

'Dakar here I come!' shouted one of his friends.

It was a favourite pastime for the boys of our village to make fantastic toys from wire coat hangers – mostly scrounged from Monsieur Letouye's shop. Sushie, Richard and Monsieur Boubacar were also regularly pestered for coat hangers each time word got about that one of them might be travelling to the capital. The heavy wire would be used to create elaborate outline forms of all manner of vehicles – complete with moving wheels, axles, doors and even sometimes what the boys called 'working suspension'. Some even had drivers – little see-through figurines, desperately clutching tiny steering wheels in see-through pick-ups, *camions* and Jeeps. One or two of the boys in particular were exceptionally skilled at creating detailed models; so much so that they were considered lieutenants in Adamou's gang. Attached to the rear of each of these truly impressive vehicles was a wire pusher and handle, allowing them to be raced competitively through the dusty alleys of Wadata.

As a child, Abdelkrim, like every boy in our village, had

spent many hours making and racing his own creations – dreaming of one day owning a real vehicle, or of participating in the *anasaras'* races even. We had often seen images of such races on Monsieur Letouye's television set, but these mostly stirred up interest only among the boys. The craze for these toys was widespread across the country, and Abdelkrim said that the children of our capital were particularly fond of, and accomplished at, creating models of modern rally cars.

Miriam's brother Dendi began to chase Adamou around the main throng, kicking up great clouds of dust as they passed Mother and me.

'Yours is a pile of junk!' he shouted.

'No!' Adamou protested, 'Yours is!'

Abdelkrim looked up at my mother and beamed.

Mother shook her head and said, '*Walayi!*' She chastised the boys for wrestling too close to our water pots, but she too was smiling broadly.

For a moment I observed them both as if they were strangers, or actors in a movie; these two people whom I loved more than life itself, reflecting each other's smiles in that way that only a mother and her child can. It was a moment I wish I could have captured somehow – frozen it in time forever: not as a photograph, but as a tiny, physical fragment; one to which I might actually have reached out and touched whenever I felt troubled. Would that I could have had such a talisman for the dark times that lay ahead of us.

The moment was shattered by the arrival of my father. 'Get out of here! All of you!' he bellowed.

8

'Do you mind telling me exactly what you thought you were doing yesterday, Haoua?' my father demanded, when things had quietened down in the compound.

'Salim,' my mother said, 'I have already reprimanded the girl.'

I knew that it had been a mistake for her to speak at all.

My father glared at her, intensely, a sinewy vein bulging at his temple. 'I did not ask you to interfere,' he said, coldly, his hands wringing the staff of his hoe. 'Why don't you do something useful, Azara, and prepare some water for me? I must wash again before prayers.'

From the far side of the compound I heard Abdelkrim draw air in through his teeth.

My father looked furiously towards him, but said nothing.

'Come, Adamou,' my mother beckoned to my brother. 'You can help me.'

Adamou remained standing beside Abdelkrim's crate. 'But we have to finish my car, Mother!' he protested.

'*Walayi!*' She pointed towards the house.

Abdelkrim gave him a gentle push.

'*Boori arwasu.* Good boy,' my father said, patting Adamou's shoulder as he stomped by sulkily. 'I have to discuss this matter with your sister.'

'I'm sorry I was so late, Father,' I said, warily, when they had gone. 'I wanted to send Katie and Hope a picture. Miriam and I wanted a magic picture – like Abdel's. . .'

'Katie and Hope! Katie and Hope!' my father mimicked. 'That's all we ever hear from you these days! If the *anasaras* really want to help us, why don't they send us money, eh? Real money! You'd do better to settle down and concentrate on your work, girl!'

I was stunned. 'But, Father,' I said, 'I am concentrating on my work. Monsieur Boubacar says. . .'

He cut me short. 'Monsieur Boubacar says. . . pah! I mean your real work – helping your family to put food in their bellies – not those fancy ideas from that school!'

'I thought you liked it that I could read and write, Father,' I said, quietly.

'I'm beginning to wish that I'd never agreed to any of it!' he snapped.

'But I thought you wanted Adamou to start school too, Father?'

'You see! You see how disrespectful you are!'

'But. . .'

'Silence! It is not your place to question my decisions, child. These days it is important for a young man to have an education. If it pleases God, Adamou shall go to the Koranic school. But there is much work to be done here and education is expensive.'

Abdelkrim, who was still sitting on his crate working at Adamou's truck, let out a loud, exasperated 'Aiee!'

'Is there something you wish to say?' my father asked Abdelkrim.

'Yes, Father,' my brother said, setting the model on the ground and standing up. 'There are lots of things I'd like to say.'

My father snorted, noisily, then turned his face away to spit.

Abdelkrim dusted his hands off and stretched, his movements an attempt, perhaps, to hide his agitation. 'First of all,' he continued, 'Adamou is eager to do his military service. Perhaps he will like the life and stay on – like me. He could do worse. The army educated me – in more than just the ways of the Koran.'

My father said nothing, but his glare caused me to shudder.

'Secondly, you cannot have it both ways. . .'

'What?' my father snapped.

'You are not paying for Haoua's schooling. Vision Corps – that British NGO – pays. Isn't that the way it works?'

'You ought to mind your own business, boy!' my father said.

Abdelkrim strode towards my father and looked down into his face. 'Oh?' he said. 'I am not a boy, and this *is* my business. I don't like your bullying, your lies and your deceit. I've witnessed plenty of that. Nobody likes it.'

By now my father was seething, and for the first time in my life I feared that something awful might happen between these two grown men, both of whom I loved dearly.

'Be mindful of what you say, *soldier*!' Father said, his voice shaking and tinged with sarcasm.

'I am mindful, Father,' Abdelkrim replied. 'I've thought about these matters very carefully over the last two days. I've watched what goes on here. You demand respect, but what respect do you show anyone other than your gambling friends?'

Father threw down the hoe that he had been holding and clenched his fists.

Abdelkrim looked down at the implement and then, glaring back at our father, he raised his eyebrows and tipped his hand forward, as if to say 'Well? What?'

My father's eyes narrowed, but he said nothing.

Abdelkrim nodded and gave a little smile. 'You talk about putting food in your family's bellies, yet you squander my money!'

'Mind your business!'

'You boast about taking another wife, yet you can't support the one you have!'

'How dare you. . .'

'You ought to thank Haoua, Father. In truth she puts food in your belly, but all you can do is scold her!'

'She is forbidden to go near the river!'

'She has apologised.'

'I might have lost her!'

'At least that would be one less mouth for you to have to feed!'

In a flash, the shouting was over. With a loud smack, my father brought his hand hard against Abdelkrim's face. 'I want you out of here!' he hissed.

I stood, trembling, before them. My mother and Adamou were standing in the doorway of our house, looking shocked.

Abdelkrim put his hand to his cheek and smiled again.

I had never before seen anger on a face that smiled.

'Don't worry, Father,' he said, his eyes shining. 'I'm going.' He turned away and walked out of the compound, pausing only to spit.

My father turned towards me and pointed. 'You!' he said. 'Go and find your sister!'

9

It was not difficult to find Fatima. She was playing with her friend Amina near Monsieur Letouye's shop. I beckoned to her to come quickly, then took her by the hand before she had time to protest.

'Where are we going?' she said.

'I have to take you home,' I answered. 'But first we must call on Miriam.'

We walked out briskly to the east side of the village until we came to the Kantaos' compound, a large enclosure with four small dwellings housing Miriam's large extended family. There was no sign of the halved fish which I had presented to Monsieur Kantao the previous evening. Three or four goats were tethered in one corner of the compound, waiting to be milked. Everything seemed to have returned to tranquil normality.

I had always liked visiting Miriam's house and family. Despite the fact that there was always a lot of activity, there was also a calmness and order here that I found reassuring and comforting. The Kantaos always seemed well organised, friendly, hard-working and generous. There was a kindness about these people which made visiting them a joy.

I could not bear the thought of anything coming between myself and Miriam. We had grown up together. We talked about everything. Monsieur Kantao said that, one day, his daughter would become a doctor, and neither Miriam nor I doubted it for a moment. It was easy to see that he was equally proud of his other four children, all of whom, he said, would have an education, whether boy or girl.

Miriam's compound was a place of intrigue and colour too. Often the Kantaos hosted interesting visitors from all parts of the Sahel. Miriam's Uncle Memet was a Touareg who had done business with Monsieur Kantao for many years and then given up his nomadic way of life to be with Madame Kantao's sister, Ramatou. It seemed to me to be such a noble, selfless, fine thing to do: to give up one's way of life for the sake of love.

I had been standing quietly, hand in hand with my sister, in the middle of the Kantao compound for some time, wondering whether or not to approach the threshold, when Madame Kantao appeared.

'*Ira ma hoi bani*,' we greeted each other.

'Madame Kantao. *Mate fu?*' I said, with my head bowed. 'It was my fault that Miriam came home so late last night. I'm sorry.'

Her eyes rolled in her great, happy face and she nodded, then set to work on one of the goats. 'Go on inside,' she called to us. 'Miriam is just finishing Narcisse's hair.'

Little Narcisse Kantao was considered something of a miracle baby in Wadata. She had just turned two and was plump and healthy and happy, but the Kantaos had almost lost her a year earlier. She had barely put on weight during the first year of her life but Sushie had given her special milk and medicine which Madame Kantao said had saved the child's life.

We girls found Narcisse adorable, amusing and, at times, infuriating. She was everyone's favourite and always got her way, even with Monsieur Kantao. We took great delight in styling her hair in outlandish plaited and braided designs: the more elaborate we could make it, the more Narcisse liked it. If Madame Kantao plaited two elegant swirls into Miriam's crown, Narcisse would demand three.

Miriam was just completing her latest creation when my sister and I entered the house. She pointed at the two large horns which she had given Narcisse and gave us an immense smile. A great sense of relief washed over me when I realised that we did not even need to discuss the events of the day before. This was a new day.

Narcisse was peering into a little scrap of tarnished mirror glass which Madame Kantao usually kept propped up on a battered set of drawers in their living area. She beamed at Fatima and me and then, twiddling her new horns proudly, she proclaimed, 'I'm cow!'

We all fell about laughing, so much so that Madame Kantao took a break from her work to see what all the fuss was about.

'*Toh*,' she said, smiling, when finally we settled down. 'There is food to prepare, Miriam.'

'Yes, Mother,' Miriam replied, then turning to me she rolled her eyes and said, 'We're having smoked fish!'

'Yes,' I said. 'I think we are too. We'd better get back to help Mother before there is more trouble at home.'

As Fatima and I bid our farewells, I realised that I was full of apprehension about the thought of facing my father again, and wished that my sister and I could somehow borrow a little of the Kantaos' warmth; that we could wrap it carefully in palm leaves, like a baby bird fallen from its nest, and hide it in the folds of my *pagne* to take home with us.

10

A strange blue mist hung over the river as I approached it. I heard no voices, and yet I knew that someone was waiting for me there. As I drew closer, the sound of wet clothing, slapping against rocks, broke the silence. I pushed on through the thickening, soupy haze and at last caught sight of a solitary figure, ankle-deep in water and stooped over what appeared to be a huge, craggy log. Beside the figure, a half submerged pile of garments quivered in the eddies of the river.

I waded cautiously through the silt until I was just a few metres from the working figure. I could see now that it was a woman and was about to call out to her when all of a sudden the log began thrashing about in the water. I realised then that it was not a log at all but a gigantic crocodile. It twisted its head from side to side and smacked its huge tail against the surface of the water. Then, with a final lurch, the beast turned towards me and bared its great jaws, before swimming off in the direction of the other shore. As the animal submerged, an array of red garments, which had been attached to its knobbly back, floated to the surface and bobbed there forlornly for a few moments, before they too sank into the deep.

All this time, the woman had stood, rock steady, with her back to me and the shore, but now she turned silently to face me. It was my grandmother.

'Bunchie!' I said, my voice shaking with emotion. 'Bunchie!'

'Little One.' She spoke softly. She reached out and took my hand, but I could not feel her touch.

'Where have you been, Bunchie?' I asked her.

'I don't know.'

'Why did you have to go away?'

'I don't remember,' she said, sadly. 'I didn't want to go away, my child.'

'Then stay here,' I said. 'Just stay with us now. Please, Bunchie.'

'I have to go, Haoua,' I heard a different, urgent, voice say. 'I have to go right now, Little One.'

When I opened my eyes, I found that I was looking into the face of Abdelkrim.

11

It was still dark outside, but I could just make out the crouching, silhouetted form of my brother. A cockerel crowed impatiently in the distance, yet I knew that it was really too early to leave the warmth of my bed. I sat up and rubbed my eyes. The rest of my family were still sleeping.

'Little One,' Abdelkrim whispered, 'come through to the other room for just a moment. I want to talk to you.' He stood up and stretched, then drew back the curtain that separated our two rooms.

A dizziness enveloped my head; perhaps part of my spirit was still standing at the river with my grandmother. Without a word, I crawled off my bed and stumbled behind my brother through to our living area. In the faint glow of the kerosene lamp, I was surprised to see Sushie sitting at our table.

She gave me a little wave. '*Ça va*, Haoua?' she whispered, her pale skin glowing in the lamp light.

My fatigue may have overridden my manners; I am not sure if I answered her. 'What's going on?' I asked my brother.

'I can't stay here any longer,' he said, removing a chewing stick from his mouth. 'Mademoiselle Sushie is going to drive me to the *camion*.' He pointed at his kitbag, which was lying by the door. I realised then that he was dressed in civilian clothes for the first time since he had been home.

'There is some medicine coming in from Niamey,' Sushie explained, 'so I have to go out there anyway.'

'Oh.' I fidgeted with the little wire knob on the lamp.

'You were already asleep when I came back last night,' Abdelkrim said.

'Father sent me to bed early.'

'Yes.'

I looked at him, crossly. 'The others will be upset that you have left without saying goodbye!'

Abdelkrim put his hand out towards me, reassuringly. 'I told them I was going last night,' he said. 'It's for the best.'

'But why do you have to go so soon, Abdel?'

'Because. . . it's for the best.'

'But. . .'

'Hush now,' he said. 'Go back to sleep. I just didn't want to leave without saying goodbye. And I will come back – soon. I promise.'

I wheeled around towards Sushie. 'Let me come with you, Mademoiselle?' I urged her, pouting, I hoped, like baby Narcisse.

Abdelkrim sighed. 'Haoua!'

'Please, Abdel,' I said. 'I would be company for Sushie on the way back.'

Sushie looked at my brother and shrugged. 'It's quite a distance,' she said.

'And there'll be a lot of waiting about. The *camion* to Niamey should be through by midday but the one bringing our medicine won't arrive until much later.'

'I don't mind,' I said. 'Please let me go, Abdel?'

We heard movement from the bedroom and then my father and mother appeared from behind the curtain.

Abdelkrim glanced at my father. 'That wouldn't be up to me, Little One,' he said. 'You would need to ask our father.'

My mother mumbled something in Father's ear.

'May I go with Mademoiselle Sushie, please, Father?' I said.

'And your work?'

'I will do it, I promise. All of it.'

'Your mother needs help,' he said.

'I know it, Father.'

'She could help me later, Salim,' my mother said, quietly.

Everyone looked at my father. 'You'd better get dressed quickly then,' he said, returning to the bedroom without a further word to Abdelkrim.

I had been in a car before, of course – several times, in fact – but it was still something of a novelty for me to be riding along in Sushie's. The sun was only just beginning to think about rising, so our journey to the camion pick-up point was easier than the return trip to Wadata would be. Later, the air inside the vehicle would be breathless and hot and the firm sand on which we were now travelling would be much softer.

As we bumped along, I could not help but think of my mother. She had taken Abdelkrim's decision to leave very badly, although I knew that he had no real choice. I was sure that my mother knew it too. I leaned my head back on the rear seat and closed my eyes, content for the moment to be near my brother at least. Despite the lurching and jolting of Sushie's Vision Corps Toyota, I soon drifted off into a shallow half-sleep, in which neither *Egerou n-igereou* nor my grandmother featured. Instead, only the voices of my brother and Sushie, as she wrestled with the steering wheel and cursed the furrows of soft sand, soaked into my consciousness.

At first, their conversation seemed little more than the awkward but polite exchanges of two people who barely knew each other, but as their tones became more hushed, I realised that it was my mother, my father, my siblings and me that they were discussing. It soon became apparent that this was not the first such conversation they had had. I abandoned any notion of sleep then and, keeping my eyes closed, strained to catch every word.

'I could drive for a while, if you'd like me to,' I heard Abdelkrim say.

'No. I'm fine, thank you,' Sushie replied.

'*Toh.*'

'How's Haoua doing?'

'I think she's still fast asleep.'

'She's a spirited girl,' Sushie said, over the whine of the engine.

'For sure.'

'Strong. Determined. Clever,' she said.

I felt a little embarrassed but also quite proud, and perhaps slightly guilty for my deceit.

'She was always clever,' Abdelkrim said. 'I hope that she will remain strong, Mademoiselle Sushie.'

'I will keep an eye on her, Abdel,' Sushie said. 'And the rest of your family. I really do care about all of my Wadata children, you know,' she added, with a little laugh.

'I know,' my brother said. 'But you will not always be around, Mademoiselle. You will return to your life in America and forget all about Wadata.'

Sushie tutted. 'Abdelkrim, I'm not the only one looking out for your people. There is Boubacar, Richard – not to mention the other Vision Corps workers. They're all good people, believe me.'

I heard a muted grunt from my brother.

Sushie's voice took on a more serious note. I opened my eyes, slightly, and caught sight of her leaning over towards Abdelkrim. 'I'm mainly concerned about your parents for now,' she said, her words somewhere between a hiss and a whisper.

He nodded. 'Indeed, Mademoiselle. As I said before: my father is not to be trusted.'

'Hmm. . .' She paused, as if deliberating whether or not she should say any more on the matter. Then, 'Abdelkrim. . .' she said.

'Mademoiselle?'

'He really can't be trusted. . .'

'I know it.'

Sushie took a deep breath. 'Yes. . . but. . . I didn't say

anything before because I didn't want to risk making a bad situation worse.'

'Uhuh.'

'Your father – and he's only one of many – well, to be frank . . . I'm not sure that he is *careful*, if you get my meaning?' She was barely audible over the din of the engine now.

'Continue,' Abdelkrim said.

'I spoke to all of Wadata's menfolk, some time back. About protection, you know?'

'It's all right,' Abdelkrim said. 'The *waykuru* women. I've heard the stories.'

'Yes. It's hardly a secret. Wadata's not very large. And, like I say, Salim's not the only one who goes to. . . that place.' Sushie glanced over her shoulder and I squeezed my eyes shut. 'The thing is, Abdel, the men in the village have the idea that they are not susceptible to infection, that protected sex is not for them and that if they are 'quick' there can be no problem!'

'Yes,' my brother said.

'It alarms me greatly that they choose to ignore my advice and warnings,' Sushie continued, as the vehicle hit a deep pothole, '– and the women they go to are just as reckless about the whole thing!'

Abdelkrim sighed. 'As you say, Mademoiselle Sushie, Wadata is a small village, and such has been its way for a very long time.'

'Dangerous ways!' Sushie said. 'Dangerous ways!'

The *camion* post consisted of little more than a large, rickety shed and a latrine house. Parked nearby was a badly beaten up Land Rover. A tall, shiny communications mast was attached to one end of the main building and, at the other, a makeshift canopy had been erected under which passengers could wait for the *camion*. An array of baggage and belongings lay scattered about on the sand in no particular order, creating a sense that my brother's fellow travellers and their possessions had recently been dumped there. From a battered speaker mounted on a wooden pole, the tinny sound of *La Voix du Sahel* assaulted our ears, even though we had parked some distance away.

It was mid-morning by the time we arrived and uncomfortably hot inside the vehicle.

'I'm sorry the air conditioning isn't working,' Sushie said.

I had drifted in and out of sleep throughout the journey and now had a throbbing pain in my head. My back was soaked with sweat, my *pagne* peeling from the vinyl seat each time I wriggled in an effort to get comfortable.

Sushie reached into a large, green, plastic cool box at Abdelkrim's feet and handed me a bottle of bitter-tasting water. I thanked her and was glad of the refreshment but could not help but screw my face up.

'It's the purification tablets,' she said, in an unapologetic, matter-of-fact way. She fumbled in the little compartment in front of Abdelkrim. 'Where the hell did I put those documents?'

'I think you put them in your bag, Mademoiselle,' Abdelkrim said.

'Of course. I'm so tired I can't think straight.'

'You ought to have let me drive.'

'Hey!' Sushie said, winking at me. 'I saw you driving those toy trucks with Adamou – we had to get here in one piece, you know!' She grabbed her bag and got out of the vehicle.

'Are you all right, Little One?' Abdelkrim said.

'I'm fine. Thank you.'

'You had quite a sleep.'

'Hmm.'

'Maybe you're still asleep?' he teased.

'Hmm.' I took another swig from the bottle and handed it across to him.

By now Sushie was talking to some other travellers, her long, pink arms flailing wildly as she worked her magic charm: she had a forwardness, a confidence with my people which few *anasaras* have and, judging by the gleeful expressions on these Touaregs' faces, I could tell that it had not failed her with them either.

'Abdel,' I said, as my head began to clear.

'Hmm?' he mimicked.

'Do you think she's pretty?'

'Who?'

'You know who!'

He turned in his seat to face me, mischief in his eyes. 'Mother? Fatima?'

'Sushie!' I said.

'Oh – *Sushie*. . .' He looked out towards the gathering and then leaned back. 'I think she's a remarkable woman,' he said.

As if she'd heard our conversation, Sushie looked over at us and, smiling, gave a little wave.

'Let's see what's going on,' Abdelkrim said, opening his door and stepping out into the baking heat.

We sat on the ground in the shade with the Touaregs for what might have been several hours, but to me it seemed like minutes. I did not want my brother to leave. Abdelkrim told us stories about his army comrades – about getting drunk with Sergeant Bouleb, fights in the barracks, witnessing floggings. He told us of his hopes to become a member of the elite Presidential Guard, about his dream to travel to Europe and America and about meeting girls at the dances in Niamey's Rivoli Hotel.

Sushie shook her head after my brother had recounted his tale about an encounter with two French female back-packers. 'You mark what I said earlier!'

Abdelkrim grinned. 'Oh, Mademoiselle,' he said, flirtatiously, 'I take great care. When it rains I always wear a raincoat!'

'I am so glad to hear that, Monsieur,' Sushie replied, also smiling.

I was a little irritated that they considered themselves to be talking in code, and even sometimes as if I was not there, but I said nothing. Had they forgotten that I too was almost a woman?

'Perhaps one day I will find a wealthy European lady,' Abdelkrim continued. 'Or, indeed, a beautiful American!' he added, with a wink in my direction.

Sushie nodded. 'Uhuh. Wealthy European, beautiful American, you say?'

'Did I say that?' said my brother. 'Beautiful, ugly, fat, thin – whatever. But she must be wealthy!'

They laughed together. It was a togetherness which both pleased and annoyed me. Perhaps it was jealousy. I don't know.

'And what about you, Mademoiselle?' my brother asked, following a lull in the conversation.

'Me?'

'Your life. Your story. How you came to be here – far away from home. Far away from America, the great Land of the Free.'

'There's not much to tell, really.'

Abdelkrim raised his eyebrows and enticed her with his open palms.

'Well, let's see,' Sushie said. 'Grew up outside Boston. Father a medic. Mother in real estate. No brothers, no sisters. Finished High School. Trained to become a nurse. Met guy. Fell in love. Got engaged, got dumped. Thought "fuck it", joined VCI and here I am. . .'

'You were running away, eh?'

She did not reply.

'Thought you'd help the poor Africans?' Abdelkrim said.

'Whatever.'

Abdelkrim lit a cigarette and then offered one to Sushie. She shook her head.

'I'm playing with you, Mademoiselle,' he said. 'I can see that your organisation has helped my people – truly. And I know that you have a good heart.'

Sushie sighed. 'I think there are a lot of my people who would like to help more. To be able to force countries like the US to waive debt, increase trade with countries like Niger – that sort of thing. We can stand up and shout for what we believe in, sure, but it's not always enough for some people. Major changes like that occur over a long period of time, I guess. Some of us just want to do something *now* – anything.' She spoke wearily, as if she'd had to justify her presence in our country often before. She shrugged and looked at my brother. 'That's why I'm in your country, Abdel. It may seem naïve, but that's why I'm here.'

There was a long silence. I felt too tired to even try to join in with their conversation. Instead, I leaned my head on Sushie's shoulder and watched the Touaregs opposite. There were five of them in all. Males. Their ages unclear due to the dusty blue *cheches* which covered all but their bloodshot eyes and the bridges of their noses. They looked like they had been travelling forever. The Free People. The People of the Veil. Mysterious, proud, strong. I thought of Miriam's uncle and the stories that he told about his great journeys. They kept themselves to themselves, speaking to us only occasionally in Djerma between excited exchanges in Tamashek. They drank mint tea and *eghale* and played *tiddas* with small stones and twigs which they had laid out with care on a reed mat.

I had just begun to doze off again when Abdelkrim broke the silence.

'So,' he said, 'tell me about this man who broke your heart – if you'd like to, that is. . .'

I looked up at Sushie and rubbed my eyes.

She smiled at me. 'He was just a guy,' she said. 'He was an artist. An asshole, really. Nothing else to tell.' She drew her knees up close to her chest and hugged her legs.

'I think this man was a fool!' Abdelkrim said.

One of the Touaregs stood up and walked a few metres across the sand. He squatted down and pulled his *jellaba* taut across his knees and, using only his thighs to afford himself some privacy, began to urinate.

Sushie gave a little laugh. 'They can even make that look elegant!' she said.

The Touareg finished his business and then began walking back across the sand towards us. After a few strides, he stopped and pointed north towards the horizon.

Abdelkrim stood up and followed the Touareg's gaze. 'Something's coming,' he said.

'Is it the *camion*?' I asked.

'I can't tell yet.'

Sushie and I got to our feet and peered out across the vast expanse of desert towards the erratically zig-zagging dust cloud.

'It's stopped again,' Sushie said, after we had watched the incoming vehicle for some time.

'Probably stuck,' Abdelkrim said. 'It's very hot now. The sand will be very soft. I don't think it's the *camion*.'

I went back into the cool shade of the canopy and lay down, resting my head on my brother's army-issue kitbag.

12

I awoke to find a small, scruffy boy standing in front of me. At his feet stood a large, metal pail, the top of which had been covered with an off-cut of jute sacking, folded into a thick square to form a makeshift lid.

'Drink some of this, Haoua,' my brother said, handing me a tin can half filled with water and shredded stalks of ginger.

I drank the liquid greedily. It was tepid but delicious. 'Thank you,' I said, handing the tin back to Abdelkrim.

'You will have some, Mademoiselle?' he said, holding the empty container up to Sushie.

'I can't drink that, I'm afraid,' she said, patting her flat stomach. 'Did once. Big mistake. I've been here for a while but my guts still aren't tough enough for that!'

Abdelkrim lobbed first the tin and then a few coins towards the boy. With a grin, the boy deftly caught everything before lifting his pail and approaching the patiently-waiting Touaregs.

'Where on Earth did he come from?' Sushie said.

'Good question,' my brother replied. 'The closest village is at least fifteen kilometres from here. Llingaberi, probably.'

Sushie rubbed at her eyes. 'All I can see is sand – miles and miles of it!' She lifted her water bottle from the ground, unscrewed the top and took a swig. 'Yeuch!' she said, 'It's hot enough to bathe in!'

'I'll see if Youssef has anything else,' Abdelkrim said, nodding towards the large shed and standing up. 'Sometimes he buys in crates of sodas.'

'Hmm. I noticed the Sprite sign,' Sushie said, 'but, really, I'm okay with my nasty water, Abdel.'

'I need to stretch my legs, anyway,' he said, heading off in the direction of the shed.

'Watch out for those jerks!' Sushie called after him.

I looked at her, questioningly.

'The owners of that car,' she said, pointing towards a heavily-laden Citroen estate that I had not noticed previously. 'They arrived while you were asleep. French. Arrogant. Let's just say I didn't like their attitude.'

The car seemed to be packed to near bursting, with boxes, holdalls, jerry cans, tools and the like. Strapped to its roof rack were a set of sand tracks, several spare wheels, a large canvas bag and still more tools. Mounted above its windscreen was a great array of lights.

Abdelkrim returned a few minutes later and handed Sushie a Coka. 'Heeey!' she said, with a grin. 'It's cold!'

'He has a generator in there,' said Abdelkrim.

'Wow!' said Sushie, stuffing a thousand CFA note into my brother's hand. 'Thanks.'

'Mademoiselle Sushie!' he protested. 'I have bought this for you.'

'Take it, please, Abdel,' she said. 'You said yourself that you didn't know when you'd see your next wages.'

He feigned a look of displeasure before folding the note and putting it into his pocket. 'Thank you,' he said.

Sushie took a gulp from the bottle and then smacked her lips. 'God bless America!' she said, cheekily.

Abdelkrim nodded. 'Your French friends are playing cards with Youssef.'

'Those two look like they're more used to playing with themselves!' Sushie snorted.

Abdelkrim laughed. 'They're probably harmless.'

'What happened?' I said.

'Nothing, Little One,' my brother said. 'These boys' manners are not so good. That's all.'

Sushie spat, expertly, onto the sand. 'A couple of smart-ass, colonial-minded pigs, Haoua!' she said, offering me her soda. 'I've met so many like them. They treat your country like a playground.'

'Beautiful women should learn how to accept a compliment,' Abdelkrim said, with a twinkle in his eye.

'*Walayi!*' Sushie shook her head, as if despairing of my brother.

Abdelkrim winked at me and then took a few strides towards the other end of the canopy. 'By the way,' he said, turning again to address Sushie, 'if you're at all hungry, Youssef also has a big pot of goat stew on his stove.'

'Good idea,' she replied. 'Let's go.'

I had not realised how hungry I had begun to feel until there had been mention of food. I stood up, eagerly.

'*Attends!*' Abdelkrim said, waggling a finger at me.

'What's the problem?' Sushie asked.

Abdelkrim held his open palms out towards her. Then, with a little shrug, he patted his pockets.

'Come on,' Sushie said. 'I'm paying.'

Inside the large building, another radio speaker spewed out a constant, tinny barrage of news and traditional music from *La Voix du Sahel*. Two long, wooden tables – scrubbed grey – were set end to end so that they ran the length of the interior. On either side, a number of benches provided seating for perhaps up to thirty people. I could smell the aroma of bubbling meat as soon as we entered the building. At the far end of the room the two French men and the owner, Monsieur Youssef, were indeed playing cards. A fog of cigarette smoke hung over them.

Youssef excused himself from the company and approached us. 'Young Monsieur?' he said, addressing Abdelkrim politely. 'I welcome your friends.' He was a burly man with white hair and watery eyes that were somehow at odds with the rest of his kindly face.

'We'd like some of your stew, please, Youssef,' said my brother.

'*D'accord.*'

One of the French men gave a shrill whistle as Sushie untied her hair and began to fix it.

Sushie sucked her teeth at them, before sitting down beside me at the table, her face like a broody camel.

'Mademoiselle,' one of the men called, leerily. 'Why don't you join us here?' His fine-boned face looked dirty and unshaven. He wore heavy spectacles and a tatty red tee shirt with the word *Ferrari* printed on the front.

His friend was sitting on the same side of the table as us, so at first I could see only one side of his pale face. Strands of lank, wispy hair jutted out from beneath a green baseball cap, while his shirt was a riot of flowers – prettier than any *pagne* I had ever seen.

I suppose I must have stared for too long. The man with the glasses mumbled something to his partner. He looked up from his cards, turned his head towards me and stuck out his tongue.

'Don't pay them any heed, Mademoiselles,' Monsieur Youssef called from behind his stove.

Abdelkrim had been waiting by the stove to carry our food to the table. He walked towards us, fiddling in his breast pocket as he crossed the room. 'Let me take care of this,' he whispered. He walked to the far end of the long room and, standing with his back to us, spoke quietly to the French men.

Sushie looked down at me, pulled a funny face and shrugged. I smiled, and then strained to catch the conversation. We were not close enough to hear easily and the radio continued to blare, but it soon became obvious that Abdelkrim had said something to displease them.

'*Merde!*' exclaimed the one with the spectacles, putting out his cigarette. The man with the patterned shirt mumbled something across the table and then, standing up, handed a piece of paper to my brother. Clearly, he too was agitated.

I was beginning to feel a little apprehensive, until Abdelkrim saluted the two men in a theatrical way and I heard him say, 'Monsieur Franck, Monsieur Michel.'

Then he turned, smartly, and returned to our end of the table, taking a seat opposite myself and Sushie.

'What was that all about?' Sushie said.

'Oh, nothing. It's dealt with.'

Sushie coughed and began drumming her fingers on the table. 'What did you say, Abdel?' I demanded.

He shot a glance at the two *anasaras* and gave a little smile. 'Let's just say that they won't be bothering you again.'

'Uhuh?' Sushie stopped drumming and held out her open palm, to indicate that she expected more information.

'I showed them my military ID and then made sure that their documentation was in order – you know, *carte de passage*, passports, visas, that sort of thing.'

'Can you do that?' Sushie asked.

'I just did.'

'They didn't sound happy about it.'

'No. They weren't. But when they challenged my authority, I told them that we might meet again. And that next time it might be when I really *was* on duty. . .'

'Ah,' Sushie said. 'You mean to tell me that you're just another corrupt official, Abdel? – always on the lookout for a little bribe here, a little deal there?'

'Not at all,' my brother said. 'In fact, Mademoiselle, I despise any countryman of mine who behaves in such a manner!' He rolled his eyes towards the French men and gave a little sideways nod. 'But they don't know that.' He looked very pleased with himself.

Monsieur Youssef set three battered aluminium bowls, containing a thin, dark, steaming stew of goat meat, cow peas and peppers, in front of us. '*Bon appetit, mes amies*,' he said.

'It looks good, Monsieur,' said Sushie.

'You came at the right time, Mademoiselle,' he replied.

'The *camion* will be full of hungry people, so I slaughtered this goat just yesterday.' He smiled, broadly, revealing more space than teeth.

As we ate, the radio announcer declared that students in the capital were protesting at the delay in the payment of their allowances and that several mid-ranking military officers had been arrested, following rumours of plans to mutiny.

'Mainassara has had his day!' Abdelkrim said under his breath. He nodded towards a framed picture of our president at one end of Monsieur Youssef 's building.

'You really think so?' Sushie said.

'For sure. I know lots of *gendarmes* and soldiers who would dearly like him to stand down. He's never been forgiven for scrapping the electoral commission. And who really trusts the so-called Union of Independents for Democratic Renewal?'

'And yet you've applied to become a member of the Presidential Guard?'

Abdelkrim shrugged. 'He's the president. That's just the way things are for now. We have a parliament – of sorts. Some of us may not like how it came about, but there you have it. One day we will be able to vote again. And vote we will.'

Abdel's *camion* was indeed full, as Monsieur Youssef had predicted; not only with workers and travellers but with furniture, tyres, bundles of clothing, bedding, rugs, fuel canisters, water containers and food provisions, all coated in a veil of fine dust. Anything that could not be piled into the groaning truck's cargo hold was tied to the side of the vehicle. Any passenger who could not find a place on top of this cargo would cling instead to the roof of the cab.

It was not until Monsieur Youssef had fed and watered all of the passengers and they had prayed and toileted and begun to clamber back on board the creaking hulk, that I really began to believe my brother was leaving.

'Who are all these people?' Sushie said, as we stood next to the huge truck. 'Where are they all going? Where have they been?'

'All kinds of people,' my brother said. 'People like me, visiting their families. People giving up on rural life. Some of them will be illegal workers – returning from Algeria or Libya, perhaps. They'll have no passports or papers and won't have seen their families for a very long time. The *camions* travel right through the night, taking detours to avoid checkpoints.'

'There is no room for you, Abdel!' I said, staring up at the vehicle in amazement. It was the first time I had been so close to a *camion*.

'There is always room on the camion,' he said.

The French men came out of Youssef 's shed and wove their way through the throng of travellers towards their Citroen. The bespectacled man nodded towards us as he passed. '*A toute à l'heure*,' he said, cheekily.

Abdelkrim scratched the back of his neck, but said nothing.

'Monsieur!' someone called from the peak of the truck's cargo. 'Pass up your baggage.' Sushie lifted the kitbag and passed it to Abdelkrim and seconds later it was disappearing over the tailgate.

Suddenly there was a spluttering from the vehicle's engine. The truck shuddered as a great cloud of blue-black smoke belched from its skyward-pointing exhaust. There was a cheer from the top of the cargo and then, all too quickly, we were bidding Abdelkrim bon voyage.

I wiped a tear from the corner of my eye as Abdelkrim squeezed my shoulder and rubbed my back.

'Soon, Little One. *Ça va?*' He turned towards Sushie then and shook her hand. 'Thank you, Mademoiselle. . . I. . .Thank you.' Although the handshaking had stopped, they continued to hold on to each other.

'You're sure that you can find your way back to Wadata?'

Sushie nodded. 'I'll keep to the *piste*, don't worry. And I have my compass – and Haoua here.'

Abdelkrim looked at me and grinned. There was the roar of another engine and the tooting of a horn as the French men's Citroen pulled away from the *camion* post in a cloud of dust, its passengers saluting my brother and blowing kisses towards Sushie as they passed us. Abdelkrim sucked air in through his teeth but there was no time for words.

As if in reply, the *camion*'s great klaxon emitted a series of loud blasts.

Abdelkrim touched my face and then clambered like a lizard up the vehicle's tailgate. Moments later the truck moved off and my brother was gone; no more than a waving speck on top of that strange, groaning, rattling, creaking hulk, moving wearily across the sands.

'Let's get into the shade again,' said Sushie. 'We've got a long wait ahead of us.' I followed her under the canopy, all the while peering southeast at the diminishing cloud of dust. She sat down and leaned back against the gable end of the building, patting the sand beside her. 'Don't be sad, Haoua,' she said as I leaned against her shoulder.

I tried hard to be strong but, eventually, just like my mother earlier that morning, I sobbed. 'It was such a short visit,' I said, through my tears.

Sushie put her arm around me and kissed the top of my head. 'Hey,' she said. 'You'll see him again soon.'

13

Haoua Boureima   Boyd
Child Ref. NER2726651832   Member No. 515820
Vision Corps International   Ballygowrie
Tera Area Development Programme   Co. Down
C/O BP 11504   N. Ireland
Niamey   BT22 1AW
Republic of Niger
West Africa

21st October, 1998

Dear Haoua,

Sorry I haven't written for quite a while. I have been thinking of you, though, and wondering how you are getting on at school. I'm so glad you liked the photographs and books we sent. They are in English, of course, but hopefully your friend Richard will be able to help you read them. This time we are sending a book in French, which our father bought when he was in Paris last month with some of his pupils. Perhaps your teacher will want to read the story to your class. It is one of our favourite books – 'Harry Potter and the Philosopher's Stone', by J. K. Rowling. It's a bit weird at first, but funny too. I hope you like it. All our other friends think it's great.

Love,
Katie. X

Dear Haoua,
How cool that your brother came to visit your family! He
sounds nice. I think that having a brother must be great. I hope
the rest of your family are doing well also. Our mother says that
perhaps, one day, we might have a baby brother, but our father
says that we girls are enough! Our parents are well, but our
great grandfather (we call him 'Papa') has been quite sick. As
you know, he is very, very old.

It would be lovely to hear from you again. Please give our
regards to your family.

Oh yes – we put the little picture of you, which VCI sent us, in
a frame. It sits on top of our TV, in the kitchen. So now you are
really like one of our family!

Your friend,
Hope. XOXO

My heart ached for weeks after Abdelkrim returned to the
capital. It was obvious to everyone that my gentle mother felt
the same way. It seemed to me that the gleam in her beautiful eyes began to fade, and she carried herself differently, so
that with every new day she seemed to become more like her
own mother and less like mine.

Each afternoon on the way home from school, I checked
with Richard or Sushie to see if a letter had come from my
brother, but none did. Katie and Hope continued to write to
me, and of course I was glad to receive their letters, but I
would have given up a year's worth of their kind thoughts
for just a line or two from Abdelkrim. Before his visit I
had not worried about him much; now I could not get him
out of my head. Perhaps I picked up on my mother's anxiety
– for anxious she certainly was – but, somehow, it was no
longer possible for me to ignore occasional snippets of
news from Niamey on Monsieur Letouye's television or
Sushie's wind-up radio. Although Wadata was far removed
from the unrest in the capital, we were all aware that

any upheaval there could crucially affect our village too.

I had been finding it difficult to concentrate at school too, but the prospect of reading Katie and Hope's storybook with my class filled me with excitement. So I was greatly disappointed when Monsieur Boubacar, having read the book himself, announced that it was not suitable reading for us because it was largely about sorcery and witchcraft. Furthermore, he did not offer the book back to me and I was too timid to request it from him, and so it was lost to me forever. The idea that my friends had sent me a book about such matters seemed very strange, but there was nothing I could do but try to forget about it and hope that they would send me another, different story soon.

I had also taken my little adding machine into school and this had caused great excitement. Even Monsieur Boubacar was impressed.

'Yes, I have seen these machines before,' he said, 'but never one so small! You are a very fortunate young lady to have such a useful item – and such good friends. Unfortunately I cannot permit you to use it in counting class; you must use your own brain instead, Haoua!' He said this as if he was angry with me, but the whole class laughed, knowing that he was not. 'Can anyone tell me about an experience they've had when being able to count was useful?'

Oduntan, a boy two years younger than Miriam and me, raised his hand.

'Yes, Oduntan.'

'Please, Sir, when I am doing my homework, Sir.' There was a titter around the room.

'*Toh*,' Monsieur Boubacar said. 'But what about besides school and school work?'

Oduntan looked blankly at our teacher.

'He's so stupid!' Miriam whispered – unkindly, I thought.

Monsieur Boubacar shook his head and looked around the class. 'Anyone else?'

A boy named Samuel, who walked eight kilometres to and

from home each day to attend class, shot his hand up eagerly.

'Yes, Samuel?'

'Please, Sir, when I have to check the goats for my father!'

'Good. Right. Now,' said Monsieur Boubacar. 'Moving on. . .'

And, as usual, we sat on our mats with our exercise books on our laps, pencils at the ready, eager to learn. I liked mathematics very much, and I was good at it, but Miriam and I were especially fond of reading. Certainly we were disappointed that our teacher considered the Harry book inappropriate for us, but I was somewhat relieved; for I had looked through it and felt a little daunted by the number of words that I did not recognise. Besides, the VCI people had provided Monsieur Boubacar with a small selection of beautiful picture books and I had read only half of these. And Monsieur Boubacar was an excellent and engaging storyteller; we all listened, enthralled, when he read to us or made up a story from his own head. I often imagined myself in front of a classroom full of boys and girls, and I prayed for the day when I too would actually be a fine teacher and make my mother and Abdelkrim proud.

Miriam put her hand up to attract Monsieur Boubacar's attention. 'May we read *The Story of the River Island People* again please, Sir?' she said.

'Not today, Miriam,' he answered.

More hands shot up. '*The Hunter and the Ebony Tree*, please, Sir!' '*The Tale of Harakoye Dicko!*'

'Perhaps later.' Monsieur Boubacar shrugged, apologetically, and then turned to the rickety blackboard and scrawled the words *Personal* and *Project* in big, chalk letters. 'For now I want each one of you to consider this: in one week's time I shall expect you all to do a little presentation to the rest of the class – to talk, for a short while, about a subject that really interests you.'

A wave of murmurs and groans rippled through the classroom. Miriam looked at me with a scowl on her face, but I felt quite excited at the thought of this project. My class-mates had been intrigued with Katie and Hope's letters and gifts to me (even those of them who had their own sponsors) and I was often asked about them outside the classroom also. I knew that, like me, they were fascinated by the fact that my sponsor's daughters were twins, but I was sure that it was the gifts in particular that interested them. (I had shared my candies around the class on a number of occasions). Still, I was already planning my presentation and couldn't wait to speak to Richard about the ideas that were bouncing around inside my head.

As I walked home with Miriam later that day, we met 'Aunt' Alassane walking towards us. I recognised the dress she was wearing as being an old one of Sushie's: plain, blue, much too short for a Wadata woman – and it made her belly look lumpy. She was carrying a bag made of red netting, full of supplies from Monsieur Letouye's shop.

'I'll bet she didn't have to pay for those!' said Miriam under her breath.

'Hush!' I said. 'She'll hear you!'

We stopped and exchanged greetings, politely. I knew that this was a mere formality; she had very little time for me or my friends, really. When one spoke to Aunt Alassane one always sensed that she was anxious to be elsewhere.

Aunt Alassane was not married. Nor, in fact, was she my aunt. She lived in a large, brick house on the edge of the village with her two younger sisters – Flo and Hamidou. They were not originally from Wadata. It was said that their late parents had been nomads who had settled in the village after losing their livestock to persistent drought. Even so, their household had more goats, sheep and chickens than any other in Wadata, with the exception of Monsieur Letouye's. It could not have been said that these women were liked in our village. In fact, we children took great delight in concocting outrageous tales about them. Yet, all over

GAVIN WESTON

Wadata and as far away as Goteye and Konni, there were men beholden to Alassane and her sisters, and when they snapped their fingers, a man would always come running.

It was my father who had encouraged us to address Aunt Alassane in such a formal manner. My mother never spoke about her. Once, when I had taken Fatima to the *dispensaire* to have a damaged toenail removed, I had overheard Sushie and some visiting VCI officials discussing the 'health risks of the Big House'. I was not then certain that it was Aunt Alassane's home to which they were referring, but I had a fairly good idea that it might be.

'You remind your father that he promised to fix my roof, girl. Okay?' she said, as we continued on our separate ways.

'*Toh.*'

'Tell him to come and see me soon.' She gave us a great, toothy smile. Like a crocodile, I thought: a pretty, dangerous crocodile.

Miriam and I watched her as she continued on her way. Her broad hips swayed like those women in movies and she swung her bag, plump with onions and peppers, like a schoolgirl.

'What age do you think she is, Miriam?' I said.

'I don't know,' she replied. 'Who cares? She's a witch!'

I didn't want to admit it, but she had said exactly what I was thinking.

At home, Fatima was watering Mother's okra patch. She was not in good form.

'What's wrong with you, Bébé Boureima?' I said. She did not answer. I tried again. 'Why do you scowl so?'

'I want to go to school too!' she said, sulkily. 'You get to go to school and I have to do all your work!'

'I have to go to school *and* work,' I said.

'It's not fair,' Fatima said. 'Can't you ask those *anasaras* to let me go to school too?'

'I don't think it is quite as simple as that,' I answered. 'Besides, I think you are still too young.'

She kicked at the empty pail by her feet. 'Hmmphh! Father says even Adamou is going to go to school soon – and he's a stupid boy!'

'Perhaps,' I said, setting my schoolbag down. 'And perhaps you will go to school one day also, Fatima.'

She looked at me sceptically. 'Now I have to help Mother pound the stupid millet!' she said.

'I will help you.'

She allowed herself a little smile.

I put my hand on her shoulder. 'Come on, Bébé Boureima,' I said. 'Let's find Mother.'

'*Toh*,' said Fatima. 'But I'm not a baby!'

I should have noticed how silent the compound was when we entered it. Apart from the clucking of our few chickens as they scratched around in the dust, there was no sound.

'Mother?' I called, expecting, I suppose, to see her emerge from the house. There was no reply.

'Azara?' Fatima called out, cheekily, a great grin on her face. Again nothing.

'Are you certain that she was not going to the river?' I asked my sister.

'She was pounding millet when I went to tend the okra,' Fatima said. 'She told me to hurry back to help her.'

'*Toh*.' I stood still for a few moments, wondering where she might be.

I walked instinctively around to the back of our house, not expecting to find her there at all.

But find her there I did. She was lying, face down, in a mess of millet and sand.

'Mother!' I cried.

Fatima came running to my side. 'What's wrong with her, Haoua?' she said.

I was already on my knees, shaking the limp body. A faint groan told me that she was alive. I turned quickly and grabbed Fatima by the shoulders. 'Listen, Fatima,' I said.

'She's going to be all right. But we need Sushie. Now! Run as fast as you can!'

Fatima nodded, tears welling up in her eyes. In a flash she was gone.

I did not know what to do. 'What if Sushie has gone to Goteye?' I asked myself. 'What if. . . oh please don't die, Mother!' I thought. I wanted to turn her on to her back, but something told me that I should wait. Instead, I eased my hand under her head and cradled her face in my palm. Gently then, I brushed the dust off her other cheek with the end of my *pagne*. I squeezed my eyes closed and begged Allah to spare her, promising Him anything, if only she should live. But it was Sushie I wished for most, in truth. 'Come on, Sushie!' I whispered, trembling with fear. 'Come on!'

When I opened my eyes, I saw that Mother's were open too. 'Mother!' I said, overjoyed. I bent down and kissed her forehead.

'My Haoua,' she said, her voice a faint, dry crackle.

I gently stroked her face. 'Sushie is coming. Be still.'

'A little water, child.'

With my free hand I untied my head wrap. Then, folding it into a pad, I eased it under my mother's head. As I went to fetch the water, I continued to pray, all the while glancing at the entrance for any sign of Sushie.

'Your water, Mother,' I said, easing my knees under her head and putting the plastic cup to her lips. Her eyes seemed to brighten a little as she sipped at the water. Two thin rivulets snaked their way across her still dusty cheekbone, leaving shiny streaks of skin. She gave a little nod, then brought her hand up weakly to her mouth. 'My Haoua,' she whispered again.

I cradled her head in my arms and put my forehead against hers. Her finger gently, rhythmically, tapped my elbow as we waited. I could not have been alone with her for very long, but to me it seemed like an eternity.

At last I felt a hand on my shoulder. It was Sushie. Behind

her, a small crowd had gathered. I looked for Fatima, but could not see her.

'What have you been up to, Azara?' Sushie said, panting a little. 'Let's get you onto this blanket.' She helped me up, then quickly steered me away towards the crowd.

Near the back, Adamou was standing, looking frightened and bewildered. Beside him, I saw Fatima's tiny frame. She clutched at the end of his tee shirt. I weaved my way through the onlookers to join my brother and sister.

'What happened?' said Adamou, his voice faltering.

'I don't know.'

'Will she be okay?'

'Yes,' I said. 'She has to be okay.' I looked back just in time to catch sight of my mother being whisked away by my father and three of the other menfolk, each of whom held a corner of the large, coarse blanket. Sushie followed them out of the compound. I pushed my way through the throng of people and caught up with her.

'May I come too?' I said.

'No, Little One,' she answered. 'You stay here and look after your brother and sister. You're the woman of the house until your mother returns – *toh*?' She put her hand to my cheek and gave a little smile.

I nodded. 'But you'll tell me when I can see her?'

'Of course,' she said. 'I'll tell you as soon as she's well enough.'

14

When my father returned from the *dispensaire*, late that evening, he told us that Mother was fine. We were all in bed, but none of us had been able to sleep.

'Does that mean she can come home?' Adamou said, sitting up.

'Not yet,' my father replied, turning to me. 'Sushie will tell you more tomorrow, Haoua. She wants to see you alone first.'

'Haoua?' my brother said. 'Why does she want to talk to Haoua, Father? I am the eldest.'

My father did not reply.

'I want to see Mother too!' sobbed Fatima.

'Hush,' my father said. 'You will all see her. Now go to sleep.' With that, he turned and left the room.

'Why would Sushie want to talk to a little tick like you?' Adamou demanded.

'I don't know,' I said. 'Perhaps because Mother has requested it, or perhaps because I am almost a woman.'

'Aiee!'

At the far side of the room, Fatima was still sobbing. I clambered off my own bedding and crawled in beside her. Immediately she snuggled up to me.

'Go to sleep, Little One,' I said, stroking her forehead – much as I had stroked my mother's, earlier that day.

15

Haoua Boureima
Child Ref. NER2726651832
Vision Corps International
Tera Area Development Programme
C/O BP 11504
Niamey
Republic of Niger
West Africa

Hope Boyd
Member No. 515820
Ballygowrie
Co. Down
N. Ireland
BT22 1AW

20th November, 1998

Dear Haoua,

Thank you for writing to us again. It was really nice to hear from you.

This is just a very short note from me (Hope) – Katie says she will write again soon – because we have had some very bad news and are all feeling sad here. My great grandpapa ('Papa') died last week. He was just a few days away from his 100th birthday! I can't believe that he has gone. My mum says that he is with Jesus now. I hope so. Papa was a very good man, and very clever too. He was great at making and fixing things. He was a sailor during the second war against Germany. He used to tell us about the terrible things he had seen! I will miss him.

My dad says that during the war Germany took control of France and that your country had been ruled by the French before that, so Niger kind of became part of Germany for a while! How strange to think that your country and mine were on opposite sides! Have you been to France? We went camping there a few years ago. It was fun! I so liked the swimming pool at our campsite.

The rest of my family are well. We are going to go to Spain quite soon for a holiday. Katie and I are really looking forward to that.

I hope that your family are all well.

Lots of love,
from Hope Boyd

True to her word, Sushie sent for me the following afternoon. Richard came to the house to fetch me. Fortunately, Adamou was working with my father and Fatima had gone to play with Amina and their other little friends, so there was no fuss.

'Ready?' Richard said.

'Yes,' I answered. 'Will my mother be coming home today?'

He raised his eyebrows and shrugged. 'You'll need to talk to Mademoiselle Sushie about that, Haoua.'

We were halfway to the *dispensaire* when we met Aunt Alassane and her sister Flo at the corner near Monsieur Letouye's shop. I did not want to stop, or talk to anyone just then – least of all Aunt Alassane – but I knew that it was necessary to do so.

'How is your poor mother, dear?' Flo asked me. For the first time I noticed that her face was more weathered than Aunt Alassane's.

'I don't know, Mademoiselle,' I said, 'I haven't seen her yet today.'

'*Toh*. You must be so worried, you poor child,' said Aunt Alassane.

'Excuse us, Mademoiselles,' Richard said, politely but firmly. 'We are on our way to see the good lady now.'

'*D'accord*. Do give her our regards.' 'Of course.'

I was glad that Richard had intervened. As we walked on, he patted me gently on the shoulder and then looked down at me and winked.

As we approached the *dispensaire* compound, I could see that there were several people sitting on beer crates outside a rattan screen, waiting to see Sushie or one of her colleagues.

'If you'll wait here just a moment please, Haoua,' Richard said, giving my shoulder a little squeeze. He greeted the patients at the entrance to the small consultation room and then went inside.

I too nodded politely at the patients.

'Your mother is a good woman,' said Madame Hacheme, who was leaning against the door frame and breathing heavily. 'God will watch over her,' she panted. She looked like she might give birth at any moment.

Madame Dekougbonto, her neighbour, nodded in agreement. She clucked her tongue, loudly, as if to say, 'What a shame.'

I did not want small talk. It was as if everyone else in the village knew something that I did not, and it both irked and frightened me.

I did not have to wait long before Sushie appeared at the door and beckoned me in. The *dispensaire* consisted of an extra room which had been added to a two-room dwelling. The house was unusual for Wadata in that one entered it through a hallway rather than directly into a room. This arrangement meant that a level of privacy, at least, could be maintained by Sushie. Living and working in the same place ensured that she got very little peace, but we never heard her complain.

Instead of leading me to the door at the end of the hall, she drew back a striped curtain and entered her living quarters. 'Come through here first, please, Haoua,' she said. 'I want to talk to you before we go through to your mother.'

I had been in this room before. Its dimensions and general

appearance were similar to the living area of my parents' house, but still I was intrigued by its unfamiliarity. There were only a few objects in the room that might not have been found in any other house in Wadata, and yet, as my eyes became accustomed to the muted light, the space both excited and unsettled me. The little chest of drawers that Sushie had painted the colour of newly emerging shoots, the wind-up radio standing on a plastic chair by the side of her raised bed, the framed photograph of her parents with their smooth, silvery hair and ivory white teeth, the large, orange backpack leaning against the wall and the little shelf with its array of expensive toothpaste, water purification tablets, mosquito repellent creams and other potions – all of these things had a mesmerising effect on me.

As I followed Sushie into the room, something brushed against my cheek. I clawed at the air, fearing that it might be a spider or scorpion, or a praying mantis dropping down from the rafters of the house.

Sushie turned in time to see me flinch. 'It's a wallet,' she said, a great grin on her face. She reached up and unhooked the object from a nail, then shook its tassels in my face. 'The Chief of Tahoua gave it to me last year! I was his guest of honour,' she continued, rolling her eyes. 'He gave me some sandals too, but they fell apart long ago.' She handed it to me and I studied it carefully. With its pouches, heavy decoration and neck string, it was indeed a very beautiful thing.

'It is very fine,' I said.

'Hmm. We ate couscous together with some of the other village elders. My Hausa isn't so good, but I'm fairly sure he wanted to bed me!'

We laughed together. Then her face became serious.

'Have a seat, Haoua,' she said.

I did as she instructed, somehow already aware that my life was never going to be the same again.

16

'I'm not going to lie to you, Haoua,' Sushie said. 'Your mother is very sick indeed. She has been for some time now.' She paused, perhaps for me to say something in response.

Instead, my fingers continued to work the tassels on the Chief of Tahoua's wallet, all the while my eyes remaining firmly fixed on the dust floor.

'Haoua?'

Our eyes met for just a moment.

'Did you hear what I said?'

I nodded. 'Mademoiselle.'

Sushie sighed. 'The thing is, I want her to have some more tests carried out. . .'

'Tests?' I said, my voice shaky.

'Yes.'

'What kind of tests?'

'We need to see what's going on with her blood, her immune system. Find out why she's losing weight. Why she's coughing, fainting, vomiting sometimes.'

'Mother works too hard. Fatima and I can help her. We can work harder. She will be all right,' I said. I could almost taste the panic, steadily rising within me.

'No. It's not just that. She needs special treatment.'

'Medicine?' I said, looking at her directly now.

'Yes. Probably. Medicine that I don't have here.' She seemed to read the question on my face correctly. 'I have to take your mother away, Haoua.'

'Where will you take her?'

'To the hospital in Niamey. She'll get proper attention there.'

I nodded.

Sushie crossed the room and put her hand on my shoulder. 'You understand what I'm saying?' she asked.

Again I nodded. My head was reeling. 'Mother will be all right,' I whispered. 'God is good. God is great. We will look after our father until Mother is well again. Adamou and Fatima and. . .'

Sushie gave me a little shake to interrupt me. 'Haoua,' she said. 'I need to take your sister to Niamey too.'

I looked up at her through brimming tears, which now began to cascade down my cheeks. I thought of my school and of visits from other health workers and serious talks from Monsieur Boubacar about Health Education. My lip trembled and I shook my head from side to side. For what seemed like an eternity, I could not bring myself to utter the word. Then, 'AIDS?' I said.

Sushie squeezed my shoulder. 'Hopefully not. But it could be. We have to be sure.' She took a roll of tissue paper from the shelf and tore some off, handing it to me. 'You must be strong for your mother, Little One,' she said. 'Let's go and see her.'

I stood up. Sushie took my hand and made to lead me out of the room. 'Wait,' I said.

She turned to face me, still holding my hand. 'Is it Fatima?' she asked.

'Yes,' I said. 'Why do you need to take her too? She isn't sick, is she?'

Sushie shook her head. 'No. She seems very well, Haoua. But remember what you learned about HIV/AIDS in school: the virus can only be transmitted sexually, or through blood, but a pregnant mother can pass it to an unborn child.'

'But Fatima is five,' I said.

She nodded. 'Yes. But your mother may have been HIV

positive for some time before Fatima was born.' She gave my hand a little squeeze. 'We just have to check.'

'And me. . . and Adamou?'

'No. Neither of you are in danger – because of your age. I have asked your father to have the tests carried out, though, but he seems unwilling to do so.'

'AIDS is a very bad thing,' I said, daubing my eyes. 'It brings great shame on a family.'

There had been many other villagers who had been taken to Niamey for tests and never again set foot in Wadata, but no one ever admitted that they had died from AIDS. We all knew about this cursed disease. We had all watched members of our families grow thin and weak and sickly.

But Bunchie used to say that our people had lived and died in this way since the dawn of time. 'Always working towards the next meal,' she would tut. 'Working ourselves to death.' *AIDS*, she believed, was nothing but a label that the *anasaras* had given to illnesses that they themselves could neither understand nor cure. She said that they could do nothing about visitations from evil spirits from the *Thin Places*, whereas, with the old ways, one could seek the help of a witch doctor and know that he would try to chase them away.

'Look,' Sushie said, 'we don't know yet. We just have to wait and see. It may be something else.' She took my face in her hands and smiled at me kindly. 'Don't let your mother see that you have been crying.'

But Sushie was a nurse who had seen many such cases before. Of course she knew.

With a heavy heart, I trudged behind Sushie to the treatment room. I was familiar with this room too; it was here that my grandmother had died. The combined odours of disinfectant and medicine and a faint waft of vomit hit me immediately. Memories of Bunchie's last hours rushed at me also, but I fought them back. A metal grille, fitted over a single small window, caused the room to be bathed in a gloomy half-light. Directly beneath the window, a bowl and jug for washing hands had been placed on a small table. Opposite this stood a battered, grey filing cabinet in which drugs, syringes and medical books were kept safely locked away. Dotted about the walls, happy, smiling faces beamed down from Vision Corps International posters: children drawing water from wells, farmers tending crops, fishermen repairing nets, doctors holding babies. To the right of the doorway, a rattan screen had been placed between two single beds and on one of them lay my ailing mother, covered to the neck with a thin white sheet.

'Hey, Azara,' Sushie said, cheerily. 'Look who's here to see you.'

My mother was awake and looking just a little stronger than when I had last seen her. She smiled and held out a feeble hand to take mine.

'How do you feel, Mother?'

'I will be on my feet again in no time, child,' she said. 'Are your brother and sister all right? Have you been seeing to my crops? And our animals?'

'Yes, Mother,' I said. 'Your crops are fine. The animals are fine. And we are all fine. Fatima is at Amina's house and Adamou is working with Father. You must not worry about anything.'

'That's right, Azara,' Sushie said, stooping down to remove a basin at the bedside. 'You must concentrate on getting strong again.' She draped a cloth over the basin and stood up.

My mother looked Sushie in the eye. 'Uhuh, Mademoiselle. That is true. There is a great deal of work to be done. Salim will never cope alone.'

'Really, Mother,' I said. 'Everything is fine at home. We will manage perfectly well until you are well enough to return.'

Sushie moved towards the door, but my mother coughed

110

and gestured for her to remain in the room. The thin, clear tube running from a metal stand to the back of her hand swayed as she covered her mouth.

I held a plastic beaker to her lips, to allow her to sip some water.

'And when *can* I return to my home, Mademoiselle?' she said, when she had regained her composure. Sushie paused by the door, the basin still in her hands.

I caught her eye and realised only then that she had not yet broken the news to my mother.

Setting the basin on top of the filing cabinet, Sushie crossed the room again. She propped herself against the edge of my mother's sick-bed and put an arm around me. 'Azara. . . I've just been telling Haoua that we will need you to go for some tests.' She paused.

My mother continued to fix her gaze, silently.

'To see what's making you so weary, so sick. . . you understand?'

'Uhuh.'

Sushie continued. 'The thing is. . . I don't have the facilities here, Azara. Or enough beds. Wadata is full of pregnant women. There are cases of malaria, dysentery and even one of what may turn out to be river blindness. Who knows what this little room will be needed for next? We'll need to shift you – when you've regained your strength a little.'

'Shift me?' my mother said, suspicion in her voice. Sushie nodded.

I stroked my mother's hand. 'It will be all right.'

She looked at me, then squeezed her eyes shut and shook her head. 'No.'

'You will get proper treatment in Niamey,' Sushie said, still trying to sound cheery, but failing.

My mother opened her eyes. 'I always knew this day would come,' she hissed, her face suddenly veiled in anger. 'I knew that my husband would bring this shame to our door!'

17

The thought of being without my mother filled me with dread. I had pleaded with her – and Sushie – to let me accompany them to Niamey but my pleas fell on deaf ears.

'But I can help to keep Fatima occupied,' I argued. 'She will be less frightened if I am with her.'

'I have other business to attend to,' Sushie said, as she helped my mother tie some of her belongings into a bundle for the long journey. 'I don't even know when I'll be coming back to Wadata. And your father will need you here, for sure. I'm going to try to find Abdelkrim too. I'm sure he will help if he can.' She looked towards my mother who was wheezing heavily. 'That's right, isn't it, Azara?'

'That is right. You will be the woman of the house while I am gone, Little One.' Mother's tired face smiled sadly. 'Adamou is just a boy. And your father. . .' Her words trailed off and were replaced by a series of violent coughs.

With both Mother and Fatima gone there was indeed a great deal more work to be shared out at home. I thought of what my grandmother had said about 'always working towards the next meal' and never before did her statement seem more true. For the first few days we seemed, somehow, to manage quite well. I got up earlier, went to bed later, yet still managed to continue with my school work. My mother had been right about Adamou though: he needed to be reminded to carry out his chores constantly. At first my father encouraged and praised my brother. Occasionally he would even comment on the meal I had prepared. But after a week or so had passed, he appeared to lose interest and spent less and less time in and around our compound.

I had just finished clearing away our utensils one morning and was about to get myself ready for school when I heard a voice at the door.

'Hey there!' It was a woman's voice, shrill and impatient and only vaguely familiar to me.

I went to the door to find Aunt Alassane standing there, dressed in a flamboyant green and yellow *pagne* and blue sunglasses.

'Listen. . . girl. . .'

'It's Haoua,' I said.

'That's right. Haoua. . .' She nodded vigorously in such a way that I knew my name was of little concern to her at that particular time. 'Anyway. Your father sent me over to tell you that you must help your brother tend to the livestock and crops today. He's busy.'

I was a little confused. I had not seen my father that morning but had presumed that he had come in late the previous evening and had left his bed before either Adamou or I had risen. He had been doing this increasingly, even before my mother had been taken to Niamey.

'I have school,' I said.

'You'll have to miss it,' Alassane said, turning to spit out some kola nut juice. 'My roof won't wait any longer.' Suddenly her face struck me as hard – unwomanly somehow – and I wondered that I had ever thought of her as pretty.

'But we're working on our projects!' I protested. 'Father knows that. I will be in big trouble, Mademoiselle! Tomorrow I'm to make a presentation to the whole class. I've been writing about my friends in Ireland and studying their country. Richard has been helping me. He found some beautiful pictures in a magazine. It really is very important!'

She shrugged and looked down at me through her blue lenses. '*Walayi!*' she said, curling her lip. 'Do you think I give a damn about your stupid school, or that oaf Boubacar, or your stupid project? Why don't you have some respect for your poor father – and for me?' She was shouting now. I was determined not to cry.

'I've a good mind to teach you a lesson myself!' she snapped. For a moment I really thought that she was going to strike me. Her anger had risen quickly and taken me by surprise. 'Just do what your father has told you to do. Who knows, it may be possible for you to attend your precious school tomorrow.'

I was even more alarmed by this statement. 'But I have to go to school tomorrow! I simply *have* to!'

As I spoke, Alassane looked quickly over her shoulder.

I continued to protest. 'Please listen, Mademoiselle. Monsieur Boubacar says that. . .'

Before I knew what was happening I had been pushed back into the house and on to the floor. Alassane was straddling me, her broad knees pinning my shoulders to the ground. One hand clenched my jaw while she jabbed me in the ribs with the other.

'Now you listen to me, you little bitch.' Each word accompanied another jab. 'Don't answer me back again or you'll be sorry. Just shut up, do what you're told and – if you know what's good for you – don't mention this little discussion to anyone. Not even that brother of yours. Understand?'

I nodded.

Alassane slapped my face, lightly, as if I was someone about whom she cared.

'Good girlie,' she said, a false smile on her face. She stood up and brushed off the dust from the hem of her *pagne*. 'Look what you've done to me,' she clucked, straightening her sunglasses. She turned then and strutted to the door. 'I'll call again soon.'

I had not moved from where I had been pinned down. I was so terrified that I could neither move nor make a sound.

'Did you hear what I said?'

I sat up and nodded.

She paused by the doorway, just long enough to peer

disdainfully around the room. Then she grinned at me. 'You've got a lot to do, girlie,' she said. 'If I were you I wouldn't sit about!'

Then she was gone.

18

Haoua Boureima
Child Ref. NER2726651832
Vision Corps International
Tera Area Development Programme
C/O BP 11504
Niamey
Republic of Niger
West Africa

Katie Boyd
Member No. 515820
Ballygowrie
Co. Down
N. Ireland
BT22 1AW

4th February, 1999

Dear Haoua,

I'm so sorry to hear that your mother is not feeling very well. Hopefully she will be up and about and back from hospital very soon. I'm sure that you are worried about her, but it's good that your father is there with you anyway. We are all thinking about you and your family and I say a little prayer for you all every evening before I get into bed. I know that Hope does also.

I was reading the magazine that we get every now and then from VCI, and there was a story about how lots of children in West Africa have to walk miles to school. The story said that many children do not own shoes! I can't imagine not having shoes. I talked to my dad about it and he said that it would be okay if we sent you some shoes. He said that if you could draw around your foot and send us the paper, we could send you back a nice pair of trainers, if you'd like that?

Hope and I are very excited because we are doing a very important exam at school soon, and Dad says that if we do well we can get a pony! I have always wanted a pony. Do you have many ponies or horses in Niger?

I think it's great that you are doing a project on our country in school. I hope your teacher likes it. Perhaps your father will treat you if you do well. My friend Lucy says that she wants her parents to sponsor a child too.

Well, I must go now, because I have lots of homework to do and I have to help Hope to set the table. Don't forget about the foot drawing.

Your friend,
Katie. XXX

I never did get to make my presentation. My father did not appear at home again for several days, so Adamou and I had no choice but to carry out all of his chores as well as our own, Fatima's and Mother's. We were exhausted.

Richard called to see why I had not been attending school, but had no news about Fatima's tests.

Aunt Alassane would call at the compound too from time to time; not from any concern but simply to check that we were doing everything that my father expected us to do. Once or twice she brought us a little *boule*. And always she made a point of tweaking at Adamou's hair and saying, 'Such a handsome boy. Just like his father,' or some such.

My brother did not say much about Alassane, but I could tell that he did not like her either and that he was frightened of her too. One evening when we were sitting drinking tea, he looked me in the eye and said wearily, 'Everything is going to be all right, isn't it, Haoua?' My big brother looking to me for reassurance!

'We'll be all right,' I said, yawning.

'It's just that. . . you know. . . Mother is sick. Really sick, isn't she?'

'She's going to be fine. Father said so.'

'But what if she isn't?'

I didn't answer.

Adamou continued. 'I mean, what if this is the way it's going to be?'

'What do you mean?' I said, crossly. I knew what he meant. I had been worrying about the same thing myself.

'If she doesn't come back. . .'

I shook my head. 'That's not going to happen to us. We have to be strong. We have to ask God to help us. God is good. God is great. We must ask for his help.'

'. . .and if Father stays away. . . or gets sick too?'

I was really angry now. 'Be quiet, Adamou!' I yelled. 'Just shut up! Sushie will be back with Fatima any day now. Mother will be back soon too. Everything will be as it was before.'

Adamou stood up. 'I'm going to bed,' he said. It was dark, but along with the firelight reflected in his eyes I was sure that I caught a glimpse of tears too. 'Maybe tomorrow I'll just go up to the Big House and tell Father to come home.'

But we both knew that to do so would only bring us more trouble.

I sat for a long while after he had gone, poking at the embers while the mosquitoes nipped at my ears and the cicadas sang their never-ending song. Sparks flitted into the night sky and mingled with the stars overhead, and I thought of my mother's poor, gaunt face.

Adamou was right, of course. I had been thinking the same thing for days. We had seen it happen to other families who had lost parents, or been abandoned by a surviving parent after the death of the other. We had watched children struggle to survive; come to rely on pickings, scraps, hand-outs from their already poor neighbours, while kindly officials like Richard and Sushie did what they could to help. It happened less frequently now in Wadata, but it happened. I knew that Adamou's fear was identical to mine: it was the fear of the unknown, of vulnerability, of abandonment.

Yet suddenly it seemed ridiculous. A ludicrous thought. I knew my father. He was not ill. Nor would he abandon us. He would not do such a thing. And so what if he married again? Lots of men had more than one wife. He would still care for us – and for Mother. I knew my father.

And sure enough, the very next morning, I awoke to hear the sound of firewood being chopped outside and the clattering of our old black kettle against the flat stones. I kicked my bedding away and leaned across to give Adamou a shake.

'Adamou,' I said. 'He's back!'

There was a grunt from beneath his blanket. 'It's Father!' I said.

We went outside together and found Father – and Aunt Alassane – sitting on mats in front of our house. Flames were just beginning to lick around the base of the kettle.

My father was cleaning his teeth with a stick. 'I was just about to waken you,' he said when he noticed us. 'Let the animals out, Adamou.'

Adamou stretched, then turned without uttering a word.

Alassane looked at me and winked. 'Hey, girlie,' she said. 'You want some tea?'

I shook my head.

'Where are your manners, Haoua?' my father said. 'Aunt Alassane is talking to you.'

'No. Thank you,' I said. I did not like this woman being here like this. I turned to go back inside to dress, then hesitated, realising that there might never be a better moment to discuss my floundering school work. 'Father,' I said. 'I need to go back to school.'

'I know, Little One,' he answered. 'But there is so much to do here. When your sister and mother return, we will manage much better.'

I considered protesting but he had turned away from me and I was aware that Aunt Alassane was glaring at me meaningfully.

Despite my father's apparent disinterest in my schooling and the increasing menace I felt from Alassane, I was not about to give up my education without a fight. It seemed perfectly reasonable to me that I should return to school, now that Father was home again. After all, Adamou and I had looked after the animals, the crops and the house for more than a full week. I had missed my presentation and a great deal of lesson time and, although I was always pleased to see Miriam, it had pained me greatly to hear her talk about school each day when she called at our compound in the afternoons.

Besides, I knew that it would also be Mother's wish that my schooling continue.

The day after my father's return, I rose early and slipped quietly out of bed in the dark. I had left my *pagne* and head wrap folded carefully on a chair in the outer room of the house the previous evening and had hidden my school bag in the corner of the room, behind a sack of millet. I did not dare to light the kerosene lamp, dressing instead in the grey half-light which had begun to creep under the door. Without a sound, I removed the cloth from the bucket on the table and poured some water into a plastic beaker. Then, grabbing a fistful of dried dates, I went to fetch my school bag.

It was not there.

My first thought was that I had changed my mind about hiding the bag there, but I could not think where else I might have put it. Was it Adamou up to his usual tricks? But I had not mentioned my plan to anyone – not even to Miriam.

I rummaged around in the gloomy light but the bag was nowhere to be found. It would be pointless to go to school without my exercise books and the pretty pencil case that Katie and Hope had sent me. Besides, even though I had been absent for the project presentation day, I still wanted to hand my work in to Monsieur Boubacar, and it too had been carefully packed in my school bag.

I had just sat down at the table to consider what best to do when I heard a cough behind me.

'Is this what you're looking for?' It was my father. He was standing in the inner doorway, holding out my school bag. I pretended not to notice the gruff tone in his voice.

'Yes, thank you, Father,' I said, crossing the room and reaching out to take the bag from him.

Instead of letting go, he gripped the straps firmly. 'What do you think you are doing?' he hissed.

'I have to go to school, Father,' I said, somewhat shaken now.

He wrenched the bag from me and threw it on to the floor, behind him. With his other hand he grabbed my wrist. 'What did I tell you?' The whites of his eyes pierced the gloom.

'You're hurting me, Father,' I said.

He let go of my wrist then and crouched in front of me, grasping my shoulders in his big strong hands. 'Would you defy me, Haoua?'

I looked down at my feet.

'Would you defy me, girl?' he said again, shaking me now.

'I *have* to go to school, Father. It is what Mother wants for me too.'

Suddenly his face took on the look of a stranger. It was as if he had donned some ancient mask and was about to perform a terrible ritual, calling on our ancestors for strength and guidance. His teeth were bared and his eyes were wide and, I noticed now, badly bloodshot. 'I have to go to school! I have to go to school!' he mimicked.

I tried to pull away from him but he pulled me back, grabbing my head and pushing his contorted face close to mine. His breath stank. This was not my father.

'Don't you understand? Didn't you listen? There is too much work to be done! I need your help here!' He was shouting now. 'I should never have listened to the *anasaras* –

or to your mother! Look at you now! Look what you've become! Defiant, disrespectful, lazy. . .'

For a moment the image of my brother Abdelkrim – strong, self-assured, resistant – flashed through my mind and I wondered if my father might be possessed. I knew that he was not a devil, but was sure that he could be at the mercy of a devil. I was frightened, but not so much that I could stop myself from at least trying to defend my actions.

'Lazy? Father! I work hard – always. I. . .'

He shook me again. 'Disrespectful! So disrespectful! You can forget that damned school and your precious books and letters and nonsense! You can forget all of that! There are going to be changes around here. I can't do this by myself! You are going to help me! You are going to help me!'

He was ranting, but still I could not give up. 'Please, Father. I will do my work, but. . .' The shaking continued. 'Shut up! Shut up! I say! I've had enough of your insolence! I've had enough talk about ways which are not ours! I've had enough of interfering *anasaras*!'

'What would you do without the *anasaras*' seed programme?' I blurted out through my tears. 'They have helped you too, Father!'

As soon as the words had crossed my lips, I knew that I had pushed him too far. A tortured gasp heaved from deep within his chest and he raised his right hand to strike me.

'Stop it!' Adamou's voice called out from behind him. 'Stop it now!'

In a moment it was over. My father lumbered out of the house and Adamou and I stood facing each other in grim silence.

19

I did not challenge my father's decision about my education again. Instead, I continued to tell myself that Mother would soon be well again; that she would return to Wadata with Fatima and that everything would return to normal. Then I would go back to school. Father would stay at home and tend his livestock and crops. Adamou would do his chores but have time to play with his friends also. Alassane would stay away from our compound and Miriam and I would resume referring to her as one of the witches from the Big House.

My father had left instructions for Adamou and me to resurface the floor of the main room in our house. 'It will please your mother when she returns,' he had said.

It was hard, slow, back-breaking work – collecting bucketfuls of cattle and goat dung, mixing it into a thick paste, then spreading and tamping it evenly with off-cuts of wood scrounged from Monsieur Letouye. We had, of course, carried out this job before, but never without the help and guidance of our parents. Even so, we were pleased with our handiwork and we were close to completion by mid afternoon.

'Do you think that Father is sick too?' Adamou asked, as he ladled out great dollops of the mixture with his hands for me to spread towards the door.

I stopped working and looked up from where I knelt. 'His face, Adamou. . . it was not like Father's. It was as if he had a demon inside him or something. . .'

Suddenly his eyes filled with tears. 'We're going to lose Father too, aren't we?'

'Stop it.'

'It's true!' he said, forcefully. 'We're going to be orphans – like the Gandemey children. . .'

'No!'

He was sobbing now. I set down my piece of timber and shuffled across the dusty part of the floor, on my knees, towards him. 'It's going to be all right,' I said, putting my filthy arms around him. It felt a little strange to be comforting him like this. For him too, I think. It was more usual for us to squabble. After a few moments, though, he leaned his head in towards me and we just stayed still and silent for a time.

'We'll sleep outside tonight,' Adamou said later, as he scraped the dried excrement from his hands and forearms. 'You can be sure that we won't see Father until tomorrow.'

I put my finishing touches to the floor around the doorway and stood up. Flies swarmed around us, driven insane by the lure of baking dung. Adamou was pouring water from a large plastic jug, first over one hand, then the other. I was just about to tell him to save some of it for me to wash too, when we heard the roar of an engine as a vehicle pulled up outside our compound. We looked at each other, hardly daring to breathe. There was the sound of doors opening and closing followed by muffled voices and giggling.

'Fatima!' I said.

We met her, hand in hand with Sushie, at the entrance to the compound.

'What in good God's name have you two been doing to yourselves?' Sushie said, in her odd, lazy drawl. 'You stink to high heaven and you look like shit!'

Adamou laughed. 'It *is* shit, Mademoiselle! We've been fixing the floor in our house.'

'*Toh.*' Sushie looked at me, quizzically. 'And school?' she said.

I shrugged. 'It's Father. . .'

Fatima was bouncing around us, eager to tell us all about her trip to the city.

Sushie gritted her teeth. 'Right. We'll talk about that later.' She bent down and pulled Fatima towards her. 'The main thing now is to let you know that this little madam is fine.'

Fatima giggled as Sushie tickled her.

'She's not going to get sick?' I said.

'No. She's fine. The tests were negative.'

'And Mother?'

'We'll talk about that later, too. Right now you two need to get cleaned up. Gather up all your buckets and gourds and we'll drive down to the river. Fatima can tell you all about her adventures as we go. You can have a proper wash and stock up on water supplies at the same time.' She let go of Fatima and stood up, then clapped her hands together. 'And I'll keep an eye out for that monster, Fawako, while you're bathing,' she added, winking at Adamou.

We clambered into the back of Sushie's truck with as many buckets, gourds and jars as we could find and, squeezed between boxes of medical supplies and blankets and cases of imported spring water, we set off for the river.

20

Haoua Boureima   Abdelkrim Boureima
Wadata   Military Barracks
Tera Area   Avenue de Seyni Kountche
Republic of Niger   Niamey
                        Republic of Niger

9th February, 1999

Dear Haoua,

Here is a little radio for you, as I promised some time ago. I think that it is not so fine as the one that your friends sent me, but I hope that you will like it anyway.

Please give my best wishes to Fatima and Adamou and tell them that I will send them something also when I can.

Pray for our mother.

Your loving brother,
Abdelkrim

That night we had a fine supper of dried meats, cheese and soft, sweet-smelling bread, the likes of which I had never before tasted.

'It's from the French supermarket,' Sushie said. 'Those bastards really know how to fleece us *anasaras*!' She grinned as she spoke and I felt warm, not just from the fire which flickered before us but because, for the first time in ages, I felt safe.

Fatima lay with her head on my lap, drifting in and out of

126

sleep. Adamou sat cross-legged on his mat, poking at the fire and belching occasionally while Sushie told us about the shanties in Niamey, the markets heaving with illegally acquired aid relief goods and warehouses full of ill-planned consignments of rotting Spanish tomatoes. Her speech, although full of venom and foul language for what she said was a flawed and corrupt system, was also passionate and sincere; so much so that had any stranger wandered into our compound that evening they would have been left in no doubt as to the fact that this woman truly loved Niger.

But, though her stories were, as ever, funny, scary and engaging, I longed only to hear about Mother. Adamou was also becoming restless and, eventually, Sushie knew that she could hold out no longer.

She nodded, then screwed her big, steel coffee cup into the sand. 'Your mother,' she said, 'is a very ill woman.' She paused and looked hard at us. Firelight danced across her pale, anxious face.

We did not speak.

'I am sorry.'

'How long?' Adamou said, after another silence.

Sushie opened her hands towards him, as if asking for his forgiveness. My brother jumped to his feet, kicking dust into the fire, and in a flash he disappeared into the night.

'He is angry,' I said, wiping tears away from my eyes.

'Yes.'

'But not with you, Mademoiselle.'

'It is okay to be angry. I was angry when my grandmother died,' Sushie said.

'And me,' I said. 'But Bunchie comes to me in my dreams sometimes.'

'That's good. She was a good woman. I liked her very much – even though she didn't trust me a pick!'

We both smiled, sadly.

'I don't dream much. At least if I do, I rarely remember.' Sushie nodded towards Fatima, who was snoring gently. 'I wonder what she's dreaming about. The big city, perhaps. . . the president's palace, riding on your brother's motor-cycle. . . vegetables growing under Kennedy Bridge – who knows?'

'Abdelkrim is well? Really?' I asked.

'He's well, Haoua, but he doesn't get to visit your mother often. Mainassara's people have to keep on their toes at the minute; there's been quite a lot of trouble. We only saw Abdel briefly, one afternoon. One of his friends had been injured during a student riot and he was able to combine driving him to the hospital with seeing your mother. It's not nice for her either.'

'I have to see her,' I said.

She sighed. 'I don't know if that is possible.'

'Please, Mademoiselle. You must speak with my father. Please.'

She stood up and stretched. 'I'll try. Tomorrow I'm going to find your father and get your schooling sorted out again, at least. Let's see what mood he's in then.' She bent down and lifted my sister from my lap. 'Let's get this little one to bed,' she said, struggling with our newly-issued VCI mosquito nets, which Adamou had rigged up over a rough timber frame. Together, we managed to wrestle my sister on to her straw mattress.

As Sushie was leaving, Adamou marched into the com-pound and threw himself down on his own bedding without speaking to either of us. I made myself comfortable, under the open sky, while Sushie stood silhouetted at the compound entrance until all was still.

I wanted to ask her to stay, to look after us, to be part of our family. I had not dared mention Alassane's treatment of me. Suddenly I felt frightened and cold. I had no desire that night to be visited in my dreams by anyone, living or dead.

But, of course, I did not ask Mademoiselle Sushie to stay. How could I? She was only one nurse in a village of nearly three hundred children. Sent by the *anasaras* to train birth attendants and healthcare workers and to provide basic treatment for every ailing citizen of Wadata, many of whom would be on her doorstep at first light, demanding to know why she had been away for so long.

Of course she could not stay with us.

21

My father appeared again, late the following afternoon, angrier still than when we had last seen him.

Sushie had indeed found him.

'That woman. . . *Walayi!*' he muttered. 'Who does she think she is?'

As we went about our chores – making sure to keep busy and out of his way – he would catch my eye from time to time and mutter, but I dared not say a thing.

And it soon became apparent that Sushie had spoken not only with my father, but with Aunt Alassane also. Clearly they had had a difference of opinion. Later that evening, Fatima and I served the meal that we had prepared in silence, aware that Father was still seething, but thankful that at least the muttering had stopped. When he had finished his food Father went into the house without speaking to any of us.

But there was more trouble to come.

Adamou had gone to check on our livestock and Fatima and I were clearing away our utensils when I heard a familiar voice call out my name. I looked up and was surprised to see my teacher, Monsieur Boubacar, standing in our compound.

'Haoua. *Ça va?*'

I was a little flustered. 'Monsieur Boubacar! Sir!' I said, both pleased and anxious. I dried my hands on my *pagne* and clasped them to my chest.

His square, genial face beamed at me and at once I felt less ill at ease. 'I see you're keeping busy, young lady,' Monsieur Boubacar said.

I nodded. 'Oh yes, Sir.'

'I'm here to see your father,' he said. 'Mademoiselle Sushie spoke with me this morning and explained your difficult situation. I had, of course, heard about your poor mother, but Mademoiselle Sushie filled me in with the details.' As he spoke he slapped an exercise book against his thigh. 'I am very concerned that one of my best students might fall behind with her work, so I thought that perhaps we could work out some kind of plan whereby you might keep up your studies at home – until things return to normal.' He smiled again, his strong, white teeth impressive in the fading evening light.

That this wonderful man cared enough to come to my home filled me with a great surge of hope and happiness. I smiled back at him and then turned to Fatima, who was still cleaning our utensils. 'Fatima, will you fetch Father, please?'

My sister made an irritatingly good impression of an adult sucking her teeth and for a moment I thought that she was going to embarrass me by protesting, but she did as she was asked and disappeared into the house.

'Can I offer you some water, Sir? Or tea perhaps?' I said, indicating that he should sit on one of the mats that we had spread out around our cooking fire.

'Thank you, Haoua. Tea would be very welcome.' He answered not in French but in Djerma. I guessed that he had switched languages to ensure that I felt more at ease and I was most grateful to him. Monsieur Boubacar had come to Niger from Mali, some years earlier, and spoke in an unusually precise way. This, along with his education and impeccable manners, the care that he gave to his general appearance (he was wearing a smart two-piece bush suit) and the fact that he was, as yet, 'unspoken for', ensured that he was held in high esteem by every woman in Wadata.

Just as I placed our old black kettle on the fire, my father emerged from the house, looking ruffled.

Monsieur Boubacar, who had just sat down, uncrossed his legs and stood up again, offering his hand to my father. 'Monsieur Boureima. . .'

To my shame, my father did not take the extended hand of my teacher. 'You needn't sit down again, Monsieur,' he said. 'We don't have a great deal of business, you and I!'

'Father!' I protested.

He glared at me. 'Go inside, Haoua – now!'

Hesitating briefly, I considered the situation, but Monsieur Boubacar raised the fingers of his right hand and squeezed his eyes tight, indicating that he was not perturbed and would not be put off by my father's rudeness.

I retreated to the house, glad of the opportunity to hide my embarrassment, yet anxious that my father was about to make matters worse still.

Fatima was standing just inside the doorway, looking tearful. 'He shouted at me too,' she said.

I put my arm around her and leaned against the door-frame, straining to hear the conversation outside. 'Monsieur Boureima. . . Salim. . .' I heard Monsieur Boubacar say.

'I don't want to hear it, Boubacar. My family has had enough interference from outsiders!'

'I don't like to think of myself as an outsider, Monsieur.'

'I don't care how you think of yourself!' my father snapped. 'I wish I'd never listened to any of you. Not you, not the *anasaras*, not anyone!'

'Your daughter is a bright student. She has learned a great deal over the last few years and continues to make good progress in her studies. I have high hopes for such a promising girl.'

'She is needed at home. My wife is sick. I can't manage my crops, my animals, my house and three children alone.'

'Salim,' Monsieur Boubacar implored, 'your daughter's education is very important. You must not take it away from her now, please. With an education she can help to make things better. She could be a doctor or a teacher or a great writer, or an interpreter like Monsieur Richard.'

'She can make things here better now – by helping me and her family and by putting those *anasara* ways out of her head,' my father said, scornfully.

'These are not *"anasara"* ways,' Monsieur Boubacar continued, 'they are the ways of the world, my friend.'

'They are not *our* ways! My daughter has grown indolent and disrespectful since she went to that school – questioning everything. . . answering out of turn. I tell you, I will stand for it no longer!'

There was a short silence before my teacher spoke again. 'Look, Salim,' he said, 'I didn't come here to anger you and I understand that things are difficult for you at present. I can see that you have a lot to contend with just now. I just thought that perhaps we could discuss a work programme for Haoua – one that she could continue here at home, until things settle down. It is essential that she does not fall behind in her studies any further. She needs to keep up with the rest of the class.'

'And I tell you, Monsieur, my daughter does not need school work, you or the *anasaras*. I have decided.'

A cold chill ran down my spine. 'No! No!' I whispered, clutching at my sister more tightly.

Monsieur Boubacar coughed. 'With the utmost respect, Monsieur Boureima: is it not true that you also have a lot to lose should you remove your daughter from the Vision Corps programme?'

'That is my business!' my father bellowed.

'Indeed. But how do you intend feeding your children without the benefits of the loan scheme and the cereal bank, Monsieur? Mademoiselle Sushie has categorically explained to you, I'm sure, that Haoua's sponsorship from abroad is directly related to your participation in both her education and in the seed loan programme. And with the possibility of

⁺he new ox-plough project getting started in Wadata there is still more potential for farmers such as yourself, I would have thought.'

'Enough!' my father shouted, so loudly that I plucked up courage and peeked around the doorframe, fearing that something still more awful was about to happen. It already had: to my horror he had grabbed Monsieur Boubacar's lapels and was marching him, backwards, towards the compound entrance. 'I want you to leave now,' he hissed, 'and I don't want you or any of your sort prying into my family's affairs again! I may not be an educated man, but I am not stupid. None of this was what I wanted for my daughter. It was my wife's idea – and she is no longer here. My family will not starve, let me assure you!'

Monsieur Boubacar did not resist. He stood now, at the compound entrance, with his hands forlornly by his sides. Then, looking over my father's shoulder, he noticed Fatima and me standing petrified in the doorway of our house. He raised one hand and with it patted the air towards us, while, with the other, he offered the exercise book to my father. 'At least let Haoua have these exercises that I've prepared for her – please, Salim.'

'Get away from my home,' my father said, and turned his back on my wonderful teacher.

22

Weeks went by. After the incident with Monsieur Boubacar, I hardly dared mention my poor mother, lying in a hospital somewhere in the capital, to my father. I knew that Abdelkrim had sent some money home with Sushie, to enable Father to visit Mother, but he did not seem in any hurry to do so. On the contrary, with me working at home all day, he seemed more relaxed, settled. Sometimes he even seemed happy, and I began to wonder if he had simply forgotten about Mother; a notion that grew as steadily as the number of days that Aunt Alassane spent in my father's company, skulking around our compound. The talk in the village was that he had no intention of visiting Mother – that he was scandalised by her illness and that he did not acknowledge any part in either it or her care. In spite of everything that had happened, I could not believe this of my father.

We heard occasional, vague reports about Mother's worsening condition through Monsieur Richard or Sushie but, with the growing unrest in the capital, fewer people around Wadata were making regular trips to Niamey then.

'It's kind of getting a bit hairy there right now,' Sushie said to me one morning at Wadata's little market where I was selling ground nuts.

I did not know what she meant.

'A little bit dangerous. There are a lot of very angry people running around Niamey at the minute – cursing Mainassara, shouting a lot and staging riots. Who can blame them? Many haven't been paid for months. The military are pretty twitchy too by all accounts. They're expected to keep things under control – and *they* haven't been paid either! I heard on the radio that they arrested some journalists yesterday!'

I'd heard it too. I could not imagine living without my little radio set now, but the more news I heard about the unrest throughout the country, the more I worried about my brother. 'Do you think Abdel will be all right, Mademoiselle Sushie?'

'Yes,' she said. 'I do. Abdel's a big boy. He can look after himself. You've got enough to worry about without worrying about him, Haoua.'

'*Toh*,' I said, more anxious than ever.

By March, my brother and sister and I were so distraught that we finally decided to risk my father's anger. Fatima and I had been watering Mother's okra that morning and Adamou, on his way to tend to our livestock, had stopped to discuss our situation yet again.

'You do it, Haoua,' Adamou insisted. 'You are better with words.'

'He'll be angry with me, I know it,' I said, 'especially if that witch is hanging around again.'

'Our poor Mother will be feeling abandoned,' Adamou said. 'He must know that too. If he doesn't go to see her, one of us ought to.'

'Why don't you speak to Father, Adamou?' said Fatima. 'You are the oldest.'

'No,' I said. 'I will do it. If he is angry, so be it. God will guide me.'

I was writing a little note to Mother later that day when Father came into the house. I made a half-hearted attempt to shield it from his eyes; even though he could not read it, I knew he would quiz me about it. And he did.

'What are you doing?' he said quietly. 'I thought we had agreed that you should put all of that behind you.'

'All of what, Father?' I said, cautiously.

'You know what I mean, Haoua – school, writing, all of that nonsense. It can only bring trouble your way.'

I tried to read his face. He seemed calm enough, but I wondered if this was just the beginning of yet another fierce rage.

'I just want to let Mother know that we have not forgotten about her, Father. She has been away for nearly three months now, and only Abdelkrim has visited her. Sushie says that even he cannot manage it often because of the trouble in the city.'

My father looked agitated. 'Your mother can only read the few words that you taught her, child. It is pointless to waste your time on such things – especially when there is so much to do here!'

It was true. The toil was never-ending. And yet he seemed to spend more and more time playing *tiddas* and dominoes with his friends and less time helping us.

'This will not take long, Father. I'm just letting her know that we are all fine. Someone will read it out to her in the hospital – one of the doctors, perhaps.'

'I wouldn't count on it. If you'd ever seen these big hospitals you'd know that the doctors and nurses have no time for such things. They are very busy places.'

'You have seen them, Father?'

'I have seen them,' he said, looking to the ground. 'And I have no desire to see them again.'

I took a deep breath. There would never be a better moment. 'Father,' I said, gently, reaching out and touching his sleeve, 'Mother needs you.'

He said nothing, but closed his eyes tightly.

'You could take my letter to her. . .'

He opened his eyes again. They were glazed with what I thought for a moment might be tears. He kneaded them with the tips of his fingers. 'This dust gets everywhere!' he said. Then, pursing his lips, he nodded. 'I will go to her. As it happens, I have to discuss some important matters with your mother – and I have other business to attend to in Niamey.'

I was elated. I hugged him tightly around his middle, my tears soaking into his *jellaba*. 'Thank you, Father, thank you!'

He patted my back and then, taking my shoulders in his hands, he moved me gently back so that he could see my face. There was, somehow, a distant look in his eyes, but he was smiling. 'Finish your letter, Little One,' he said. 'But, Haoua. . .'

'Yes, Father?'

'Don't write down any of that business about your teacher, please. We don't want to worry your mother, do we?'

'No, Father.'

23

Azara Boureima
Salle Quatre
National Hospital of Niamey
Republic of Niger

Haoua Boureima
Wadata
Tera Area
Republic of Niger

14th February, 1999

Dear Mother,

This is your daughter Haoua writing. I am so pleased to
know that Father is seeing you. He has been very busy but
Adamou and Fatima and I have been helping with the work
here as much as we can.

Fatima has told me all about your hospital and the doctors
and nurses there and I hope that one of them will read my
letter out to you.

While Fatima was away, Adamou and I fixed the floor for
you and then we slept outside. Father says we did a fine job.
We are looking after your crops too, so do not worry. Our
animals are fine also.

Mademoiselle Sushie gave me the little radio which
Abdelkrim bought for me and I listen to it at night and hear
about things happening where you are. And I hear about
things happening in other countries too and I love it. My
friends in Ireland are going to send me some proper shoes! I
am so happy.

Monsieur Boubacar and Monsieur Houeto are very
well, and so is Miriam and all of her family. They all

pray for you, Mother, and so do I. May God bless you.

Affectionately your daughter,
Haoua

My father was away for ten whole days and when he
returned to Wadata he did not do so alone.

Fatima, Miriam and myself were carrying water back
from the river when we spied the two figures walking
towards the village from the north.

'It's him! It's Father!' Fatima shouted.

Keen to hear news of our mother, we set our pails and jars
down and hurried to meet him.

'I'll see you later,' I called to Miriam, as the dust flew from
my heels.

'*Toh*. Are you going to watch television?' she called after
me.

'Yes.'

'*Toh*.'

Fatima was ahead of me, but she stopped short, a few
metres before the two men. I stopped beside her and put my
hand on her shoulder.

'Father,' I said.

'My daughters.'

'How is Mother?' Fatima said.

Father stepped forward and put his bundle on the ground.
Then he stroked our heads and said, 'Have you forgotten
your manners?' He turned to indicate his companion – a
short, stocky man with yellow eyes. 'This is my cousin
Moussa.'

'Mademoiselles, *ça va? Mate ni go?*' Moussa said, smiling
through broken teeth.

'*Iri ma wichira bani,*' we said together.

'My daughters – Haoua and Fatima,' Father said, placing
his hand on our shoulders as he said our names.

'Very beautiful. Very beautiful young ladies,' Moussa said,

smiling his strange smile again and fixing his gaze on me. 'You've grown into a fine young woman.'

I could not recall ever seeing this man before.

'You were about this little one's age when I saw you last,' he said, pointing at Fatima.

I felt awkward and shy and, somehow, unsettled. Perhaps it was Moussa's teeth or his sickly, darting eyes. I don't know.

Father was standing behind us now, so I turned to face him. 'You saw Mother, Father?'

'Yes.'

'When will Mother come home?' Fatima demanded.

He did not answer. Instead, he turned and walked towards the village.

Moussa picked up my father's bundle and walked towards us. 'Your poor father is very anxious about your mother, girls. She is a very sick woman. You must look after your father.' He handed Father's bundle to Fatima and his own to me. Then he followed Father.

'But, Monsieur,' I called. 'My sister and I are carrying water to the house.'

'*Oui, oui!*' he shouted. 'You can come back for it.'

'*Walayi!*' I said, and both Fatima and I sucked our teeth in disgust.

It had been bad enough having to deal with Aunt Alassane's unannounced visits and her bullying ways while my father had been in Niamey, but with Moussa staying in our home things quickly became worse. It was like having to look after a very young child. He did nothing to help around the compound and fully expected to be waited on throughout the day, no matter how busy anyone else might be. To make matters even worse, none of us had any idea how long he planned to stay in Wadata – nor did we dare raise the matter with our father, who seemed to become more like his selfish cousin each day. We knew our place and what was expected of us, and so had no choice but continue to work the ground, carry water, tend the crops and our animals, wash clothes, cook and clean.

I was missing school badly. I missed the classroom and my lessons with Monsieur Boubacar, but I also missed my friends. Few of them visited our compound any more and only Miriam kept me informed about what my classmates were doing in school. In the evenings, as we walked to the river to draw water or wash clothing, she would tell me what she had learned that day, or try to remember the story which Monsieur Boubacar had read to the class. In this way I tried to keep up.

At the river, Souley and her cronies would taunt me and throw handfuls of black mud to try to dirty my clothes, but most of the time I was too tired to care or to fight back.

Most evenings I was too exhausted to think about television at Monsieur Letouye's compound – or, when I did, Moussa or my father would suddenly demand some more tea or an article of clothing repaired, and before I knew it, it would be too late.

Worst of all, Moussa had borrowed my radio and Father had told me that I must remain silent about the matter when I had complained to him.

We had been told that Moussa was an important businessman in the city, but I had quickly grown to dislike him, and Adamou and Fatima were not happy with our situation either.

'That man is a bastard!' Adamou declared one night, as we tried to sleep, while, outside, the sound of Moussa's high-pitched laughter and filthy jokes echoed around our compound.

Most nights, he and my father would disappear into the darkness and would not return again until the following morning. It was only too apparent that they made regular visits to the Big House, but the three of us had grown to prefer to be without Father rather than with both he and Moussa.

'They'll hear you!' I whispered to Adamou, as Fatima tossed and turned and groaned again in the darkness of the room.

'I don't care. I've had enough of him. What's he doing here anyway?'

'He thinks he's helping Father.'

'Huh!'

The laughter outside subsided and there was silence for a brief while. Then I heard Moussa's voice again.

'Your children have respect for you, Salim. That is good.'

My father grunted. 'You think so?'

'The boy is strong-minded, though – like his brother,' Moussa continued.

'Yes. But not so hot-headed, I think.'

'Perhaps.'

'Let's hope so, anyway,' my father said.

'Indeed.'

Suddenly, my brother kicked furiously at his bedding and sat upright.

'*Walayi!*' he said, the word hissing through his teeth like the whisper of an angry snake, 'One of these days I'll show him who's hot-headed!'

A short while later, we heard the sound of women's voices, shrieking and singing, followed by the clinking of bottles.

'Saaaliiiiim!' one of the voices called out from the compound entrance.

I recognised it as Aunt Alassane's immediately.

'What are you two lovely creatures doing dropping by at this unearthly hour?' Moussa said, loudly.

'My sister and I came to see the cloth that your good-for-nothing cousin has been promising to show me,' Alassane replied.

I could tell that she had been drinking.

'And we brought cold beers,' the second woman said, chinking bottles together.

'Mind who you're calling good-for-nothing!' my father said. 'Didn't I fix your roof? And that's not all I'm good for!'

More laughter.

'Well,' Alassane said, 'where is this wonderful cloth then? Every night you promise to show it to us, and every night you appear at my house empty-handed. What's wrong? Is it so cheap that you're afraid to let us see?'

'Yes,' her sister leered, 'show us what you've got, Monsieur Boureima!'

Adamou sat up again. 'Which one is that?' he whispered.

'I don't know,' I said. 'Hamidou? No, Flo, perhaps. Who cares? They're all witches.'

'They've brought alcohol here!'

'Father won't touch it. Moussa's already consumed a lot of sorghum beer, but Father declined.'

'Yes, but *now* he'll tolerate it in his home.'

'Because of *them*,' I replied. 'It's *their* fault.'

'It's not what he taught us.'

'No.'

'It's not our way!'

'No.'

'And it's not what Mother would want. None of this is!'

'No.'

'Father's a hypocrite!' he said, slapping the ground, hard.

'Be quiet, Adamou,' I said. 'Even if you don't get us into trouble, you'll wake Fatima again!'

He kicked at his blanket and then lay back down.

'You know, Adamou,' I whispered, some time later, 'Abdelkrim drinks alcohol sometimes. I saw the bottle.'

But Adamou did not say anything.

The laughter continued outside.

'Where's the lovely Flo?' Moussa called out.

'She's busy.'

'Busy, eh?'

They cackled like hens.

Alassane and Hamidou began a tuneless chant. 'Get the cloth! Get the cloth!'

'Get the damn cloth, Salim,' Moussa said.

'Yes, Salim. Monsieur Moussa wants to see this wonderful cloth too, of course!' Alassane said.

'I'm getting it! I'm getting it!' I heard my father say. 'I told you I'd get it and I'm getting it!' He made a curious noise – like a wild animal yawning – and then added, 'You won't be able to see it properly in the firelight anyway!' Then the faint light of a kerosene lantern swept across the curtain which divided our two rooms, and I heard him enter the living room. 'Where is it? Where did I leave it?' he muttered, as he rummaged around noisily.

I knew what he was looking for. He had returned from Niamey with a large bolt of fabric, more beautiful even than anything I had ever seen Monsieur Letouye display at his shop. He had left it in the corner of the room in a big, black, plastic sack and, when he was out one day, I had sneaked a look inside. The fabric had a fine pattern of pink and white flowers, with pretty wisps of green foliage trailing across the entire design. There was enough material in the bag to dress a whole family – in both *pagnes* and head wraps. It must have been very expensive. I could not imagine how Father had paid for it.

I knew what it was for and it filled my heart with dread.

As the light disappeared from view, Adamou sat upright again. 'So,' he said, 'it *is* true. He is going to marry that witch!'

I lay awake for hours that night, listening to the jokes and laughter of my father and his friends and worrying about my poor mother. I tried not to picture her lying frail and ill and lonely in a hospital in the city. Instead, I recalled memories of her singing as she toiled, smiling as she watched television at Monsieur Letouye's, dancing at the end of Ramadan. It was not easy. The images in my head altered themselves – like in a dream – and each time I saw my mother looking well and strong, my mind took her face and twisted it, and left it with an expression of pain and weariness. Perhaps, at times, I *was* dreaming, but in order to dream one must sleep, and if this was sleep, then it was a sleep which offered no rest.

I tried to imagine what the shoes that Katie and Hope had promised to send me would be like, but I could not concentrate on such things. And it was then that I cried.

Gasping great lungfuls of air, in an attempt to stifle my sobs, I shook uncontrollably. In truth I wanted to scream at my father. There were other Wadata women whose husbands had taken more than one wife, but none of those women were lying in a hospital in Niamey, and none of them were my mother. I was angry with my father, and had he not been outside that night, I think I might have walked into the desert and howled at the sky. Instead, I lay there praying that God would save my mother and bring her back to Wadata, and tried to ignore the demons inside my head that told me this was never going to happen. Perhaps I was angry with God too.

Sleep was finally beginning to embrace me when an angry exchange of words outside jolted me to my senses. Aunt Alassane's voice was loudest of all.

'No, Salim! You cannot!' she screeched.

'Oh, take it easy on my cousin, woman!' Moussa said. 'Not five minutes ago you were all over him!'

'You keep out of it, little fellow! Don't tell me what to do! You're nothing but a leech, anyway!'

'Alassane!' my father said. 'Moussa is my guest. All I said is that you should stay here with us. . .'

'And why would I want to stay in your filthy little hut when I have a perfectly good house of my own?'

'With a perfectly good roof. . .' Moussa added.

'And no brats!' Hamidou said.

There was the sound of a bottle breaking. 'You pig!'

'I've had enough of you people!' Moussa said. 'If I'd wanted trouble with women I could have stayed at home!'

'Well,' Alassane said, 'why don't you slither off back to the city – like the little snake that you are?'

'Calm down,' my father said. 'You're all drunk!' He spat, loudly, and then continued, 'As I said, we'll come back with you then.'

I heard Alassane suck her teeth. 'And – as *I* said – you can't!'

'*Walayi!* You're so argumentative tonight! Why don't you just sit down again and relax?'

'No, Salim. I mean it. You've got little enough to offer me – and I'm not the kind of lady who's used to very little. . .'

'Lady?'

'Shut your face, Moussa!' Hamidou said.

More breaking glass. Then Alassane's voice again. 'Sort it out or I'm not interested, Salim. I mean it!'

There was a flurry of activity, followed by the sound of muffled voices. Then, finally, silence.

24

We all needed new clothing, really, but I knew that that was not about to happen – especially when Father had just spent everything he had on cloth for his betrothal.

Sometimes Sushie or Richard brought bundles of garments back from the aid agency depot for distribution from the *dispensaire* but, as Sushie had said, with things as they were in the capital, there were fewer trips being made now. So, when it was quiet one afternoon (Father, Moussa and Adamou had gone off to pray and Fatima was playing with Narcisse and Amina) I sat down on my mat and began to repair Father's frayed pants and a torn Mickey Mouse tee shirt, which had first been worn by Adamou and then by me. The garment was thin and faded but the tear under the arm was small. I decided that Fatima might as well get some wear out of it.

I had not seen a great deal of Sushie for quite some time. My father had forbidden her to come to our compound ever since he had quarrelled with her, so I only saw her occasionally at the market and sometimes waved at her vehicle, as I made my way back from the river and she made her way to Goteye. I rarely got to speak to her.

This arrangement suited me in one respect: each time I caught a glimpse of her I feared that she might be the bearer of bad news – if not about my mother, then possibly concerning my undoubtedly precarious place on the VCI sponsorship programme.

These thoughts were racing through my mind as I stitched when I suddenly realised that someone was addressing me.

'Anyone in there?' It was her.

I stood up to greet her, relieved to see that she was beaming brightly at me. She did not look like the bearer of bad news.

'Pardon me, Mademoiselle Sushie,' I said, smoothing down my *pagne* and trying not to appear flustered.

'I know I'm not meant to be here,' she said, 'but I've got a package for you, Haoua. Remember Maggie, the Peace Corps nurse you met at Goteye? Well, she was out at the *camions* post this morning to pick up some medicines and Head Office had sent this too.' She handed me a rectangular package about the size of a goat's head. 'I think it's been lying in Niamey for a week or two.'

I recognised the writing on the heavy brown paper immediately, and the familiar stamps with pictures of the Queen of Ireland, looking sideways and wearing a crown that looked like it was too small for her. Miriam had said that perhaps the queen's mother had had a much smaller head, because she had heard that such fine jewels were often handed down from one family member to another – much like our Mickey Mouse tee shirt. 'It's from Katie and Hope,' I said.

Sushie nodded.

'Shall I open it now, or wait until the others come home?'

'It's your call,' Sushie said, sitting down on a plastic crate.

I sat back down on my mat and examined the package. It had been wrapped carefully, the paper folded neatly over and then taped at both ends. Two blue and white airmail stickers had been placed below the row of queens' heads and I now noticed that my friends' names and sponsor number had been written in thick, black letters on the underside of the package. On the front, underneath the airmail stickers, my name and the Vision Corps International address had been written in the same black letters. There was something beautiful and mysterious about it, even though I had a fairly good idea what it contained.

'What do you think, then?' Sushie said. 'Do I get to see what's inside now?'

'Katie said they were going to send me some shoes,' I said. 'I think it's my new shoes!'

'Wow!'

I smiled as Sushie handed me her pocket knife and winked. Together, we carefully removed the wrapping paper and tape, and inside there was a white box, with a sturdy lid which I removed.

I had never owned a proper pair of shoes before. All my life, I had walked on my bare soles or in a pair of plastic sandals which had previously belonged to Adamou. And yet lying there, before my eyes, in a nest of thin, white paper, were the most beautiful shoes I had ever seen. And they were mine!

'Aren't you going to try them on?' Sushie asked, after I had stared at them for some time. 'In the US we call them *sneakers*.'

I lifted one of the sneakers out and held it close to my face. It smelt clean and new.

'May I?' Sushie said. She took it from me and held its sole against my foot. 'Looks like they'll fit. You must have made a good drawing.'

'Yes,' I said. And yet I still did not dare to put them on. Although they were clean and new and white and pink and wonderful, they were also hard and strange to me. I examined the perfect stitching running across the smooth surfaces, the tiny holes punched along the seams, the ridged soles and the three pink stripes on either side of the main body of each shoe. Then I looked at Sushie. I had seen her wear similar ones. 'I will wear them later,' I said, deciding that I wanted to be alone when I squeezed my feet into them for the first time.

She shrugged. '*Toh.*'

'There are other things in the box,' I said, setting the shoes down carefully on my mat and wrapping them in the thin paper again.

We found a plastic frog with a tube attached to it. Sushie

showed me how to make it jump, by squeezing air through the tube with a little bulb. There was a label, which said 'Adamou', attached to one of its legs. There were some more magic bubbles, with no label attached, six little packages of candies and a book for Fatima.

I was playing with the frog when Sushie waved a piece of folded paper in front of my face.

'Did you see this, Little One?' she said.

I took the paper from her and unfolded it. It was a letter. A small photograph fell on to my mat. I picked it up and looked at it. The face of an old man – an *anasara* man – stared out at me. He wore thick-rimmed spectacles and a long, pointed moustache which was curled up at the ends. He was wearing some kind of uniform and had medals pinned to his chest. I showed it to Sushie.

'Goodness!' she said. 'He looks kind of important. Like the president or something!'

I handed her the letter. 'Will you help me with this, please, Mademoiselle?'

'Sure.'

Haoua Boureima	Hope Boyd
Child Ref. NER2726651832	Member No. 515820
Vision Corps International	Ballygowrie
Tera Area Development Programme	Co. Down
C/O BP 11504	N. Ireland
Niamey	BT22 1AW
Republic of Niger	
West Africa	

26th March, 1999

Dear Haoua,
We were really pleased that you sent us the outline of your foot, as Katie suggested. Dad took us to the shopping centre yesterday and we chose these trainers for you. I hope you like

them. (Katie and I argued about which ones you'd like best, but finally we agreed on these ones. My friend Sorcha has a pair just like them.)

I have enclosed a photograph of our Papa, who died a few months ago. I photocopied it in our school library at lunch time today. He was our father's father's father and he was a very brave, clever and funny man. (He used to read a lot, and work in his garden, but he was almost blind for the last year or so of his life, so he could not do his favourite things any more.) He is quite young in this photograph. It was during the war. (My dad says I have to tell you which war, because there have been lots of wars in Africa too. It was the Second World War and Dad says that some of that was even in Africa!)

We've been wondering how your mother is now. I'm sure she missed you and your family while she was in hospital. I hope you are still enjoying school, and that your project was successful. Write soon, if you can. We love hearing from you! Lots of love,
Hope.

Sushie folded the letter again and handed it back to me.

'Thank you,' I said. I opened it and peered at the un-familiar scratchy blue marks on the paper, not French and certainly not Djerma. I felt saddened by Hope's news about this great man who was her father's father's father. I had not even known my father's father because he had died before I was born. I laid the letter out on the mat in front of me and looked again at the little photograph. 'He looks stern in this photograph,' I said.

'Yes. He's got that *Salim* look about him!' Sushie said.

We both laughed – myself a little nervously.

'Hey, you look stern in the photograph I took of you for the VCI records.'

'Yes.'

'I guess we can all read a face wrong sometimes. These kids obviously loved this old man.'

I nodded. Then I sat in silence, lost in my thoughts while Sushie trimmed her fingernails with one of the little tools on her pocket knife.

Somehow I had not expected to hear that my friends' great grandfather had died. It was as if I had – foolishly – believed that no harm could befall these children and their family. That, somehow, they were protected from pain and suffering.

It was then that I felt a great wave of fear and panic wash over my entire being.

'Sushie!' I said.

She looked up.

'I *have* to see Mother!'

Sushie sighed. 'I did try talking to your father about that, Haoua.'

'What did he say?'

She shook her head.

I stared hard at the photograph of my friends' dead relative, but I did not speak.

After some time had passed, Sushie broke the silence. 'Hey. Haoua?' she said, cupping my cheek in her hand.

I opened my mouth, but instead of words, a great surge of anxiety and pain erupted. I closed my eyes tightly as I felt Sushie's arm pulling me towards her, and when I opened them again I saw that my tears had dripped on to the letter and smudged Hope's name.

'I am not crying for myself,' I said.

'I know that, Little One.'

'Why will he not let me go there?'

'He said you could not go alone and that he has no money.'

I sat upright and looked at Sushie.

She leaned back and wiped tears from my face with her pale, bony thumbs.

'I wish Abdel would come and take me to Mother,' I said.

Sushie nodded, then spoke quietly. 'Haoua. You do know how ill your mother is, don't you?'

'But she is going to get better!'

Sushie sighed. 'I know Monsieur Boubacar has spoken to you in school about HIV/AIDS. I know you understand what is happening to your mother.'

I shut my eyes, put my hands over my ears and tried not to listen, but Sushie gently eased them away from my head.

'Even if you could go. . . you might not get there on time.'

I was about to answer when we heard voices at the entrance to our compound. It was Fatima, accompanied by Amina and little Narcisse Kantao. I was delighted to see that Miriam had joined them. They looked happy and excited as they skipped across the dust towards us.

Sushie leaned over, winked, and quickly gave my face another wipe with her palm. 'What have you all been up to?' she said.

The girls giggled, as if they had agreed to keep some great secret to themselves. Little Narcisse began singing to herself, dancing around to her own rhythm, until Sushie began to clap along in time and approval. Suddenly Narcisse became shy, and stood plucking at her *pagne* and staring only at her feet.

Fatima grabbed at her and began to tickle her under the arms. She wriggled furiously, like a monkey caught in a snare.

'Hey, you girls,' Sushie said. 'Haoua's had a letter from her friends in Ireland, haven't you, Haoua?'

'Yes,' I said. 'And they've sent a gift for you, Fatima.'

They all clambered around my box and began to examine my shoes and Adamou's frog. I gave Fatima her book and shared out some of the candies. Sushie took a little green one and told us that they were called Jelly Beans and that they were her favourite. I was glad that Miriam was there to keep an eye on Narcisse, otherwise her little fingers might have dirtied my shoes or torn the beautiful wrapping paper or bent the pages of my sister's book.

After she had flicked quickly through every page, Fatima

looked up and addressed Sushie. 'This is a very strange book,' she said.

I peered over her shoulder and wondered if it contained stories of witchcraft and evil spirits, like the one which Monsieur Boubacar had thought inappropriate for my class.

Much to the delight of Amina and Narcisse, Sushie had been blowing bubbles, and the girls were in awe of their oily colours and the way they popped. 'I think that's a counting book,' Sushie said. She reached out to take it and studied the front cover. 'Hmm,' she said, setting the bubbles down, '*When Sheep Cannot Sleep* by Satoshi Kitamura. Looks interesting.'

On the cover was a picture of a *mouton* – a sheep – lying in a proper human's bed. It was dressed in a shirt with blue and white stripes. Flowers and grasses were growing all around the bed, and in the distance were some trees and an evening sky of blue and orange.

'Why is the animal in a bed?' Fatima asked.

'And why is it wearing clothes?' Amina said.

'I guess it's tired.'

'But it's a sheep!' I said.

'I think Satoshi Kitamura is just having a bit of fun.'

Narcisse had the book now and was turning the pages a little roughly while Fatima looked on in concern.

'Gently, Narcisse!' Miriam said, easing her sister's fingers from the book.

'Is Sat-osh-i an Irish name?' I asked.

'I shouldn't think so,' Sushie said. 'Sounds Japanese to me.'

'Oh.'

Narcisse made a baa-ing sound and pointed at a picture of the sheep talking to some cicadas.

'Will you read it to us, Mademoiselle?' Miriam said.

Sushie stood up and shook her head. 'I can't, my friends. Sorry. Maybe you can bring it to my compound later on and I'll read it then. But I'm not supposed to be here at all.' She snapped closed the lid of the bubbles and handed them to me. 'We'll talk again soon, Haoua, okay?'

'*Toh*,' I said. 'Thank you for bringing the package, Mademoiselle.'

After Sushie had gone, we girls sat looking at the book for some time. I thought the pictures were very strange but I liked Fatima's book nevertheless. The animal looked quite sad in some of the pictures, frightened in others. In one picture, it was standing at the end of a long corridor of many doors. In another, it was sitting at a small table – similar to the few we had in my school – drawing pictures with brightly coloured pencils.

'Look!' Miriam said, 'It's drawing one of the pictures in the book!'

She was right. On the next page the animal was looking at a wall of pictures – all of which were tiny copies of the pages of Fatima's book. I leaned forward and counted the tiny pictures. There were fifteen. Then I counted the coloured pencils on the previous page.

'There are fourteen pencils and fifteen pictures,' I said. 'Sushie was right. It is a counting book.'

Miriam flipped back through the pages until she came to an image of the sheep standing before a large, eerie house. 'And this house has twelve windows!' she said.

'*Walayi!*'

Narcisse pointed to the next page. 'Shoes!' she said.

The animal was running down a grassy hill between thick, dark trees and bright red flowers.

'Hah!' Miriam said. 'This *mouton* is wearing shoes like yours, Haoua. Two pairs of them!'

'I think that it just has white feet,' Fatima said.

'Shoes,' Narcisse repeated.

The others continued to flick through the book, discussing each picture in detail and discovering something to count on each page, but my mind had begun to wander. As I looked at the pictures of the animal climbing a ladder, or cooking chickpeas, it struck me that this shoe-wearing sheep could do just about anything. And it was then that I made my decision.

I shared out some more of the candies and then gathered up my sewing tools and half-repaired garments, Adamou's frog, the bubbles, my shoes and the letter and photograph from Hope.

'Where are you going?' Miriam asked as I stood up.

'Inside,' I said, 'to think.'

I hid the rest of the candy in my bedding and put my letter and photograph safely away with my other treasures. Then I put the little plastic frog on Adamou's bedroll. I had left the shoes in their box on one of the chairs in the living room and now, as I lifted the lid to look at them again, I felt myself waver. I sat down on the floor and took one of the shoes from the box. I decided to try them on, but not walk in them. My feet slipped into them with ease. Although they felt strange, it was also as if my feet knew and felt safe inside them. I imagined myself running to school or walking to the river for water in such a fine pair of shoes. They had straps with fuzzy material on the underside that caused them to attach themselves like magic to the top of the shoe. When I pulled at these straps there was a noise – like ripping fabric – and I thought for a moment that I had damaged them. I wanted so much to keep them on; to walk through the village, parading my fine shoes and to see Souley's face when she saw me wearing them. I wanted to be able to write back to Katie and Hope to tell them how useful they were, how beautiful and strong. How happy they made me.

Instead, I took them off, wrapped them up in the fine paper, put them back in their box, tucked the box under my arm and went to look for my father.

25

On the far side of Wadata, just beyond the flat ground where the market traders gathered, the boys of the village often congregated for bouts of wrestling or soccer matches. No one had a proper ball – Monsieur Richard had promised to bring a new one back from Niamey the next time he went there – and the sprawling teams played barefoot, but often these events were exciting enough for the menfolk of the village to be found on the sidelines, placing wagers on one team or the other or urging on the grappling wrestlers. We girls sometimes joked that it seemed difficult to distinguish one sport from another.

It was here that I found Father and cousin Moussa. They were sitting crosslegged on a large mat, playing dominoes with several of the elders.

'What are you doing here, Little One?' my father called above the hullabaloo of the ball players nearby.

'I need to speak to you, Father,' I said.

'Can't you see I'm busy? Haven't you got chores to do?'

'I will get back to my chores immediately, Father. But first I want to show you something.'

At this, Moussa slammed a domino piece down onto the mat and then fixed his gaze on the box under my arm.

My father stood up, shaking his head, and excused himself from the party. As he walked towards me, the boys' soccer ball – a raggedy sphere of tightly rolled rags – landed a metre or so in front of him, scattering dust towards the domino players.

'*Walayi!*' he said, lifting the ball and kicking it back over to the boys, 'What is it, child?'

'Can we go somewhere quiet to talk, Father?' I said.

'We can talk here,' he said firmly.

'It's about Mother.'

He sighed, then indicated that I should follow him, and when we had walked down the slope to the edge of the Tokunbo family's compound, he stopped and turned to face me again.

'Well?' he said, eyeing up my shoebox.

I was nervous but determined. 'This is from Katie and Hope – my friends who write to me – remember?'

He nodded. 'Yes, yes,' he said impatiently, 'but what's this about your mother?'

I looked him in the eye. 'Father,' I said, 'I need to see Mother.'

At first I thought that he was going to start ranting – such was the look of disapproval on his face – but when he spoke his voice was calm but stern.

'Haoua, I have discussed this with your *anasara* friend. I have explained that I cannot let you travel to the capital alone and that I also have no means of paying for such a journey for you. I have seen your mother. She is not a well woman, I admit it, but she will get well, and when. . .'

'No!' I said. 'You know that is not true!'

My father looked stunned.

'Mother is not going to recover. Mademoiselle Sushie has made it clear to the rest of us, Father. And Monsieur Boubacar and Monsieur Richard have taught me all about AIDS. Mother is going to die and I must see her!' I stared up at him, hard. '*Please*, Father!' I said, and tasted the salt of my own tears.

My father looked at the ground and said nothing for what seemed like a very long time. I wanted him to put his arms around me, but he did not do so. Instead, he put his hands over his face and stood motionless until a voice called his

159

name. 'Salim? Salim? *Ça va?* Are you all right?' It was Moussa.

'I am fine, cousin,' my father said, dropping his hands, 'but my daughter here misses her poor mother.'

'Ah.'

'I've been trying to explain that I cannot let her go to Niamey. It is too dangerous, too far, too expensive. I cannot risk losing her also.'

'But, Father,' I said. 'I have thought of a way of providing for my journey.' Before he could say a word I lifted the lid off the box and folded back the pretty paper to reveal my precious shoes. 'We can sell these. Katie and Hope sent them for me, but Mother is more important. Please, Father.'

He lifted one of the shoes out of the box and examined it closely, while Moussa took the other. 'Very fine workmanship.'

Moussa nodded. 'Indeed.'

'But there is no one in Wadata who could pay a good price for these, Little One.'

'Monsieur Letouye?' I said.

My father continued to stare at the shoe in his hand while he considered my suggestion. 'I would doubt it, child.' Then he shook his head as if coming out of a deep trance, and when he spoke, his voice was stern again. 'Besides, as I have said, I cannot let you make such a journey alone.'

'I would be fine, Father!' I insisted. 'I could travel on the *camion* and I could stay with Abdelkrim.'

'No.'

'But, Father!'

'No, I say!' He threw the shoe onto the ground. 'God only knows what your brother is doing at present. Didn't you pay attention to the news on Monsieur Letouye's television set the other night? Niamey is a dangerous place at the minute. Mainassara's people are arresting anyone who even looks like they might be *thinking* of causing trouble. And there have been more rumours of mutiny! It was difficult enough for Moussa and me to get back here. It's certainly not safe for a child to be travelling alone.' He stepped forwards and, taking my chin in his hand, tilted my head back so that I was looking into his eyes once again. 'You must forget this idea, girl. You are needed here.'

I knew that I should give in, but I no longer cared. 'And Mother needs me!' I said, pulling back from him. 'Besides, aren't you always telling me that I am almost a woman?'

My father clapped his hands together in frustration and then bent down so that his face was close to mine. 'You've accepted that no one can help her!' he said, angrily. 'Now accept that I will not permit this journey.'

I buried my face in my hands and sobbed, frustration and rage now vying with my feelings of fear and sadness.

Behind us the excited cries and shouts of the boys playing soccer continued and, for a few moments, I tried to block out all other sounds and thoughts and concentrate only on those of the game. Then Moussa spoke again.

'Forgive me, Salim,' he said, stooping to pick up the shoe. He dangled the pair on his fingers. With his free hand he took my father's arm and led him a few metres away. His hushed, urgent manner made me suspicious. In truth, all of his actions made me suspicious. 'Salim. Cousin. I do not mean to interfere, please believe me, but may I speak with you on this matter?'

'*Toh.*'

Moussa glanced back at me awkwardly as he spoke. 'You know, I really need to return to Niamey very soon – as I've said. I think you will agree that our business here is concluded for the time being?'

My father nodded.

'And my own family needs me.'

'Of course.'

'And then there is my shop. . . I really don't trust that young oaf I've left in charge. He's bone-idle, and Doodi can't watch him all the time!' With this, Moussa turned to look at me again and then stroked the gleaming shoes. 'But I may be able to help you out with this problem.'

'How so, cousin?' my father said.

'I could escort the child to the capital, Salim,' Moussa replied. He held the shoes up in front of my father's face. 'Many people come to my shop. I can easily find a customer for this fine footwear. It would cover all expenses and. . .' he motioned towards me without actually turning his gaze, '. . . it would do your daughter no harm to see my home, meet with my family.'

My excitement immediately pushed aside my instinctive mistrust of Moussa. 'Yes, Father!' I said. 'That is a good idea!'

But my father's response was more measured. 'I don't know. . .' he said, quietly.

'*Please*, Father. . .'

He held his hand up to silence me, but looked at Moussa as he spoke. 'You would take her on the *camion*?'

'Of course,' Moussa replied. 'And she could stay with my family. That goes without saying.'

'And afterwards – when she has seen her mother – how would she return home?'

'We can work something out,' Moussa said.

I could not contain myself. 'Perhaps Abdel could bring me back, Father.'

Again he held his hand up. 'Quiet, child. Your brother will be too busy to have to worry about you.'

'We can work something out,' Moussa said again.

And so it was decided. We were to leave for the capital in a few days' time. I was to ask Sushie for a ride to the *camion* post and, once we arrived in Niamey, Moussa was to contact Abdelkrim. If my brother was unable to escort me to the hospital, Moussa himself would take me.

I was to see my dear, sweet mother again!

26

The following morning I awoke before the cockerels began to crow. I had been dreaming again of my grandmother, my mother – and of Moussa. Now, as I lay awake in the darkness, I could not recall the details of my dream; only the vague notion that Moussa had been smiling his broken-toothed smile at me.

Somehow I felt unsettled by the dream, and yet I also felt guilty that I should still bear suspicion towards my father's cousin – a man who was clearly prepared to help me.

Slowly, as I began to collect my thoughts, I realised that it was not my dream which had wrenched me from slumber, but physical discomfort. I reached down and, fumbling beneath my blanket, felt a thick, warm wetness between my legs. The *jingar ceeri* had come upon me.

I was not frightened. I knew what had happened and I knew what to do.

Mother had prepared me for this moment and, as my body had changed, I had waited for it for a long time. Even so, I was perturbed that my bedding should be soiled, and determined to get it out of the house before anyone else should notice.

Beside me, Fatima was fast asleep. From the other side of the room I could hear Adamou's snores. I sat up and craned my neck to peer at the lumpy silhouette in the darkness. (Father had occupied his own bed more frequently ever since Aunt Alassane's outburst.) It was a sight that would usually have given me some comfort, but now it only caused me frustration. It meant that Moussa had spent the night in our living room and that I would have to get past him without drawing attention to myself or my bedding.

I cleaned myself as best as possible, dressed hurriedly and then quietly gathered up my bedding. Fatima stirred, ground her teeth and then muttered Adamou's name. I guessed that our brother's taunts and torments had even followed my sister into her dreams. With two steps I was at the curtain that divided our two rooms. I stood in the darkness for a few moments, straining to hear some indication that cousin Moussa was still asleep too. From outside, as if to thwart me, the low moan of a fresh wind drowned out the gentle sounds of our sleeping household and then ceased almost as suddenly. At last, I heard the rhythmical breathing of our guest, whose dark form I could just make out lying on the floor in front of me. I would have to step over him.

I checked the bloody bundle in my arms and then lifted first my left foot and then my right over the slumbering body. I had made it! All I had to do now was take a few more paces towards the outer door and then head for the river. I could have my bedding laundered and well on its way to drying before anyone else even stirred.

I put my hand carefully on the door and pushed it out-wards. Suddenly, a beam of light enveloped me from behind. Startled, I looked around and, dropping my bedding, raised my hands to shield my face from the glare.

'Who's there?' Moussa called, gruffly. He was leaning on one elbow and holding a small flashlight above his head.

'It's me. Haoua, cousin Moussa,' I whispered, anxious that no one else in the house might be disturbed. 'Forgive me for waking you.'

'What are you doing, girl?' He moved the light down my body, from my face to my feet, and then on to the unfurled blanket.

'I – I – nothing. . .' I said. *This is my house*, I told myself. *I don't have to explain myself to him!*

But Moussa's light was fixed on the soiled bedding in

front of me. Frantically, I threw myself onto the blanket and began to bundle it up again.

It was too late. 'Ah, so you're a real woman now – eh, girlie?'

I looked up and saw that he was now shining the beam on to his own face, the harsh light making his features and broken teeth eerily prominent, his eyes still more yellow. He was leering.

'It's nothing to be ashamed about,' he said, chuckling to himself. 'It just means that you're ready!'

I did not answer him. Instead, I backed out through the door and, running through the darkness, headed for the river.

I was not ashamed. I knew that what was happening to my body was perfectly natural. I wanted to be able to talk to my mother more than ever, though I was glad that she had prepared me so well. As I ran, I thought about Fatima and wondered if our mother would be granted the time to prepare her also. I knew that it would fall to me to do so should my mother not survive her illness. Bunchie had told me stories about the old ways – when 'showings' were made public and the bedding of virgin brides was displayed for the whole village to bear witness. I was glad that those ways had changed.

I slowed to a brisk walk and put the bundle on my head. By now, the sun was beginning to peek over the horizon and the air was beginning to lose its chill. I looked down at my bare feet, kicking through the cool dust, and wished that I had remembered my sandals. I thought again of the beautiful shoes that Katie and Hope had sent me. My friends in Ireland were about my age. I wondered if they had become women yet. The image of Moussa's leering face stuck in my mind and I suddenly felt more apprehensive about travelling with him to the capital.

. . . *It just means that you're ready!* His words echoed around in my head. A shiver ran down my back.

It was light by the time I reached the river and a persistent wind had developed, scuffing up snake-like wisps of sand across the reedy banks and causing ripples on the surface of the water. Without even checking to make sure that I was alone, I set down my bundle, stripped off my *pagne* and stepped into the cool, dark water to bathe. After several minutes, I suddenly became aware that I was being watched. I was submerged to the neck with my back to the riverbank, yet still I sensed eyes boring into me.

I spun round in the water, half expecting to see Moussa standing there. Instead, a small troop of monkeys scattered in all directions, startled by my splashing. I realised then that they had been playing with my clothes and pulling at my bundle, and one of them was now dragging my blanket towards some bushes to my left.

'Aiiiee!!!' I screamed and hurled a rock at it. The creature let go of the blanket and disappeared into the bushes after its companions. I stumbled through the silt and on to the riverbank, where I quickly gathered up my belongings. Without pausing to dry myself, I pulled on my *pagne* and then carried the bloody – and now muddy – blanket down to the water's edge where I scrubbed it against some rocks.

As I worked, I realised that it was a school day and wished that I could go home, fetch my schoolbag and then call for Miriam. I wished that I could find my mother at home, cooking boule and serving tea to my father. I wished that Abdelkrim was not away from home and that Moussa was not staying with us. And I wished that Alassane and her sisters would leave Wadata forever and go far, far away.

As I worked, I sang a song that Bunchie had taught me when I was little. *Nil, Niger, Congo, Senegal, Orange et Limpopo, Zambeze. Azikiwe, Awolowo, Una na nya ran na, Orange et Limpopo, Zambeze.* And I wished also that Bunchie could be there beside me, telling me stories about Harakoye Dicko, Goddess of the River Niger, the mother of genies who could transform themselves into the bodies of possession dancers; that we could be washing our clothes together, as we had so often in the past. Then I thought of Katie and Hope and I wished that their father's father's father had not died.

I knew that I could not ask God to reverse these things, that what was done was done, but I thanked Him for His greatness and asked Him, once again, to spare my mother.

As I walked home, I sang Bunchie's song again. I recalled standing beside her in the muddy waters, my head barely reaching her exposed thigh, copying her actions as she scrubbed and rinsed; eager to learn. *That was my childhood*, I thought. *But now I am a woman.*

27

When I got home the house was quiet, and both my father and Moussa had gone. I draped my blanket over the compound fence and then drank some water and ate a little millet paste. As I took my cup and dish back into the house, I noticed my shoebox on the floor beside Moussa's untidy bedroll. I looked out through the door to make sure that neither Moussa nor my father were nearby and then lifted the box and set it on the table. I reminded myself that the shoes were still mine and that I did not need to feel guilty about looking at them again.

I lifted the lid off the box and set it on the table. Again the clean, new smell hit me. I folded back the thin paper and was about to take one of the shoes from the box when I noticed, in one corner, the little radio that Abdelkrim had sent me. I hesitated for only a moment then, quickly looking over my shoulder, I lifted out the radio instead.

The earphones knocked gently against the inside of the box as I coiled the cable around the radio. I stared at the beautiful little object in my hand for a moment, in awe of its precision and curious numbers, until a movement from the bedroom brought me to my senses and I stuffed it quickly under my head wrap.

'I'm telling.' It was Adamou.

'What?'

'You shouldn't be poking through our guest's things,' Adamou said.

'They're *my* shoes, actually,' I said. 'They're mine until they're sold.'

He walked towards me and then reached behind my head. I flinched a little. 'Wait!' he said. 'What's this?'

The earpieces of the headphones had been dangling down from beneath my head wrap and Adamou now gave them a gentle tug.

'That's mine too,' I said, pulling the radio out. 'Moussa was only borrowing it.'

'Still, I don't think he'd like you poking around.'

'You're always poking around my things!' I said.

'And you're always complaining about me doing that!' He picked up one of the shoes and let out a shrill whistle. 'I think they'd fit me,' he said.

I grabbed the shoe away from him. 'You mustn't put them on! They must be new shoes if we are to sell them.'

Adamou made no reply. He put his hand into the box again but I held his wrist tightly. 'Don't touch that one either, Adamou!' I hissed.

'*Walayi!*' he said. 'Will you calm down? It's this I want to see.' He withdrew his hand, holding in it Moussa's flashlight.

'You'd better put that back,' I said. 'That *is* his.'

'I'd really like one of these,' he said. 'Think what fun Youssef and I could have – upsetting the little ones with spirit games! Tell your stupid friends to send me one of these.'

I snatched the flashlight off him and put it and the shoes back into the box.

28

Mademoiselle Sushie did not respond to my request in the way I had hoped. In fact, I could not help feeling that – even if it had been possible for her to drive Moussa and me to the *camion* post – she might not have agreed.

'I'm sorry, Haoua, but my colleagues and I have arranged to meet the *Sous-Préfét* and his entourage tomorrow morning. Work is finally to begin on our borehole!'

I was fidgeting with a pen which had been lying on the little plastic table in her compound.

Sushie put her hand over mine to stop the tapping. 'Just think,' she continued, her eyes twinkling with enthusiasm, 'if all goes well, soon you won't have to walk far to draw good, clean, safe water ever again!'

I nodded. It was indeed good news. Moussa had also promised my father a fine bicycle from his shop in Niamey, which would have helped with the fetching of water until the pump was completed, but somehow none of us really believed that he would honour his word.

'Are you listening, Haoua?'

'Yes,' I said, sulkily.

She gently wrenched the pen from me and poked the back of my hand with it. 'Hey.'

I looked up.

'You know that I don't think this journey of yours is a good idea. But, aside from that, I really do have to meet with these officials.'

'I know that, Mademoiselle.'

'*Toh*. I have to admit that I don't much care for that Moussa fellow – and I don't like the idea of him being responsible for you. I haven't seen much evidence of responsibility from him while he's been staying with your father, either. All he ever seems to do is smoke and play dominoes – that's when he's not quaffing beer and hanging around with those whores! Why can't he help your father to fix his fences or something while he's here?'

'He's not so bad,' I said, surprising even myself. Sushie raised her eyebrows.

'It's the only way my father will permit me to travel to Niamey, Mademoiselle,' I said. 'Moussa is my father's cousin. He will look after me.'

'Hmm.' She seemed unconvinced.

'I have to see Mother,' I said, fixing her eye. 'How else can I do so? If you were to travel to the capital, Mademoiselle Sushie. . .'

'I have no business there at the minute, Haoua.'

'*Toh*.' I stared at the tabletop again.

Sushie stood up and placed her chair beside mine. 'Hey,' she said.

I looked up and she took my face in her hands.

Her strange, pale blue eyes peered deep into mine. 'Please don't make this trip, Little One. I know you are worried about your mother. We all are. But going to Niamey will only distress you both.'

'But she is going to be okay. . .'

'No, Haoua.'

'Yes!' I shouted. 'My mother is going to be fine! They told us in school about drugs that can be administered.'

'There are no drugs to cure your mother, Haoua. They will make her as comfortable as possible in the hospital, but she is very weak and her immune system is not working. . . and drugs cost a great deal of money. . .'

'Abdel will help,' I said.

'He can't.'

'What do you mean? Of course he can. He has a good job. He will pay for the medicine. I know my brother, Mademoiselle.'

She shook her head and wiped my tears away with her thumbs. 'I talked to him in Niamey. There's been a lot of trouble, you know? He hasn't been paid for months, Haoua. And, like I said, the medicine cannot cure her anyway. Besides, your mother told me that any money your brother had sent was gone.'

'Gone where?' I said.

'You would need to ask your father about that.'

'But if we had the money my mother would live?'

'She might live a little longer.'

'*Inshallah*. God will provide,' I said. 'God is great!' but my words sounded hollow somehow.

Sushie let go of my face and shrugged.

'My shoes!' I said. 'We can use the money from the sale of my shoes.'

'It wouldn't be enough. Besides, do you really think that fellow would sell your shoes and then hand over the money for medication for your mother? I've heard about him and his ways, believe me. The walls have ears in Wadata. That's not going to happen, Haoua.'

I dried my eyes with the end of my *pagne* and looked into her eyes again. 'Can't you help us, Mademoiselle?' I said very quietly.

She held her palms out towards me and I knew that she was hurting too. 'Stay here, Little One,' she said. 'Fatima needs you, Adamou needs you and – God knows – your father needs you too!'

'I have to go,' I said, standing up. 'Wouldn't you do the same if it was your mother?'

Sushie nodded, sadly. 'I'm sorry I can't help you. How will you get to the *camion* post then?'

'We will walk, I suppose.'

'It's a long way. You will need to leave very early. Can't you ask Moussa to wait until the following day? I could give you a ride to the *camion* then perhaps.'

'He says that he is leaving tomorrow.'

Sushie stood up and, smiling, kneaded the back of my neck. 'Well. . . take care, Little One. Be safe. Watch that snake, Moussa. And don't go anywhere alone in Niamey. That place is crawling with crooks and pimps.'

'*Toh.*'

'And say hello to your handsome brother for me.'

I grinned and nodded.

'Give my regards to your mother too, please,' she added, stroking my face.

Weeks later, when I thought about this conversation again, I realised that she had probably doubted that her greeting would ever reach my mother's ears.

29

I considered Mademoiselle Sushie to be a true friend; not just of mine, but also of my whole family. Nevertheless, I could not deny the fact that I was a little angry with her. I understood her concern for my well-being, but considered her pleas for me not to visit my mother in hospital irritating and pointless. I knew that her VCI business with the elders and the minister and his officials was extremely important – not just for our village, but for other neighbouring villages, such as Injala and Boreemah, whose inhabitants would soon be able to draw clean water closer to their homes too – but nothing seemed more important to me than my poor mother. I would have continued to walk to the river for the rest of my life if it could have helped her in any way.

As I walked down the hill from Sushie's compound, I was met by a stream of excited children, their school day over. It was only the worry of my mother's illness which had prevented me from missing my friends, my teacher and my school work more – this and the fact that I was kept so very busy. But seeing this sea of happy faces now made my heart heavy. Some girls from my class greeted me; one of them, Aisha Gooti, paused to tell me that Miriam was not far behind. A group of boys ran past, shoving each other and sucking their teeth at me, but I put my head down and ignored them, only looking up again when I heard someone call my name. For a moment I thought it was Miriam, but my gaze was met not by the warm smile of my best friend but by the twisted scowls of Souley and her cronies coming from the opposite direction.

'Hey, Boureima girl!' Souley shouted, running up the hill towards me, closely followed by her gang. She stopped in front of me, her face looming down, close to my own. 'Look, everyone,' she sneered. 'It's little Haoua Boureima, who's been kicked out of school!'

'I haven't been kicked out of school!' I snapped. 'Get out of my way, Souley!'

I made to pass her, but she grabbed hold of my *pagne* and spun me back around to face her. 'Stand still, *boro dungurio*, you silly little bitch. I want you to tell us all about your possessed mother.'

I was furious. 'You're the bitch,' I said. 'My mother is not possessed!'

Souley sucked her teeth while her cronies giggled mercilessly. 'Uhuh. I heard that she has an evil spirit inside her and that not even the *anasara* could exorcise it. So the elders sent her off into the desert to wander alone – like a filthy leper!'

'That's not true! Let go of me!' I struggled to free myself but two of the other girls grabbed my arms and held me fast.

Souley was really enjoying herself now. 'Really?' she said. 'So, what is the truth, Boureima girl? Could it be that she has AIDS?' As she said the word she pushed my chest and the other girls released me and took a few steps away from me.

I felt like a hunted animal, surrounded, trapped by vicious, snarling, hungry beasts. 'Let me go,' I said.

'Where will you go?' Souley persisted, her face close to mine again. 'What will you do, little Haoua? Your whole family will have it, you know. You should go. All of you. You should get out of Wadata right now. My father says that your sort have brought a curse to our village.'

'No!'

'Yes. Everybody knows what your father is like, Haoua. He too is cursed!'

'The only cure is to fuck a young virgin!' one of the other girls shouted.

'. . . Instead of those wizened old whores!' Souley added.

They all laughed.

My head was reeling. 'If you were smart enough to go to school you'd know that Monsieur Boubacar has taught us the truth about AIDS!' I said. 'And you've heard it from Mademoiselle Sushie too!'

'The *anasaras* don't know!' Souley snapped. 'And neither do their slaves. They only say these things because they fear our spirits!'

At last I managed to push through the huddle, just as Miriam and Oduntan came running up the hill towards us.

'What's going on here?' Oduntan demanded, squaring up to Souley.

'What are you going to do about it, idiot?' Souley spat, and then turned her back on us, her cronies giggling and shoving each other as they left us standing on the slope.

'Maybe Adamou Boureima will talk to you about this!' Miriam shouted after them.

'I'd like to see that worm try!' Souley called back. More laughter.

Miriam hooked her arm into mine as we watched them go. 'What a little witch that Souley is!' she said. 'Are you okay?'

'I'm okay,' I said, despite the fact that I was shaking. I turned to Oduntan. 'Thank you. God bless you.'

I walked back to the Kantao's compound with Miriam, explaining my plan to her with a combination of excitement and dread.

'I think Mademoiselle Sushie is right to be concerned about your father's cousin,' she said. 'I don't think he is a very good person.'

'What choice do I have, Miriam?' I said, imploring her to encourage me in my decision.

Madame Kantao was concerned also. She was pounding millet when we entered the compound, baby Narcisse tied to her back, rocked to sleep by the rhythm of her mother's movements, but she put down her pestle to welcome us.

'How's your poor mother, dear?' she said, a great warm smile on her broad face.

Miriam spoke before I had a chance to answer. 'Haoua's going to visit Madame Boureima in Niamey!' she said, throwing down her schoolbag.

Madame Kantao looked surprised. 'Come inside and tell me all about it,' she said. 'You can both have some of the delicious guavas that Mahamadou Alpha brought me today.'

As chance would have it, Mahamadou Alpha, the brother of Miriam's Uncle Memet and brother-in-law of her Aunt Ramatou, had made plans to leave our village early the following day to meet up with the camel train. Miriam had often told me how Memet had given up the nomadic way of life to settle in Wadata with Ramatou, Madame Kantao's sister, but his brother Mahamadou had continued to work the salt caravans across the great Ténéré Desert, as their family had done for generations. I had met Miriam's relations many times before and liked her family immensely, so when it was suggested that Mahamadou might agree to transport cousin Moussa and me to the *camion* post, my heart soared. At last, I would be on my way to see my mother.

It was agreed that, for a small sum, Monsieur Mahamadou would offer us the services of his camels, provided we were at the Kantao compound at first light.

As I walked to the entrance of the compound, Madame Kantao pressed a little brown paper package into my hand. 'Take this, Little One,' she whispered. 'But do not let my husband know that I have given it to you! It will bring you luck and keep you safe during your journey.' She glanced quickly over her shoulder and then indicated that I should open the package. It was a cockerel's foot, threaded with fine cords and brightly coloured buttons. I thanked Madame Kantao for her kindness and, with the gift of a ripe guava each for my brother, sister, father and his cousin tied in a little bundle, I raced home to tell my family the good news.

30

Despite Moussa's apparent determination to leave Wadata before dawn the following morning, he was still sleeping when I was ready to leave. I squatted in the shadows next to his bed, clutching my bundle and listening to the sounds of my family snoring peacefully in the next room. All of our farewells had been said the previous evening and there was nothing keeping me from setting off on my journey now but cousin Moussa's slumber.

The cockerels were beginning to crow and, my frustration getting the better of me, I leaned across and shook Moussa's shoulder vigorously.

He sat up suddenly and snapped at me. 'What do you want, child?'

'Monsieur,' I said, 'it is time for us to go. Monsieur Mahamadou will be leaving the Kantao compound very soon. I do not think that he will wait for us.'

He grunted, slammed himself back down onto his bedding and pulled his blanket over his head.

'Monsieur!' I protested.

Just then my father entered the room, carrying a lighted oil lamp. He looked at me without speaking, then poked at Moussa's legs with his bare foot. 'Come on, cousin,' he said. 'Get up now.'

Moussa grunted again. 'The girl can go on without me,' he mumbled angrily through the blanket. 'Mahamadou will have to take water for the journey.' He showed his face now before continuing, 'She can tell him to stop at the village on his way back from the river.'

I was about to protest further, but my father put his hand
up and shook his head gently, his face a combination of
amusement and sleepy agitation. 'That won't do, Moussa.
Mahamadou will head east after taking water.'

We waited outside while Moussa dressed and gathered his
belongings together. 'You have the shoes?' my father said.

'Yes, Father.'

'And you will give your mother my regards?'

'I will, Father.'

Moussa appeared at the doorway, looking grey and weary.
He yawned, cleared his throat loudly and then spat into the
previous evening's ashes. 'You have the shoes?' he said to me.

'I do.'

'*Toh.*' He turned to my father and embraced him limply.

My father slapped him on the back and then, holding his
cousin by the shoulders, he looked him in the eye. 'You'll
look out for my daughter?'

'Of course, Salim.'

'May God go with you. *Inshallah.*' He patted my
shoulder, then turned and went back into the house.

And so it was that we missed Monsieur Mahamadou and his
camels; when we arrived at Miriam's compound there was
no sign of life. It was half light now, and at first I thought the
Kantaos had not yet stirred, yet the beasts were nowhere to
be seen.

'Don't just stand there, girl,' Moussa said. 'Go and find
out how long ago he left.'

'We ought not to disturb them,' I said. 'If we head for the
river we may be able to catch up.'

'Go on!' Moussa insisted, nudging me forward.

I approached the house reluctantly, wary of waking baby
Narcisse and thus the entire Kantao family. But, as luck
would have it, before I reached the doorway, Madame
Kantao emerged from the house carrying a large basin. I
could tell that she was a little startled by my presence.

'Oh, child! I didn't notice you at first!' she said.

'*Fofo*. I am sorry to frighten you, Madame.'

'But you have missed Mahamadou, Little One!'

I leaned towards her, whispering, 'It was cousin Moussa's fault. I could not stir him!'

She smiled at me, warmly, her scent – as always – somehow a heady mix of cooking and love. 'A lazy man, eh?'

I smiled back and nodded. 'Do you think we can catch up with Monsieur Mahamadou?'

'A fit young woman like you, Haoua? Certainly I do.' She bent down to squint at me and lowered her voice. 'I'm not so sure about that no-good cousin of your father's, though!'

We stifled our giggles, then Madame Kantao hugged me tightly and wished God's blessing on me. 'And keep the amulet close to you,' she added.

'*Toh*. Please tell Miriam I'll see her soon.'

'Of course, dear. And you give your poor mother my best wishes. *Toh, kala a tonton.*'

'What was all that cackling about?' Moussa demanded, as we headed for the river.

'Nothing,' I said.

'It didn't sound like nothing.'

'It was nothing, Monsieur, really.' I did not like to lie, but I wanted to concentrate on catching up with Monsieur Mahamadou rather than making small talk with cousin Moussa, so I decided to put a stop to the conversation there and then. 'Madame Kantao was just telling me a funny story about Miriam's baby sister.'

'So tell me the funny story.'

'I'm very tired, Monsieur,' I said, skipping ahead of him through the scuffed camel tracks on the sun-softened piste.

'*Walayi!*' he said, under his breath.

We did not speak again until we were approaching the river. I was scanning the bank in an effort to catch sight of Monsieur Mahamadou and his animals when I felt myself wrenched backwards and found myself face to face with an irritated looking Moussa.

'Wait!' he said, dropping his head. 'There's something I meant to ask you.' He was somewhat breathless and sweating heavily.

The sour odour of his body wafted around me and I longed to step away from him but knew that I could not. To distract myself I listened to the shrieks of monkeys squabbling in the distance.

At last he straightened himself. A large, black fly landed on his wet brow and followed a deep furrow to his temple. 'Why did you take the shoes?' he said.

I was surprised by his question. 'Monsieur?'

'Why did you take the shoes?' he repeated, giving me a little shake. 'I don't like it when people touch my things!'

'Monsieur, I put the shoes in my bundle because I thought it would be easier for you if I carried them.'

'Uhuh?' he said, suspicion in his voice.

'I left your flashlight beside your bed. . . and I only lent you my little radio, and missed it so. . . and the shoes are mine, after all. . .'

He grabbed my chin then, and angled my face up towards his; not roughly, but still it unsettled me. 'It's good that you are carrying them. But they are not yours, child. I'm to escort you to Niamey. The shoes are my payment. Don't forget it.' He drew a gritty thumb across my lower lip then gave an odd smile before releasing me. 'You ought to have asked me for the radio too,' he said.

As I stood with my back to the river, I realised that I was trembling slightly.

Moussa had continued towards the riverbank and now called out, 'Come on! Let's find this Touareg.'

I wiped the back of my hand across my mouth and turned to follow him.

31

The dispute over ownership of the shoes troubled me, without a doubt, but soon it retreated into the deepest recesses of my mind. Ahead of me, Moussa was making straight for a clearing on the riverbank, to the right of where we usually washed our clothes and bedding. We heard the animal before we saw it: the strange, strangled lament of a camel at odds with its master.

Mahamadou Alpha was the owner of two camels; at least two that I knew of. One of these beasts, a good-natured, white female with lashes more beautiful than those belonging to any woman, was now standing, heavy laden and hobbled and waiting patiently for its master, while it chewed at the wispy branches of a locust bean tree near the riverbank. The other, a larger, younger, brown male, which had sprawled itself on the riverbank, was obviously not about to comply so readily.

Monsieur Mahamadou had his back to us as we approached him. I had rarely heard him speak when I had visited the Kantaos and, any time he did, it was in a most genteel manner. Now, seeing this tall, light-skinned, elegant man furiously prodding the male camel in the ribs with a short, straight stick and hearing the barrage of abuse which he hurled at the creature, I could scarcely believe that it was the same person.

'You stinking bastard!' he screamed, as the animal attempted to yank its head away from Monsieur Mahamadou's grip. 'Get up, you lazy, good-for-nothing swine!'

As if answering, the animal shook its head again and uttered another furious bellow. Monsieur Mahamadou jabbed the stick into its ribs once again but the creature's legs remained stubbornly folded beneath its bulk.

'Do you need some help there, brother?' Moussa called out over the awful noise.

Monsieur Mahamadou looked over his shoulder. 'Just stay back there!' he called. 'I know how to get this son-of-a-devil on to its feet!' He grabbed the animal's lower lip with one hand and then, spinning the stick swiftly and skilfully in the other, he dropped a loop of cord attached to the end of the stick over the creature's muzzle. 'Stay well back!' Monsieur Mahamadou advised again.

It had not occurred to me to do anything else.

Monsieur Mahamadou then proceeded to twist the end of the stick so that the cord tightened quickly on the camel's rubbery flesh. The animal was indignant and roared once again. Monsieur Mahamadou brought the flat of his hand hard against the animal's neck, at the same time pulling roughly on the corded stick so that the camel's head was forced upwards and sideways in a most unnatural manner. At the same time, he kicked at the animal's torso, jabbing its ribs with his sandaled foot.

'Get up, you son-of-a. . .'

At last the poor creature struggled to its feet, all the while moaning like something possessed by bad spirits. Monsieur Mahamadou continued to clutch the stick. He glanced over his shoulder towards us, a victorious look on his face. Yanking at the stick once more, he cuffed the creature around the ears before releasing it from the noose.

This was a mistake. I had witnessed ill-tempered animals before, many times, but never anything like what happened next.

Monsieur Mahamadou turned to face us, a great, broad smile on his face. 'Got to show these beasts who's boss,' he said.

'*Walayi!* For sure!' Moussa said.

But the creature was obviously far from satisfied with the outcome of the situation; it shook itself violently and then quickly deposited a huge, steaming lump of faeces in the dust.

Now, with his back to the animal and holding on to it only with the rope attached to its nose ring, Monsieur Mahamadou did not foresee the camel's next actions: it had been angry before; now it went berserk. Uttering another of its demonic roars, it suddenly began to buck and rear, twisting and kicking in all directions. I had never seen a camel move so fast before. Too fast for Monsieur Mahamadou, who was dragged towards the river, slithering through mud and reeds, cursing wildly all the time until he managed finally to slip the noose back over the creature's muzzle.

Moussa ran towards Monsieur Mahamadou. 'How can I help?' he called.

Monsieur Mahamadou was panting heavily. The camel wheezed too and, white froth dripping from the corners of its rough lips, its ribcage heaved and its spirit seemed broken – for now at least.

'Hold this for me for a moment, please,' Monsieur Mahamadou said, nodding towards the stick and giving the noose another turn. 'I just need to catch my breath.'

'*Walayi!*' Moussa took it with little enthusiasm. 'Please God it won't start again, will it?'

Monsieur Mahamadou puffed and shook his head. 'He's young. Foolish. Goes off like that every once in a while. But he should be all right now.' He looked at me and shrugged. 'He'd better be, or I'll serve him to the dogs!'

I smiled, nervously. I had met Monsieur Mahamadou on several occasions, and had always liked him, but seeing him beating this animal had unsettled me. Suddenly it struck me that I was about to set off on the first stage of a long journey with two men whom I barely knew.

With the big male calmed, it did not take long for

Monsieur Mahamadou to add my bundle and water gourd to the camel's burden. I had not ridden a camel before and was a little apprehensive about it. Seeing the male at his worst had not made me feel any more at ease about the prospect, but Monsieur Mahamadou quickly reassured me. 'Don't worry, Mademoiselle,' he said. 'You won't have to ride alone.'

Moussa was tying his own bundle on to the female. He was quick to speak. 'No, indeed. You can ride up in front of me.'

I was not sure whether Monsieur Mahamadou had read my face or had another reason for not complying with cousin Moussa's idea, but – despite the fact that I had witnessed the ill temper of both he and his camel – I was relieved when he took me by the arm. 'No,' he said. 'My female has only a blanket on which to sit, whereas look at the fine three-pronged saddle we shall sit upon!'

As if sensing that it really was now time to set off, both creatures dropped down obediently when their master bid them. Lead rope in hand, Monsieur Mahamadou guided Moussa safely onto the female before straddling the big male and leaning over to haul me up on to the beast's back too. I was struck immediately by the powerful odour of the animal's coarse coat. Monsieur Mahamadou tapped his stick against the camel's neck and clicked his tongue in encouragement. Then, with a great lurch and a flurry of dust and hair, we were on our way.

32

The journey to the *camion* post was to take the best part of the day. Monsieur Mahamadou's camels settled quickly into a steady, sure-footed stride and, perched between Monsieur Mahamadou's thighs, high above the scorching sands, I soon got used both to the unfamiliar odours of man and beast and the odd, rhythmic swaying. At times I even found myself drifting off into a light sleep, always aware of the animal's movement and the closeness of this relative stranger, but comfortable enough, *safe* enough, to allow myself to doze. And, when I took the trouble to look around at the arid expanse, I realised that this was a wonderful way to see my beautiful country.

Monsieur Mahamadou was an extremely devout man and so it was necessary for us to make frequent stops to allow him to pray. The first few times the camels were drawn to a halt and hobbled, cousin Moussa followed Monsieur Mahamadou away from me and the animals and dropped down onto his knees in prayer beside him. I knew I was expected to stay away from the men during these interruptions in our journey, and that if I wanted to pray I would have to do so while making myself useful. And so, while I repeated lines from the Koran and asked God to protect my mother, I busied myself unwrapping tea, mint leaves and plastic tumblers from our bundles and scrambling around for anything flammable that could be added to the small supply of firewood that we had brought with us.

I soon realised that Moussa was frustrated by the constant stopping and starting; after a while, he stopped going through the motions and, instead, sat silently a few metres away from the animals – smoking and spitting and watching me.

I wished that he would join Monsieur Mahamadou. I was torn between the desire to keep my back to him and the necessity to show him the respect due to an elder. As I went about my business, it seemed like I could feel his eyes boring into me. On one occasion I was distracted from preparing our refreshment by the sound of splashing. I looked up to see Moussa urinating, not far from where I was kneeling. He had been squatting, in the acceptable fashion, with his *jellaba* and thighs affording him some privacy, but when he caught my eye, he stood up quickly and shook himself towards me. I looked away and immediately made myself busy. I pretended not to have noticed, but Moussa's cackle made me shiver. I was sure that Monsieur Mahamadou would not have approved of this behaviour, but, of course, I did not mention the incident to him.

Monsieur Mahamadou kept himself to himself. Although, when we were astride his camel, he would occasionally point out an abandoned vehicle or an animal's skeleton, I got the feeling that he barely noticed Moussa and me and that he was certainly not prepared to change his habits for us in any way. He seldom spoke to me and said less still to Moussa, and with each stop the tension between the two men seemed to grow.

As the sun became less intense and the soft sand cooled, our progress was made easier and our camels seemed to settle into a swifter pace. The prayer stops became less frequent and, with the fall of darkness and a slow half moon in the sky, I soon lost track of any real sense of time. Certainly it must have been well after midnight when, at last, we glimpsed the flickering oil lamps dotted around Monsieur Youssef 's shed at the *camion* post. Relief washed over all of us, I think; it had been a relatively straightforward journey, but I, for one, was exhausted.

Unlike the last time I had come here with Sushie, to see off my brother Abdelkrim, there was no sign of life apart from the lamps and certainly no welcoming smell of cooking. We dismounted and, while Monsieur Mahamadou and Moussa untied our bundles, I stretched and drank some water before walking a few paces into the darkness to find somewhere to relieve myself.

When I returned to the *camion* post I was both surprised and concerned to find that Monsieur Mahamadou and his camels had gone, their tracks trailing off northwards into the cool blackness of the night.

'I thought he would rest here for a while,' I said to cousin Moussa, who was sitting cross-legged on his blanket under the canopy, the glow of his cigarette like a single, eerie, misplaced eye against his silhouette.

'We're only a short distance from Djamaro,' Moussa replied. 'He said he wanted to get there before sunrise.' He sucked his teeth. 'Anyway. . . good riddance to your Monsieur Mahamadou Alpha! He tried to charge me twelve hundred CFA!' He flicked his cigarette and blew a great cloud of blue smoke in my direction. 'Twelve hundred CFA for a little camel ride? The man's a crook!'

'*Toh.*' I picked up my bundle and looked around. I wanted to speak up for Monsieur Mahamadou, to protest that he seemed like a fair man to me, but decided that it was probably wiser to stay quiet.

That was it then. There was no other sign of life. Monsieur Youssef had obviously retired for the night. I would have to rest here until morning, alone with Moussa. I set the bundle down again hesitantly and unrolled my blanket. I looked at Moussa and shivered.

'Cold, girlie?' he said.

'No, Monsieur!' I said, quickly. I leaned forward to drag my bundle over for a pillow, then gasped and pulled back as something small, dark and shiny scuttled towards my blanket.

Moussa was beside me in a flash. 'Scorpion!' he said, his

lips curled back and the faint moonlight dancing across his broken yellow teeth. Kneeling now, he took a small, straight knife from his belt and put his face close to the cool sand. I assumed that he meant to kill the creature swiftly with the knife and, even though my grandmother had taught me to respect all forms of life and I would happily have let the beast go on its way, I was not about to argue with Moussa. Instead, he used the flat of the blade to pin the insect down and, before I knew what was happening, his cigarette was searing into the tormented creature's thrashing abdomen. At last it was over. The scorpion lay still and Moussa stood towering above it, grinning cruelly.

I could not share his pleasure. 'I don't think it would have harmed us, Monsieur. . .' I said, warily.

He tutted, spat towards the dead insect and then pushed sand over it with the side of his foot. 'You'll sleep safer now,' he said, then bent down and dragged my blanket closer to his own. I felt uncomfortable but did not say so.

'Don't stand there gawping, girl!' he said. 'Bring your bundle over here and get settled. It's late and we have another long day ahead of us tomorrow.'

I picked up my bundle and moved towards him. Before I could set it down again, Moussa had snatched it from me. He untied it hastily and withdrew Katie and Hope's shoes, still in their box, which was now a little battered. 'I'll take care of these, girlie,' he said.

I nodded. As I sank to my knees he put his face close to mine and leered, his hot breath once again wafting over my face. I quickly scrambled on to my blanket and lay with my back to him, my knees pulled up tight to my chest.

'Let me know if you get cold,' Moussa said, poking a finger into my ribs.

I prayed that morning would come quickly.

To my relief, Moussa quickly slipped into a heavy slumber. I lay awake for a very long time, thinking about my mother and marvelling at the open sky beyond the canopy, the peacefulness of the night spoiled only by my travelling companion's deep snores. I turned my head to look at Moussa: he lay with his face towards me, a thin trickle of drool spilling from the corner of his crumpled mouth. He did not stir as I shuffled my blanket further away from him.

The sound of unfamiliar voices woke me. I opened my eyes and felt both a not-yet-angry sun and a light wind caressing my face. For a moment I was concerned that I had slept through the *camion*'s arrival and departure, but Moussa's belongings lay nearby, his blanket covered in fine sand.

A group of men were standing near the entrance to Monsieur Youssef 's shed – chatting, spitting, cleaning their teeth with chew sticks. I recognised a few of them as being from Goteye. Moussa was amongst them. He glanced towards me and pointed, then said something under his breath to his companions. The men looked over their shoulders and laughed. There was no time for annoyance. Suddenly I realised that someone was addressing me.

'Hello again, little Mademoiselle. *Mate ni kani*? Did you sleep well?'

I looked up and was pleased to see Monsieur Youssef beaming down at me, his face warmer than the morning sun.

'I hear you're off to the capital?'

'Yes, Monsieur,' I said. 'My mother is poorly and I am going to visit her in hospital.'

Monsieur Youssef scratched his head. 'Yes.' He nodded towards the building. 'Yes, I heard that from your cousin. May God watch over her – and you also, little sister.'

'Thank you, Monsieur. God is great. And may He watch over you too.'

Monsieur Youssef nodded. '*Inshallah*. Well now. . . you'd better get up, Mademoiselle. The *camion* will be arriving very soon.'

After a brief prayer, I bundled my things together and breakfasted hastily on dried dates and a thin millet gruel.

There were more folk gathered at the *camion* post than the last time I had been there with Abdelkrim and Sushie, but around mid-morning when the truck finally arrived, it carried only a few passengers and was not heavily laden.

We climbed aboard and tried to make ourselves comfortable. I pushed my way through bundles of clothing, past tools, plastic buckets, basins, fuel canisters and sacks containing goat meat and freshly slaughtered *moutons*, some with legs protruding through tears in the jute, and scrambled onto a pile of tyres, wedging myself into a corner at the rear of the vehicle, my back to the tailgate. Moussa lay down on some sacking next to two women whose faces were covered. At the other end of the truck, the Goteye men also covered their faces with their *cheches*. A few of them wore sunglasses: I could not see their eyes but felt sure that they were observing me.

With the first lurch of the vehicle, my head was thrown back and bashed off the tailgate. It was the first of many discomforts that day, made worse by the fact that my water supply was running low. Our driver was, perhaps, not so devout a man as Monsieur Mahamadou; nevertheless he stopped to pray several times. It was only then that I managed to doze for a short while, declining tea from the women despite my intense thirst. When the praying had finished, we would clamber back onto the *camion* and try, once more, to find the least painful position amongst the cargo.

Darkness had settled upon us once again by the time we approached the ferry embarkation point at Bac Farie. There was a great deal of commotion as the truck lumbered up the gangway but I was too exhausted to pay much attention to what was happening on the deck below. I began to think that our journey would never end. I thought of asking cousin Moussa how much longer we would have to endure such hardship, but we had barely exchanged words all day and, somehow, I felt more at ease with things that way.

At last, the rugged piste led us onto a smooth bitumen strip and the going was made considerably easier, but by the time the vehicle trundled into Niamey I was worn out and my body ached all over. Even so, as I stood peering out over the tailgate and my gaze followed colonies of bats flitting between majestic date palms, tamarind and mahogany trees and the tall electric lights and fine buildings either side of the highway, I felt relieved – excited even – but most of all happy that I was soon to be with my mother again.

33

I barely remember the short taxi ride to Moussa's house, which was unlike any I had ever visited before. It was big – bigger even than Alassane's – with straight walls and windows with metal grilles and mesh to keep the mosquitoes out. The house was set within a gated compound which, though smaller than my father's, contained several other buildings. Moussa led me into one of these – a store house, strewn with old bicycle frames and dismantled parts – and indicated that I should make my bed up on the hard, dirt floor. He then disappeared into the house, without introduction to his family or any offer of refreshment. My water gourd was empty and my throat was dry, but I was so tired that all I really wanted to do was sleep.

The following morning I opened my eyes to find a young woman standing over me. I sat up with a jolt, unsure of where I was at first.

'Excuse me, Mademoiselle,' I said.

'You are Haoua Boureima,' the woman said. It was not a question.

'Yes, Mademoiselle.'

'*Je m'appelle* Yola,' she said. 'And it is *Madame*; I am Moussa's wife.' She spoke French in a strange, thick accent, quite different to any that I had heard before. The light filtering in from the doorway behind her seemed to glow around her darkened form, and although I could not yet clearly see her face, I was certain that it was handsome.

'I'm sorry, Madame,' I said. 'I did not know.' I stood up

and brushed myself down. My clothing was caked with dust and I felt filthy.

Yola looked me up and down. 'You are to wash and then come into the house.'

'Yes, Madame.' I followed her out into the compound, squinting as the sunlight hit my face and suddenly aware of the noise of heavy traffic and the thick scent of unfamiliar blooms in the air. I stopped and Yola turned to address me.

'Why are you standing there, girl?' she said.

'I'm sorry, Madame,' I said, realising that it hurt my throat to speak. 'I am so very dirty. Where is the river, please?'

Madame Yola laughed loudly and jabbed her thumb behind her shoulder. 'The river is two miles in that direction,' she said, 'but you can wash yourself here.' She led me across the compound to the gable end of the main building. A thin pipe emerged from the ground and was fastened to the wall with metal clips. At the top of the pipe a small, round wheel was attached. 'Here,' she said, tapping the wheel.

I looked at her, but said nothing. Unfamiliar sounds and smells came at me from all directions.

'You haven't seen a faucet before?'

'Madame?'

She stepped forward and turned the wheel. A bright cascade of clear water gushed from the pipe.

It was my turn to laugh now. At school, Monsieur Boubacar had told us about such things but I had never seen anything so wonderful. I bent down and gulped the water greedily, while Madame Yola fetched a plastic pail. When I had drunk my fill, Yola allowed the pail to half fill before turning the wheel in a clockwise direction.

'If you want to use the latrine, it is over there,' she said. 'Wash yourself and then come inside.' With that she disappeared into the house.

Alone, I stood gawping down at the water, shards of morning sunshine reflected on its slowly settling surface, my head dizzy with thoughts and tiredness, until a movement to the right caught my eye. A plastic-green chameleon moved, lazily, a short distance along a low wall at the back of the compound, before stopping as if to observe me. I scooped water up in my hands and scrubbed my face and neck vigorously, then removed my head wrap and rinsed it well, before reaching underneath my *pagne* to daub at the sweat on my body as best I could. When I had finished washing, I approached the entrance of the house and lingered for a moment, trying to decide whether I should call out or knock, and listening to the sounds of utensils banging. The smell of cooking wafted around me and suddenly I realised that I was hungry.

'Madame?' I called.

'Come in, girl.'

I pushed the half open door and entered the house. Yola was bent over a stove, ladling out portions of *boule* from a large pot. A metal chimney fixed to the wall disappeared upwards through the ceiling and drew wood smoke away from the room.

Yola pointed to a long, narrow wooden table at the other side of the room, around which stood four plastic chairs. A copy of *Le Sahel* lay spread open on the table, the headline TEACHERS CALL THREE-DAY STRIKE in large, black letters across two pages.

I sat down and fidgeted nervously, and was wondering if I ought to offer to help when I heard the sound of muffled laughter coming from beyond another doorway opposite the entrance. Yola turned and looked at me without speaking, agitation clearly visible on her face. For a moment I thought that I had offended her in some way, but then she moved a few paces towards the door.

'Madame! Monsieur!' she called out abruptly.

'What is it?' Moussa's voice answered gruffly.

'The food is ready.'

More commotion from what I guessed was a bedroom.

Although Yola had her back to me, I could tell that her irritation was growing. She continued to clatter her utensils and I sat quietly, nervously, taking in the room. It was an airy room with two other wooden doors leading off it in addition to that of the entrance. Despite the fact that it was somewhat untidy, I decided that I liked this room. The walls had been painted bright blue and although patches of the paint were peeling badly, it was still a cheery space I thought. Beside an array of pots, buckets and cardboard boxes, a battered metal sign with the word *Dunlop* leaned against the wall. A shaft of morning sunshine cut through a small, square window, framing my dusty feet and plastic sandals in golden light. Behind me and to my right, their backs facing outwards like a little herd of petrified *moutons*, a further assortment of plastic chairs had been pushed, haphazardly, into the corner. To the left of the chimney hung a portrait of President Mainassara, smaller than the one in my father's house, but presented in a smart black frame. Below it, hanging from a nail, was a small Agadez Cross similar to the one which Abdelkrim had presented to my mother.

I was just about to try to strike up some kind of conversation with Madame Yola, when cousin Moussa entered the room, an unlit cigarette protruding from behind his ear. He looked first at his wife and then at me, sucked his teeth and sat down without a word.

'Monsieur,' I said.

He yawned and murmured something under his breath, then began to pick at his teeth.

Yola set food on the table and disappeared out of the room.

'You ought to have helped Madame Yola, girl,' Moussa said.

I was about to answer that I would have been glad to do so, when an older woman entered the room and sat down beside Moussa. 'So, this is cousin Haoua,' she said. No introduction was offered, but I knew that this was Doodi, Moussa's first wife; my mother had talked about her often and, although she was not one to speak ill of others, she had not done so with any affection.

I stood up and thanked Madame Doodi for her generous hospitality and asked God to bless her for her kindness towards me.

'Don't thank me,' she said, waving me down with a bony hand and shooting her husband a cold look, 'I didn't even know you were coming.'

'I'll take her to Abdelkrim once I've opened the shop,' Moussa said. 'I told you.'

Madame Doodi did not respond. Instead, she looked me up and down and began eating.

It was customary in our village that men and women did not eat together, and although there were times when communal meals could not be avoided, I still felt unsettled by the lack of formality.

'Eat,' Moussa said, pushing a plastic plate towards me.

'Thank you, Monsieur. Should I take my food outside?'

He dismissed my question with a gesture and continued eating, scooping up a handful of millet paste and pushing it into his mouth. 'You like my house?' he said, spitting morsels of food in my direction.

'It is a very fine house, Monsieur,' I said. 'You must be very rich.'

Moussa laughed. 'My bicycle shop is quite famous in Niamey. My family has full bellies. But children are what makes a man wealthy!'

I thought that it was an odd thing for him to say; he did not seem particularly fond of children.

Madame Doodi scowled, and muttered '*Walayi!*' under her breath.

There were no signs of children in the household, but the thought that there might be somehow comforted me. 'You have children, Madame?' I said.

Moussa sucked his teeth. 'This one is barren!' he said,

poking Doodi in the belly, 'But my Yola will bear me many children.'

As if beckoned, Yola came through the doorway, her eyes meeting mine briefly as she made to cross the room. Moussa reached out and grabbed at her buttocks, then laughed heartily and slapped the tabletop with both hands as Yola shrieked and scurried outside.

I fixed my gaze on the painted concrete floor, uncomfortable, anxious, awkward in this unfamiliar world and with these unfamiliar people. Across the scarred and scrubbed wooden table I sensed Doodi's displeasure and allowed myself a glimpse upwards.

The older woman's face had barely altered, but there was no mistaking the fury in her eyes.

34

I was very glad to leave cousin Moussa's house that morning. I had helped Yola to wash the dishes and was crossing the compound, to change my *pagne* and retrieve my belongings from the store where I had slept, when I heard my name called out. Next to a fenced off enclosure, where a few goats and *moutons* huddled together in a vain attempt to find shade from the strengthening sun, Moussa was wrestling with a jumbled assortment of bicycles.

'Come and help me here, child!' he said.

I hurried across the compound and took hold of the handlebars of a large, slightly scruffy, black specimen, while Moussa attempted to disengage a mess of pedals, cogs and chains.

'You *can* ride one of these?' he said, his voice tinged with irritation.

I shook my head. 'I am sorry, Monsieur.' The closest I had ever come to owning a bicycle was when my brother Abdelkrim had made me a little coat hanger toy.

Moussa sucked his teeth and carelessly took his hands off a second vehicle, causing it to crash back down on to the pile from which it had just been retrieved.

'*Walayi!*' he hissed, pushing a pair of heavy-framed sunglasses back up his nose. 'You'll just have to ride with me then.' He took the black bicycle from me and wheeled it across the compound, leaning it up against the wall beside the gate. Despite its rough treatment and obvious neglect, it was a handsome thing, with dirtied white tyres and chipped gold lettering on its crossbar, spelling out the words *Tianjin Flying Pigeon*.

'Monsieur,' I said. 'Are we going to see my mother?'

Moussa fiddled impatiently at the breast pocket of his clean beige shirt. 'I have spoken to your brother. He will meet us at the Grand Marché later this morning.' He clamped a chew stick between his teeth, adjusted his glasses again and then threw his leg expertly over the bicycle frame. 'Come on,' he said. 'I have to open up my shop.'

I was overjoyed to hear the news about my brother, but before I could give it a second thought, Moussa reached out, wrapped his arm around my waist and lifted me awkwardly onto the bicycle's crossbar so that my legs dangled, like those of a slaughtered animal, above his left foot. Frightened by the unfamiliar movement, I grabbed at the handlebars to steady myself. Moussa leaned forward, an arm each side of me, and pushed down on the pedals and before long we were on the hard, smooth surface of the Boulevard de l'Independence, winding our way through a terrifying, deafening confusion of bush taxis and *camions*, motorcycles, bicycles, camels, donkeys and carts. Ahead of us, nestling behind the Palais des Congres and the Hotel Gaweye and stretched across the river and its gentler traffic like some gigantic beast, I caught sight of the magnificent Pont Kennedy for the first time. Pedestrians streamed across the huge bridge, their heads laden with wares and possessions. Traffic herded towards Gaweye and Niamey Haut, this great stampede of tyres and feet and hooves churning up a blanket of fine dust which seemed to cling to the bases of the strange, yellowy-grey buildings all around us. High above us, huge black and white signs – their meanings unknown to me; Sonara, El Nasr, Citibank – crowned massive box-like structures, reaching up through Niamey's hazy skies and beckoning its multitudes like so many otherworldly mosques. After a few minutes I began to relax a little, despite the discomfort in my rump and Moussa's stale breath against my ear, and as the hot, tarred road shot by below us and the cool air caressed my face, I allowed myself to lean back into

Moussa's chest and tried to imagine my mother's look of joy at our reunion.

We turned off Avenue de l'Uranium at Place Kennedy and headed north along Avenue Ouezzin-Coulibaly, stopping while a convoy of military trucks thundered by.

I craned my neck in the vain hope that I might see my brother among the huddles of soldiers.

We passed row after row of smiths and artisans working by the roadside.

Moussa pointed his now ragged and soggy chew stick to his left and said, proudly, 'The National Museum,' and through a thinly scattered group of market stalls, a flash of reflected sunlight drew my eye to some large, metallic panels erected near the building. I was about to ask him about the structures, but was distracted suddenly by smells so foul that I let go of one of the handlebar grips to pinch my nose tightly.

'It stinks of animals here, Monsieur,' I said, craning my neck around so that he could see my face.

'The zoo,' he said, panting. As he pedalled, a bead of sweat wobbled on the tip of his nose.

We passed more buildings – Air Niger, U.T.A., Nigeria Airways, Air Afrique – some of which seemed, impossibly, to be made only of glass. I wondered if this might be the place that Abdelkrim had told me about – where the boys with polio did their dance. I stared in amazement under and over Moussa's arm as we glided by one strange sight after another. Here, among the traditionally dressed citizens and raggedy beggars, men and women in formal western clothing bustled in and out of vast doorways. Further along, the overwhelming stench of animal faeces was replaced by the cutting odour of human urine, mingled with Moussa's own now-familiar scent. A huddle of tin shacks seemed to prop each other up at the foot of yet another mountainous concrete building. Neatly tended strips of grass and bitumen cut through forecourts of rubbish-strewn orange dust.

As we turned onto Avenue Nasser, just before the Hotel Rivoli, a scratchy, dry voice called out to Moussa. 'Patron!'

I looked across the road and was shocked by the appearance of the man who had hailed my cousin. He did not, somehow, seem like an aged man, yet he was stooped forward, leaning heavily on a long pole. He wore a thin *jellaba* which was torn badly and had obviously not been scrubbed for a very long time. He called out again, a short greeting in Hausa, from ruined lips.

Moussa returned the man's greeting, swooping past his outstretched hand without slowing.

'Who is that, Monsieur?' I said, without taking my eyes off the fellow.

'He's called Gado,' Moussa said. 'He hangs around the Rivoli begging scraps from the prostitutes and pimps and plaguing the *anasaras* for *cadeaux*, but he's harmless really.'

I peered back over my shoulder as we lurched along Avenue Nasser. I had seen the yellowed hair of the malnourished before – in my own village – but never before had I stared into the hollow eyes of a face like this one – noseless, half eaten away by disease. As he disappeared from view, I thought that I had never seen such a lonely figure. I wondered if he had ever known the love of a family.

The sign above Moussa's shop was quite unlike those I had seen near Pont Kennedy. We had turned off Avenue Nasser into a small side street, where Moussa pulled his bicycle up in front of a tired-looking, single storey, green-painted block.

'This is it,' he said.

I slid off the bicycle quickly, my buttocks and thighs throbbing as my body pumped blood back into them.

Nailed to the crumbling wall of Moussa's shop, high above a corrugated tin door, a badly drawn bicycle and the words *à vendre* had been daubed, poorly, onto a square of white-painted wood. Below the bicycle, in smaller letters and also painted in black, I read the name *Boureima*. It was strange to see my family name up there on a shop front in a great city like Niamey.

Moussa had been fumbling with a large metal lock on a bar which slid across the door, but stopped now. Suddenly I realised that he had been talking to me. 'What are you gawping at, girl?' he said.

'I was looking at your sign,' I said.

'Do you like my sign?'

I shrugged.

Moussa nodded in the direction of the shop next to his, which was already open for business: suitcases and satchels, kettles, flasks and buckets, oil lamps and footballs all displayed neatly around the doorway and stacked on rattan mats. It was, I felt, the kind of display that our own Monsieur Letouye would have appreciated.

'My friend Monsieur Emmanuel Kountche did it for me,' Moussa said. 'He can read and write – like you.' As he spoke, a huge, bespectacled man in a vivid blue *jellaba* and white skull cap emerged from the adjacent shop, an enormous suitcase in each hand and a smaller one tucked under each arm.

I averted my eyes, certain that Moussa had not intended his comment as a compliment to either Monsieur Kountche or myself. It struck me that Monsieur Kountche had taken a good deal more care with his own sign: it too was decorated with a picture of his wares, but the letters which spelled out his name were straight and bold, whereas the paint on cousin Moussa's had dribbled and run and the last two letters of the name *Boureima* had been squashed into the corner.

'Hey! Emmanuel!' Moussa shouted, as Monsieur Kountche stretched across his shop front to arrange his goods to his satisfaction.

When the suitcases were in place, Monsieur Kountche stood up and straightened his spectacles, but did not so much as look in our direction. A taxi driver sounded his horn, trundling past in a cloud of dust, and Monsieur Kountche waved in recognition before disappearing back inside his shop.

For a moment I considered the possibility that Monsieur Kountche had not heard Moussa, but when my cousin shook his head and sucked air in through his teeth I found myself wondering how he had offended Monsieur Kountche. Somehow it never crossed my mind that it might be Moussa who had been offended.

As Moussa swung open the door, a young man, not much older than Adamou, with a damaged eye and a slight limp, crossed the dusty road and approached us.

'Ça va, Monsieur?' he shouted. 'Ça marche?' He wore an earnest, frightened expression, that, it seemed to me, he was trying, desperately, to wrestle into a smile.

Moussa turned to face him, a sour look on his face. 'What time do you call this, idiot?' he snapped.

The young man held his palms open, imploringly, towards Moussa, his head tilted to one side. 'Monsieur,' he said. 'My father is unwell. I had to help my mother carry her vegetables to the market.'

'I've told you before,' Moussa said, his face more stern than I had seen it before, 'I don't give a damn about your troubles! I don't pay you to do your mother's work! If you want this job, do it properly!' Now he was really in a rant. 'I suppose you opened up just whenever you fancied while I was away?'

'No. . . Monsieur!'

'Don't think I won't check!'

The young man cast me an apologetic smile and hobbled past us into the gloom of the bicycle shop.

'I'll be checking my stock too!' Moussa shouted, after his employee.

'But I did as you instructed, Monsieur,' the young man said, as he wheeled a tatty red bicycle out onto the street. 'I took the money to Madame Doodi at the end of each day.'

Moussa snorted. 'She told me, but I hope that everything's

in order here – for your sake. You can give me back the spare key now too.'

'And I sold two new Raleighs and the second hand Hangzhou, Monsieur!' the youth said, fumbling in the pockets of his shorts.

'Yes, yes. That's all very well,' Moussa nodded impatiently, snatching the key from the boy and then turning to address me. 'You stay here and help this oaf. I have some business to attend to.'

'When will you take me to my brother, Monsieur?' I called after him, as he strode off in the direction of Avenue Nasser.

'When I get back!'

I stood facing the young man, feeling awkward and unsure. After a few moments he shuffled towards me with his hands clasped to his chest.

'Mademoiselle. My name is Jacob.' Despite the horrible gash which ran across his forehead and eyebrow, melding into his discoloured socket like the mouth of some offensive river, I thought that he had a gallant face.

'I am Haoua,' I said.

He smiled and then stood back to look me over. 'This bothers you, Mademoiselle?' he said, touching his face.

I shrugged. 'What happened to you?'

'Let's just say I'm better at selling bicycles than riding them! – Not that your uncle would agree. . .'

We both laughed.

'Moussa's not my uncle. He's my father's cousin,' I said.

'I see.'

'He doesn't treat you fairly I think.'

'He's not so bad. I've worked for worse.'

'*Toh.*' I looked again at Jacob's wound. 'Shouldn't you have seen a doctor about that?' I said.

He rolled his palm out towards me. '*Walayi!* Who can afford doctors? I will be fine. I still have my vision, praise God.' He slapped his thigh. 'And I thank Him that I didn't lose my leg. Then I really would be in trouble.'

He disappeared back into the shop and re-emerged with another bicycle a few moments later; this time a shiny new model. 'You know, Mademoiselle,' he said, gesturing towards the Citibank building which towered over us, 'I've seen many accidents out there. Often a cyclist or pedestrian with a broken limb or two has no option but amputation!'

I shuddered at the thought and then set to work, helping Jacob to wheel out and display the rest of Moussa's stock. The shop itself was small, dark and cluttered. The unfamiliar smell of rubber was a welcome change from the stench of urine outside.

On every wall, shelves overflowed with saddles, tyres, pumps, cogs, chains and oil cans. Jacob hauled a large folding wooden sign outside and stood it in front of the shop. When we had arranged everything to his satisfaction, ready for the day's trade, he lit a little kerosene stove and offered me some sweet tea. We sat outside on two plastic crates and, although I had only just met this boy, I told him all about Wadata, my brother Abdelkrim and the plight of my poor mother.

He set down his plastic cup and looked at me, a serious frown on his battered face. 'Mademoiselle,' he said, 'I will pray for you and your family.'

I thanked him and was about to ask him about his own family when Moussa appeared again, a cigarette hanging from his lip. Jacob jumped to his feet and frantically began polishing the handlebars of a green Hangzhou with the end of his torn tee shirt.

Moussa blew a great cloud of smoke into the air and sucked his teeth. 'Hey!' he said.

Jacob looked up from his pointless and thankless task.

'I'm taking the girl to the Grand Marché,' Moussa said, nodding towards me. 'You make sure that everything's in order here. I just spoke to Monsieur Djennbe and he wants to collect his machine this morning.'

'Toh,' Jacob said. 'I have it ready for him, Monsieur.' He

turned to face me then. 'May God smile upon your family. *Kala a tonton.*'

I thanked him and followed Moussa back out on to Avenue Nasser.

The Boulevard de la Liberté is a fine, broad, straight road which passes in front of Niamey's famous Grand Marché. I trudged along behind Moussa, staying close to him and feeling a little frightened, for we were now surrounded by hordes of people, all making their way towards the market. Hundreds of clay pots and dishes of all shapes and sizes lined the roadside. A vendor wobbled by on a bicycle, a clutch of live chickens, their feet lashed together with cord, dangling from his handlebars. Another fellow ran alongside the bicycle, trying to keep up, on his head a tray with hunks of flayed meat laid out on brown paper. Groups of women, their heads piled high with baskets, gourds or bundles of fabric, wove their way through the throng. A tall, thin man, wearing several pairs of dark glasses stacked up over his forehead, barred our way and thrust another armful of his wares towards us. Moussa pushed him aside and muttered under his breath. As he disappeared into the crowd, I heard the tall fellow's laughter mingle with the vendors' cries of *Solani* and *Coka* and wondered if it was at my expense.

At the junction of Avenue Ouezzin-Coulibaly and Boulevard de la Liberté, traffic had slowed almost to a standstill, as whole families struggled from taxis and trucks, wrestling their goods onto the dust before lugging them up the gentle incline towards the Grand Marché. Furious car drivers honked their horns, pedestrians swore at cyclists, animals brayed and squawked and bellowed unheeded.

We followed a boy towards the heart of the market, on his head a huge, vibrantly coloured assortment of buckets and basins, kettles and cups, all tied together with string. An old woman stopped him to purchase an item, and I stared as the boy lifted this great jumble off his head and set it on the ground. As he stretched across to cut free a blue pail, I realised that, together, his goods stood as tall as his chin.

We passed stalls of chillies, beans, peppers and millet. There were sacks of rice stamped with the letters 'UN', table-tops strewn with boxes of baby milk, Nescafé, Lipton's tea, women deftly fingering freshly mashed peanut butter into jars, blue-grey slabs of meat, busy with fat, black flies, groups of tiny, scruffy children begging for *cadeaux*.

A one-legged cyclist propped himself up on a crutch, while peddling cigarettes and matches. An agitated gendarme pushed through the crowd, flailing his baton to clear a path: ahead of him a boy around my age, wide-eyed with terror, zig-zagging to escape.

'Stop that thief!' the gendarme shouted, as the boy dashed across our path, the sour odours of both pursuer and pursued mingling with all the aromas of the Grand Marché and the overpowering reek of urine, and lingering in the air for a brief moment. Suddenly I recalled my poor, dead grand-mother telling me that it was possible to smell fear. She was right.

'He is taking a great risk,' Moussa said. 'If he's caught they'll chop his hands off!'

Theft was not a huge problem in Wadata – perhaps because my village had too many other problems, and because everyone knew everyone else, as well as a great deal of their business – but all my life I had heard such things said about crime and punishment in our cities. I was unsure whether or not they were true. It struck me that for a place brimming with the wealth of a fine city, there seemed to be a great deal of poverty here also. Perhaps the boy had stolen simply because he and his family were going hungry. I knew this did not make his actions right but, as I watched him weave through the crowd and disappear behind the gleaming French *supermarché* on the west side of the market place, a flurry of dust churning up around the bleached soles of his bare feet, I hoped, secretly, that he would not be caught.

We continued our slow progress through the hubbub until

we came to a long, pockmarked table laid out with plastic beakers, glass tumblers and large metal flasks decorated with floral designs. Hitched to a white enamelled box trailer, a dilapidated three-wheeled cycle had been parked next to the table. Nearby, a large, black kettle bubbled and spat over an open fire. A small, stooped man with an ancient, creased face was busily lifting more utensils out of the box trailer and arranging them on the table. The thick white mat of hair on his head – as white as the snow in Katie and Hope's photograph – seemed somehow at odds with his crumpled, leathery face.

Moussa stopped and nudged my shoulder. 'Just wait 'til you meet this old goat!' he said. 'No-one in Niamey can spin a yarn like old Nourradin.'

The man with the creased face looked up and nodded at us. There was a warmth about this face, in spite of its deep furrows and the fact that the eyes were glazed with a thin, watery film; the whites yellow with age and dust. It squeezed itself into a great, broad smile and opened a toothless mouth. 'Hello, hello, my friends,' the old man said, pulling back a wooden bench and indicating that we should sit.

Moussa took the extended hand and the two men exchanged their greetings. 'Monsieur Nourradin.'

'You have returned from Tera, Monsieur!' the older man said, continuing to pump Moussa's hand.

'I have.'

'And, God willing, you found your family well?'

'I did,' Moussa said.

I wondered if he had forgotten about my poor mother, or if perhaps he did not actually think of her as part of his family.

'Praise be to God!' the older man said. 'God is merciful! God is great!' His fixed smile seemed to unnerve my cousin as it beamed up at him.

'God is great,' Moussa repeated, his eyes flitting back and forward from the old man's face to his feet.

'Uhuh. Uhuh.' The leathery hand remained clamped around Moussa's. He did not let go until Moussa had, more or less, steered him in my direction. 'And who is this fine young woman?'

'This is my cousin, Haoua, from the village of Wadata in Tera,' Moussa said. 'Haoua, this is Monsieur Nourradin.'

'*Fofo*. Hello, young missie.' Monsieur Nourradin said.

'Monsieur. *Foyaney*.'

The thick white mat on his head bobbed furiously as he considered me, and his smile did not falter. 'A pretty girl. A pretty girl, indeed!'

We sat down at Monsieur Nourradin's deeply scarred table while he busied himself around us.

Moussa ordered a Nescafé for himself, placed a packet of cigarettes and some matches on the table and then fumbled in his shirt pocket, withdrawing a beautiful cell phone. (I had only ever glimpsed such a fine thing once before; when the *Sous-Préfet* had visited Wadata with his entourage, strutting around our village, shaking hands with our griot and the other elders, nodding and making promises and important announcements after an infestation of locusts had destroyed our millet and sorghum crops.) Moussa struck a match and inhaled deeply, then nodded towards Monsieur Nourradin. 'He's an artist, that one. Here from dawn 'til midnight, come what may.'

I watched as the old man dipped a glass into the hot water without scalding his fingers. 'Some tea for the little lady, perhaps?' he called from his fireside.

My throat was indeed dry, but Moussa spoke up before I had a chance to answer for myself.

'She's all right,' he said. 'We're just waiting here for her brother.'

'*Toh*.'

'Abdelkrim will be here directly?' I said.

'Perhaps.'

'You spoke to him?'

'He's coming here, girl!' His tone was abrupt.

I considered silence, but only for a moment. 'Did my brother mention my mother, Monsieur?'

'*Walayi!*' he snapped, through a puff of blue smoke. 'He's coming! I told you!' He poked at the cell phone on the table, so that it spun several times, like a donkey cartwheel. Then he sighed. 'I spoke to him, yes. I don't know about your mother.'

Monsieur Nourradin was standing upright now – insofar as he was able – the glass raised high above his head. From this he began to pour the hot water into another tumbler which he held at waist height. With all the ceremony of the performers at the *Cure Salée*, whom I had watched with interest on television, he carried out this procedure several times, transferring the hot liquid from one vessel to the other in great precise arcs; his aim true every time. When he was satisfied that the liquid had cooled sufficiently, he slammed the empty glass on to the table, spooned in a measure of Nescafé, some thick, syrupy milk from a little red tin can, added the water and then stirred the mixture vigorously.

'*Voila!*' he said, placing the steaming coffee in front of Moussa. He gave a little bow and then turned his attention to the needs of some new customers.

As Moussa picked up the glass, his sleeve brushed across the cell phone on the table. It wobbled gently for a moment and then lay still and silent, as before. I watched him sip at his Nescafé. I watched him suck at his cigarette. I watched Mousieur Nourradin preparing mint tea for the two fellows who were seated at the other end of the battered table. Beyond the French *supermarché* I could just make out a rickety row of tailors' shops, their proprietors seated outside, feet frantically pedalling their ancient Singers. I was minded again of my mother, and her dream of owning a sewing machine.

I kicked my feet out of my plastic sandals and gouged my toes into the warm, gritty sand. I drummed a *djembe* rhythm on the tabletop. I considered the phone as it wobbled again.

I sighed. I fidgeted. Suddenly, before I could stop myself, the words were out of my mouth. 'Perhaps you ought to call my brother again?'

'I can't!' Moussa snapped loudly, as if he had been waiting for me to make the mistake of uttering these words.

Monsieur Nourradin and his customers turned their heads towards us before resuming their conversation.

I bowed my head and worked my fingers into the folds of my *pagne*.

'I can't!' Moussa leaned towards me and hissed again, his words agitated still, but his voice more controlled. 'Do you hear me, child? Look at me when I'm talking to you!'

I raised my head to meet his cold gaze.

'I have no time left on my phone,' he said.

I was not sure what this statement meant exactly, but I knew not to ask about the cell phone again. He drained the dregs of his Nescafé and belched loudly.

The attentive Monsieur Nourradin was by his side in a moment. 'Another, Monsieur?' he said, gesturing towards the table. It was only then that I noticed the mangled fingers of his left hand. I tried hard not to stare at the buckled claw and the stumpy, nail-less fingers, but by the time I had forced my gaze towards my feet he had noticed and now let out a loud, bellowing laugh.

'It's all right, young woman,' he said, his face half disappearing into the folds of his great, warm smile. 'You may look!' He thrust the hand towards me. 'That's shrapnel for you! A souvenir of the French Indochina war, that is; my *medal* from Général Navarre for helping him out at Dien Bien Phu in '53!'

'Coffee, yes,' Moussa said, a scowl on his face.

Monsieur Nourradin nodded. 'And something for you now, Mademoiselle?' he said, still chuckling.

I was very thirsty. Deciding that if I did not actually meet Moussa's gaze it could not intimidate me, I spoke up. 'I would like some tea, please, Monsieur.'

'*D'accord.*'

'You can pay for that yourself,' Moussa said, as the old man returned to stoke his fire.

'Monsieur?' I said. 'I have no money!'

'You think I have?'

'But, the shoes, Monsieur. . .'

He leaned across the table towards me again. Had it not been between us, perhaps he might actually have pounced on me. 'Have you seen me sell them yet?'

He grabbed at his cigarettes and lit another.

'I just thought. . .'

'Who asked you to think?' he snapped, smoke billowing from his nostrils and fire in his eyes. He fiddled with the carton, his features clearly laden with irritation and impatience, increasing as surely as the arc of the morning sun. 'Your brother can pay!'

Monsieur Nourradin hobbled back over to our table and set the drinks in front of us. 'Have you heard about our ghosts?' he said, rubbing the back of his head.

Moussa exhaled and rolled his eyes. 'Ghosts?'

'Indeed, my friends. Evil spirits. Terrorising folk here – especially young women!' he added, his eyes flitting in my direction.

A shiver ran down my back. When Bunchie had been alive she had spoken of spirits often. It was the way in Wadata. Mademoiselle Sushie could explain ailments away and treat them with her medicine and *piques*, but there were few in my village who could honestly say that they did not hold our sorcerors, herbalists and bleeders in fearful high esteem. *The old ways*, my family said. But I knew that while my father might bow his head to Allah and beseech Him to request help with our crops, he might just as readily present our witch doctors with a sacrificial chicken on the same day. And my poor mother had always done what was necessary for a quiet life.

Monsieur Nourradin had shuffled back over to his trailer

and now returned, slapping a copy of *Le Sahel* on the table in front of us. He tapped the lesser of two headlines with a stumpy finger. 'Read this,' he said, as another customer sat down further along my bench.

Moussa looked even more irritated now and very uncomfortable. He pushed the paper towards me. 'You read it, girl,' he said. 'I'm smoking.'

As I scanned the front page, I could not help but enjoy his discomfort. I picked up the paper and considered it carefully. Printed in French. I would struggle, but I would manage. I had seen newspapers before, but not often. Occasionally Monsieur Boubacar would have produced cuttings from *Le Sahel* or *Le Républicain* and instructed us to translate them into Djerma in class, and Mademoiselle Sushie sometimes had copies of a publication called *Herald Tribune* brought back from the capital, but despite recognising some English words from Katie and Hope's letters, I was unable to read these properly.

'*Le Sahel. Quotidien Nigerien D'information. Jeudi Avril le huitieme, 1999,*' I read aloud.

Cousin Moussa flicked the stub of his cigarette into the air and shook his head. 'Just read the article, you stupid girl!' he said. 'You're not in school now!'

I ignored his comment. '*Mayor Tells Sorcerors to Banish Evil Spirits,*' I continued, my finger following the bold, black headline. '*The Mayor of Niamey has ordered qualified sorcerors to chase away evil spirits reported to be making terrifying appearances at night. Nightlife lovers in Niamey have repeatedly complained of a woman who appears from nowhere, curses and threatens them before vanishing as if she had evaporated. Courting couples and women in skimpy, Western style outfits have been particular targets for the evil spirits.*

"Given the rumour, which has been circulating for at least three weeks now, of strange apparitions stalking people, notably young women, I have ordered all the elderly of

Niamey to resort to the traditional sacrifices, with qualified people, to stop this," Mayor Jules N'Dour said yesterday. "People should be reassured: if there are any evil spirits, they will be dealt with," the mayor told radio station R and M.'

'What rubbish!' Moussa said.

Monsieur Nourradin was chuckling to himself again. '*Walayi!* It's true, Monsieur. Just down there, behind the Sonara Building two nights ago, I was pedalling home with the tools of my trade and I witnessed just such an incident!'

'Uhuh.'

'On your children's lives!'

'I don't have children!' Moussa said, sourly, casting a look towards me.

'Nevertheless,' Monsieur Nourradin continued, 'I saw a fellow in the bushes, with his *jellaba* up around his armpits, his great naked backside busily pumping away at some young floozy when, all of a sudden – as God is my witness – this very apparition appeared right in front of me on the road!'

'What god is that, Monsieur Nourradin?' Moussa said.

'*Walayi!*' I said. 'What happened, Monsieur?'

'Well,' the old man continued, with a glint in his eye, 'she gave me a great wink and then turned, took a run at the fellow and kicked him right up his rump. There was such a cloud of dust churned up in that young couple's commotion that they all just seemed to evaporate!'

Moussa heaved a sigh and spat over his shoulder.

Monsieur Nourradin's sides were shaking as he turned to attend to his latest customer, who had been tugging at his skullcap, sucking his teeth and beckoning him impatiently.

'Can it be true?' I said, addressing my cousin.

'It's nonsense. He's a ridiculous old fool. Almost as ridiculous as that story.'

He swung his leg over the bench and stood up, pocketed his belongings and shouted over to Monsieur Nourradin. 'The girl's brother will settle this with you,' he said, waving his hand over the table.

Monsieur Nourradin threw another piece of wood on to his fire and then approached my cousin. 'Monsieur?'

'My cousin will pay you, I say. He'll be along shortly.'

Monsieur Nourradin looked confused. 'It's three hundred CFA, Monsieur,' he said.

'Yes, I know!' Moussa snapped. 'My cousin will be along shortly.'

Monsieur Nourradin said nothing, but looked from Moussa to his table and back again.

'Abdelkrim Boureima will give you the three hundred, old man. All right?'

Monsieur Nourradin shook his head, his dusty brow knotting into a serious frown for the first time since I had met him. 'You are leaving the young lady here, Monsieur?'

'*Eh bien oui!* Now you have it!' Moussa said, like he was talking to a simpleton.

I was no happier about the prospect of being abandoned than Monsieur Nourradin was of not being paid.

'It's three hundred,' the old man said, firmly. He straightened his back a little, rearranged his features and held out his good hand. 'Three. . . hundred. . . CFA, Monsieur!' he said, firmly, like he was issuing a military command.

Moussa stared down at him for a moment, then swore and thrust his hand into a pocket. He poked at a handful of coins; pushed some into Monsieur Nourradin's. 'There's two!' he snapped, then jabbed a thumb towards me. 'Like I say, her brother will be along shortly!' With this, he turned on his heel and, without a further word, stormed off down the hill towards the Boulevard de la Liberté.

I was not surprised by my cousin's lack of manners. And, indeed, I was relieved to see him leaving, due to his behaviour. Nevertheless, as the bustle of the market place continued all around me, I suddenly felt quite small and alone. Had it not been for the fact that I was already anxious about my mother, I might also have felt frightened.

Monsieur Nourradin cupped his hands around his mouth and called out, through the crowd, 'Thank you, Monsieur. And don't worry about the girl's tea: it's on the house. . .'

He turned to face me and shrugged, the warmth returning to his face as suddenly as it had disappeared. 'He puts on a good act, but I think he's not such a nice fellow, that one,' he said.

I nodded. 'Thank you for the tea, Monsieur. You are very kind.'

'That's all right,' he said. 'And you may wait here as long as you need to. I'm quite sure your brother will be here in no time.'

It can't have been very long before Abdelkrim did indeed turn up, but to me it seemed like an eternity. I was so over-joyed to see him that I wept.

I spied him as he pulled up on a little grey motorcycle on the road below, and, almost forgetting my own manners, had taken off down the hill to greet him before turning to address Monsieur Nourradin. 'My brother is here, Monsieur!' I called, pointing to the road. 'I will come back.'

Monsieur Nourradin nodded.

Abdelkrim had dismounted and was making the motor-cycle secure in the middle of a jumble of bicycles by the time I reached him. He pocketed his sunglasses, stood up and brushed the dust off his smart uniform, then rolled up his beret and pushed it under one of his epaulettes. 'Abdel! Abdel!' I called, as I stumbled down the hill. A great smile broke across his handsome face and he bent down and opened his arms to catch me as I threw myself at him.

'Hey, Little One!' he said, lifting me off my feet for a moment. '*Foyaney*. Look at you!'

'You have a motorcycle!' I said, running my hand over the cushioned saddle of the dusty grey machine. 'Fatima said she'd ridden on it with you!'

'It's Bouleb's. Recently I've had to borrow it often. It's meant that I can travel between the barracks and the hospital a lot more easily. Bouleb has been very good to me.'

'How is Mother?' I asked, without further ado.

'You'll see her soon,' Abdelkrim said, then quickly steered the conversation towards the topic of our cousin.

I told him all about my morning with Jacob and Moussa and then, taking my brother by the hand, began leading him back up to Monsieur Nourradin's tea table.

Abdelkrim was muttering as we trudged up the hill. 'Leaving you here alone!' he said. 'That Moussa is a no-good swine!'

'Monsieur Nourradin was very nice to me,' I said. 'You mustn't worry about me, Abdel.'

Monsieur Nourradin was rinsing out some glasses in a pail of greasy grey water as we approached his pitch. When he saw us coming he stood to attention and saluted Abdelkrim.

'This is my brother Abdelkrim, Monsieur,' I said. 'Abdelkrim, this is Monsieur Nourradin.'

'An honour, young sir,' he said. 'I served four years as a sergeant under Général Navarre.'

'At ease, Monsieur,' my brother said, giving him a half-hearted salute. 'Not only do you outrank me, but you served a different master.'

For a moment I was concerned that Monsieur Nourradin might think rudeness a trait of my family, but when I looked up I saw that both men were smiling, as if this was not, in fact, their first introduction.

'Indeed, young sir,' Monsieur Nourradin said with a nod, his lips puckered into a thoughtful twist. 'You serve that buffoon, Mainassara, who's going to cause our nation to boil over with despair!'

'A Nigerien buffoon, at least – whereas you served a bunch of imperialist bastards who raped and pillaged their way to power!' Abdelkrim said.

There was a brief silence, then both men laughed as if, having mentioned their differences, they had resolved them.

Monsieur Nourradin picked up some glasses and began shuffling towards his kettle. 'You'll have some tea?' he said, over his shoulder.

'Thank you, but no, Monsieur.'

'Don't worry about the cost, young sir,' Monsieur Nourradin said, winking at me. 'It's no secret that our great leader, in his infinite wisdom, has frozen salaries all over the country.' He tapped the newspaper that I had read from earlier and was still lying on the table. *Monsieur Tandja's MNSD Party Calls for Restoration of Electoral Commission*, the principal headline announced. 'Your president can't be sleeping soundly these nights! I hear there's been another mutiny in Diffa!'

Abdelkrim shrugged. 'We'll have to discuss the matter another time I'm afraid, my friend. We must go. Thank you for taking care of my sister, Monsieur.' He saluted again and turned towards me, his face suddenly serious. 'We have to get going, Haoua.' His voice sounded shaky. 'I was with Mother last night when Moussa phoned the hospital, and I promised her that I would bring you to her as soon as I could.'

'She is all right, then?'

'She is far from all right, Little One,' he said, taking my hand as we began to descend towards the road.

'God go with you!' Monsieur Nourradin called, holding a ragged cloth up in his ragged hand.

'Thank you, Monsieur,' I called back through the throng. '*Au revoir. Merci. Kala a tonton.*' My head was reeling by the time we reached Sergeant Bouleb's motorcycle.

35

I had never ridden on a motorcycle before, but as we sped away from the Grand Marché, I clung tightly to my brother's waist and gave little thought to the blur of bitumen below us. With my eyes squeezed tight and my cheek pressed against Abdelkrim's back, I pictured my mother's face and prayed that she would grow strong again. I took comfort from the closeness of my brother and, by the time the motorcycle came to a halt, I was in a state somewhere between trance and sleep.

'Are we at the hospital?' I called, over the dying revs of the machine.

'No.'

'Then why have we stopped?'

Abdelkrim pointed towards the river. 'Another student protest,' he said. 'They are blocking the bridge again. That's the second time this week!'

'Why are they blocking the bridge?' I said.

'Like many of us, they are angry that they have not been paid their allowances.'

'Won't they let us through if we tell them we're on our way to the hospital?'

He sighed. 'I'm in uniform, Haoua. They're more likely to tear me limb from limb! And it's not safe for you.'

'But you haven't been paid either, Abdel!' I reminded him.

'I doubt if they'd stop to check,' he said. 'Besides, it's also crawling with gendarmes and soldiers down there. If I didn't get mauled by the protesters, I'd most likely get seconded into duty. Sergeant Bouleb said he'd watch my back for a couple of hours, but in truth I'm AWOL, so I can't afford to be explaining myself to some irate captain. It could get ugly down there. Angry students, trigger-happy militia. That bridge has hosted a blood bath before today!'

'What is AWOL?' I said.

'It means I don't have an official pass. We'll just have to cross further up.'

As we sped away from Pont Kennedy, a convoy of military vehicles thundered past us, heading for the river.

36

April is the hottest time of the year in my country. Even the rush of the motorcycle did little to cool me; the air baked breathless by a fierce midday sun. The machine dipped and leaned and zig-zagged and I clung to Abdelkrim as we sped along Niamey's grand, wide roads; the urgent, beseeching words of my prayers trailing behind us like so much smoke. I took comfort in the sight of the majestic towers and minarets of the Grande Mosquée as they rose before us, strangely familiar to me, even though I had only ever seen a picture of the magnificent building in one of Monsieur Boubacar's reference books. The engine screamed below us as we charged past taxis, cars and trucks, and still this wonderful, sacred giant seemed to linger to our left, floating on its vast – now deserted – forecourt of diligently trodden dust and sand. I tried to imagine its swarming congregation, flocking here to worship the Almighty God above. There and then, I vowed to witness such a spectacle. Releasing my grip on my brother's waist, I clutched behind my rump at the motorcycle's seat, leaned back and peered upwards into the empty, parched sky, the breeze snapping the tails of my head wrap about my cheeks and eyes like angry serpents.

'Merciful God,' I said, 'watch over my mother!' I felt Abdelkrim's hand, searching, questioning my shift in weight.

'What are you doing, Haoua?' he shouted over the whine of the engine.

'Nothing.' I wrapped my arms around his waist again, closed my eyes and waited.

Somehow I had expected l'Hôpital National de Niamey

to be grander: a building to rival the Grande Mosquée, or at the very least a large, clean, white structure – like Citibank or Sonara. Instead, its exterior was yellow, like bad teeth, and shrouded in a mantle of hopelessness and dread. Despair seemed to seep from these very walls as we approached and a sickly stench, perhaps of fear masked with disinfectant, reached my nostrils even before I had dismounted.

Small groups of bewildered-looking citizens loitered around on the hospital steps and veranda. A queue of people – mostly pregnant women and small children, some with orange hair and distended bellies – meandered into the foyer and through a set of scuffed double doors.

A tatty white pick-up truck with a canvas top and a faded blue cross marked on each of its doors had been parked near the entrance. An orange-roofed taxi pulled into the shade of the building, just ahead of where Abdelkrim had parked the motorcycle. The driver was shouting excitedly in Hausa but I could not make out exactly what he was saying. As we approached the vehicle, I saw him lean across his seat to spring open the rear door. Immediately, a pair of dust-caked feet spilled out towards us and began kicking and thrashing about wildly. The driver craned his neck towards the opening and called out in French as we came alongside his taxi.

'Can you help me with this fellow, brother?

Abdelkrim leaned into the car. 'What's wrong with him?'

'A teacher over at La Poudrière flagged me down and asked me to bring him here,' the driver said. 'Apparently he collapsed during class.'

I squeezed up beside Abdelkrim and was immediately gripped both by pity and disgust as I gazed at the boy on the back seat. He looked a little younger than Adamou and, despite the tortured grimace that he now wore, I could tell that his face was handsome. His eyes were wide with terror and pain. Rivulets of sweat trickled from his brow and into their sockets. His lips quivered, thick dollops of gluey spittle spilling from the corners of his mouth.

The driver had clambered out of the vehicle now and opened the other rear door. He put his hands on the boy's shoulders and tried to prevent him from knocking his head against the car seat.

'Isn't there anyone with him?' Abdelkrim asked.

The driver shrugged. 'None of the teachers could leave their classes. They told me he walks from his village to the school every day – two hours each way. Help me get him out, Monsieur!'

Abdelkrim nudged me gently out of the way and then took hold of the boy's sodden tee shirt. 'Bring him towards me,' he said to the driver.

The boy was shivering, his torso heaving uncontrollably and, as the two men tried to manoeuvre him out of the car, he drew his knees up and curled himself like a ball, his frame now wedged.

Abdelkrim stood up and shook his head. 'We're going to need more help,' he said, wiping his hands on his tunic.

The taxi driver was about to speak when two hospital porters in green tunics appeared, one of them carrying a rough board.

'We'll take him from here,' the youngest of the porters said, throwing the board on to the dust and going around to the far side of the car.

His colleague looked at me and gave a little chuckle, then he leaned into the car, grabbed at the patient's ankles and yanked. Again the boy began flailing his limbs around.

The taxi driver came and stood beside my brother. He clapped Abdelkrim's arm and tutted. '*Walayi!*' he said. 'Thank you, brother.'

Abdelkrim nodded. 'What do you think is wrong with this boy?' he said.

'I'm no doctor, my friend,' the driver said.

'Clear case of malaria, I'd say,' the younger of the porters called from within before he and his colleague managed to wrestle the still thrashing body out of the car and on to the wooden board.

'Of course, he's no doctor either!' the older man said, chuckling again. 'But I shouldn't think this one will have long,' he added, lifting one end of the board as his colleague did the other and lugging the unfortunate village boy up the hospital steps, past the queuing people and through the gaping doors. It was only then that I noticed the heavy staining on both men's uniforms.

'Can't they be more gentle with him, Abdel?' I said, as we watched them disappear.

Abdelkrim put his arm around my shoulder. 'Let's find Mother,' he said.

37

During the months that my mother had been in hospital, my brother had visited her as often as his job allowed. Before we climbed the steps to the hospital's main entrance he drew me close to him, took my hands in his and went to considerable lengths to ensure that I understood just how ill she really was. His words had frightened me but, now, as I followed him through the stark, empty corridors and up several flights of stairs, the click of his leather boots and the slap of my plastic sandals echoing through the eerie gloom, I had no doubt that I was only moments away from being reunited with my poor, sweet mother.

The sight of the malarial boy outside had disturbed me greatly, yet already I was focussed on the gravity of my own family's situation and I took comfort from the fact that soon I would be able to hold my mother's hand – however weak it might be.

At the top of the stairs, we passed a sign with large, neatly painted blue letters and an arrow directing us to Salle Trois. My brother led me through another set of double doors that opened into a hellish, crowded room full of metal-framed cots and beds packed together so tightly that in places there was barely room to squeeze between them. The smell, which I had first noticed beyond the steps of the hospital, had not seemed as offensive on the stairwell, but now it hit me again with an intensity that surprised me. Worse still was the noise: a disturbing babble of flemmy coughing and wailing babies. Abdelkrim stopped in the doorway, turned to look at me and put his hand to his nose and mouth; I did the same.

Our passage through Salle Trois to the foyer of Salle Quatre seemed to take forever. I inched my way through the long, stinking, white-washed room as if in a dream, filled with shame at being fit enough to do so. No bed or cot was occupied by less than two women and several also supported two, or sometimes three, young children. Drip stands and tubes, like the one I'd seen Mother hooked up to in Sushie's *dispensaire*, stood at the end of several beds. The women's faces were wan, their eyes empty. Their tight, hardened mouths looked like they might never again be capable of conversation or pleasantries, or a gentle mother's smile or kiss. Many of the babies lay staring listlessly at the flaking ceiling, while their mothers fanned them with their hands or tattered copies of *Le Sahel*. A tiny tot, naked from the waist down, stretched out his hands towards me as we passed the end of his shared cot; his face contorted with misery, layers of tears encrusted on his thin, dusty cheeks, his cracked lips pale and grey. I paused for a moment and looked up at Abdelkrim. He nodded and then took me gently by the elbow, just as the child gulped a deep, raspy breath and issued a piercing shriek of desperate protest.

The relentless crying and hacking coughs heralded us into Salle Quatre like a nightmarish fanfare. The stench of diarrhoea and vomit again hit me as we entered this ward, similar to the last, but more crowded still. The left hand side of the ward was crammed as before with white painted, metal-framed cots and beds, but the right hand side was laid out only with thin mattresses, placed directly onto the hard, tiled floor. For months, my brother had been bringing food to the hospital for my mother – it was a requirement that families made such provisions for their kin – and now, as he pushed purposefully and quickly towards the far end of the room, I felt a strange sensation: anticipation, excitement, dread – all combining, so that suddenly I broke into a cold sweat.

'Oh, Almighty Father,' I prayed, my eyes closed tightly as

I trudged behind Abdelkrim. 'Deliver our mother from this place!'

When I opened them again, my brother had stopped before one of the cots. An empty drip stand stood at its end, like a little toppled silver question mark. I followed Abdelkrim's puzzled gaze and was confused to find that an old woman and two tiny babies occupied the bed. I peered deep into the woman's hollow, vacant eyes, momentarily wondering if this might indeed be my mother. She looked through, rather than at me.

'Where is Azara Boureima, Madame?' Abdelkrim said to the old woman.

She did not raise her eyes to meet his.

At the next bed, two healthcare personnel were discussing another patient.

Beside them, a woman sat rocking backwards and forwards and muttering to herself.

Abdelkrim reached across the bed and touched the young nurse's arm. 'Where is my mother?' he said, and now I thought I could hear fear in his voice.

The nurse fidgeted with her clipboard and shrugged apologetically before turning to look at her superior, an older, burly woman, heavily adorned in jewellery and trinkets and dressed in a white coat and the most beautiful blue and green *pagne* and matching head wrap I had ever seen.

'Young man,' the older woman said, abruptly, (she spoke French in an accent which by now I had realised was particular to Niamey), 'I'm Doctor Aissata Palcy. If you and this girl will be so kind as to wait in my office, I will speak to you presently.' She pointed her stethoscope towards a booth at the far side of the room, took her other hand out of the pocket of her unbuttoned coat to prod a listless form on the bed and then turned to address the nurse again. 'What do we have here?' she said.

The nurse gave a little apologetic smile in our direction before responding to Doctor Palcy's question. 'This bush

228

woman arrived earlier with her two children,' she said, pulling back a blanket. 'This one has just died.'

'And what about the other one?' the doctor said, untying the rocking woman's *pagne* and extracting a tiny baby from a bundle. She fingered the few tufts of orangey hair still left on the baby's head. 'Have you given this child some water?' she said, addressing the mother.

The rocking woman steadied herself, then shook her head. 'No, Madame,' she said, shrugging and spilling one hand out towards the doctor. 'She has diarrhoea. I thought it best not to.' She dropped her head and began to rock again.

Doctor Palcy tutted impatiently, as if she had heard such a response many times before. She pinched the skin around the now squealing infant's belly button. 'On the contrary, my dear! You must give such cases liquids!' She turned to the nurse again. 'Rehydrate her and give her the malnutrition treatment to begin with,' she said. 'Let's hope that she doesn't end up like her brother.'

She turned briskly then, but the rocking woman caught her coattail. 'I sold all my clothes to pay the marabout!' she wailed. 'I sold all my trinkets to pay the healer! He told me that my son was possessed by the spirit of his dead twin Dominick! He told me that Yanou would live!' She released her grip on the doctor's coat and buried her face in her hands.

Doctor Palcy smoothed down her coat and shook her head. 'That has nothing to do with your children's illness,' she said, moving on to her next patient.

Doctor Palcy's office is a place that I will remember, vividly, for the rest of my life. Separated from Salle Quatre only by a thin partition with a glass door, Abdelkrim and I were in no way protected from the sights, sounds and smells of the hell outside. The familiarity of the room surprised me: it was quite different to Sushie's treatment room in Wadata, but many of the objects with which it was furnished were similar to hers.

Abdelkrim had remained standing in the same spot, staring vacantly at the bed previously occupied by our mother for quite some time after Doctor Palcy had addressed him. The elderly woman on the bed had not acknowledged us. As I stood waiting for my brother to do something, I found myself wondering if she were the grandmother of the tiny, wailing babies who also occupied the bed and wished that – even if she were not – she, or someone, would comfort them. Briefly, I considered doing so myself, but I was frightened by my brother's expression and, though pleased that God had heard my prayers and ensured that my poor mother recover in a more suitable place, I was also frustrated that I could not yet see and touch her. Eventually, I had taken Abdelkrim by the hand and led him across the ward to Doctor Palcy's office.

This is how things looked just before my life changed forever: the scene that I relive, like a dream, every day of my life.

Abdelkrim was sitting on a tubular metal chair in front of Doctor Palcy's desk. I was standing near the door, leaning on a rickety table and playing with a set of chipped white-enamelled scales. The shutters were open and a buckled ceiling fan lurched above us, but still the air was thick and heavy and tainted with other people's grief. I looked about the room; at the files and healthcare posters, the examination bed, the half full waste paper bin, the blank forms on Doctor Palcy's desk, the striped cup full of pens and pencils, the rubber stamps, the little dish of paper clips, and I wondered if, some day, I could be a doctor and spend the greater part of my life working in a desperate place like this. For quite some time I had pictured myself as a teacher, helping other people through education, but I thought that to help people by saving lives would surely be a great thing.

On one wall, displayed high above an array of framed certificates, my eyes lingered on a portrait of our president. It was a much grander image than those I was used to seeing in my home and school and Mademoiselle Sushie's *dispensaire*. And larger too. Against a golden background, he was standing proudly before my country's beautiful flag, the folds of which caused the orange, sun-like disc in its centre to look more like a bruised and battered guava. He wore a fine, embroidered, ivory-coloured tunic with a matching skullcap and the presidential sash of green and yellow. His right hand rested on a leather bound copy of the sacred Koran. On his left hand he wore a large, jewelled ring. The text below this impressive image read: *S.E. Le Général de Brigade, IBRAHIM Mainassara Bare, Président de la république du NIGER, Chef de l' État.*

I remember that I had been staring at the face of our president, thinking that – somehow – he looked surprised to find himself there, posing for this photograph; just as I now felt somehow surprised to be waiting in this doctor's office when all I wanted to do was embrace my sweet mother.

Dr Palcy had entered the room and my brother and I both turned to face her. Abdelkrim stood up and crossed the room to stand beside me with his hand on my shoulder. He took a deep breath as Doctor Palcy picked up a document from her desk and fixed it to a clipboard.

'Where is our mother, Doctor?' he had said, his voice wavering.

Doctor Palcy had shaken her head. 'Monsieur Boureima,' she said, a blank expression on her broad face, 'you know that your mother was a very ill woman. I'm sorry to say that she passed away early this morning. You will need to sign this and take your copy to the morgue for the body to be released.'

She had held the clipboard out towards my brother, but I did not see him take it or sign the document.

As my head began to spin and my knees buckled beneath me, the last thing I remember is Abdelkrim's hands clutching at me and his voice calling my name, 'Haoua! Haoua!' over and over again.

38

When I opened my eyes I found that my face was pressed hard against my brother's tunic and that the insignia on his shoulder was digging into my cheek. My body had been propped up against Abdelkrim's, and now, when I cautiously sat upright, I saw that we were seated outside on the steps of the hospital veranda, flanked by other despairing or bewildered people.

Abdelkrim was slumped forwards, eyes closed, his fingers interlinked behind his head, elbows resting on his knee.

I rubbed my eyes and sniffed, aware that my face was tight, tear-stained and dirty, yet without any memory of having actually wept. The knowledge that I would never again be warmed by my mother's smile, or hear her gentle, patient voice, or feel her arms around me, had already set – like sun-baked clay – deep within me. I was thankful that I barely recalled the initial shock.

I leaned back into my brother's shoulder and tried to speak his name. Only a faint, unfamiliar crackle crossed my lips, and I realised that my throat was dry and raw.

He sat up and put his arm around me. He gave me a little squeeze and said, 'She is gone, Haoua. *A ban.*'

Immediately, the awfulness of the situation hit me again. I clutched at my brother and wailed; a desperate, lonely screech tinged with fury.

And Abdelkrim wept too. 'I hoped that you would see her before the end, Little One. She talked about you and Adamou and Fatima every day. She loved you all very much.'

He gripped me tight, patting my shoulders in his strong hands and rocking me gently.

In time, my desperate, heaving panic became quiet sobbing.

Abdelkrim took me by the elbows and gently pushed me upright. 'We have to retrieve her body,' he said.

I nodded. The dreadful truth. 'She must be buried within twenty four hours.' For a moment I thought that he might pour scorn on our traditional ways. Indeed, I was alarmed to realise that my own heart was full of anger and doubt towards our God. I pushed these thoughts to the back of my mind, deciding that such matters would have to be addressed another time. 'And it must be in our village, Abdel,' I added. 'She must be taken home to be with Bunchie.'

'Yes,' he said, pinching his nose. 'In our village.'

I felt a new kind of dread grip me. 'How can we do that?'

He stood up and dusted down his uniform with his palms. Then he stepped off the veranda and walked towards Sergeant Bouleb's motorcycle. 'Come on,' he said. 'There's no time to lose!'

I pushed myself up, dizzy, weak, and followed him. By the time I reached the motorcycle, he already had the engine running.

'Where are we going, Abdel?' I said, over the revving engine. 'Shouldn't we try to let Father know before we do anything else?'

'You're right.' He put his hand to his face, then shook his head vigorously.

'Got to think straight!' He cut the engine and swung his leg over the saddle, then heaved the machine back onto its stand. He fumbled in a pouch on his belt and extracted a cell phone, similar to the one I had seen Moussa carry. 'Aiee! *Walayi!*' he said, as he stared at the phone's screen.

'What is it?'

He held it out towards me. 'I have very little time left.'

There was that expression again. 'Time?' I said.

'Time, credit – money to make the call.'

'Oh.'

'My regiment clubbed together to buy this phone. But it doesn't work well, and who has money to buy credit now?' He rubbed his eyes. 'I'll try anyway. I have a number for your *anasara* friends. If it doesn't work I'll just have to go to the *cabine téléphonique*,' he said, and moved off into the shade.

I clambered onto the seat of the motorcycle and waited. At the edge of this new nothingness. I wondered if my mother had been reunited with Bunchie. Somehow it still did not seem possible that she was dead. We had not seen a body. I stared at the hospital entrance and watched the constant flow and hobble of the sick and the despairing. Many of the women who came and went during those few slow moments were just like my mother in so many ways; in age, in stature, in the way they dressed. It was as if all I had to do was choose one of them to be her. A woman in a blue and red *pagne* and head wrap crossed the veranda and came towards me. I half closed my eyes and tried to fashion my mother's warm face from the woman's harsher features.

As she neared the motorcycle, she noticed me staring at her and her face softened to a gentle smile. '*Ira ma wichira bani*,' she said.

'*Foyaney*. Good morning to you too, Mother,' I said.

The sound of bickering distracted me. Nearby, two small boys were attempting to transport a large block of ice on a flat cart; one pulling, the other walking alongside and steadying the load with a rusty metal hook. The scorching sun and soft sand were not making their progress easy.

When I looked around again there was no sign of the woman in the blue and red *pagne*. Abdelkrim appeared at my side again.

'Did it work, Abdel?' I said.

He sighed. 'I spoke to Richard, very briefly. Then we got cut off.'

'But you told him?'

'Yes. At least they will know now. And Father can organise the funeral.'

'What do we do now?'

'We have to find my friend Archie.'

'Archie?'

'Archie Cargo. He has a car.' I was about to ask more questions but Abdelkrim was already clutching at the bike's handlebars. 'Shift back,' he said, squeezing onto the saddle and kicking the machine into life.

39

I did not look back at the hospital as we sped away. I hoped that I would never again look upon the place where my mother's life ended. Nor was I interested any longer in absorbing the detail of this bustling city. For as long as I could remember I had dreamt of drinking in the wonders of such a place, of even becoming a part of it. Now, as I pressed my cheek against Abdelkrim's back and closed my eyes, I had no idea of or concern for our location or direction. If I opened my eyes, all that I saw was the khaki expanse of my brother's tunic, a small, damp patch of sweat between his shoulders and a blur of buildings and open spaces as the motorcycle sped along. I wished that I were at home, in Wadata. Then I wondered if Wadata, or anywhere for that matter, could ever really be home without my mother.

When we came to a halt again, I discovered that we were in the shaded parking bay area of L'Université Abdou Moumouni de Niamey. Abdelkrim tapped my thigh and I slid back a little to allow him to dismount.

'Why are we here?' I said.

Abdelkrim pushed his sunglasses onto his forehead and picked dust from his eyes. 'This is where Archie Cargo works,' he said. 'He's a technician here. Teaches a few classes too. I met him one night in the Rivoli.' He smiled sadly. 'We got very drunk together.'

I climbed off the motorcycle and followed him to the entrance. Abdelkrim pushed open the heavy, green door and we entered a cool, dark foyer, the walls of which were covered in flyers advertising student meetings, wrestling bouts and musical events, and posters highlighting the benefits of safe sex and warning of the risk of HIV. The faces on these posters were smiling, happy, carefree.

Inside, a tall, thin man in a grey uniform stepped forward from a desk and asked if he could help us.

'I'm looking for Monsieur Archie Cargo,' Abdelkrim said. 'He teaches woodwork here.'

'They've gone to the bridge,' the concierge said.

Abdelkrim spilled his hand outwards, inviting more information.

'The students. They've all gone off to join the protest.' He jabbed a thumb towards a small portrait of the president above his desk. 'You are one of Monsieur Archie's students, are you not? There's hardly a soul about today!'

Abdelkrim shook his head. 'No, Monsieur. I'm a friend of Monsieur Archie's. I need to find him urgently. Do you think that he went to protest with his students?'

'I wouldn't know. I haven't seen him today at all.' He shrugged. 'It's possible. I daresay he hasn't been paid – just like the rest of us!' With that he put a chew stick in his mouth and went back to his desk.

Back outside, Abdelkrim straddled the motorcycle and lit a cigarette.

'What now?' I said.

He took a long draw on the cigarette and shook his head. 'We'll just have to find him.'

'But you can't go near the bridge in your uniform!' I said. 'It's dangerous! You said so yourself . . .'

He nodded.

'Perhaps Mademoiselle Sushie will come for us all.'

Abdelkrim shook his head. 'No, Haoua. Even if she had already set off from Wadata, by the time she got here and back it would be too late. Besides, Mademoiselle Sushie has many other matters to attend to in the village, and Father will not allow her to be involved.'

I felt unnerved by the truth of the situation, but glad, once again, that my brother had chosen not to question our people's ways. I could not bear to think of our mother's soul wandering restlessly. We *had* to lay her to rest within twenty-four hours of her death. 'Does your friend have a cell phone?' I asked.

'He does. But I have no time left on mine – and even if I did, my battery is dead.'

'Can't you phone from here?'

Abdelkrim shook his head. 'His number's stored on my phone. I can't switch it on now, so I can't get his number.'

'Ask the concierge for Monsieur Archie's number,' I said.

'He wouldn't be allowed to give out staff information like that. We'll keep looking.' He threw down the remains of his cigarette, crushing it into the dust with his boot, and started the motorcycle. Then we were off again. The frantic rush around the city lulled me into a kind of numbness, which all but took my mind off the very reason for the urgency. As we hurtled along, I started to recognise places we had criss-crossed earlier in the day: Avenue des Djermakoyes, Rue Maurice Delens, Avenue de l'Uranium. I began, once again, to take note of things that I might never see again: Le Lycée Coranique, Plateau Ministeres, billboards announcing soccer matches, horse and camel races, street entertainment by the local Samaria community groups. We zig-zagged our way along Avenue du Président Luebke, past Cinéma Vox, to which Abdelkrim had promised to take me during his last visit to Wadata, and I looked back over my shoulder, sure that I would now never enjoy such an experience; sure, in fact, that life held nothing for me now. I felt no pang of disappointment as the building retreated in a flurry of dust; only the already familiar mantle of shock, the clawing, gnawing chill of grief.

We had just passed La Mission Catholique and were approaching a busy junction, when Abdelkrim leaned back and called out over the racket of the engine, 'Hold on tight!'

I clutched at his tunic and suddenly the bike careered off

to the left, dipping at a precarious angle and screeching alongside a blue pick-up truck which had been travelling directly in front of us.

As we nosed past the big vehicle, Abdelkrim looked over his right shoulder and put his arm out to indicate to the driver that he wanted him to stop. At first the driver, an *anasara*, appeared only to be irritated by my brother's actions, his bloodless-looking face a storm, but then Abdelkrim raised his sunglasses and a look of recognition came over the driver's face. He waved and pulled onto the hard shoulder and Abdelkrim pulled up ahead of him.

By the time the motorcycle engine was dying, the *anasara* was standing beside us, a great toothy smile on his pale face. 'Hey, Abdel, my friend!' he said, in the most peculiar attempt at French that I had ever heard. '*Ça va?*'

My brother shook the *anasara*'s hand. '*Ça va, bien.*'

'Sorry I didn't recognise you, man. What's happening? And who is this?' he said, nodding towards me. 'Bit young, even for you, Abdel!'

My brother could not disguise his displeasure. 'That's my sister,' he said, coolly. I was not introduced.

The *anasara* grinned and slapped my brother on the arm as if to indicate that he had not meant to cause offence.

'Look,' Abdelkrim said, 'I need to find Archie. It's urgent.'

The *anasara* shrugged. 'Don't know, man. I haven't seen him about much lately. Isn't he at the college?'

'We've tried there. The students have joined the civil servants in another demonstration at Pont Kennedy.'

'Oh, yeah, *that*. . .' He put his hand into a pocket, withdrew a pack of cigarettes and lit one, before offering them to Abdelkrim.

Abdelkrim took a cigarette and tucked it behind his ear. '*Merci.* You haven't seen him then?'

'Not for a while. What's the problem, anyway?'

'Do you have his cell number?'

'Sorry. I suppose you could try the Rec. Center. If he's got a day off he might be hanging around there. I think he sometimes goes there to swim and play tennis with a couple of those apes from the Marine House.' He sucked on his cigarette and then exhaled a great cloud of smoke. 'Are you in trouble, man?' he said.

My brother hesitated for a moment before shaking his head. He thanked the *anasara* and kicked the engine into life again. We were back on the road.

I leaned forward and put my mouth close to Abdelkrim's ear. 'Who was that?'

'His name's Robert,' Abdelkrim shouted. 'He's from Scotland. Owns a biscuit factory out at Gamkale, to the east of the city.'

I thought of Monsieur Boubacar's beautiful book of maps. An *atlas*, he had called it. I knew where Scotland was because, like Ireland, it was a very small country. And close to Ireland too.

'Why didn't you just ask him to take us to Wadata, if he's a friend of yours? That is a very fine car.'

'I wouldn't exactly call him a friend. I've met him through Archie Cargo a few times – at nightclubs, parties, that sort of thing. Lots of money. Pompous. Let's just say I don't trust him much.'

'Uhuh. And this Monsieur Archie. . . he is a true friend?'

'I think he is.'

'And he is from Scotland too?' I yelled, as we flew past scores of cyclists on Avenue du Général de Gaulle.

Abdelkrim strained his head back again. 'Actually, he's from Ireland – like your friends!'

Now I was intrigued.

40

Mademoiselle Sushie had spoken of the American Recreation Center. I knew that it was a place where Americans and Europeans – aid workers, visiting engineers, Peace Corps and VCI volunteers – went to relax, eat and play, but I could not have imagined such a place.

We pulled up at the entrance and parked beside a dulled white Mercedes with rusty fenders. Mounted on a heavy wrought iron gate, a brightly painted metal shield with the symbol of a beautiful white-headed eagle indicated that we were about to set foot on American property. Great walls of heavily-scented red bissap towered above us, the roofs of other vehicles peppered with its discarded leaves and petals and a thin veil of dust. I noticed that my brother was smiling as he dismounted.

'He's here!' he said.

'How do you know?'

He gave a little snort and kicked at one of the Mercedes' worn tyres. 'That is his car.'

Just inside the gates, by a little wooden hut with a sign, in both French and English, declaring that the centre was for the use of Americans and their guests only, an official-looking man with shiny grey hair was frantically brandishing a broom, doing little other than shifting dust from one place to another, or so it seemed to me. He looked up and nodded as we entered, and for a moment I thought that he was not going to challenge us. But as we approached a tall, white pole from which an American flag hung listlessly, he called out and pointed to the sign.

'It's members only, Soldier.'

Abdelkrim stopped in his tracks and turned to face the older man. 'I know that, Brother,' he said, genially, 'but you've seen me here before – with the marines and with Monsieur Archie Cargo, the Irishman.'

The older fellow shook his head. 'I don't think so, Soldier.'

'Look,' Abdelkrim said, 'we're just here to speak to Monsieur Archie very briefly. About an urgent matter. Then we'll leave. *Ça va?*'

The guard seemed uncertain. He looked all around and then took a few steps towards us. 'Fifteen hundred CFA,' he said, putting his hand out, his voice little more than a whisper.

My brother was in no mood for dealing with petty bureaucrats. 'You're a robber, old man,' he said. 'That would buy me *membership*!' He took out a five hundred note and stuffed it into the open palm. 'Take that and keep your mouth shut or I'll have a word with your employers – and mine!' He took my hand then and we marched on before the guard could protest further.

'How is it that your friend can come here unchallenged if he is not an American?' I said, as we followed a neat, winding path towards a café and bar area.

Abdelkrim looked down at me and shrugged, as if to say that it was not he who decided such things.

'I don't understand.'

My brother sighed. 'Haoua,' he said. 'Don't you know that there is one set of rules for one kind of person and another for the likes of us?'

Across a canopy of flowering snake plant, I could just make out a throng of children, playing happily behind a tall, wire grid fence. They were taking turns at throwing an orange ball at a hoop. Black faces. Pink faces. The sound of their laughter like a song in the perfumed air.

Further along the path, an elderly Wodaabe – forty, at least – was watering shrubs and trees with a yellow hose. He nodded towards us and continued with his work. I looked back over my shoulder to see if I could follow the winding yellow hose to the water supply – the marvel of the faucet – but the overhanging flowers and fronds obscured my view.

Abdelkrim tugged me along as we approached the eating area. Here too everything was in order: the tiles were swept clean and the white plastic tables and chairs were stacked in neat towers. The smell of cooking meat wafted around us and wrenched at my stomach. I had not partaken of meat of any kind for many weeks and had not even considered my hunger before this, but the smell was so alluring that I found myself searching for the source.

A handsome, sullen-looking fellow, perhaps the age of Abdelkrim, dressed in a smart, white tunic, was standing nearby at a pristine glass-fronted bar, prodding busily at thick, round slabs of juicy meat on a huge gridiron. On a shelf by his side sat a large silver basket of fat breads. Behind the glass, displayed like one of the pictures in Mademoiselle Sushie's fine magazines, an array of fruits and vegetables – some of which I had never seen before – tomatoes bulging with redness, clean, shredded carrots, fresh dates, guavas and pears carefully carved into the shapes of stars. Glass jugs, brimming with crystal clear water and little bricks of ice, stood on shelves in a chiller cabinet. Bottles of liquid the colour of gold, the colour of fire, the colour of the sky, lined a mirrored wall. I stood, mesmerised before this cabinet, the anguish and pain which I carried momentarily lifted by the sheer wonderment of it all.

A small group of young, adult *anasaras* shuffled past me, interrupting their chatter to smile pleasantly at me, their pink, half naked, wet bodies dripping onto the clean tiles. They threw down their bundles of colourful, damp cloths and began wrestling chairs from the stacks.

I was only vaguely aware of my brother's voice. He had let go of my hand and was addressing the cook.

'. . . the Irish guy,' he was saying. 'Works at the university.'

The cook was eying him with some suspicion. 'You're a member?' he said.

'No, friend,' Abdelkrim said. 'I just need to speak with Monsieur Archie briefly.'

The cook looked at me with disdain before answering. 'He's over there,' he said, barely moving his head to one side before returning to his preparations.

Abdelkrim took my hand again and yanked me away from the bar. 'Jumped up Peulh dog!' he snapped.

We walked across a clipped blanket of grass – so green that it looked unreal to me – and joined another winding path flanked by mango trees that led to a large, tiled, rectangular pool in which a few people were swimming. The water was bluer, clearer, than any I had ever seen before; not a leaf or twig floated on its surface. At one end of the pool a strong-looking *anasara* threw a tiny white baby into the water, and for a moment my heart stopped. I let go of my brother's hand and covered my face in horror. No one else seemed concerned and after a few seconds the baby broke the surface of the water and began paddling, furiously, towards a woman at the other end of the pool, who was beckoning the child enthusiastically. She scooped the infant up in her arms as it reached her and they both giggled and waved at the man at the other end.

More tables and chairs were scattered around the edge of the pool, a few of them occupied. Abdelkrim waved to a man at the far side: a fine-boned, wiry *anasara* with long, straight hair, who held up a beer bottle and smiled through a mouthful of crooked teeth.

'That's him!' Abdelkrim said, hurrying towards his friend.

Monsieur Archie Cargo: a man whose kindness and warmth I will recall until my dying day.

41

Here I was then, standing in front of someone from the same part of the world as Katie and Hope. Had it not been for the circumstances, I would probably have been bursting with questions. As it was, I felt exhausted, hungry, thirsty, scared, shy and, of course, numb.

Monsieur Archie did not rise to his feet immediately when we reached his table. He slapped his newspaper down (a copy of the *Herald Tribune*, which Mademoiselle Sushie sometimes read) and lazily tilted his plastic chair back on two legs, then thrust out his hand towards Abdelkrim. 'How are you, my friend?' he said, grinning with pleasure, in an accent every bit as odd as that of the Scottish man in the pickup, but with a great deal more eloquence and a much better command of French. He pointed at some chairs. 'Sit down. Join me. Will you have a drink?'

There was a silence from my brother, which surprised me. When I looked up I saw that Abdelkrim was shaking his head, a pained expression on his face. For a moment I thought that he was going to weep.

Only then did Monsieur Archie get to his feet. 'What is it, Abdel?' he said. 'Is it your mother?'

'She died before dawn today,' Abdelkrim said, quietly.

Monsieur Archie put his arms around my brother and clapped his back. 'I'm so sorry, my friend,' he said.

We sat opposite Monsieur Archie and, even before I was introduced, I felt a great sense of warmth towards him. It was clear that Abdelkrim trusted this man. Even through the sadness of their discussion there was a sense of brotherhood.

He fetched soft drinks from the bar for us and offered us food. I had been deeply disappointed when Abdelkrim had declined the offer, but understood why he had done so.

'I am really hungry, Abdel,' I complained, while Monsieur Archie was away from the table.

'We will eat later, Little One,' was all that my brother said.

On the way back from the bar, Monsieur Archie stopped briefly to talk to a young mother at another table close to ours. The woman was dressed in a traditional, expensive looking *pagne* and was nursing perhaps the most beautiful child I had ever seen. She was sitting with her right side towards my left, so that I had to crane my neck to watch her soothe her baby as she laughed and chatted with my brother's friend.

Normally, the prospect of a cold Sprite or Coka would have excited me. Now, it seemed merely a small detail in a very bad dream. Even so, I sat up straight and smiled as he set the drinks on the table. 'Thank you very much, Monsieur Archie,' I said.

'You just call me Archie, d'you hear? Everyone else does.' He winked, and I nodded shyly, uncertain that I could bring myself to do so.

He sat down and motioned towards the nursing mother. 'Do you know Binta?' he said to my brother. 'She's married to that Canadian guy, Walter, who works for CARE.' He pointed to an *anasara* who had been slowly swimming up and down the pool since our arrival. I had taken note of him earlier, on account of his fat, brown moustache and the fact that he was wearing gold-rimmed spectacles while he swam.

Abdelkrim shook his head and looked in the direction of Binta once again.

'She is very beautiful,' he said. 'That Walter is a lucky man.'

Archie laughed. 'Indeed he is,' he said, shaking his head. 'I think he'd follow her to the ends of the earth and back again. In fact, he kind of already has!'

Abdelkrim raised his eyebrows a little. 'She's Nigerien, no?'

'She is. Walter met her a few years back, at some function that the American ambassador was throwing down at the Hotel Gaweye. She was a chambermaid there and he was just about to finish his first season in the country. Fell head over heels with each other. Next thing you know they've tied the knot and he's whisked her off home with him.'

'They went to Canada?'

'Yes. But beautiful Binta there wasn't happy in Quebec. Too cold. Snow and all that,' Archie said, widening his kind, green eyes and flashing his crooked teeth at me. 'Wanted to come back home to be near her family.'

'And now they've got their own family,' Abdelkrim said.

Archie smiled. 'Yes. That's little Dorette. Canadian born and citizen of the République du Niger!'

We all glanced at Binta as she covered her breasts and leaned her golden-skinned baby across her knee to wind her. She looked towards our table and smiled.

Archie held up his beer bottle and smiled back, then chinked our bottles. 'To good friends – and to departed ones.'

'To our mother. May she meet our ancestors soon, and may God show us each other again,' Abdelkrim said, tilting his bottle back.

Archie pushed his chair back. 'I'll introduce you. Walter's just getting out of the pool.'

Abdelkrim reached across the table and put his hand on Archie's wrist.

'Another time, my friend. We have a big problem and I need your help.'

'Of course I'll help, if I can,' Archie said, pulling his chair back towards the table. 'What can I do?'

Abdelkrim lit a cigarette and sighed.

Archie pulled a funny face and pretended to hold his nose as Abdelkrim's blue smoke wafted around us. I smiled back and fanned the air in front of me.

'We have to get our mother's body back to our village by tomorrow morning.'

Archie opened his hands and nodded, his expression serious now.

'She must be laid to rest immediately. If we are unable to do this, her spirit will never be at peace.' Abdelkrim sat back in his chair and glanced at me. 'That is what my people believe.'

'Right,' Archie said, thoughtfully. 'And what? You need money to get to Wadata?'

'I need you and your car, my friend.'

Archie stared blankly for a few moments, first at Abdelkrim and then at me. 'My car? You want me to transport your mother's body?'

'I'm sorry to ask,' my brother said, 'but I can't think of any other way.'

Archie scratched the bridge of his pale nose. 'You've seen my car, Abdel,' he said. 'It's a wreck!'

'It's a Mercedes,' Abdelkrim said, a little smile softening his grim expression. 'Mercedes Benz is a very reliable make of car. And with your students on strike you are not so busy, I think?'

Archie Cargo was fiddling with a lock of his hair now. 'I don't know,' he said. 'I bought that car three years ago – from a French guy who fancied himself as a Paris-Dakar rally driver. Somehow he'd managed to get it across the Ténéré Desert, but it was already half destroyed by the time he arrived in Niamey!' He lifted Abdelkim's plastic lighter and began playing with it. 'As for my students, I'd like to think that they'd be back at the college tomorrow.'

'I wouldn't count on that,' Abdelkrim said. 'Have you seen what's going on out there? There are gendarmerie and soldiers everywhere!'

'Why do you think I'm staying here out of the way?' Archie said. He eyed my brother up and down. 'What about you, Abdel? Won't your superiors be looking for you?'

Abdelkrim shuffled. 'I'm kind of on a half day's compassionate leave – unofficially. There's someone watching my back but, yes, I'll need to notify my unit that I'm burying my mother.'

Archie set the lighter on its end, then flicked it with his finger. 'Wadata. That's Tera country, isn't it?'

'That's right.'

'How far is it? One hundred and fifty kilometres?'

My brother nodded. 'Something like that.'

'A long drive. Even if we left now, we'd be driving through the night.'

'There's a good road, part of the way. Of course, I will cover all costs,' Abdelkrim said. 'That is. . . when I get paid.'

Archie Cargo waved the comment aside. 'Hmm. And my car's hardly equipped. . .'

'I wouldn't ask, Archie,' Abdelkrim said, 'but it's either you or the *camion*.'

The thought of my poor mother's shrouded body being thrown about on the back of one of the huge desert trucks like the one that had transported me to the city only the previous evening filled me with horror.

'I suppose I could try to find a bush taxi driver who would be willing to take a cadaver and give me credit,' he added.

Archie gave a little snort. 'It's a wonder most bush taxi passengers don't end up *as* cadavers. Most of them are death traps!'

Abdelkrim put his hands to his chest. 'My friend,' he said. 'My good friend. We would need to organise things now.'

Archie looked at me, blankly. There was a long silence. 'How do we do this, Abdel?' he said, eventually.

My brother put his cigarette out and patted my arm. 'Go and wait for us by the entrance, Haoua.'

For a moment I considered protesting, but the sudden, business-like mood of the two men persuaded me otherwise. As I was leaving the pool area, I looked across at Binta's table. Her bespectacled husband was standing dripping before her now, patting his pale body with a large, thick towel the colour of the bissap flowers by the entrance. Binta held up one of her baby's fat, golden hands and waved it in my direction. I smiled and waved back, even though I was sure that the child's deep, beautiful eyes could not possibly have registered me.

I made my way back along the shiny wet path, past the bushes with leaves bright and green, like plastic, past the guard's hut and the drooping flag and through the great iron gates, all the while thinking about Fatima and Adamou and wondering how my father would break the news to them about our dear, sweet mother.

42

I am not sure how long I waited outside the gates of the American Recreation Center. From time to time, the guard would pop his head out of his hut to spit into the foliage or to clear dust from his nasal passages, but he did not speak to me. Overhead, in the boughs of magnificent and ancient mahogany trees, angry birds screeched and scraked their displeasure at the heat and bustle below. I sat on the seat of the motorcycle, watching the relentless traffic: saloon taxis, bush taxis, cars, buses, *camions*, convoys of military vehicles, ox carts, donkey carts, camels, horses, bicycles, motorcycles, wheelchairs, pedestrians. An endless stream. And high above, like giant dragonflies, three helicopters buzzed angrily across the sweltering, dust-filtered haze, disturbing the birds still more.

When my brother and Archie Cargo eventually appeared, they seemed to have agreed a plan. Archie unlocked his car, popped open the trunk, wound down all of the windows and opened a hatch in the roof, then held open the creaking back door for me. 'Hop in, Mademoiselle,' he said.

I looked at Abdelkrim and he nodded affirmation. The interior of the car was stiflingly hot and the distinct smell of layered, stale sweat wafted from the fabric of the seats and head cloth. Archie kneed my door closed, before bending over the motorcycle and taking a firm grasp at the forks. Abdelkrim had hold of the rear of the bike and together they wrestled it up and into the large trunk.

'Do you think we need to tie the lid down?' Archie said.

My brother shook his head. 'No. The barracks isn't very

far. Just drive slowly so that it doesn't bounce out. Bouleb will have my hide if that happens!'

The barracks was a bleak and imposing kind of place adjoining the city's main prison, about which there were many terrifying stories told – even in Wadata. We had parked some distance away from the main entrance and Abdelkrim and Archie had removed Sergeant Bouleb's motorcycle from the trunk of the car. I was sitting in the back, fanning myself with a magazine which had been lying on Archie's window shelf and observing the forbidding exterior of the barracks over the shoulders of the two men who were now back in the car. An odd little green, plastic man with a white beard and yellow stockings dangled from the rear view mirror and made me smile momentarily.

Archie Cargo's kind eyes caught my smile, reflected. 'Are you okay, back there?' he said.

'Yes, thank you, Monsieur.'

'Archie.'

'Archie,' I said, hesitantly, and smiled again.

'That's my leprechaun.'

'Leprechaun?'

'Kind of a good spirit. *The Little People*, we call them. My silly cousin sent him to me from home. He's my talisman, my amulet, you know?' he said, whacking at the figure so that it rebounded off the windscreen. 'Everybody in Niger needs an amulet before making a journey!'

I nodded and leaned back against my seat, feeling at my bundle to make sure that both the cockerel's foot which Madame Kantao had given me and my treasures were safe. Ahead of us, at the entrance of the barracks, two sentries stood rigidly to attention, rifles by their sides. I noticed that, by blinking first one eye and then the other, I could make the little green man appear to jump, back and forth, between the two sentries.

In the front, to my right, Abdelkrim was busy scribbling a note to Sergeant Bouleb, a grubby exercise book on his lap.

When he had finished writing, he tore the page out of the book.

Archie took an envelope from a little locker beneath the dashboard and handed it to him. 'Seal it and write your sergeant's name on the front,' he said.

Abdelkrim did as he was told and then handed the envelope back to his friend.

'Back in a moment,' Archie said, getting out of the car.

'What is he doing?' I said, as we watched him cross the road and walk in the direction of the sentries.

'We're just letting Bouleb know that his bike is here,' Abdelkrim replied, slumping down in his seat. 'It's best if I keep out of sight.'

Archie was talking to one of the sentries, his hands waving about and occasionally pointing towards the motorcycle, which was now parked a few metres behind us. When he eventually persuaded the soldier to take the envelope, he crossed the road again and got back into the driver's seat.

'Okay,' he said. 'That's that. Where to now?'

'We'll need water, fuel, that sort of thing,' my brother said. He looked at Archie, a great frown on his face. 'I don't have much money left.'

'We'll sort that out again, Abdel,' Archie said, starting the engine. I remained in the car while Abdelkrim and Archie shopped in a French *supermarché*. Through the dirty rear window of the vehicle and the perfectly clear glass of the shop front, I could make out an abundance of foodstuffs and beverages the likes of which I had never seen before. Tins stacked to the ceiling, shelf after shelf of brightly coloured boxes, beautiful photographs of succulent meats and fish, and fruit and vegetables so flawless they did not look real.

The men emerged from this wondrous place carrying a tray of bottled water and several brown paper bags. 'Throw my jacket over the water, will you, Haoua,' Archie said, placing the tray on the back seat beside me. 'Keep it in the shade.' He dropped a chocolate bar into my lap and got back into the driver's seat.

I thanked him and tore open the packaging. Part of me wanting to savour this most wonderful treat: instead, I bit into it greedily, surprised to discover that the chocolate was not just delicious, but cold and brittle. I was happy to allow the awful pain deep within me to be pushed aside, if only for a few moments.

Abdelkrim was lighting another cigarette. 'You don't mind, do you?' he said, addressing his friend.

'I'm not bothered,' Archie said. He tilted his head back towards me. 'Just so long as your little sister there doesn't mind.' They both looked at me.

I shrugged, my cheeks bulging. Cigarette smoke was the least of my worries at that moment.

Abdelkrim exhaled and shook his head. 'I suppose there's nothing else for it but to collect the body now.'

The body.

Archie leaned across and patted my brother on the shoulder, then pursed his lips and sat back. He drummed a rhythm on the streering wheel. 'What about a. . . casket?' he said.

'*Walayi!* I hadn't even thought of that!' Abdelkrim said.

'It's only just crossed my mind,' Archie said. He glanced at me briefly and lowered his voice. 'Presumably she'll be wrapped in some kind of shroud at the mortuary, of course. But, you know, Abdel, we're going to have to carry her on the roof. We can hardly do that without some kind of receptacle.'

'*D'accord.*' My brother blew smoke out of the window and then cradled his face in his free hand. '*Merde!*'

'And we'll need some ropes.'

'Yes.'

Until then I had not considered this indignity for my mother. And a casket was not only necessary for transportation. In the past, my people had buried their dead in shrouds only, but wild dogs had become an ever increasing problem in and around Wadata.

Abdelkrim sighed heavily and threw his cigarette out of the window. 'What about the university, Archie?'

'The university?'

'Your workshop. You have timber there, *n'est-ce pas*? I can't afford to buy a coffin.'

'Hmm.'

'Could we make something ourselves?'

Archie leaned forward and rested his forehead on the steering wheel. 'This is getting crazier by the moment! I make furniture, not coffins,' he said.

'I'm sorry,' my brother said.

There was a brief silence, then Archie slammed back into his seat. 'Right. I guess we can knock something up. It's going to take a while though.'

'How long do you think?'

Archie shrugged. 'I suppose we can rip a couple of sheets of chipboard and cobble something together in an hour or so. If you're helping me. It's not going to be very pretty though.'

My brother held his hand out to shake Archie's. 'Thank you, my friend,' he said. 'I will repay you for your kindness.'

'Hey, you know I'm always looking for money-making ideas for my students. Who knows; perhaps this could be the beginning of another little sideline!'

I do not remember resting my head on Archie Cargo's jacket and the tray of bottled water, but that is where I found myself: emerging, crusty-eyed and sticky, from a thick slumber. Once again I was in the vehicle by myself. All of the windows and the roof had been left open, but my clothes were wet with perspiration and my head was throbbing.

In front of me, the back of the empty passenger seat came into focus. Already the interior of the car felt familiar: safe somehow, despite my discomfort and the hollow feeling in my gut. I considered a little tear in the fabric and, for a moment, wondered how it had happened. Suddenly, an image of my mother repairing clothing flooded my memory and, just as quickly, despair surged through every part of my being once again.

I sat up to take my bearings, blinking back tears. The car was parked outside Archie Cargo's place of employment: L'Université Abdou Moumouni de Niamey. It appeared that the demonstrating students had not returned from their protest at Pont Kennedy and, despite the sound of distant traffic, an unnatural stillness hung in the listless air. The green doors would swing open occasionally to allow someone to enter or exit but there was not the bustle one might generally expect at such a place. I wondered how long I had slept for and how long Abdelkrim and Archie had been inside. It was well after midday, for sure; the sun had peaked some time earlier and already the shadows were beginning to lengthen.

The concierge who had spoken to us earlier emerged from the building and looked up and down the road, then stretched his thin arms slowly towards the silvery sky. I put my head out of the window and waved towards him.

'Monsieur. Have you seen my brother and Monsieur Archie Cargo?'

At first he did not answer, a look of puzzlement on his bony face. 'Ah! Mademoiselle!' he said at last. 'Monsieur Archie and his friend have gone to the workshops.'

I thanked him and considered whether I should stay in the car or venture into the building.

The concierge had his hand on the door and was about to go back inside when he paused. 'Would you like me to show you where they are?'

'*Oui. Merci*, Monsieur.' I stepped out of the car and followed him into the foyer of the college.

He pointed down a long, grey, dimly-lit corridor. 'Just keep going down that hallway until you get to the end,' he said. 'It's the last door on the right. You can't miss it.'

I thanked him again and set off down the corridor, a strange, acrid smell filling my nostrils. Despite the shiny, grey walls and the gloomy light, I decided that this building was a good deal more cheery than the hospital. Each of the large, wooden doors I passed had a wire mesh, glass-encased panel, which allowed pockets of natural light from the rooms beyond to seep into the corridor. Door signs boldly announced: *Laboratoires de Sciences, Mathématiques, Métallurgie.* Still more leaflets announced student activities: lectures, dominoes championships, bus schedules, a Vietnamese restaurant, a visiting hypnotist from France, movies at Cinéma Vox; pamphlets calling for wages from the civil servants' unions and posters demanding immediate payment of allowances for students fluttered from a cork pin-board as I breezed past a long, recessed area. On the floor, at regular intervals, buckets filled with sand had been placed beneath bright red, wall-mounted fire extinguishers. At the end of the corridor, just below the yellowed ceiling, a single dormant bell seemed to lie in wait to break that eerie silence unbefitting any school.

The last door on the right was, sure enough, the wood workshop. Through the meshed window panel I could see Abdelkrim and Archie Cargo moving busily. I tapped at the glass but they did not hear me, so I pushed open the heavy door and entered the room. It was dusty, but there was a fresh, sappy scent in the air that I liked. Four or five large benches stood in line, and at one of these my brother and Archie Cargo were putting the finishing touches to the rough casket which was to bear my poor mother to her grave. I swallowed hard and forced myself to smile when the two men looked up at me from their work. Archie was daubing a square piece of board with thick, white glue while, at the other end of this chilling construction, my brother was busy with a hammer and tacks.

Archie finished his job and then inspected Abdelkrim's work. 'Oh,' he said, 'I had planned to glue that first.'

Abdelkrim slid a dirty fingernail into the joint and made a half-hearted attempt at prising it open. 'It will be fine. We'd best get going.'

Archie chewed at his lip, then nodded. 'I'll just lock these tools away again.'

I walked over to the coffin and ran my hand along its lid. I did not speak. Somehow I felt part of some great betrayal of my mother.

Abdelkrim came and put his hand on my shoulder and I turned and buried my face in his tunic, concentrating on the sounds of cupboard doors opening and locks turning and trying to hold back my tears.

'You have a lot of fine machinery here,' I heard my brother say.

Archie's voice moved towards us. 'Yes. Pity most of it doesn't work. They sent us thousands of dollars worth of equipment and we don't have the correct wiring facilities installed. It's a scandal!'

'Toh.' Abdelkrim patted my back and I moved towards the door while the men lifted the casket off the bench.

'You can get the doors for us, Haoua,' Archie said, lifting a bundle of cords from one of the tables.

We must have looked a curious sight: a white man, a black man, a twelve-year-old girl and a coffin, tied upright in the open trunk of a battered Mercedes Benz car, moving slowly across the city through the heat and haze of that awful afternoon.

The city mortuary was situated not far from the main hospital block, a single storey concrete building with a corrugated tin roof in its own little discreet compound on a rise overlooking the river. A pair of metal gates opened into a dusty forecourt and a strip of asphalt allowed vehicles to back right up close to a set of double doors. A small sign inside the hospital's grounds had led us to this place but the shuttered windows along the façade gave no indication of the building's purpose: a storage place for the dead. I had never before considered the possibility of there being such a place.

As I sat in that vehicle, looking out over the majestic river below, I was seized by cold fear once again. The sun, still fierce and pulsating, descended steadily through the haze. Marking time. Reminding me of the task ahead. Of the need to be strong. To carry the burden. Help my brothers, my sister, my father. Wadata seemed very far away.

My head reeled; a great drop seemed to open before me, a chasm stripped back by these tempestuous, violent events over which I had no control. What would happen to my family? Who would now bind us together? How would we survive? Try as I might, I could see no way forward. We had lived without my mother for several weeks now but only the hope that things would return to the way they had been before had driven us. We had tended crops and animals, fetched water, cooked, cleaned, washed clothes and bedding, mended fences, woven mats, traded goods in the market, forfeited school and much contact with friends, all the while fending off unkind remarks and cruel looks from the likes of Souley and her gang, and with barely a word of praise from our father. The idea that we should henceforth embrace that existence as our normal way of life – possibly even with Aunt Alassane in the place of our poor mother – was unbearable.

Archie Cargo turned the engine off. He looked across at my brother and the two men nodded silently at one another.

'You stay in the car,' Abdelkrim said, twisting around in his seat to address me.

I looked out of the side window, avoiding his eyes. 'You are going to put her in the box now?'

He nodded, his lips a tight line of sadness.

'Shouldn't I help you?'

Abdelkrim sighed, and Archie Cargo sat rigid with his arms folded.

'No, Little One. You must remember her as she was.

Happy. Warm. Kind. Good-hearted. Loving. Not like this.'
He turned to his friend. '*Ça va?*'

In the blink of an eye, Archie was out of the car.
Abdelkrim reached out and brushed my cheek with the back
of his hand. Then he too was gone. I leaned back into my
seat and squeezed my eyes shut. I shuffled my feet, worried
at my fingers with my teeth. Tried to ignore the banging and
rattling and slapping of cords coming from the open trunk.

At last there was stillness: quiet but for the occasional
cheep of the cut-throat finches in the trees above and fragments of the pirogue boatmen's voices rising up from the
great muddy slide of the river below; the torpor of a breathless and terrifying afternoon. I leaned against the car door,
trying to drink in this moment of calm. My heart pounded
like a pestle. I considered praying again. A bead of sweat
snaked its way down my spine. I put my head out through
the window and peered up at the now pale, empty sky and
wondered if my gentle mother's spirit was looking down on
me; but there were no signs. Nothing. Emptiness.

I looked over my shoulder at the scuffed doors of the
mortuary. Inside, my brother and a man I had only just met
were taking hold of my mother's body and laying it in a
casket. I would never see my mother's face again. Panic
gripped me. What if I could not remember what she looked
like in the weeks, months, years that stretched before me?

I do not remember getting out of the car or pushing my
way through the mortuary doors. I was standing in a narrow
vestibule, next to a desk on which lay some papers with my
mother's name at the top. On one of them, my brother had
printed his name and scrawled his spidery signature at the
bottom. A battered metal trolley stood next to a tower of
little open-ended compartments, most of which were stuffed
with papers similar to the one on the desk. Ahead of me,
another set of doors attempted, unsuccessfully, to contain the
stench within. I was familiar enough with the smell of death.
Animal, human, it was all the same. They could try to lace it

with detergents and disinfectants but nothing could truly mask its unsettling, sickly sweet and somehow familiar scent.

I stumbled forwards. Voices beyond the doors. My brother's, Archie Cargo's and another man's. Suddenly I found myself inside the main chamber – cool, dank, dark and putrid.

Hell itself.

'What are you doing in here, child?'

Abdelkrim and Archie were crouched over my mother's casket, fixing the lid in place.

Another man – large, fat, stinking of sweat and alcohol – loomed over me, a white surgical mask covering his mouth and nose.

'What are you doing in here?' he repeated.

'Haoua!' I heard my brother call out, just as the fat man took hold of my forearm and spun me towards the vestibule.

In the corner of my eye I caught sight of more trolleys and shelves laid out with cadavers, some draped with grubby sheets, others waiting, exposed, drained of life and dignity.

'I want to see my mother again!' I said, wrenching away from the fat man.

Close to my brother, the grey, tortured face of what looked like a drowned man grimaced pitifully through a rent in the fabric of his shroud. A mother and child, laid out on the same board, had been abandoned carelessly in a rigid knot of diseased limbs. Rack after rack of the empty husks of humanity lined the dingy room.

'Get out of here! Now!' my brother shouted.

The fat man had my arm again and, before I had time to protest further, I found myself standing, blinking in the hazy sunlight next to Archie Cargo's car, hot tears coursing down my cheeks.

'It does no good to go in there unless you have to, young mademoiselle,' the fat man said.

I turned angrily to face him, prepared to hurl a torrent of abuse his way. But something stopped me. I looked up and found that he had removed his mask and that he was smiling at me. His unshaven face was gentler than I had expected.

'Believe me,' he continued, 'I wouldn't if I didn't have to!' He dug his hands into the pocket of his grubby white coat and shrugged. An embroidered label, next to a pocket bulging with biro pens, read: *Doctor Mackenzie, Guy's Hospital.*

'You're a doctor?' I sniffed.

He laughed and shook his head. 'No, no! This is nothing but an *anasara*'s cast-off.' He flicked at the label disdainfully. 'Doctor *Death* – that's me. Now you just wait there. These fellows will be right out with. . .' Then he turned and disappeared inside.

I leaned against the car and sobbed quietly, my shoulders heaving until there was nothing left, and I stood, numb, empty, without even the will to swat away a fly that had landed on my tear-streaked cheek.

My mother's coffin scuffed against the mortuary doors as Abdelkrim and Archie wrestled it into the open, the thud jolting me to my senses. While the box was being slid onto the roof of the car, I crossed the compound and, sinking to the sand, sat cross-legged against the wall with my head down and my fingers locked behind my neck.

'We need a blanket or something, to stop it slipping around,' I heard my brother say.

'There are some old sheets in the trunk,' Archie said. 'I'll get the ropes too.'

I looked up in time to see the fat mortuary attendant disappearing into his horrific workplace once again.

Abdelkrim was passing a rope to Archie through the rear of the cab.

'Let's make sure that the doors will close over before we make it fast,' Archie said. 'This is quite sturdy rope.'

I watched them make a loop over the coffin and the roof of the car.

'I'll keep some tension on it, Abdel,' Archie said. 'You try closing the door.'

Abdelkrim put his hand flat on the panel and tried slamming it over. The door juddered violently and then bounced back towards him. '*Walayi!*'

'*Merde!*' Archie came around to Abdel's side. 'You know what we're going to have to do?'

'What's that?'

'We're going to have to leave the windows open enough for the rope to pass through with the doors closed.'

'That means the doors will be tied closed.'

Archie opened his palms and tilted his head. 'What choice do we have? What we really need is a roof rack.'

Abdelkrim gave a great puff and scratched his head. 'So we'd have to get in and out through the windows?'

'Exactly.'

There was a brief silence. The two men looked over at me. Archie Cargo gave a little wave and I waved back.

'Let's do it,' Abdelkrim said, unravelling the rope.

43

A chill, not normally noticeable until much later in the evening at this time of year, enveloped us, and I wished that I had retrieved my unwashed *pagne* from Moussa's house. A strange calm had befallen the city just before we had set off, followed soon after by a light breeze that whipped up the orange dust along the roadside and made me think of harmattan season and the storms at home. Never again would I hide away with my mother and brother and sister, safe from the fury outside.

'Do you think we made it tight enough?' Archie asked, as he negotiated the evening traffic exiting Niamey.

We were heading northwest, along Route Nationale Deux, in the direction of Tera, the car now also laden with the corpse of my mother. Like Monsieur Nourradin's tea, traffic and pedestrians seemed to pour from every side road and junction. Car horns and *camion* klaxons blared constantly. At the roadside, beggars and small children implored passing commuters for 'cadeaux' and hawkers bombarded our vehicle at every halt along the way. From the roof of a new building a group of Touareg builders lowered a bucket on a rope down to one of the hawkers and then hoisted a selection of soft drinks back up. We passed the tannery, the camel market and the race track in a blur. On either side of us, the shanties seemed to stretch forever, the combined stench of human and animal urine filling the air.

Abdelkrim put his hand up to the taut rope that ran across the car's interior, just above his and Archie's foreheads. He gave it a gentle tug.

'It's fine,' he said. 'We'll stop in an hour or so and check the box again.' He shuffled around in his seat to speak to me. 'Check that one too please, Haoua.'

Another rope ran directly above my head, from rear window to rear window. I raised both my hands and pulled myself upright on the rope, like a monkey on a branch. 'It seems all right.'

I caught Archie's eyes in the rear view mirror. 'Don't swing on it too much, Mademoiselle. I don't have all that much faith in my knots!'

'*Toh*,' I said, sulking a little. I ducked out of sight behind his seat and put my hand through the gap between the top of the window glass and the doorframe. The cooled air stroked my fingers and I hummed a little melody quietly to myself.

Abdelkrim looked over his shoulder at me again. '*Ça va?*'

I shrugged.

'You may help yourself to some water if you want it, you know?'

'*Merci.*'

He turned to face the windshield again and twanged at the rope where it disappeared out through his own side window. 'I guess that means we can forget the luxury of your air conditioning when we need it, Archie?'

Archie laughed. 'The air conditioning hasn't worked in this old heap for a long time, my friend!'

A few kilometres beyond the city boundary, we came across a military checkpoint. We were filled immediately with a sense of panic; there had been no time for Abdelkrim to gather together civilian clothes and the validity of his compassionate leave seemed unclear.

'Just let me do the talking,' my brother said, his voice faltering a little as we glided to a halt near an army Land Rover. Further down the road, an identical vehicle lay in wait, flanked by several armed soldiers. From out of nowhere a stooped man appeared, plastic bottles full of gasoline strung around his neck and shoulders. He waved and began limping towards us until his path was blocked and he was chased away by a heavy-set fellow in a torn tunic. A young, slightly scruffy soldier stepped towards the car and leaned in to scrutinise us, the butt of his rifle clanking against the car door. Beads of sweat glistened on his forehead and beneath his right armpit a dark, damp patch of fabric was clearly visible. Even from the rear of the car I could smell him.

'Monsieur. Your papers, please.'

Archie Cargo groped in the little compartment beneath the dashboard and handed some documents to the soldier. 'Trouble?' he said.

The soldier took the papers but did not reply. Already he had eyed my brother's now disarrayed uniform. He flicked through the papers and handed them back to Archie.

'You are off duty, brother?' he said, addressing Abdelkrim.

Abdelkrim put his arm out through his window and tapped the box on the roof.

'Compassionate leave,' he said. 'Our mother.' He turned to draw attention to me.

'We're on our way to Tera.'

'*Toh*.' The soldier stepped back from the car and looked it over, warily. Then he moved towards us again and leaned across the roof, the cords twanging above our heads like a gurumi as he plucked at them.

Across the road another soldier, older than the first and wearing dark glasses, grinned at me as if I had just told him a great joke.

The sweaty soldier leaned back in towards Archie and looked my brother in the eye. 'And your papers are also in order, of course?'

'Of course, brother.'

'Only there have been mutinies in Tahoua, and other places as well.' He leaned back and tapped the roof of the car. 'Who knows what you could be carrying up here.'

'Oh great!' Archie whispered. 'They're going to fuck us about!'

Abdelkrim waved his hand discreetly towards Archie. 'As God is my witness. . .' he said, 'it's my poor mother.'

The soldier held his gaze again for a moment and then withdrew from the car. He spat, and then crossed the road, deserted but for the army vehicles, and spoke to his comrade with the dark glasses. After conversing for a few moments the older soldier approached my brother's side of the car.

'*Ça va, mon frere?*' he said. '*Ça marche?*'

'*Ça va bien.*'

'*Non, ça va pas!* My brother says that you have your poor mother up here.'

'Yes.'

The soldier moved closer. '*Walayi!* I know you, don't I?' The broad smile had returned to his face. He pushed his sunglasses down his nose to reveal his eyes. 'It's Boureima, isn't it?'

'Yes. And you are. . . Kassato?'

'Kassato, yes. Third Company. You're with old Bouleb's squad, right?'

'That's right.' Abdelkrim put his hand out towards him. 'Look. Can we get under way, brother? My family is expecting us in Wadata by morning.'

'*D'accord, d'accord,*' Kassato said. He looked over the roof of the car at the first soldier, who had taken up his position by Archie's window again. 'Let them through, Julius.' Then he ducked back down to address Abdelkrim. 'God go with you, brother.' He waved us on, nodding at me as Archie accelerated and we pulled away in a cloud of dust.

'Whew!' Archie said. 'I didn't enjoy that! Your comrades scare the shit out of me, Abdel! Every time I take to these roads I wonder if I'll ever reach my proposed destination.' He gave a little snort. 'That's the first time I've ever got through one of your checkpoints without having to pay tax!'

'It's all right, though, isn't it, Abdel?' I said. 'I mean, you're not going to get into trouble, are you?'

Abdelkrim did not answer. He reached across and switched on the radio, then put his cheek against his fist and leaned out of the window.

It was not long before we had to turn off from La Route Nationale Deux and the road became rougher, the asphalt worried away by countless trucks, buses, *camions* and bush taxis. Either side of us, vast plains stretched away towards the wavering horizon, the sameness of the landscape interrupted only by an occasional baobab tree, a rocky outcrop, clumps of parched brushwood or the skeletal remains of a car wreck.

Abdelkrim had folded his jacket into a pillow and was dozing in the front, despite his head being buffeted against the door pillar. Archie reached across and disengaged my brother's ear from the seat belt, pulling the buckle out and down across his chest and clicking it into place. He looked up and caught my eye in the rear view mirror.

'I'm sorry there is no seat belt for you back there, Haoua. They were cut away when I bought the vehicle. I don't know why.'

'I am fine, thank you,' I said.

Archie glanced at me, a great grin on his reddened face. 'Just hold on tight when we hit a pothole! I'll do my best to miss them!'

'*D'accord.*'

The sun ate its way through the haze and once again left the air inside the car heavy and thick. In time, the road dipped into a scorched valley, cutting through massive, blood-red rocks and re-emerging once again to carve a swathe through vast plains of thorn scrub and savannah. On the eastern horizon, the sky, drained of colour and sapped by searing heat, merged into a pulsating band of nothingness; a shimmering, vibrating ribbon of white hot air which seemed also to consume the land itself, creating the mysterious illusion of floating trees and re-forging boulders and hillocks into curious, hovering, molten forms.

All of the car's windows were down but the heat was still intense. If I leaned a little to my left, I could feel the afternoon sun baking down on my eyelids. Already, my face was covered in a fine layer of dust and my tongue was sticking to the roof of my mouth.

As if reading my mind, Archie glanced up at his mirror again. 'Why don't you open one of those bottles of water for us?'

I stuffed his jacket onto the rear window shelf and began to poke at the tough plastic wrapper that encased the tray of bottles.

'Here,' he said, handing me a tiny, squat little knife with a sliding blade. 'Handy thing, that. I never go anywhere without it.'

I thanked him and began hacking at the packaging until one of the large, heavy bottles could be freed. I grasped its neck and began twisting at the cap, but the sweat on my palms prevented me from getting a proper grip.

'Here, let me open that for you,' he said, reaching his hand back between the seats and flexing his fingers impatiently.

I handed him first the little knife and then the bottle.

He dropped the tool into his shirt pocket and then, clamping the bottle between his thighs, cracked the seal open and took a long swig before handing it back to me. 'Yeuch!' he said. 'It's already warm. But better than nothing, I suppose.'

I tilted the clear, clean liquid into my mouth and drank. It was true that the water was warm, but it was also without the brackish, metallic taste and the cloudiness that I was so used to. I was about to offer it to him again when, far off in the distance, a movement caught my eye.

'Look, Monsieur!' I said. 'Giraffes!'

It was a small herd, five in total. Moving across the mirage band of the horizon, their improbable necks all but disappearing, then reappearing momentarily, their fine, chiselled heads like wingless birds, dipping above the plain as their spindly legs carried them towards the edge of the earth. Seconds later they were gone.

'Beautiful!' Archie Cargo said, stopping the car and peering into the vibrating void. 'You don't see that often these days. Not in this country.' He glanced across at Abdelkrim, who was still sleeping. 'Pity your brother didn't get to see them.'

'Yes.'

Abdelkrim's face was tilted away from us. A bead of sweat had cut a thin line across the dust on his temple and dribbled into little tributaries over the high ridge of his cheekbone. He shuffled in his seat and then was still again. For a moment I felt awkward, shy, and wished that he would waken.

Archie Cargo cleared his throat, shook his head and screwed a finger into his ear. 'This dust gets everywhere, doesn't it?' he said, pulling on to the crumbling road again.

I considered telling him about the baby giraffe which Miriam and I had found near the river when we were younger; instead I leaned my head back and let it bounce against the seat as we bumped along. I closed my eyes momentarily, but opened them again with a start when I found myself confronted with the image of the drowned man in the mortuary. I thought, too, of my mother; her poor, empty body now concealed within the box above us, and my eyes filled with tears. I blinked hard and sniffed, my heart filling too – but with a seething rage rather than sorrow. Suddenly I pictured Alassane, laughing with my father in our compound in Wadata, and I wanted to scream at her to get out, to go home to her Big House, her sisters and her filthy way of life. I thought too of Souley: of her taunts about my mother and my family. I pictured her face in front of me – close to mine. And although I knew that it was wrong, in my mind's eye, I brought my hand hard against her cheek.

These were thoughts that shocked me. It was as if some malignant spirit had momentarily possessed me, taken hold of my heart and twisted it. I thought of the healers and the marabout in our village, and the woman in the hospital who had been told that her baby had been possessed by the ghost of his dead twin. Despite the intense heat the sweat on my brow felt suddenly cold again.

I recalled the teachings from the Koran. I knew that I needed to forgive as well as to be forgiven. There was Allah's forgiveness and human forgiveness. I knew that I needed both, because we do wrong in our relations to Allah as well as in our relations to each other. I thought of Bunchie and the beliefs that she had held on to all her days, that she said had existed long before our people looked to Allah for forgiveness. I knew that I had to be strong.

Confusion mingled with my fear and anger and at last I could hold back no longer. A great spasm seized my chest. My head felt as if it had been gripped by a huge pair of hands and squeezed like a mango. I opened my mouth to gasp for air and from deep within my chest a wretched, guttural croak erupted, along with the bubble of mucus which burst forth from my nose.

Archie Cargo seemed unsurprised by this display of emotion in the rear of his vehicle. 'Hey there, Haoua,' he said. 'Are you all right?' He slowed the car down and offered me a soft, white cloth, which he took from his pocket. 'It's okay to cry, you know,' he said, checking me in the mirror. 'Your mother was a good, kind woman and she deserved your love.'

I nodded, padding my eyes, nose and mouth and then holding the soiled cloth out to him, my heaving body causing my hand to shake.

'H-how do you know?' I sobbed, the hollow words of this stranger whose shoulders I spoke to suddenly fuelling my anger further.

'You can keep that!' he said, glancing over his seat to pull a face and then flashing me a smile, the kindness in his eyes quelling my agitation a little. 'Actually, I did meet your mother – once – and although I didn't really know her, I could tell that she didn't have a bad bone in her body.' He shrugged. 'You can just tell when people are good.' He peered into his mirror again. 'Would you like me to stop?'

I shook my head. 'When did you meet my mother?'

He drummed his fingers on the steering wheel. 'Hmm, let's see; ten. . . twelve weeks ago maybe? At Efrance's house.'

'Efrance?'

Archie cocked his head towards Abdelkrim. 'Your brother's friend. Lives in Pays-Bas, Niamey's shanty area. She has a little daughter, Momi. Didn't he tell you about them?'

'No.'

'Oh. I see. Well, probably best if he does so himself.' He shrugged. 'Anyway, your mother stayed with Efrance and Momi for a few weeks, to be relatively close to the hospital. Then of course, when her condition worsened. . .' he broke off.

'And that's where you met her?' I said.

'It is.' He leaned across and opened the little compartment in front of my sleeping brother. 'I should have a photograph in here somewhere,' he said, glancing up at the treacherous road every few seconds as he rummaged around. At last he handed me a brightly coloured envelope on which the word *Quikacopy* had been printed. 'I'd dropped Abdel off there that day; Pays-Bas is some distance away from central Niamey. Mainassara's people like to keep its inhabitants out of sight, well away from the Presidential Palace etcetera, you know?' He looked over his shoulder and pulled a mock smile on only one side of his face. 'Efrance insisted I take some tea with them and I happened to have my camera with me.'

There were some twenty photographs altogether. In other circumstances I would have paid more attention to the images of *anasaras* whom I did not know and young, Nigerien men working in what I recognised as Archie Cargo's workshop. Now, however, I shuffled through them impatiently until I found the single picture of my mother. Seeing her face again after so long wrenched at my heart, and my eyes welled up once more. She was seated in front of a small, shabby hut, on her head a wrap which I did not recognise. Her face was thin, gaunt, tired, but her eyes were full of life and love. It was, unmistakably, my mother. To her right sat my brother, his face serious, handsome, his arm around her shoulder protectively. On her left, a young, pretty woman – Efrance I guessed – leaned in towards my mother and the child on her lap.

'This is Momi?' I said, shuffling forward to hold the photograph towards Archie, and then tapping it.

'Yes.'

Momi had a pretty face too. I guessed that she was about three years old. She was seated on my mother's lap and her tiny hands were clutching the sleeves of my mother's *pagne* as she cradled the child. Like one of her own, I thought.

'I couldn't get them to smile,' Archie said, shaking his head.

'*Toh.*'

'And little Momi wriggled like a snake!'

I leaned back and held the photograph close to my face. Together, these four individuals looked like a family, albeit a small one. My mother could easily have been mistaken for the child's grandmother. Here was a very real part of my mother's life – of the last part of my mother's life – about which I had known nothing. What had she felt for this woman and her child? Had she grown to love them? Had she put aside thoughts about me, Fatima and Adamou? Had she given up on my father? I gazed again at her face and searched for some clue. Abdelkrim would provide me with some answers, but I dared not risk waking him. Again, a wave of anger washed over me, causing a prickling sensation in my temples and a burning feeling around my ears. Could it really be that I felt anger and jealousy towards my poor, dead mother and my beloved brother, I wondered. Just as suddenly as it had seized me, my anger receded and was replaced by guilt. I sniffed and replaced the photograph in its envelope.

'Thank you for letting me see this, Monsieur,' I said, handing the packet across the back of the seat.

Archie shot me a stern look. 'Archie!' he said.

I smiled. 'Archie.'

'That's better.' He had not taken the photographs from me. 'You can keep the one of your mother – if you'd like to.'

I took the photograph back out of the packet and examined it again.

'Thank you,' I said. 'I would like to.' I untied the little bundle which I had knotted around my waist and added the photograph to my collection of treasures, slipping it carefully between one of Katie and Hope's postcards and my 'magic' picture of Abdelkrim in uniform on the Bac Farie ferry. In front of us, Archie's little plastic leprechaun jiggled about furiously with every bump and swerve of the road, his pale, pink face smiling, come what may. I twisted the bundle back onto my hip and left my hand resting on it. For a moment I felt reassured, calmed. A warm glow seemed to emanate from my fingertips and pulsate up my arm towards my heart, my soul. I was glad enough of Madame Kantao's cockerel's foot but my treasures were my true amulets.

I wanted to know more about this Efrance and Momi, but Archie Cargo's loyalty to my brother was obvious. There and then I decided to disclose some of my secrets to him, perhaps because I felt that I too could trust this man, or perhaps because I felt that he might offer more information if I did so first. I told him all about Miriam, Fatima, Adamou, my father, Monsieur Boubacar, Richard and Sushie. About my photographs and postcards, about the letters to and from Katie and Hope, about the joy of being able to read and write and my dreams of seeing the world and of being a school teacher or a doctor. Archie Cargo listened intently as I spoke, never once interrupting me or yawning, or shaking his head or sucking his teeth.

When I had finished my excited ramble he nodded, turning the side of his pointed face towards me as he drove. 'It is very good to have friends all over the world,' he said, pushing a few strands of his straggly brown hair back from his damp brow. 'I have made lots of friends since first coming to your country eight years ago, Haoua.' He motioned towards my still-sleeping brother. 'Abdelkrim is one of the best!'

I told him about the photograph that Abdelkrim had given to my mother and that she had then given to me on her departure from Wadata, and of the day Miriam and I had gone in search of Monsieur Longueur and his 'magic' camera.

'Monsieur Longueur!' he laughed. 'That's a good name for him. I know that guy. Sometimes he comes in to the Rec Centre for a swim. Ha!'

I agreed that I would show him my treasures at the earliest opportunity.

We drove on for several kilometres until finally the car struck a pothole with such force that it juddered almost to a halt, my brother's head bouncing against the doorframe. Wrenched from his exhausted slumber, he swore and, scowling through gritty eyes, rubbed the crown of his head.

'What's going on?' he said. 'Where are we?'

'I'd guess about eighty kilometres from the river crossing,' Archie said.

Abdelkrim sat up and rubbed his eyes. He stretched, the stink from under his arms suddenly wafting around the cockpit of the car. He spat out of the window and rubbed his neck. 'Aiiee! I feel like I've been kicked by a camel!'

Archie laughed. 'You smell like one, too, my friend! Do you want some water, Abdel? Where's that bottle gone, Haoua?'

I handed it across the seat.

'It's warm already, I'm afraid,' Archie said.

Abdelkrim took the bottle and removed the lid, then

275

steadied it between his thighs. 'I'll show you a little trick I learned in the army,' he said. He reached down to the floor of the car and extracted a packet of Lipton's mint teabags from one of the *supermarché* bags. He ripped open the packaging, took out two teabags and poked them into the narrow mouth of the bottle, then he screwed the lid back on and gave the bottle a great shake before setting it on the dash of the car, in full view of the sun. 'Better than drinking tepid water!'

'That's clever!' Archie said.

Abdelkrim leaned out of the open window and scanned the sky. 'We have a few hours of daylight yet. I'll drive for a while, if you want?'

Archie shook his head. 'I'm all right for now. But later, thanks.'

I shuffled forward and leaned an elbow on each of the two front seats. Although I had felt quite at ease with Archie Cargo, I was glad that my brother was now awake. 'We saw some giraffes, Abdel,' I said.

'Uhuh.'

'Quite far off,' Archie said. 'Four, maybe five, heading south.'

Abdelkrim nodded. 'They'll be trying to outrun the desert!' He twisted around to face me. 'You know, I read an article in *Le Sahel*, not so long ago, about some oaf – a royal from Britain, I think – who was visiting with the World Wildlife Fund. He was quoted as saying that there is no wildlife in Niger!'

Archie put his head down and slapped his brow. 'Aiiee, aiiee, aiiee!' he said. 'I think I know who that will have been!'

'Yes?'

'Yes. Philip – the Queen's husband. *Walayi!* He's famous for his gaffes! He once told the president of Nigeria, who was dressed in his traditional robes, that he looked like he was ready for bed!'

I sat back and thought about the abundance of creatures that we encountered on a daily basis: jerboas, rats, siafu ants, termites, wild dogs, monkeys, bats, bees and hornets, scorpions, buzzards, lizards and chameleons, crocodiles, egrets, dung beetles, river horses, gazelle, yaffil, praying mantis, vultures; creatures who wore the mantle of the desert like an invisible *jellaba*, who could hide themselves on the vast, scorched desert plains and scrublands of the bush, or slip into the muddy waters of the river and wait for hours disguised as rotting logs. Creatures who had resisted the southerly push of the desert. Creatures who had not abandoned the Sahel, who waited, along with the now formerly nomadic tribes such as my own, in the hope of an easier life.

'How can a king be so ignorant?' I said.

Archie snorted. 'Good question, Haoua.'

And so the conversation continued as we bumped and edged our way along the ruined road. A news bulletin came over the car radio declaring that shots had been fired at Pont Kennedy in the capital. Archie was clearly agitated by this news and fretted about the safety of his students, despite the fact that there were no reports of injuries.

'It's a bad situation,' Abdelkrim said. 'The government sends in militia and gendarmerie who haven't been paid to quell troublesome civil servants and students who also haven't been paid.'

Archie nodded. 'Some of my guys are just about ready to spill blood. Can't feed their families. Can't concentrate on their work. They're like pressure cookers!'

'The whole thing is a mess!'

'Mainassara should step down, don't you think?'

Abdelkrim sighed. 'Ask me after I've been paid, my friend. For now, I suppose I'm one of the lucky ones – at least the army has to feed me.'

The broken road meandered through a desolate, lonely landscape, and was now just a dusty, rock-strewn track. Fissures in its surface sent the vehicle hurtling towards the ditch at times, the wallowing tyres spinning furiously against little more than grit and red sand.

All three of us had taken on ghostly complexions, our faces coated in layer upon layer of the fine, red-grey dust that billowed through the open windows and settled on our lips and eyelids and inside our nostrils and ears. Archie had been wearing a pair of heavy plastic sunglasses for some time. He now removed them to reveal a band of pinkish, pale skin.

'Weird, eh?' he said, looking in the rear view mirror and frantically pushing two fingers in and out of his nostrils, so that when he looked towards us again he also had a little pink moustache.

'Man, you are ugly!' Abdelkrim said, and we all laughed as Archie puffed up his cheeks and crossed his eyes. For a moment he reminded me of Adamou, and I was at once filled with dread and excitement at the prospect of returning home to my village. It seemed like much longer ago than a day and a half that I had set off on foot from Wadata with cousin Moussa. In fact it seemed like a lifetime ago.

By now my *pagne* was saturated and sticking to my body. I reached up to the rope above my head and hooked my fingers around it, the warm breeze wafting around my armpits as the car bucked and vibrated its way along the empty road. The interior of the vehicle was airless, heavy with the stinking heat of the afternoon. My throat was parched. Even Abdelkrim's mint tea did little to help. I tried laying my throbbing head on the package of water bottles again but it was too uncomfortable to sleep. I rubbed the grit out of my eyes once more and sat up. 'Can't we stop for a while, please?' I whined.

'Sure,' Archie said with a grimace, as the car dipped into a steep incline. 'We'll pull over just ahead – where those other vehicles have parked.' Half a kilometre ahead, the remnants of an array of ravaged vehicles lay scattered forlornly by the roadside. We slithered down the hill towards them, stones pinging off the underside of Archie's car as the tyres scuffed along the rough terrain.

'What has happened here?' I said, as we neared the skeletal trucks and bush taxis.

'This place is known as Bukwa Fonda, Death Avenue,' Abdelkrim said. 'It's notoriously dangerous. Ambushes. Robbery. Probably best to keep going for a little while.'

We crawled through the disarray; overturned cars with their roofs ripped off, discarded doors with melted and distorted plastic mouldings, unrecognisable body panels, twisted fenders and fragments of shattered windscreens, twinkling like diamonds in the relentless sun.

'I don't remember seeing this before,' I said. 'Perhaps it was dark when the *camion* passed through here yesterday.'

'Sometimes the drivers follow other *pistes* to avoid this place,' Abdelkrim said. 'It's considered bad luck!'

'So why have you brought us this way?' Archie Cargo said, sounding suddenly alarmed.

'It's quicker.'

'Great.'

We drove on for another few kilometres until we came to a long, straight stretch of the distressed road. To the southwest, a deep red ridge had broken through the crumbling laterite and pointed towards the sun. And, just visible, protruding from behind this protective hulk of rock, we could make out the shining silver surfaces of three enormous circular plates. Signs warning intruders to stay away had been attached to a high security fence that surrounded the strange installation and then disappeared behind the great rock. There was an intense, eerie stillness about this place. Somehow it looked unreal, like a photograph in one of Monsieur Boubacar's books or the beautiful American and English magazines that Mademoiselle Sushie passed on to my school when she had finished reading them.

'What are those things?' I said.

'Satellite communications dishes,' Abdelkrim said. 'For

radio, television, cellphone signals. Keep going, Archie.'

When we did come eventually to a halt, I was so stiff and sore that I found it difficult to clamber out of the rear window of the car. I had watched Abdelkrim scramble out through his window, head first, placing his palms on the scorched surface of the road and then dragging his feet out. I felt sure that I could make lighter work of it, but the hot sheet metal of the vehicle's roof seared my palms as I struggled and twisted to get my rump onto the lip of the door. Abdelkrim stepped forward and grasped my forearm to pull me clear, one of my sandals catching on the door and falling back into the rear cockpit.

'*Walayi!*' my brother said, leaning back in through the window to retrieve the sandal. 'It's not easy with the doors tied up like this!'

He had barely finished his sentence when we heard a dull thud, as Archie Cargo tumbled from the driver's window, landing awkwardly on the ground. We hurried around to the other side of the vehicle and found him flat on his back, a cloud of dust wafting around him.

'Are you all right, Monsieur?' I said, anxiously.

'He's okay,' Abdelkrim laughed, holding out a hand to help his friend up.

'Just a bit winded,' Archie said, dusting down his baggy blue shorts. He stood up straight and swept his hair away from his forehead to reveal a great grin on his dirty, boyish face. 'No need to call out the ambulance!' He went to the trunk of the car and took out a small canvas bag. Then, without another word, he turned and started walking towards a little rocky outcrop a few metres away.

'Where are you going, Monsieur?' I called after him.

'Never ask a man in the desert where he's going with a shovel – as they say in the movies!' he called back. Then he stopped and turned to face us. 'By the way, Haoua. . .'

'Monsieur?'

'It's Archie!'

'Pardon, Monsieur – I mean, Archie.'

He shook his head and disappeared.

Confused, I looked at Abdelkrim for some kind of explanation. 'He doesn't have a shovel!' I said.

But Abdelkrim was shaking his head now too. He had been checking the ropes which held my mother's casket in place on the roof of the car. 'Don't worry about it, child,' he said. He crossed the road, unzipping his trousers as he moved, then stopped with his back towards me to piss into the dust.

I walked a few metres in the opposite direction and squatted down, hitching my *pagne* up just enough to ensure privacy. When I had finished, I returned to the vehicle and sat down beside my brother in its partial shade.

Abdelkrim looked at me and crossed his legs. 'Are you all right, Little One?'

I nodded.

He spat on his palms and rubbed them together vigorously, then took out his cigarettes and lit one.

'This doesn't seem real, Abdel,' I said, looking up at the box on the roof.

'It's real,' he said, sadly.

I picked up a twig and scratched a little drawing of a house in the sand. 'Shouldn't we pray?'

Abdelkrim snorted. 'Don't you think it's a little late for that?' He got to his feet and stretched, then leaned into the car and emerged again with the nearly empty bottle of tea. 'Want some?' he said, flicking the butt of his cigarette into the air.

I stood up and took the bottle from him and drained it while he busied himself with a fresh bottle and his teabags.

'Monsieur Archie showed me the picture of you and Mother with your friends,' I said. 'He gave it to me, in fact.'

'*Toh.*'

'It was while you were sleeping.'

'Uhuh?'

'Is that woman your girlfriend?'

Abdelkrim took a long swig from his bottle, the muddy liquid sloshing out of the neck and painting a gash across his dust-encrusted cheek. 'I suppose she is,' he said, wiping his mouth with the back of his hand.

I shuffled around to see him as he turned away from the car. 'And is the baby yours also?'

He laughed. 'Momi? No! – *Walayi!*' He was shaking his head now and making great puffing sounds. 'Her father was some kitchen boy from Zinder, I think. No, no. Nothing to do with me!'

I was impatient. 'Can't you just tell me about Mother, Abdelkrim?'

He turned to face me again. 'I'll tell you,' he said, setting the bottle on to the roof of the car. 'I met Efrance about two years ago. She was living in the shanties at Pays-Bas. Poor. Doing whatever she had to do to survive. Her baby was very young. I helped her as much as I could. I liked her a lot. When Mother came to Niamey for her tests the doctors said that she would need to continue to attend the hospital regularly. She couldn't stay with me at the barracks, of course, and we couldn't afford to find her lodgings of her own.'

'What about cousin Moussa?' I said, lowering myself onto the ground. 'Couldn't he have helped?'

'I never trusted that bastard!' Abdelkrim hissed through his teeth. 'Father suggested asking him for help but Mother had no time for Moussa – or that witch Doodi either. So she stayed with Efrance and Momi. She used Efrance's sewing machine whenever she was strong enough and looked after Momi whenever Efrance was working, to help pay her way. They all got on well. I would visit whenever I could, and Bouleb would lend me his motorcycle to take Mother to the hospital whenever it was necessary. For a little while she seemed to rally.' He looked at me and shrugged. 'Then she got sicker.'

I stared at my toes through troughs of tears and tried to imagine my mother living with Efrance and Momi in their little tin and wooden shack. 'I wish I could have met your friends, Abdel,' I said.

'You will one day, Little One,' he said, 'you will.'

'Did Fatima meet them?'

'No.'

There was a silence. Absolute. The air vibrating over the stark, baked landscape. Abdelkrim had dug the toe of his army boot into the sand and was dragging it from side to side. He stared off into the distance.

'Mother gave me the photograph of you on the ferry, also,' I said, patting the little bundle on my hip. 'I keep it here, with my other treasures that I showed you.'

He looked at me and forced his mouth into a kind of sad smile, but I was sure there was anger in his eyes too.

Archie returned with his mysterious canvas bag, whistling as he approached us. *Ça va?* Ready to go?'

Abdelkrim nodded. 'Sure. I'll drive for a while.' He drank some of the tea, made a quick check of the ropes once again and then wrestled his way, head first, through the driver's window.

Archie helped me to my feet and then put his arms around my waist, so that he could lift me clear of the door, feeding me, feet first, back into the airless vehicle.

When he too was back inside, he slapped his hand against the passenger door and said, 'Let's roll!'

44

The approach of dusk offered us some relief within the stifling car. The sun dropped low over the parched landscape and now set the sky on fire. A light breeze bowled scraps of dislocated scrub-thorn alongside our rattling vehicle, until they snared each other up, or bounced off in other directions against crusts of rock now casting long, dark shadows across the barren plains.

The road passed through a neat little village where a gang of tiny boys, naked from the waist down, chased along behind us, their little pointed penises wobbling curiously as they ran. The houses were all made of pinkish bricks, and parked alongside one of them sat an ancient pick-up truck that looked like it might have been constructed from salvaged parts of road wrecks such as those we had seen at Bukwa Fonda. A group of women, drawing water from a well at the centre of the village, waved as we swept by and, one by one, the children who had been following us trailed off to return to their mothers' sides.

'Do you know what this place is called, Abdel?' Archie said. 'I don't see any road signs!'

'I think this is Fura Daya,' Abdelkrim said. 'At least that's what travellers call it – it may have another name. There are very few young men here. Most have left to find work – in Nigeria, Cote d'Ivoire, Benin or wherever. They are known as the Kurmizey – the sons of Djerma farmers who travel to the sea coast each year, returning only for the harvests. Only women, children and old people remain. It's a favourite stop-off for some of my comrades.'

'I'll bet it is!' Archie laughed.

Just before nightfall, we came across an unlit bush taxi hauled up at the side of the road. Around it stood some twenty-five passengers while another man – the driver, presumably – worked on one of the rear wheels with a large metal foot pump.

'Should we see if they need help?' Abdelkrim said.

'I suppose so,' Archie said, leaning out of the window as the car drew up alongside the delapidated, windowless vehicle.

Some of the passengers turned to regard us as Abdelkrim pulled on the brake. A number of women, some with infants tied to their backs, milled towards us, elbowing and shoving at each other. 'Monsieur! Monsieur!' they called, each appearing to attempt to drown out the sound of the others' voices.

'What is the problem here?' Archie said.

Again the women pushed forward, but now the driver had stood upright and was chastising his passengers, his voice resonating deeply through the high-pitched babble. 'Get back! Get back! Let me speak to the young gentleman.' His teeth gleamed in the half-light.

'Monsieur! Monsieur!' one of the women cried out, defiantly. 'Give me and my child a ride, please. We have been travelling all day in this death trap!'

'I have a child too, Monsieur!' a woman in a bright *pagne* screeched. 'Take me, take me!'

The driver grabbed at the second woman's arm, wrenching her back so that he could address Archie. '*Excusez-moi, Monsieur*,' he said, hitching up his brown striped *jellaba* as he approached the window.

'Do you need some help, friend?' Archie said.

'No. No, thank you. We just have a slow puncture. It is nothing.'

'Nothing? Nothing?' the persistent woman screamed. 'We

have to stop every ten minutes for this man to pump up his stupid tyres!'

'We've missed the ferry!' another woman shouted.

'Don't you have a spare wheel?' Archie said.

The driver tilted his head to one side as if to apologise, while the women jostled him from behind. 'The soldiers took it, Monsieur.'

My brother leaned across in front of Archie. 'But you can manage here, brother?'

'*Oui. D'accord.*'

'*Toh.*' Archie slapped the side of the car and turned his face towards Abdelkrim. 'Let's go then.'

'Monsieur! Monsieur!' the woman in the bright *pagne* cried again. 'Please! Won't you take me and my child to Tera?'

'We are not going to Tera, sister,' Archie called back, 'and this vehicle is full!' He pointed ahead and Abdelkrim accelerated, the wheels of the car spinning, ripping through the cooling dust and throwing it up into the greying light to partially obscure the wretched bush taxi and its forlorn passengers.

I stared out of the back window. 'Couldn't we have taken one or two of them?'

'*Walayi!* Which one or two?' my brother said, shaking his head.

Archie Cargo was nodding vigorously. 'They might have torn either the car or us apart!'

Darkness brought more hazards. The Mercedes' lights were not good and thumping into potholes became a more common occurrence. I would not have said so aloud, but Abdelkrim's driving skills left a great deal to be desired. By midnight I felt like I had been battered by a troop of monkeys. I tried not to complain. There were too many other things to worry about. Every so often I would be lulled into a trance-like state and my mind would wander fleetingly back to happier days. But it was only a matter of time before my bones were shaken once again, or my head was bashed off the door pillar. Like shattered glass my sweet mother's face would fragment in my mind's eye, and each time this occurred it seemed to me more difficult to conjure up her image again. I patted the bundle on my hip and was thankful for the photograph that Archie had given to me.

Eventually I must have dozed off again because, when I woke, the car had stopped and I was alone in the darkness. The air was much cooler now and silence enveloped the vehicle. Someone had thrown a jacket over me. For a moment I did not know where I was and fear seized me. I sat up and rubbed my eyes and peered out of the window at the moon-whitened sands. Abdelkrim and Archie were nowhere to be seen. I twisted around on the seat and stuck my head out of the opposite window. Slowly, my eyes adjusted to the moonlight and I could just make out the silhouetted forms of my brother and his friend lying by the side of the road. Grabbing hold of the rope overhead, I struggled, feet first, out of the window. As my left foot touched the sand, my right sandal slapped against the car door and Archie jolted upright.

'Good God, you scared me!' he whispered.

I stepped away from the car a little and then flopped down clumsily onto the sand. Immediately the coldness of the hardened ground started to seep through my body.

Archie Cargo stood up and moved towards me, dragging the thin blanket in which he had been wrapped behind him. 'You're shivering,' he said, draping the blanket over my shoulders. He sat down beside me.

'*Merci*, Monsieur. . . Archie,' I said, daring to meet his smiling eyes briefly. 'It is very cold now.'

He nodded.

I looked across at the huddled form of Abdelkrim. 'My brother has been sleeping long?'

'Not long. We stopped about an hour ago. It's a very tiring journey.'

'*Oui.*'

'I thought he might not want to stop at all,' Archie said. 'He likes to get the job done, does your brother.'

For a moment I considered Archie's strange use of words, his gentle voice rising and falling like the notes from a reed flute.

'Haoua? Haoua?' he said, but I was lost in thought, battling to hold on to my dreams, and my eyes were heavy.

'*Excusez-moi!*' I pulled the blanket closer around me. 'I am still very tired.'

He nodded, cupped his hands and blew into them. 'That's all right,' he said, rubbing his palms together, his skin whispering like the hint of a breeze. 'What woke you?'

I shrugged.

There was a long silence. Our breath vaporised, rose above us, vanished, again and again. I looked at the old car that was conveying my mother's ravaged body to its resting place. The chill air vied with my grief for my attention. I clamped my jaws together tightly so that my teeth would not chatter.

'What about showing me your treasures now?' Archie said.

I was delighted that he had remembered and was interested enough to ask. I unwrapped my bundle and showed him my pictures one by one.

'So these are your friends from Ireland?' he said, shining a little torch onto the photograph of Katie and Hope in the snow.

'Yes. Do you know them?'

He looked surprised. 'Know them? Good God, no!'

'Oh,' I said, disappointed.

'What made you think that I might know them?'

'My teacher showed me a map of your country and said that it was a very small island and that very few people live there,' I said.

Archie shook his head. 'Oh it's small all right. But not so

288

small or unimportant for my countrymen and women not to fight over who governs it.'

'Like the Touaregs here?' I said.

He nodded. 'A little like the Touaregs, yes. At present both the Irish and the British governments lay claim to parts of my country. I come from a place called Wicklow. Where did you say your friends live?'

I shrugged and fumbled in my bundle for one of the letters, then handed it to him.

He shone his torch on the crumpled paper. 'Ballygowrie. That's in the north,' he said. 'Different story. Different government!' He smiled. 'Don't look so puzzled, Haoua. But the answer to your question is, I'm afraid, no. I don't know your friends.' After a while he began whistling, his feet tapping out an accompanying rhythm. 'Do you like music, Haoua?'

'*Oui, Monsi. . .* Archie.'

'I like music. A lot.' He grinned. 'And dancing. That's how I met your brother, you know? I'd taken a young lady to the Hotel Rivoli to dance the night away in their compound. Great music. I got talking to Abdel at the bar. We just kind of hit it off.'

'You have a girlfriend?'

He shook his head. 'Not as such. Not now anyway.' He gave me a little sad smile.

'Who was she?' I said, surprising myself.

'Dorette. Jamaican. She worked for the World Health Organisation. I met her at the Rec Centre.' He sighed. 'God! I love your dusty country, Haoua.'

'Do you have many girlfriends?' I said.

He put his fingers to his lips and a great grin spread across his moonlit face.

'What about my brother?' I pressed. 'He told me about his friend and her baby.'

'Efrance.'

'Yes. Efrance. Does he love this woman?'

289

'Perhaps you ought to ask him that yourself,' he said, with a nod.

I looked up and saw that Abdelkrim had woken and propped himself up on one elbow.

'Ask me what?'

'We were talking about Efrance. . . and Momi.'

'Haoua was just wondering if you are in love,' Archie said, grinning again.

'*Walayi!*' Abdelkrim rolled his eyes and lit a cigarette. 'It is bitterly cold now,' he said. He lifted his chin and blew a cloud of blue smoke towards the moon.

'But very beautiful,' Archie said. 'Like Mademoiselle Efrance!' he added, with a wink.

Abdelkrim ignored the comment. He stood up and stretched, then massaged the back of his neck with his free hand. 'What time is it?'

Archie glanced at his watch. 'Two a.m.'

'We should get back on the road soon.'

'Sure.'

'I'm hungry,' I said.

'I can fix that.' Archie stood up and crossed to the car. When he returned, he was carrying a fresh bottle of water and a package wrapped in greasy paper. 'Samosas! – From the *supermarché!*'

For a moment, he reminded me somehow of my father, in the old days when he had seemed happier. When my mother had been well and the rains came and our crops were good.

Archie handed the bottle to Abdelkrim. 'It's cool enough to drink without your teabags now.'

'*Merci.*'

The samosas were delicious, the water pure and clean. I looked up at the moon again and tried once more to imagine what life would be like without my mother. I wiped my hands on my *pagne* and gathered up my postcards and photographs, which had been lying strewn on their cloth.

When I had finished this task I tied the bundle to my waist again and began fiddling with the cockerel's foot which Madame Kantao had given me.

Abdelkrim looked at me and shook his head. 'Spirit nonsense!'

I did not reply.

'Perhaps I should have a little fidget with my leprechaun?' Archie said.

I shrugged. 'My friend Miriam Kantao's mother says that everyone needs an amulet for the road.'

'At home we also have Saint Christopher,' Archie said.

Abdelkrim sighed. 'There are no gods, no spirits.'

'There's at least one fellow in Niger who perhaps wouldn't agree with you, my friend,' Archie said.

Abdelkrim spilled his hand open. 'What do you mean?'

'I haven't told you about my journey to your country, have I?'

Abdelkrim shook his head.

Archie turned towards me. 'I first came here eight years ago,' he said. 'I was backpacking. No real plans. Just drifting. I'd travelled overland from Tangier and then hitched a ride from Tamanrasset with a French couple and their Spanish friend. They were idiots. All of them. Completely unprepared. No sand tracks. No shovels. Idiots!' He shook his head. 'Back then they were still working on Route Nationale Deux – laying a big black bitumen strip across the desert. We'd got talking to some nomads one day and they'd told us that the road crew, some sixty kilometres ahead, were a Belgian outfit with lots of equipment. This French guy – Guillaume – decided we could get a decent meal out of them. So we hauled up outside their great mobile compound and bluffed our way past their security guards.'

Abdelkrim leaned forward and gave a great, wide yawn.

'Is my story that boring?' Archie said.

'No, no, continue, please,' Abdelkrim said. 'Really. I'm interested.'

Archie continued. 'Well, the Belgians fed us all right. Plied us with wine too. I think a couple of them had their eyes on Guillaume's girlfriend, Adrienne. They seemed quite a friendly bunch. There was music, singing, story-telling, even some very drunken dancing. Eventually it got really late. The road crew was due to work the following morning. The foreman told us that we couldn't stay inside their compound – reasons to do with insurance, he said. So we thanked them, gathered up our stuff and drove a few kilometres back down the road, where we pulled over, spilled out on to the roadside and collapsed immediately.'

'You were drunk?' I said.

'We were drunk. That's right, Haoua.' Archie looked at Abdelkrim again.

'Go on,' he said.

'Well, I'd dragged a sleeping bag out of the car and forced myself into it – it was pretty cold, you know. A night very like this one. Moonlit. Chilly. I don't think I'd slept for long; it was still dark when I woke up. I was sweating profusely and my guts were churning. I thrashed around for a while and then crawled out of the bag. The other three were still sleeping soundly. I made my way around them to the car and found some toilet paper, then headed across the tarred road towards some bushes. That was the first of many such visits to that spot! I was shitting and vomiting all night. I'd break into these raging bouts of sweat and then, just as suddenly, my teeth would be chattering with the cold. Then along would come the churning guts and the hot flushes again. It seemed like the night would never end. It got so bad that I stripped naked and lay on top of the sleeping bag.'

'We know what that feels like, my friend,' Abdelkrim said, glancing at me.

I nodded. Bunchie had told us that there had been devils living in her stomach for as long as she could remember.

'Yes, but that's not the whole story,' Archie said. 'My head was throbbing, my stomach muscles ached and my ass was on fire after a final, violent episode. I was walking back across the road in my bare feet, toilet roll in hand, and realised that the bitumen surface felt nice and cool on my soles. It seemed like the obvious thing to do at the time – my companions had not stirred and there was no sound except for the cicadas. I lay down on the road and put the toilet roll under my head. The moon-cooled bitumen soothed my burning skin. I was exhausted. I went out like a light.

Bang. It was the most comfortable I'd felt in hours. I'm not sure how long I lay there, but eventually, through my feverish slumber, I became vaguely aware of some vibration and a distant rumbling sound. God only knows what I put it down to in my drained state. Certainly not a vehicle. But, of course, that is exactly what it was. The vibration increased and the sound intensified. Finally, somehow, I became aware that my naked body was being bathed in bright light. I sat up and opened my eyes, just in time to scuttle out of the path of a huge truck hurtling towards me! The driver blasted his horn as I dived into the scrub, but still the others didn't stir.'

Abdelkrim was shaking his head and chuckling. 'Bad enough that you pick up a dose of amoebic dysentery, but then to almost get flattened by a *camion* too!'

'Well, yes!' Archie laughed. 'I often wonder what the driver made of the sight of a naked white man, at night, in the middle of the desert. I like to think that he thought he'd witnessed some kind of ghost!'

We were all laughing now.

Archie covered his face with his hands, as if he were embarrassed. 'You know I definitely took some chances with the water along the way – forgot about the odd purification tablet maybe. . . couldn't resist an occasional swig of that wonderful ginger water they sell by the roadside – but my French companions had another theory.'

'Uhuh?'

'Yes. They wondered if our Belgian hosts might have added some nasty ingredient themselves. The French aren't the Belgians' favourite nationals, you know! Within a few hours of getting back onto the road, my three companions had the same thing. It was horrible, really. At one stage we had to stop for Adrienne to empty her bowels in full view of some nearby villagers. She just flung the car door open, bundled herself out and dumped her load right next to some poor bastard's hut! There was no controlling it. No dignity. Embarrassing too. It was months before we shook it.'

A serious look came over Abdelkrim's face. 'This is Africa, my friend. We know about lack of dignity. At least you and your European friends had medicines available to you.'

Archie nodded. 'Sure,' he said, genuine sadness in his voice now, 'I know, I know. . .'

Back on the road, I slept again. I had prayed that the spirit of my mother would come to me in a dream and, sure enough, God now answered my prayers. At first I could not tell if the figure in the dusty haze before me was my mother or Bunchie. A blizzard of sand swept across my vision, from right to left, obscuring the solitary form as it moved slowly towards me. The wind howled. I did not feel frightened. The experience did not then seem strange. I was standing alone, in a bleak, unfamiliar place, waiting for my mother. It seemed the natural thing to do. I stretched out my hands before me but they too disappeared in the swirling, gritty air. I dropped them by my sides again and when I looked up my mother was standing directly in front of me. At first she said nothing. As I tried to focus on her rheumy eyes – sand and dust battering my face all the while – her features became like liquid and reformed again to reveal the face of my grandmother. Then, just as swiftly, Bunchie's features melted away to reveal those of my mother again. I tried to speak, but my lips seemed tightly locked. I tried to lift my hand to touch my mother's face but found that this too was beyond my power. My eyes were full of grit now and I seemed powerless even to be able to blink. Again I attempted to open my mouth. It was set fast. The image before me was fading, reappearing, then fading again, like the picture on a faulty television set. I summoned all my strength and tried to communicate with my mother through my eyes alone. There was a great flurry of sand and a shrill, haunting whistle. Then at last, the wind dropped and my mother spoke.

'Haoua,' she said, in a voice that I did not recognise. 'There is a great storm coming.'

Although the wind had died down, the veil of dust between us remained in place. I did not understand my mother's words. In vain I tried to tell her so. There was no sound now, as if the volume control on the broken television set had been turned right down. I stood there, confused, rigid as a statue, willing my mother to speak again. *What do you mean?* I wanted to ask. *The storm is here. The storm is here.*

She did not speak again. Instead, she turned and walked away, pausing briefly to look back over her shoulder at me. Once more I strained to focus on her features. Her mouth seemed different now: her lips pinched, grey and twisted, like those of the drowned man in the mortuary. Panic surged through me as she finally disappeared.

Perhaps I would have followed her into that soundless blizzard. Perhaps the crash was God's way of preventing me from doing so. A sharp pain in my ribcage made me open my eyes. Even in the half light, I immediately recognised the interior of Archie Cargo's car. I found myself on the floor, wedged behind the driver's seat, with the remainder of the case of mineral water bottles strewn over and around me. The vehicle had come abruptly to a halt and was now sitting, nose down, at an alarming angle.

Someone was groaning in the front. 'What the hell happened?' Archie Cargo shouted.

I sat up just in time to see him untangle himself from my brother who was squashed against the driver's door.

Abdelkrim shook his head and then pulled himself up to peer over the back of the seat at me. 'Are you all right, Little

One?' There was blood trickling from a cut just above his left eye.

'I'm fine,' I said, rubbing my ribs.

'Fuck it, man! What happened?' Archie said again, dragging himself across the front seat and through the passenger's window, before falling out on to the ruined road.

'I don't know!' Abdelkrim said. 'You tell me.'

'I was sleeping, man. Maybe you were too?'

'No. One minute we're on the road, the next we're in the ditch!' Abdelkrim put his shoulder to his door and tried to force it open. 'Damn these ropes!' he hissed, groping his way through his window instead. He tumbled out and made his way towards the rear of the car, pausing to yank at my door. 'Wait a moment,' he reassured me, 'we'll have you out of there in a moment.'

Archie had already untied the second rope, which had been holding my mother's coffin to the roof, and now opened the other rear door, scooping the jumble of plastic bottles, paper wrappers, blankets and jackets out of the way.

'Give me your hand, Haoua,' he said.

I reached out and he pulled me up and out onto the sand.

Abdelkrim staggered out of the ditch and lay down on the ground, a few metres away from where I stood.

'You're hurt, Abdel,' I said, scrambling towards him.

'It's nothing!' he snapped.

Behind us, one corner of the rear end of the car protruded over the ditch.

Archie had scrambled down and was inspecting the front for damage. A torrent of foul language told us that all was not well.

Abdelkrim sat up and steadied himself. 'What is it?' he called.

'*Merde!*' We heard the clank of metal being slapped or kicked, then Archie appeared before us. He took a deep breath. 'Are you both okay?' he said, but did not wait for us to answer. 'Looks like we've had a blow-out. Driver's side, front tyre. Torn to shreds.'

'You have a spare?' Abdelkrim said, daubing at his fore-head with a scrap of cloth.

'Of sorts.'

'What does that mean?'

'It means that your military comrades helped themselves to it the last time I made a trip down to Benin. *Tax* they called it. Took my spare battery too – and charged me three thousand CFA! Bent bastards! Someone gave me a replace-ment, but I haven't really checked it out. . .'

'Uhuh.'

'That's not all.'

'No?'

'No. I don't think we'll shift the car by ourselves. The chasis seems well and truly wedged on the rubble. And there's fuel everywhere!'

'Great!' Abdelkrim said, standing up. 'Well, let's see what we can do.' He patted my shoulder and then turned to face his friend. 'I told you I didn't fall asleep,' he shrugged.

Archie put his hand on my brother's forearm. 'There's something else, Abdel.'

'*Toh*. What now?'

Archie's face contorted. 'It's your mother. . .'

We made our way to the top of the ditch and peered down at the twisted front end of the Mercedes. At first I could not see that there was a problem of any real consequence with the coffin. It was clear that the impact of the accident had caused it to slip forward so that only one end remained on the roof of the vehicle while the other now rested on the car's bonnet. But as we clambered down the ditch to take a closer look, it became obvious that the structure had partially disintegrated.

'*Walayi!*' I said, as the full extent of the situation became apparent.

Archie bent down to pick up the bottom end panel of the hastily constructed box. 'I knew it should have been glued too!' he said, holding the square piece of timber aloft.

As if to transfer blame, Abdelkrim immediately addressed me. 'I told you not to keep hanging off that rope!'

I only glanced at him momentarily. I was transfixed by the sight of the puckered shroud and my poor mother's withered feet, which were now protruding from the open end of the coffin and resting on the buckled bonnet of Archie Cargo's car.

45

It had not even occurred to me to offer my help. I had been too upset. Instead, I had turned my back and run away from the stricken car and the burst coffin. I had climbed to the top of an escarpment and sat watching a new dawn through tired and tearful eyes.

When I was very little, Bunchie used to tell me that each new day of life was a blessing. Much later, when death was drawing close to her, she had called for it to take her – every day for two whole weeks. As I watched the fierce new sun rent the horizon, I could not help but consider my mother's death. I prayed that it had not been slow or painful. I could not even contemplate the fact that she had died alone.

When, eventually, I looked down at the car again, I saw that the coffin had been removed from the roof and placed by the roadside. In the hulking shadow of the slope on which I sat, my brother and Archie, tiny as ants, were busy pushing and rocking the vehicle, with no success. It seemed obvious to me that they might as well not try; the car was stuck fast. Though I was sure that my added strength would make little difference, I decided that I should at least offer to help. I was half way down the slope when I heard the rumble of engines approaching. Instinctively I looked north – the direction in which we had been travelling – and then south, but there appeared to be no other vehicles on this stretch of the road. Not even a charred or stripped shell. As the shale fell away beneath my feet, I turned my head to the west and saw a cloud of dust moving towards us across the scrubland at considerable speed.

By the time I reached the base of the outcrop, three military Land Cruisers had already pulled up near Archie's car. Each was brimful of gun-toting men clad in *cheches* and tattered combinations of civilian and military clothing. All of them sported dark glasses, and cigarettes hung from most of their lips. They jeered and whistled as they spilled from the back of the Land Cruisers. For a moment I hung back near the rocks, sensing malevolence and a feeling that this was no ordinary military patrol. A slim soldier, who had remained on one of the trucks, yelled at me to halt as I crossed the road and swung a huge, mounted machine gun around so that it was pointing at me. For a moment, I truly thought that he meant to shoot me and a warm trickle of urine ran down my leg and spilled over the heel of my sandal before soaking into the stretched and cracked surface of the ground. There was a huge guffaw and one of the soldiers lobbed a bottle high into the air above my head. Another fired a volley of shots from a pistol. I sank to my knees and covered my head with my hands just as the bottle shattered on the rocks behind me.

'Leave her alone, you bastards!' Abdelkrim shouted.

I remained at the side of the road, huddled in a ball.

There was the sound of a scuffle, and then another voice, gruff and authoritative, ordered me to get up. I felt rough hands clutching at my *pagne*. When I opened my eyes I was being dragged across the road towards Archie's car, which had, effectively, been encircled by the Land Cruisers, despite the fact that it was actually going nowhere just then. Archie and Abdelkrim had been backed up to the bonnet of one of the trucks, where a group of the scruffy soldiers were interrogating them. A man wearing a beret and mirrored glasses was leaning menacingly towards them and brandishing a fat cigar. Rifles and pistols were shaken angrily each time he spoke. As I was led into the circle, he turned to face me and let out a shrill whistle.

'Well, now. What tasty morsel do we have here?'

'She's my sister. Just a child. Just leave her alone!' My brother sounded full of both anger and fear.

The man in the beret patted Abdelkrim on the chest and laughed. 'Easy brother, easy,' he said. He leaned closer, so that his reddish face was almost touching my brother's. 'That's a nasty cut. You ought to be more careful.'

More laughter.

Abdelkrim put his arm out to catch me as I was pushed roughly towards him. A few of the other renegades had made their way towards Archie's stricken car and were poking about in the trunk.

'I'd stay away from that car with those cigarettes!' Archie called. 'We had a broken fuel pipe. A lot of gasoline has been spilled!'

The men took a few steps away from the vehicle and turned to face their commander. Several of them were gulping water from our supply of bottles.

'Lose the cigarettes, you idiots!' the man in the beret shouted. He looked at my brother and then shook his head, as if he were sharing some great joke with him. 'I am Général Lucien Majila Ag Akotey,' he said, crushing the end of his cigar on the hood of the Land Cruiser and flicking it into the scrub, 'and we are the Free People, the Abandoned of God.' He scratched himself and sighed. 'And you are a soldier also. Are you going to tell me what you and your merry little party are doing here?'

'*Chef*,' Abdelkrim said, 'that box contains the remains of our poor mother. My sister and I are taking her to Wadata for burial. My friend here has kindly offered to help us.'

'Uhuh?' he eyed Abdelkrim up and down. 'What is your name?'

'Boureima. Abdelkrim, *Chef*.'

'You are Songhai?'

'*Oui, Chef*.'

He nodded towards Archie. 'And the *anasara*?'

Archie stepped forward and extended his hand. 'Archie

301

Cargo, technician and lecturer, L'Université Abdou Moumouni de Niamey.'

Instantly, he was slammed back against the grille of the Land Cruiser by one of Akotey's henchmen.

Akotey stepped forward and fixed Archie's gaze. 'I didn't ask *you*!' he said.

There was a brief, awkward silence. Abdelkrim pulled me closer, but by now I was shaking.

Akotey did not miss this fact. He looked at me and laughed again, then he backed away from us a few paces. He removed his sunglasses, put them in the breast pocket of his jerkin and took a pistol out of the holster on his belt. He pointed it towards the wilderness, looking down its muzzle with one eye closed. There was a click. I recognised the sound of the safety catch being released; Adamou had plagued Sergeant Bouleb to show him how his firearm worked when he had brought Abdelkrim to Wadata, so long ago. Akotey dropped the weapon to his side and let his arm dangle loosely. 'You know,' he said, 'I could do anything I want with you three.' He nodded. 'I could shoot you, one by one. I could hold the *anasara* hostage. I could have you all burned alive in your shitty car. Or, I could have you all raped!' He smiled; a vicious, cruel slit on an evil face. 'My men haven't been with a woman for weeks, you know? A goat would do! They're not fussy!'

There was a chorus of laughter. The sun had risen rapidly and already its immense power baked down on us, the ground buckling in the heat, yet I felt cold with fear.

Akotey stood close to my brother again and prodded him gently in the belly with the pistol. 'What should I do, Boureima, eh?'

'You should let us be on our way, *Chef*,' Abdelkrim said.

'You think so?'

'*Oui, Chef.*'

He waved his pistol towards the Mercedes. 'What, in that? It doesn't look to me like you'd get very far.'

'Your men could help us. . . get the car back on to the road. . . if it pleased you, *Chef*,' Abdelkrim stammered.

'Uhuh.' Akotey stepped back and eyed us all up and down once more. 'And why would I want to do that? So that you can report us to your superiors and receive commendation for helping track down yet another bunch of scum dissidents?'

'*Chef*?'

'You know what we are, Boureima – me and these *moutons*!'

Abdelkrim shrugged. 'I know that many personnel are unhappy with their circumstances at present.'

Akotey leapt forward and pushed the gun under Abdelkrim's chin, clutching at his collar with his free hand. 'We are freedom fighters! We are foes of the oppressors!' he yelled, threads of spittle spraying my brother's face. 'Enemies of the fat cats! You understand, Boureima? We are no mutineers – whatever the media may say.'

Abdelkrim nodded, his arm still around my shoulders, but his palm open, tense, his fingers pushing, clawing at the air. For a moment I thought that I might piss again.

Akotey relaxed his grip and looked down at me. He pinched my cheek between his thumb and forefinger and gave me a cold smile. Then he turned his back on us. 'You're a soldier, like us, Boureima,' he continued.

'*Chef*.'

'Answer me this. . .' He spun around to face my brother again. 'Are you loyal to the president?'

Abdelkrim cleared his throat and looked nervously at Archie. 'I. . . ah. . .'

'Let me put the question another way,' Akotey said. 'When was the last time you were paid?'

'Not for some time, *Chef*.'

'*Toh*. Not for some time. Yet still you serve these dogs without question.'

'I am just a humble soldier.'

'*Walayi!*' Akotey snapped. 'Half the country is protesting against Mainassara's rule, yet people like you do nothing! The military must unite against this corrupt system. Together we can force him to resign. He states that the only thing that can bring Niger out of its present crisis is order, unity and work, but why should we work for nothing?'

'I agree with that,' my brother said.

'Yet still you serve your president?'

'Mainassara declared himself a democrat when he seized power in ninety-six. He promised that power would be placed in the hands of civilians. He promised free elections. It is true that those things have not yet materialised. Yet it is democracy that I wish to serve.'

'Nor will they ever materialise under Mainassara!' Akotey said. He stared hard at my brother, but some of the menace seemed to have gone from his face. He slid his pistol back into its holster and folded his arms. 'If you and your kind are waiting for that to happen, you'll wait a long time.' He nodded. 'I like you, Boureima. You should join us, my friend. You know, there is only one language that that bastard will understand!' He touched the end of his shiny nose. 'There are many of us ready to take action.'

'How do you mean, *Chef*? You think Tandja will restore democracy, perhaps?' Abdelkrim's voice sounded more assured. 'Another bloodless coup? My dream is to serve under a truly democratically elected government.'

Akotey took his glasses from his pocket and put them back on his face. 'My uncle served under Kountche,' he said. 'Believe me, there's no such thing as a bloodless coup!'

While this discussion had continued, the other mutineers were plundering the Mercedes and our few possessions. One of them, a big, ugly fellow, now offered his findings to his leader. He emptied Abdelkrim's belt pouch onto the ground and stooped down to pick up the little radio which had been a gift from Katie and Hope. He held it out to Akotey now, a stupid grin spread across his broad face.

'Hey! That's my radio!' Abdelkrim put his hand out to retrieve it, but another mutineer's rifle butt caught him on the wrist.

'Get your hand down, you dog!' the soldier snarled.

Akotey stepped forward, one hand up, to pacify the situation. He took the radio from the ugly soldier and looked at it closely, before inserting one of the earpieces into an ear and switching the device on. A great grin came over his face then. '*Ça, c'est pour moi!*' he said, with a look that seemed to dare contradiction. '*Ça va?*'

My brother shuffled where he stood. He stared hard at the soldier who had struck him and then nodded at the renegade leader. '*D'accord.*'

The ugly soldier stepped forward and grabbed Archie's wrist. He lifted his hand up and flicked a fingernail against the face of his watch.

Akotey nodded his approval and the watch was removed, roughly, from Archie's wrist.

The men who had been rummaging through the trunk appeared beside us, carrying a toolbox and a spare battery. They set their finds at Akotey's feet and stepped back.

'Not my battery! You can't leave us without a spare battery, man! I've only just replaced it after the last time!' Archie said, appealing directly to the leader. 'And I need those tools! They're my *tools*, for Christ's sake! I help your own people learn how to create things they can sell.' He took a step forward in protest and was struck instantly in the face by the butt of a rifle, the dulled crack of flesh-cushioned bone connecting with timber causing me to jolt and making my blood run cold with fear. Archie stumbled back, cradling his chin, and leaned on the fender of the Land Cruiser. Abdelkrim took his arm from my shoulder and steadied his friend.

They are going to kill us! I thought.

Akotey shook his head again. 'Don't question my decisions, my friends.'

'This is your idea of a new democracy, is it?' Archie said, spitting bloodied saliva on to the sand.

The leader did not hesitate. In a flash he had grabbed Archie by the neck. He brought the flat of his hand hard across Archie's cheek, then he slammed his head down on the hood of the Land Cruiser and held it there. His face hovered just a few centimetres above Archie's ear. 'You'd do well to keep your mouth shut, *anasara*,' he whispered. He stood up and straightened his jerkin and beret. He stared hard at Abdelkrim and for a moment I thought that he was going to strike him too. Instead, he resumed his position between his henchmen.

I had shuffled in behind my brother and was clutching my bundle, fearful that they would take it from me. Now, as I emerged and Archie stood upright, I saw the imprint of Akotey's hand, like some giant spider on Archie's reddened face.

'Let us go, please, *Chef*,' Abdelkrim said. 'We are not a threat to you. We only want to bury my mother. You've got what you want from us.'

There was a long silence before Akotey spoke. 'You have money?'

Abdelkrim shook his head.

'I have some,' Archie said, croakily. He pulled a fold of notes from his shirt pocket and held it out.

'But you'll have to give us some fuel in return,' Abdelkrim said. 'We've made a temporary repair to the fuel pipe, but we've lost at least half a tank.'

One of the mutineers snatched the cash from Archie's hand and presented it to Akotey. He counted it slowly and then slid it into his pocket. Sunlight glinted off his mirrored lenses. 'I don't *have to* give you anything,' he said. 'But I'm feeling generous today. Here's what I'm prepared to do for you, Boureima: we'll get this piece of junk back on to the road for you. We'll tow you, *en piste*, to within a few kilometres of the river. Then you're on your own. *Ça va?*'

'And the fuel?'

'Your problem. Get some at the *camion* post. Whatever. We're saving you fuel by towing you.'

46

There was a flurry of activity, during which I sat on a rock, some distance away from the vehicles, just glad that the mutineers had, it seemed, decided to spare us.

Archie's car was manhandled back on to the road and jacked up so that the spare wheel could be fitted. Two of the mutineers attached a metal cable to the Mercedes and then shackled it to the tow bar of one of the Land Cruisers. The coffin was tacked back together and lashed onto the roof of the Mercedes once more.

Akotey's men gathered up their plunder, stowed it in the Land Cruisers and then ordered us back into the car.

It was obvious that Archie was still in some discomfort, so Abdelkrim had opted for the driver's seat again.

'Just select *neutral* and release the handbrake,' the ugly soldier said, leaning in towards Abdelkrim.

'I know.'

Another soldier set a plastic bucket, half filled with dried dates, beside me on the back seat. 'That's your breakfast!' he grinned, and then joined his companions on one of the Land Cruisers.

With the sun still rising, our convoy set off. Akotey saluted us from the first of the Land Cruisers as it pulled away in a flurry of dust and grit.

Then it was our turn; the Mercedes creaked and then moved off behind the second vehicle, eerily silent but for the strain of metal, the scuff of a rubbing tyre and the squeak of the axles. I looked out of the back window and saw the third of the trucks take up the rear, sandwiching us in this dangerous cavalcade.

A few kilometres north, the lead truck drew almost to a halt and then edged off the road, slowly. The other vehicles followed it closely, the underside of Archie's car scraping over the loose rubble as we were dragged down the slope and onto the heat-softened *piste*. Gathering speed quickly, we headed northwest across a vast, flat, barren plain.

'Where are they taking us?' I said.

'They're trying to avoid contact with authorised patrols,' Abdelkrim said. 'Don't worry.'

The fat tyres of the Land Cruisers churned up a great wake of sand, which ricocheted off the Mercedes' windshield and spilled in through the open roof and windows, quickly coating us in a thick layer of reddish dust. We tried closing the roof over, but the trapped air became stiflingly hot. Not only had the mutineers taken Abdelkrim's tea, but they had left only two bottles of water – now hot – lying on the back seat beside me.

'Fuckers!' Archie said, as he reached back for one of the bottles. He splashed a little of the water on to his palm and then flicked it into his face, a series of rivulets cutting through his dusty mask like threads of gossamer.

I offered him the bucket of dates but he shook his head. 'No, thank you. I think I've got a cracked tooth! It hurts like hell! I'm going to need to get to a dentist as soon as we get back to the capital.'

'*Merde!*' Abdelkrim said.

'Our marabout in Wadata can pull teeth,' I said, eager to help.

'I think I'll check out one of the French guys in town, thanks, Haoua.'

'These are pretty tough,' Abdelkrim said, chomping down on one of the dates.

'Like stones,' I agreed, clattering one of the fruits around in my mouth.

'They took all of your money, I suppose?' Abdelkrim said.

Archie shook his head and winced. 'No. I keep some inside the lining of my boot – for emergencies, you know. I'm more annoyed about my tools.'

Abdelkrim checked the rear view mirror. 'Hmm. And my radio!' He sucked air in through his teeth. 'At least we can buy some more fuel later.'

'You can borrow my radio, if you want to, Abdel,' I said.

We travelled in this manner for the best part of two hours. About thirty kilometres from the river crossing, we drew to a halt. The mutineers jumped down from their Land Cruisers and unhitched the Mercedes. We watched Akoteye step out of the cab of the lead truck and pad his way across the sand to the driver's window of Archie's car, flanked, as always, by two of his followers.

'What now?' I said.

'Just say nothing,' my brother warned.

Akoteye leaned on the door and peered over his sunglasses to address Abdelkrim. 'Just keep heading west now,' he said. 'You'll find the river easily enough.'

'Thank you. I know where we are,' Abdelkrim said.

'*Toh*. I think we'll meet again, my friend,' Akoteye said. Then he turned and walked back towards his Land Cruiser.

'I'm no friend of yours, you bastard!' Abdelkrim said, under his breath, as he turned the ignition key of the Mercedes.

We pulled away from the mutineers, bedraggled, perplexed, but glad to have come away from the situation alive.

'What will happen to those men if the authorities catch them?' I said.

'They'll be court-martialled,' Abdelkrim said. 'Imprisoned. Possibly executed. But they don't intend to be taken alive.' He shrugged. 'The thing is I agree with a lot of what they stand for. But violence is not the right path to democracy.' He looked over his shoulder towards me. 'It could have been a lot worse, you know, Little One.' I knew what he meant.

Archie leaned out of his window and cleared his nose. Then he yanked the plastic leprechaun from the stem of the rear view mirror. 'So much for fucking talismans!' he said, lobbing it out of the window.

Without Akoteye's Land Cruiser to pull us along, the Mercedes struggled on the soft sand. We were already tired and uncomfortable, and both Abdelkrim and Archie were in pain. The constant stopping and starting – climbing out through the car's windows, digging enough sand away to allow the tyres a purchase on the metal sand tracks and then climbing back in – ensured that our spirits remained low. After a while we even stopped talking and the whole tiresome process was repeated mechanically, in near silence.

When we finally reached Bac Farie we were exhausted and filthy. I lay back on the rear seat, breathless in the heat, engulfed in an aura of sweat and stale piss. I longed to bathe but, even as the car pulled up by the shore, Monsieur Bonanza Junior's ferry was churning towards us, its engines belching out black smoke and drowning the noise of angry crakes circling overhead.

Date palms and raggedy green ribbons of tussock grass hugged the river banks, an uplifting sight after the seemingly endless, stripped landscape through which we had previously passed.

This was only the second time that I had travelled on the ferry, but all of my life I had heard stories about its pilot, Monsieur Evarist Bonanza Junior and his aristocratic family. Monsieur Bonanza Junior's late mother had hailed from Agadez. His father was Togolese. Monsieur Bonanza Senior had served in the French military and, later, the Togolese navy before meeting Madame Bonanza and moving to Niger, where he'd worked as ferry pilot at Bac Farie for many years, finally handing over the position to his son. It was said that Monsieur Bonanza Senior was now one hundred and twenty years old, and that he still rode horses with the Touaregs and hunted wild animals with his rifle. It had been dark when I had made my first ferry crossing with Moussa and I had only caught a brief glimpse of the famous pilot in the dimly lit wheel house, but now we were able to watch Monsieur Bonanza Junior's stout silhouette moving about the bridge of the vessel as he guided it towards the shore.

'He must be very rich, to be so fat!' I said.

Abdelkrim turned the car's engine off. 'They say his family have always had money.'

'Bonanza?' Archie said. 'That doesn't sound like your typical Nigerien name.'

'It isn't,' Abdelkrim said. 'The pilot's father was from Togo originally, but they say the old man took it from an American television show that he used to love to watch.'

Archie laughed. 'God! I remember that show! Western. Cowboys. That sort of thing. . .'

'Indeed.'

'It was awful!'

The shoreline was fairly busy that morning. Two or three skiffs were already heading up river, away from the wash of the ferry, and a handful of other fishermen were repairing nets nearby. Further downstream splashes of brightly coloured fabric lay stretched out to dry on the rocks and a group of women hopped over the flattening wake, their *pagnes* tucked up around their shiny thighs. Once again I thought of my mother and had to fight back tears.

Only one other vehicle was waiting to cross to the western shore of the river: a C.A.R.E. truck, loaded with strange-looking digging equipment, driven by a Nigerien.

A group of people, mostly women and children, had gathered around the vehicle and were imploring the driver to take them to their various destinations. The driver sat quietly, staring through his windshield at the lazy, majestic river, one elbow jutting over the top of his door, a chew stick clamped between his teeth. Occasionally he shook his head or swatted away a fly, but it was clear that he was not going to be swayed. A few of the travellers glanced over at Archie's car and looked as though they were about to try us instead but, just then, the ferry docked under the expert control of Monsieur Evarist Bonanza Junior.

The incoming ferry carried no vehicles and only a handful of foot passengers. Abdelkrim waited until all of the passengers had disembarked and all of the westward bound passengers had gone on board, before slowly edging the Mercedes behind the C.A.R.E. vehicle and up the ferry's groaning ramp. No sooner had he applied the handbrake than three or four of the women, who had been pleading with the C.A.R.E. driver, approached the Mercedes and began babbling and arguing as to which of them we should convey and why.

I knew that my brother was in no mood to listen to such a cackle. At first he appeared to try to adopt the C.A.R.E. driver's stance, and ignored the barrage in his ear. Then suddenly he slammed his hand hard against the door panel, startling the women momentarily.

'I'm not taking any of you anywhere!' he barked and wound his window up until it snagged against the rope which held our mother's coffin in place on the roof.

There was a lull, during which a little stooped fellow with a ticket machine attempted to shoo away my brother's tormentors. He wound off a little strip of paper tickets for us – the colour of raw meat – and then turned to collect fares from the other passengers. But in no time the women were pushing their way back towards the Mercedes, pleading and bickering, even appealing to me through the open back window. A young woman with a child tied on to her back sidled up to Archie's window and called to my brother.

'Abdelkrim. Abdelkrim Boureima.'

Abdelkrim looked up. 'Who are you?' he said.

'Don't you remember me, Abdel?' the woman said. 'I'm

Monique Hassane from Goteye. Our parents are old friends. We heard about your poor mother and we are on our way to Wadata for her funeral. May God show us each other.'

Abdelkrim leaned forward to get a better look at her. He nodded. 'Ah, yes. Monique. It's been a long time. Forgive me, please.'

Monique leaned her head in through the open window, so that her face was close to Archie's. Her skin was beautiful. 'My mother is travelling with me, Abdel. And my child.' She glanced towards me in the back seat. 'You have room to take us to Wadata in your fine car, brother,' she said, trying to bewitch him with her large, round eyes.

Abdelkrim shrugged and looked at Archie, agitation registering on his face. 'I don't know,' he said, 'the doors don't open. . .'

Just then there was a frantic knocking at the driver's window. One of the other women who had been haranguing us earlier had her face pressed to the glass.

'Monsieur! Monsieur! My sister and I are going to your mother's funeral also. You can give us a ride. Please give us a ride. My sister has a bad leg. She has river worm. She cannot walk easily. Please, won't you give us a ride?'

Abdelkrim put his hands over his face and growled.

Monique had withdrawn her head from the car and was berating the other woman across the hood. 'Go to hell!' she called. 'You and your sister are liars and freeloaders! Go to hell!'

Archie nudged my brother. 'Let's take Monique,' he said, with a smirk. 'She may have a foul mouth, but at least she has a pretty face.'

Abdelkrim glanced over his shoulder. 'And a nice behind!' he said.

Before anyone could say anything further, Monique was calling to her mother and passing her baby in through the rear window to me. I took the child and shuffled over behind

314

Abdelkrim, as Monique clambered in, head first, through the window.

'Aiee, aiee!' Abdelkrim said. 'You don't take no for an answer, do you, sister?'

Monique unfolded her legs awkwardly. 'It is right that you take us, brother,' she puffed. 'Most of these people are free-loaders, God is my witness.' She shoved her large, rounded bottom up against me and gestured again to her mother. The older woman grabbed the handle of the door and gave it a yank. It opened partially and then sprang back against the taut rope.

'The door will not open, Monsieur!' she complained to Archie, throwing her hands up in the air. She pulled at the door again.

'Leave it, Madame! Leave it!' Archie said.

Monique leaned forward and clutched my brother's shoulder. 'Can't you lift her in?'

'*Walayi!* What do you think this is?'

'Please, Abdel. It would take my mother many hours to walk to your village. She is old and frail!'

I considered Monique's mother for a moment. I was unsure as to her age. Her skin was puckered and thin, but she certainly did not seem frail to me. In fact she was much the same build as her daughter – full and curvaceous. It struck me that she too must have been very beautiful once.

Archie and Abdelkrim looked at each other and shook their heads.

'I can't believe I'm allowing this,' Abdelkrim said, lowering his window again. 'All I want to do is bury my mother!'

Archie dabbed at his bloodied lip with his thumb. 'This whole thing is hardly turning out as I envisaged it either, my friend.'

They both scrambled out of the front windows and, each taking one of Madame Hassane's elbows, they tilted her backwards, cradled her thighs with their forearms and lugged her bulk into the car, feet first. There was a little fart sound as Madame Hassane's large rump slapped down on to the hot upholstery of the rear seat, and Monique, her baby and I were all momentarily catapulted upwards. The baby – a beautiful little girl named Divine – had been wide-eyed with curiosity, but now she gave a little cry, as confusion, perhaps even fear, set in. By the time my brother and Archie were climbing back into the car, she had opened her lungs fully.

'This just gets better and better!' Archie said.

Madame Hassane straightened her *pagne* and then leaned across in front of her daughter. 'Give the child to me,' she said, practically snatching Divine from my arms.

Behind us, the battered ramp of the ferry clanked and rattled and juddered as it was raised. The engines belched out more thick, black smoke and shook the vessel, and with a great lurch it pulled away from the shore. I had hoped to get a closer look at Monsieur Evarist Bonanza Junior but now, as I peered out at the throng of disgruntled foot passengers on the deck and considered my position, squashed against the rear door, I decided to stay put in the car for the crossing.

Abdelkrim and Archie were just settling back into their seats and Madame Hassane was babbling loudly to baby Divine when the car seemed suddenly to sag behind us. Archie stuck his head out of the window and yelled something which I could not make out, and when I looked over my shoulder I realised that the trunk lid had been sprung open and someone had climbed inside. In a flash, my brother was back out of his window, followed closely by Archie. Jammed in the back of the vehicle and with the trunk lid obscuring our view, we could only sit and listen to the yelling and bickering and watch the foot passengers as they scuttled across the deck to the hullabaloo at the rear of the Mercedes, like capitaine drawn to a lure.

Abdelkrim's voice could be heard above the commotion. Clearly he had had enough. 'Just get out of there, you old goat!' he bellowed. 'My friend has already told you that the car can carry no more weight. We will get stuck in the sand with you there. Out! Now!'

The tail end of the vehicle sprung upwards again, as the stowaway either removed himself or was wrenched from the trunk. The arguing and bickering continued as Abdelkrim slammed it shut and then he and Archie climbed back inside the car.

'*Walayi!*'

'*Merde!*'

'Incredible!'

'Can you believe it?' Archie twisted around to face me. 'Apparently nearly all of these folk are heading to Wadata for your mother's funeral!'

'They're mostly from Bankilare,' Monique said. 'Like I say, a bunch of scroungers!'

'Word travels fast,' Abdelkrim said. 'I can't say that I recognise one of them.'

Monique laughed. 'But you didn't recognise me, Abdel!'

My brother leaned his head on the steering wheel for a moment. Then, fumbling in his pocket, he leaned back in his seat heavily and lit a cigarette.

Archie patted him on the shoulder. 'We'll get through this, my friend.'

Across the deck, a few of the foot passengers were leaning over the handrail, discussing something excitedly that we could not see from the car. An elderly man pointed across the water and then raised his hands up in the air.

'What are they doing?' I said.

'That's the marabout from Bankilare,' Madame Hassane said. 'He's probably asking the spirits for safe passage across *Egerou n-igereou*.'

'River of rivers!' Monique said.

The ferry continued to hurtle across the murky waters. Madame Hassane looked at her daughter and pulled a face, as Abdelkrim's cigarette smoke snaked its way towards us, buffeted by the rush of cool air through the open windows. She clicked her tongue and then proceeded to make clucking sounds at her grandchild, who was still sobbing pitifully.

The river is wide at Bac Farie but the famous Monsieur Evarist Bonanza Junior's ferry *La République* made the crossing swiftly and safely, despite its flaking paintwork and battered hull. We bounced down the ramp on to the western shore and slowly overtook the foot passengers, a few of whom assailed us with looks of great displeasure and a barrage of foul language.

Abdelkrim waved to them as he accelerated along the dusty track, heading at last for Wadata. 'Ah, Monique,' he said. 'Your neighbours will be calling on the spirits to wrack your guts with pain!'

Monique laughed. 'Or yours perhaps, Abdel!'

'The spirits are already doing their damnedest to ruin me and my family!' my brother said, without a hint of humour.

'Azara was a good soul,' Madame Hassane said, after a brief silence.

I could not help wondering when she had last seen or spoken to my mother.

With the extra weight in the car, a rhythmic scud developed behind me and after a few minutes Abdelkrim drew the car to a halt on the softening piste. Madame Hassane and her grandchild had already fallen asleep, but Monique – whose head had been lolling against my shoulder – now sat up with a jolt.

'What's wrong?' she demanded.

'*Ça va, ça va,*' my brother said.

'Is it the tyre, Abdel?' Archie said.

'*Oui.*'

They both got out of the car and began kicking and pulling and bending the guard directly behind me, against which the tyre had been rubbing.

'It's practically worn right through!' I heard Abdelkrim say.

Archie groaned. 'Like I say, this just keeps getting better and better.'

'I'm sorry, my friend. I will reimburse you. I promise.'

Archie climbed back into the car, behind the steering wheel. 'Hey, don't worry about it. I told you I would help you,' he said, as Abdelkrim's knees drew level with his face. 'It's part of the deal.'

I expected my brother to say something, to thank his friend, but instead he leaned his head against the door pillar and closed his eyes. Perhaps it was exhaustion that made him forget his manners, I do not know. Nevertheless, I could not help but feel embarrassed, and so I took it upon myself to thank this stranger who had so quickly become a trusted family friend. 'May God smile upon you, Monsieur,' I said.

Archie Cargo shook his head. 'It's Archie, Haoua. Archie!'

47

I had been away from Wadata for just two days: the only time in my life, in almost twelve years, that I had ever stayed away from my home. Now, as the Mercedes limped across the scorched plain towards my village, I briefly experienced the sweet pleasure of home-coming that I had read about in the stories in Monsieur Boubacar's school books and those which Katie and Hope had sent me. The dull ache in my heart, that had remained with me ever since my friends' letters had dried up and I had been prevented from attending school, surfaced momentarily, but was replaced with dread when I recalled the ritual that we were about to carry out.

In the distance we could see that a throng of people had gathered on the outskirts of the village. As we trundled down the gentle incline, past Aunt Alassane's Big House, women covered their faces and shook their heads and men clasped their hands and nodded to show their respect. When I turned to look out of the back window of the car I watched them gather up their few belongings and then begin to follow us on the short route to my father's house. These then were the final stages of my mother's final journey to her home village. Before she went to join the spirits in the *Thin Place* she would make only one more short journey in this world.

Archie brought the car as close to our compound as possible. As we drew up alongside the entrance I caught sight of Adamou and Fatima, both of whom were shiny clean and dressed in their best clothes. They ran towards us as we struggled out through the car's windows for the last time, but stopped a few metres beyond the gate. I brushed myself down and looked at them with a mixture of relief and sadness. Truly, it seemed like years had passed since I had last set eyes on them, rather than just two days. Their lives had also altered forever, but at that moment none of us could have known quite how much things would change. I tried to smile at them but realised then that they were not looking at me but at the box lashed to the top of the car.

Behind us, Archie was already attempting to untie the ropes, while Madame Hassane and her daughter sat babbling and complaining, impatient to be released.

Abdelkrim took his hand off my shoulder and opened his arms wide and Adamou and Fatima trudged sadly towards us, their eyes glazed and red. Together we stood, the four of us, huddled and sobbing, until we heard my father's voice.

'Why did you put your mother's body in a coffin?' Aunt Alassane stood close by him, looking awkward but defiant. I could see only agitation on his face.

Before he turned to address Father, Abdelkrim rubbed our backs and shoulders and whispered, 'We must be strong and dignified.' He let go of us and met Father's eyes. '*Foyaney*, Father,' he said softly.

My father made no reply but stood staring, clearly waiting for an answer.

'It made transportation easier. And I remembered Mademoiselle Sushie saying that there had been a problem with wild dogs in the area.' He gestured towards the Mercedes, where Archie Cargo was edging the casket carefully towards the trunk.

I searched my father's eyes, but could find no warmth or sorrow. Just anger, embarrassment even. 'Tell the *anasara* to stop that! He is nothing to do with me or my family!' he snapped. 'Get your mother out of that thing. Her body must be washed and wrapped in white cloth before we lay her in the ground.'

'The body is already prepared, Father,' Abdelkrim said.

'My friend here, Monsieur Archie Cargo, has helped us immensely.'

My father paused, and for a moment I thought that he was going to thank Archie Cargo. Instead he retreated, with Alassane, to the house.

The mourners who had followed us from the edge of the village now sidled up to the car. I felt another hand on my shoulder and when I looked up I saw Madame Kantao's kindly face smiling down at me. Miriam was there too, holding her mother's other hand. Behind them, a sea of faces. The whole of Wadata, it seemed. And scores of people from Goteye, Bankilare, Kokorou and Wanzarba. But for every face I recognised there were at least two that I did not.

'Come, child,' Madame Kantao said. 'We must get you cleaned up before the burial.'

Indeed my clothes were filthy, and my body stank, as well as being sore and stiff. In the distance, the lament of an *algaiita* drifted across the village. As I trudged along beside my friends, my throat dry, my eyes gritty and rubbed raw, I looked back just in time to see my mother's body being lifted gently from the coffin by Abdelkrim and Monsieur Letouye. Then the crowd closed around them and filtered in to my father's compound.

My mother's body was carried to the high plateau. The marabout read the opening *Surah* of the Koran:

In the name of Allah, Most Gracious,
Most Merciful. Praise be to Allah the
Cherisher and Sustainer of the worlds.
Most Gracious, Most Merciful, Master of
the Day of Judgement, You alone do we
worship and Your aid we seek. Show us
the straight way, the way of those to
whom You have given Your favour, and
not of those who go astray.

Then all of the women and girls who had gathered for the ceremony stood back. Two lines were formed so that the angel of death might pass through. The men lifted my mother's shrouded body, chanting as they carried her away. We buried my mother next to Bunchie, among the rocks on the plateau. After her body had been placed in the ground, we all said: *From the earth have we created you, and into it shall we return you, and from it shall we bring you forth once more.*

Afterwards there was silence for a brief moment, during which one could almost hear the sand grains rasp against one another in the gentle breeze. The marabout, my father, Abdelkrim and the elders then led the procession back towards our village while Adamou, Fatima and I followed with the other mourners. Behind us, the mood had lifted and people were talking freely, openly.

'The grave is the first stage of the journey into eternity,' someone said. 'Death is a bridge that unites friend with friend.'

'May God show us each other.'

'This AIDS is a terrible thing,' I heard a younger voice pronounce, before being hushed.

'Our people have always died in this manner,' an old woman from Goteye said. 'The *anasaras* have just given it a name, that's all.'

'*Walayi*. The Hausa word for it means *Welcome to the Grave!*'

I wanted to cry, but I remembered that the prophet Muhammad (peace be upon Him) said, *Whosoever is wept upon will suffer as a result of this weeping.* My mother was gone but I knew that her spirit could still hear me.

Alassane had been following the procession with her sisters, but now she caught up with us and cradled Fatima's head in her bony hand. She put on a great display of shaking her head as if she had been my mother's dearest friend. 'You children must help your father more than ever now,' she said, sternly.

Madame Kantao put her arm around Fatima, protectively I thought, and gave me a reassuring smile.

Back at the compound, Fatima and I were kept busy, carrying water to the mourners to enable them to wash and drink. It seemed an unending task, despite the fact that Adamou and Fatima had filled every gourd and container they could find the previous evening. Mademoiselle Sushie turned up in her truck, with four huge plastic jars which she had filled at the well at Goteye. People stood about in small groups, or squatted on palm leaf mats, waiting expectantly. I wished that they would all go home, so that I could talk to my brothers and my sister, and perhaps even my father.

My father took Abdelkrim by the arm and led him out past the entrance of the compound, where Archie was preparing his car for the return journey to Niamey. I had just poured some water over the marabout's hands and decided that Archie might like to wash too. I followed Abdelkrim and my father and stopped a few metres behind them: just as they had not heard me behind them, I was unaware then of the figure standing behind me.

'Our guests must be fed, Abdelkrim,' I heard my father say. 'Many of them have travelled great distances in order to pay their respects.'

Abdelkrim looked at him blankly. 'I doubt if Mother knew half of these people, Father.'

My father made no attempt to conceal his anger. 'How would you know, soldier boy?' he snapped. 'You've had little enough to do with your family these past years! How dare you criticise others who wish to pay their last respects to your mother!'

'I think they've done that. They should go home now,' my brother said, pushing back his broad shoulders. 'And I'll remind you that my employment in the military has done you no harm.'

'What do you mean by that?'

'I think you know what I mean, Father.'

My father took a step towards Abdelkrim, so that their faces were up close.

Archie had finished packing the car and slammed the trunk closed. He looked at me and shrugged. For a moment I thought that he might intervene. The tinny sound of western music on the car radio raked across the dust towards me.

'What is it that you're trying to say, Abdelkrim?' my father said.

Abdelkrim took a step backwards, so that he was leaning against the vehicle. He coughed, then shook his head. 'Now is not the time for this, Father.'

'Now is fine.'

Their eyes were locked. They held each other's gaze for too long. Eventually Abdelkrim spoke.

'*Toh*. So be it.' He took a deep breath. 'I know you frittered away the money I sent to Mother. Where did it go, Father? On whoring and gambling? You can use what's left to feed your guests!' He side-stepped my father and made to move towards Archie, but my father caught his arm and spun him back against the body of the car.

'I have no money to feed these mourners!' he hissed. 'You must bear your responsibilities. You must help us. Do not shame me!'

Abdelkrim pushed him back, gently. 'Shame you? Shame you? You are the one who has brought shame to this family!'

My father looked furious now. 'How dare you!'

Abdelkrim glanced towards the compound entrance and saw me standing there, quiet and frightened. 'And don't talk to me about responsibilities.' He pointed towards me. 'There are your responsibilities: Haoua and Adamou and Fatima. Tell these people to be on their way and concentrate on looking after these children – instead of squandering everything you have on the likes of that old witch!' he pointed beyond me now, and as I followed the direction of his gesture I realised that Alassane was standing behind me.

She had a look on her face that was neither a smile nor a sneer but somehow both at the one time. At that moment, but for her expression, she looked perfectly respectable, ordinary, wholesome even. Her *pagne* and matching head wrap were sumptuously decorated in a swirling pattern of yellow and black. A chew stick jutted from one corner of her mouth. It was only then – as I examined her closely for the first time that day – that I recognised the string of beads which she was wearing around her thickset neck. They were my mother's. A wave of anger washed over me and for a moment, heady on my brother's indignation, I considered confronting her. But it was not to be.

'Aren't you going to tell him, Salim?' Alassane said, coldly.

My father composed himself. 'Keep out of this, woman!' he snapped. 'This is men's business.'

She gave a little sneer and sucked her teeth. '*Toh*. Then act like a man.'

My father shot her a look of irritation and then jabbed Abdelkrim in the chest.

'I can look after my family. I don't need you to tell me how to do so. I have the means to do so. Have some respect for your elders!' His finger stabbed out the beat of his words.

Abdelkrim pushed his hand aside. 'So, don't ask me to feed these hangers-on. And don't talk to me about respect. Mother is not even cold in the ground and already you flaunt this woman in front of the whole village!' There was rage in his voice now. 'I know all about your plans. The wedding, the bolt of cloth. I have heard about it all. Tell me how, exactly, are you going to provide for *her*' – he jabbed his thumb towards Alassane – 'and your children?'

'Tell him, Salim!' Alassane called.

My father hesitated. 'I will be able to provide,' he said. 'God will provide. *Inshallah*. But for now I need you to help your family.'

My brother tutted and shook his head. 'No.'

'*Walayi!*' my father groaned. 'All the money is tied up in the wedding. Monsieur Letouye has meat cuts ready for these mourners. He must be paid. I don't have it now. You understand?'

Alassane shuffled impatiently. 'Just tell him!'

'Tell me what? You've spent everything you had on preparations for marrying that woman. What else is there to know?'

My father looked down at my brother's feet and shrugged. 'It is true that I wish to marry Alassane. Soon, hopefully. I want more children, Abdelkrim. A man who has many children is rich indeed.'

'Aiiee!' Abdelkrim shook his head.

'But that is not the marriage to which we refer.'

Abdelkrim looked at Alassane and then back at my father. 'What?' he said. 'What is it that you're telling me?'

'*Tell* him!'

My father looked up. He too looked at Alassane, then at me, then at my brother. 'Your sister Haoua has been promised to cousin Moussa since she was six. It is *they* who are to be married.' He turned to face me. 'You are almost twelve now,' he said. 'It is time.'

My blood ran cold. Had my senses not already been deadened by the loss of my mother, I think I might have fainted again. A single word formed on my lips. A name. A plea. A cry for help: 'Moussa?' I said, my voice little more than a whisper.

Abdelkrim's displeasure was more obvious. 'No!' he shouted. 'I will not permit this!' He grabbed my father's *jellaba* in both hands and twisted it. 'You filthy old *zaneem*! Bastard! You won't do this to my sister!'

My father put his hands against the base of Abdelkrim's neck and pushed hard, but Abdelkrim spun him around and slammed him back against the door of the Mercedes.

'Abdel!' I shouted and ran forward to tug at his tunic.

Alassane had got there before me and had grabbed a handful of my brother's hair. I turned then and tried to push her arm away, just as Archie reached in and grabbed her by both wrists.

'Abdel!' Archie called over his shoulder, hauling both Alassane and me back towards the compound. 'Leave it! Enough! Stop!'

But Abdelkrim was not about to stop. 'It was you who killed Mother!' he screamed, his teeth bared and his face bearing down on my father's. 'Everyone knows that you're a carrier! It is you who has brought shame to this family! Do you think I'll stand by and let you destroy this child's life as well?' He slammed Father against the side of the car again. 'And now you tell me that you want more children! Why is that, Father? So that you can sell them too?'

My father – looking small now, frail, frightened – gave a final push and broke free of my brother. He raised his hand to strike Abdelkrim, but my brother caught his wrist and bent his arm up behind his back.

'Not this time, old man! And never again!' Tiny blobs of gluey saliva sprayed across my father's face.

Still struggling with Archie, I looked back, appalled at what was happening. 'Stop it, Abdel!' I cried. 'Stop it, please!'

Abdelkrim had Father by the chin now. Suddenly it seemed like he could crush him in his fist. 'You will not do this, old man. I will not allow it!' he hissed. 'You would steal her education from her and sell her into a life of servitude! It is not what Mother would have wanted.' He released his grip on Father's chin and then dropped his hands by his side. For a moment he stood silent, staring at my father who remained crumpled, like a rag, against the side of the Mercedes. Both of them were panting heavily.

I pulled away from Archie and stumbled back towards the car. I stood shaking between these two men that I loved; torn, dismayed, frightened. Some of the mourners had heard the commotion and had gathered at the entrance to the compound.

Abdelkrim looked down at me and wiped his mouth with the back of his hand. I could see that he too was shaking. He looked Father in the eye again. 'No,' he said, firmly. 'I will not allow this marriage. I am going now. But I will return very soon. I will prepare a place for my brother and sisters in the capital. I will come back for them. You will not try to stop me. You will not give Haoua to that bastard Moussa.' With that he nodded towards Archie and then walked around to the driver's side of the car. He opened the door and slid behind the wheel.

It seemed impossible to me that he should leave, just like that, after all that we had been through. Everything was happening too fast.

My father stepped aside as Archie approached the car. Then he too got into the vehicle. Abdelkrim leaned across his friend and called to me. 'I will come back for you, Little One.' He peered back towards the compound where a crowd had now formed. 'And the others. I promise. Tell them for me, won't you?'

I nodded, hesitantly, afraid that my father would catch my eye. 'When will you come for us, Abdel?' I said, my voice shaky and broken.

'Soon.' He put his hand up then and smiled his lovely smile. Then he started the engine and pulled away from our compound in a great cloud of dust.

The car turned in a slow, wide, dusty circle and then bounced its way back up the track towards the school and the Big House, Archie Cargo's pale hand just visible above the roof, waving a sad farewell to Wadata.

I followed along its tyre tracks until I came to the edge of the village, where I stood watching until the vehicle disappeared, taking with it my brother and my only hope.

Later that night, when all the mourners had finally dispersed and the house at last lay quiet but for the familiar sound of the cicadas and the crackle of sparks on the dying fire outside, I lay on my bedroll and listened to *La Voix du Sahel* on my little radio and tried not to think about the tumultuous events of those last few days. I was concentrating hard on the Malian musician Issa Bagayogo's strange song '*Ciew Mawele*' when the presenter of the broadcast cut in with an emergency newsflash.

Mesdames, Messieurs: we have just received news that the president of Niger, Ibrahim Bare Mainassara, has been shot dead in what some are claiming to be an apparent coup attempt. However, Prime Minister Ibraim Assane Mayaki has described Monsieur Mainassara's death as a 'tragic accident' and has announced that parliament has been dissolved and that all political activity has been suspended. A government of national unity is to be formed in a few days. . .

Suddenly it seemed that everything I had once thought of as permanent, solid, reliable, had begun to fragment; that anything could change, at any moment.

As I held my little radio tightly in the palm of my hand and tried to imagine a life with my brothers and sister in Niamey, I could not then have known that I would never see Abdelkrim again: that he would be killed in a skirmish just a few days later; and that my father – who had publicly disowned my brother and banished him from our family – would seize the opportunity to continue with his plan.

48

The assassination of President Mainassara did not affect Wadata a great deal at first but, with the new Wanke government attempting to clean up any resistance, the whole country became increasingly dangerous, and many foreign aid agencies ordered their employees and volunteers to get out of Niger. I was numb. My mother was gone. My brother was gone. I could not believe that I was to lose Sushie also.

I was married only a matter of weeks after Abdelkrim's death, and just days after my twelfth birthday. There was barely time to think about the terrible events that had plagued my family before my father and Alassane were making arrangements for the ceremony that would take place in our village at the end of the rainy season. The bolt of cloth that my father had purchased was brought out. Alassane's sisters fussed and schemed and instructed Monsieur Letouye about measurements and alterations for the various garments. Souley and her cronies taunted me relentlessly, informing me that I was still an unimportant little runt, a *boro dungurio*, even though I was to marry a rich man.

Adamou insisted that our grandmother Bunchie had been right and that our family were cursed because her mother had picked the flowers from a baobab tree when she was a young girl.

Fatima became withdrawn and argumentative.

Whenever I raised the subject of the marriage my father simply dismissed my concerns. 'Be still, child,' he would say. 'Do not question my judgement. Already I see these young boys looking at you. I will not have you falling into. . .

adventures and gaining a reputation. If that happens, no one will want you and I will have failed to fulfil my duties as a father! Cousin Moussa is a fine man with a good business. You will join his household and be a credit to our family. You will want for nothing and, in so doing, you will be helping us also. And you will obey him as your husband, just as you obey God!' He refused to discuss the matter further.

I went to Miriam's house and begged Madame Kantao to help me, but there was nothing she could do. She told me that she had talked to Monsieur Kantao and that he was not against the idea. I said nothing at the time, but I thought that the news did not bode well for Miriam and little Narcisse. The crops had been poor and there was less food in everyone's bellies.

I pleaded with Sushie to speak to my father and she did so, willingly, passionately, but he would not be swayed.

On the one occasion that I defied my father, I paid for my actions dearly. One evening, at dusk, I slipped away into the bush and hid beyond the pastures. Alone in the cold and the dark with the smell of fresh dung wafting around me and a chorus of cicadas ringing in my ears, I huddled on the dust, waiting for the warmth and light of the new day, when I planned to start walking towards the *camion* post. In truth I had no clear plan, but the thought had occurred to me that if I could find my way back to the capital, track down Archie Cargo and persuade him to take me to Efrance's house in the shanties, she might let me live with her: where I could help her with her baby daughter, work alongside her and, one day, perhaps, take Fatima out of harm's way too. Anything was better than the thought of being Moussa's wife. I could not even bring myself to think about what that might mean. I knew that I would miss Fatima and Adamou desperately, but I also knew that if my father got his wish, I would lose them anyway.

As Fate would have it, it was not to be. Despite the cold,

I fell asleep. Two of the elders found me. They bound my wrists and dragged me back to my father.

'You have let me down, Haoua,' he said. His eyes were cold, as if the *Shadow People* had taken his soul away.

'You must beat her, Salim!' Alassane said. By now she spent most nights sleeping in my mother's bed, and my brother and sister and I had to endure the sounds of she and my father rutting like goats in the darkness.

My father did not beat me. Instead he confined me in the bedroom for three days. I knew better than to protest, or to venture outside. I was left with a pot to piss in and given a small dish of *boule* and some water once a day. My radio was confiscated. I never saw it again. I think my father had begun to feel threatened by it.

I spent my time thinking about my mother, worrying about my brother and sister and imagining how our lives might have been, living together in the capital with Abdelkrim as our guardian. I read and re-read the letters in my bundle and wished that I could hear from Katie and Hope again. When I heard any sound outside, I hid them quickly, for fear that my father might remove these from me too. No one was allowed to visit or talk to me, but on the afternoon of the third day, while my father and Adamou and Fatima were elsewhere, Alassane entered the room, holding something behind her back.

'If you tell your father that I've been here I swear I'll kill you!' she hissed. She thrashed me so hard with a stick that I could not lie on my back for days afterwards. I taught myself to sob without a sound.

49

Haoua Boureima   Boyd
Child Ref. NER2726651832   Member No. 515820
Vision Corps International   Ballygowrie
Tera Area Development Programme   Co. Down
C/O BP 11504   BT22 1AW
Niamey
Republic of Niger
West Africa

27th September, 1999

Dear Haoua,
Please accept my apologies for not being in contact with you for
so long. I have been thinking about you and talking to my
children, Katie and Hope, about you. I am sorry, also, that we
have been misspelling your name in some previous letters: that
was really the fault of Vision Corps International! Anyway, I'm
sure you didn't really mind too much.

    Katie and Hope have just had their thirteenth birthdays! It
seems like such a short while ago that they were babies, and that
their mother and I had to bath, feed and change them! Now they
are taller than their mother and continuing to grow fast.

    How are you getting on at school? It would be great to hear a
little about what you are learning and what you like to do best. I
think I told you that I am a teacher, so it would really interest
me to know more about your school. Perhaps you would like to
make a little drawing of the school for us? We still have the little
map of Niger that you drew, and your fingerprint and all of

your letters. We also still have your photograph on display in our house, so you are part of our family!

I hope that your parents and your brothers and sister are well. I hope your father's crops have been good and that your mother is fully recovered and happy in her work once again. Is she still housekeeping? That's hard work too, I know: as well as my job, I am kept busy – washing, cleaning, cooking and looking after Katie and Hope.

Unfortunately their mother and I no longer live together, which has been sad for all of us, but we are trying to stay happy anyway! The children live with me for half of the week and with their mother the rest of the week. I suppose you will think that very strange, and indeed it has been strange for us too. But we are beginning to get used to it now.

I seem to remember that your father keeps some chickens, Haoua? We also have a few, which we keep as pets, and for eggs. I have a problem with one of our chickens at present: a young cockerel has declared himself 'king' and has bullied our older cockerel away from the hens! He hurt the older bird badly. The old cockerel has recovered, (Katie and Hope call him Cassidy), but he cannot live with the other hens now. One minute everything was peaceful in our garden and the next, poor Cassidy was almost dead! Maybe we'll just have to make him into soup!!! Or perhaps the younger bird should be made into soup and Cassidy returned as king: I think, however, we are all too frightened of the younger bird to try to touch him! We had some ducks too, but last year, when the snow was lying thick on the ground and food was hard to come by for many wild animals, a fox killed all of them!

Well, Haoua, I will close now. It is very early in the morning here. Outside, the birds are singing, but it is still dark! It is very cold here at present. Winter has come early. We have water piped right into our house, but when I went to get some, earlier, it was frozen solid! I have to go and do some work now, but I will try to write more often.

Katie and Hope will be home later today and perhaps they

will also write to you again. Meanwhile, you take care. Best
wishes to you, your family and your beautiful country.

Yours affectionately,
Noel Boyd

P.S. Enclosed please find some sweets, a packet of sunflower
seeds and, since you liked the first one so much, another little
solar-powered calculator – which needs no batteries! Perhaps
you will want to give this one to a friend?

Numbness enveloped me on my wedding day. I was left
alone in my father's house and covered with a large, scratchy
blanket that I had never seen before. Outside, in our compound, I could hear the village griot loudly reciting an
ancient story about marriage. Our neighbours celebrated
wildly and I felt the stomp of their feet on the ground, as they
leapt and shook and twirled in the excitement and excess of
the day. The day. My day. Their day. They howled and
shrieked and trilled into Monsieur Letouye's microphone
and, like the mating call of some deranged bird, the microphone squealed back at them.

Then the pace changed. The ground ceased to vibrate.
Accompanied by much laughter, Alassane's tuneless voice led
a chorus of women in the *Camel Song*.

Someone struck up the rhythm on a *tendi* and then a
water drum, a *tassinack* flute and an *imzhad* joined in. My
mother used to sing the same song to us when we were little.
Her voice was so much sweeter.

The door of the house lay open. Light filtered into the
room through the dividing curtain leading into our living
area. I sat forward on my little stool and, lifting my veil, tried
to peer through the curtain to the frenzy outside.
Occasionally I caught a glimpse of a whirling figure, a splash
of indigo and blue, a blur of teal and gold. A bead of sweat
trickled from my brow, down my cheek and across the

corner of my mouth. I caught it with my tongue, tasted its saltiness. The room was muggy, the air stale, yet, despite the heat, I realised that my stomach was knotted, empty, cold. I pulled the blanket close around my shoulders and listened now to the storytellers. I thought about all the weddings that I had attended with my family, in Wadata and the neighbouring villages, and about how little concern I had had for those brides as I had danced and feasted with the rest of the revellers. Bouchra Hassane, Nabila Djambe, Rekia Salamatou: where were they now? What had become of them? I shivered again.

Late in the afternoon, when the dancing and singing and storytelling had stopped, I knew that all the men-folk would be sitting outside in our compound, huddled between the clay granaries, preparing to seal my marriage to Moussa Boureima officially. I knew that Moussa himself would not be there. He would be waiting for me in his house in Niamey. I had no idea how I was to join him. I knew that his family – his mother, his brothers, his sister and cousins – were all outside. And that they had brought many gifts: fine leather sandals cured with camel piss, western-style dresses, fabric, succulent fruits, all wrapped in swatches of deep blue cloth. I knew that his family would offer my father a symbolic bride price (a small part of the total sum payable) and that then, the ceremony finally over, both families would exchange candies and kola nuts as a gesture of goodwill.

And so I became the third wife of Moussa Boureima.

All of my friends from the village filtered into our little house and sat on the floor of the outer room. From the dim bedroom I could hear and recognise their giggling and whispers. There were people there also whom I did not even like, and the voices of youthful strangers. Hordes of women scurried about busily, to and fro: many of them were unknown to me too. Finally the curtain between our two rooms was drawn back and, through the outer doorway, I could see a hired photographer in an *anasara*'s stiff suit, weaving his way through the crowd outside. The younger children – including Fatima and little Narcisse Kantao – jostled each other at the entrance to try to catch a glimpse of me, until Madame Kantao or one of the other women shooed them all away, laughing and squealing. I thought to myself: *this is what it must be like for the animals at the zoo in Niamey!* And yet I was not fearful. Not then. Not yet. I had had long enough to contemplate my situation and the true misery of loss. Bunchie had taught us to accept what Fate had decided for us, because nothing we could do could change that path. And now, when I thought about it, I realised that she was right all along and that people like Mademoiselle Sushie, Richard, Monsieur Boubacar and even my poor, dead brother Abdelkrim – for all their care and love and good intentions – could never have helped me. I consoled myself with the fact that at least I would be away from Alassane's wrath and jealousy.

Outside, the music and laughter and dancing started up again. Aisha, the old midwife, brought me a cup of water, some *manioc* and beans and a little pot of dates.

'I pray to God that this marriage will take,' she said. *'Inshallah.'*

From time to time other women would enter the room and shout *Barka!* Congratulations! or offer me some words of advice. *Give to your husband*, or *Your husband is just below God*, or *God has smiled upon you – the wife of a rich man!* But Miriam's mother just clucked her tongue and pressed my knee.

Darkness crowded in on us. I was dizzy with tiredness and hunger. Someone – I don't remember who – took me by the elbow and led me out of the bedroom, through the living room and into the compound. Through my wedding veil I noted the fires dotted about our yard, serving the little knots of women who had gathered to witness and participate in my betrothal. They huddled together in tight little groups while the sparks danced around and above them before fading away in the cool night air. There was not a man or boy to be seen now.

I was set down on another little stool in the middle of the compound. Aisha squatted in front of me. She took a piece of cloth and dipped it into a gourd, then, lifting the veil away, she began to wipe my face. Some of the other women shuffled forwards and, taking straw sponges and soap, began scrubbing my arms and legs until they stung. They dried me off and painted beautiful henna symbols onto my hands and feet to ward off evil spirits. Then, behind me, someone started to trill again. The throng of women took up the song, chanting and clapping and pushing towards me from all directions until a frenzied circle of leering, screeching faces – eyes stretched wide in the darkness, teeth reflecting the light from the fires – and shuddering limbs and prodding fingers closed around me so tightly that a mantle of body heat overpowered me and left me breathless and panic-stricken. For a brief moment I thought that I might pass out. Instead, I closed my eyes and tried to force back my tears. *Marriage is a good thing in the eyes of God*, I told myself, digging my fingernails into my thighs.

Looking back, it could not have taken long. But at the time I thought that it might never end. At last, everything went still. Aisha put her leathery hands around mine and raised me off the stool. Then a cluster of the women fussed around me like mother chickens and I was shuffled back into my father's house.

My wedding was over.

Back inside, I sat silently, dazed, with my head stooped and covered, unaware even if I had company in the room. My ears were ringing and my body ached as if I had carried water all day. When all the guests had left and the dust finally settled outside, I was led to the entrance of our compound, where two men I had never seen before were waiting in a white pick-up. Someone opened the cab door and a hand guided me towards it. Suddenly I felt terrified. I looked up and threw back the veil from my face. I peered around, my tear-stung eyes straining through the darkness, searching for Fatima, Adamou, even for my father who had sold me.

Only Aisha, tired and bent, and Madame Kantao were there with me.

'My sister? My brother?' I said, my voice like a ghost of itself.

Madame Kantao's warm eyes met mine. 'You will see them soon, child,' she said, stroking my face gently, as Aisha's bony hand clutched at my arm and pulled me towards the vehicle.

Then it was gone. All of it. Everything. The remnants of my family, my friends, my home, my village. All disappearing into the darkness as I peered through the rear window, squeezed between these silent, sweating strangers.

Ahead of me lay Niamey once again. Behind me, my hacked-off life: fading, fragmenting, like a recent dream.

Epilogue

The pain in my back and chest eases, or perhaps I grow accustomed to it. Not so the ringing in my ears and the pressure around my forehead and tear-stained temples – now dry and salty and tightened like the skin of a *tendi*. For a moment I think that I can actually hear the pounding in my head but then I realise that the sound is coming from outside. I wrap the few remaining fragments of my pictures and photographs up in my bundle and tie it back onto my waist. I stand unsteadily, one hand gripping the arm of Moussa's chair, my legs quivering, my head swimming in the stagnant air.

I peer directly, defiantly, into the warm shaft of sunlight that streams through the small, deep-cut window. The hot, blinding light is almost painful, but I resist the urge to shield my eyes. From the midst of this dazzling core, a lost dragonfly emerges and flits towards me. I blink at last, squeezing tiny droplets from the corners of my eyes. I turn my head towards the door as the insect sails majestically into the dark hallway, its blue metallic flank glinting momentarily in the light. I am reminded of the military helicopters that roared overhead the day Abdelkrim and I went in search of Archie Cargo. The day my world fell apart.

Abdelkrim. And Mother. Both gone. There is a darkness, a resolve, a hatred even in my soul which both frightens and strengthens me.

I steady myself, then take a step, pushing off against the chair. I wince, but continue towards the door. I step out of the unfinished room, limp down the hallway, my feet scudding through the dust, past the second bedroom and out into the bright kitchen with its solid, concrete floor. There is no one in the room. Outside, the thud, thud, thud continues. I lift the lid from a large plastic jug on the table and pour myself some water. My hand shakes as I lift the cup to my mouth and the liquid cascades down my chin and leaves a damp patch on my pale green *pagne*. I had liked this garment. Moussa had handed it to me without a word when I had first arrived at his house and, although I had searched his face for warmth and found none, I had accepted it graciously and worn it gladly. A present from my husband. How could I not accept it? Fate had already decreed it, just as Bunchie had always said. Besides, most of my own clothes had been taken from me – thrown away probably. I was lucky to have been able to hold on to my bundle. Now I look down and notice that there is a large rent down one side where Doodi grabbed at me as I tried to flee her latest punishment. Not the first beating I have endured since coming here three months ago. And certainly not the last.

Later. I will repair it later. There are other garments to see to also. A pile of laundry to smooth, another to scrub, food to prepare, animals to tend to, as well as all my other duties. I step out onto the veranda and then descend the steps to the yard, the afternoon sun hitting me immediately like a blast from a bread oven. A few metres to my left, Yola is pounding millet vigorously, rhythmically, humming as she works. She looks up and stops when she realises I am watching her.

'Haoua,' she whispers. 'Why did you not just get on with cleaning Moussa's room and look at your pictures later?' Droplets of sweat cling to her brow, like jewels.

I say nothing.

'Are you all right, child?' Her eyes show concern – and

nervousness. They flit about, like the dragonfly inside, before it determined its true path.

'I am all right.'

'*Toh*.' She goes back to her work.

I wave my hand to attract her attention again. 'Where is she?' I say.

Yola rests the pestle on the mortar and wipes her forehead with the back of her hand.

'Doodi,' I say. 'Where is she?'

Yola puts her finger to her plump lips to hush me. 'She is resting,' she hisses, urgently. 'Be sure you don't look for more trouble!' She points towards the house.

I look over my shoulder, half expecting to see her coming at me again. A sharp pain at the base of my neck surprises me and I flinch.

Yola takes a step towards me, but I wave her away.

I take a deep breath. 'Why does she hate me so, Madame Yola?'

She shrugs. 'I have endured her cruelty for two years. You will learn to avoid her wrath – and she will become more tolerant of you.'

'How can I do that?' I say, indignantly, kicking a sandal off and ploughing my toes through hot sand. 'What did I do wrong except stop for a moment to look at my treasures and ask if I could watch television at our neighbours' house this evening? I have worked hard all day. I would have finished the room as she had bid me.'

Yola nods. 'I know it.'

'Doctor Kwao-Sarbah gave me a ride in his car yesterday when I was returning from the market. He said that I should ask Moussa if I could watch television with his daughter Candice again this evening. They are having many guests and neighbours to celebrate *Eid al-Adha*. He said that we are all welcome.'

Yola nods again. 'Yes. Doctor Kwao-Sarbah's generosity is legendary in Yantala.'

'So I asked Madame Doodi. . .'

Yola lowers her head. Then she raises her nervous, reddened eyes again and whispers. 'It is an *excuse*, Haoua. She is jealous of you – and me. You must be quiet and careful and patient. She cannot beat me now. I am with child. Moussa will not permit it. He wants many children, but their marriage did not take. Doodi is barren, dried up, wizened. She has failed to give her husband children. But even so, he will not lay a hand on her.' She allows herself a little grin. 'I think that even Moussa is frightened of Doodi!'

My cheeks sting a little as I too smile, and the ringing in my ears rises a pitch. 'I think she is a witch!' I say. 'I hate her – and I hate him too!'

Yola attempts to wave my words away. '*Walayi!* Keep your voice down, child! Do you want another beating so soon?'

'It's true!' I say. 'May God have mercy on me, but it's true. Why does he beat me also? He promised my father that he would take good care of me. Be a good husband. These promises he breaks. What have I done to deserve these things, Madame Yola?'

She spills her hand towards me and shrugs. I know these are questions that she cannot answer.

Before me, Yola's image bends and wavers as my eyes fill with tears. I blink them back, angrily, my face flush with heat and fury. 'He hurts me at night-time also,' I say, without looking up.

'I know it.' She is staring at the ground again. 'It is the way of things,' she says, her voice barely audible. 'We held the *Marcanda* for you. We invited all the married women in Yantala. Doodi and I exchanged insults.' When she looks up her eyes are glazed and, I think, filled with memories, wishes, regrets.

I stare at the bump in her belly. 'Did he rape you too?'

She sighs and reaches again for the pestle. 'I am his wife. And so are you, Haoua. It is the way of things.'

* * *

I know that there is more work to be done. Always there is more work to be done. But I turn away from Yola and limp to the farthest corner of the compound where, listing behind the latrine, the Whistling Mgunga tree stands.

'Haoua! Haoua!' Yola calls, but I do not answer her.

I lean against the trunk and run my fingers over its scaly bark, its dappled shadow still in the breathless air as if painted on to the dust, the wall, the side of the latrine house. Its heady scent a welcome relief from the stink of human faeces. I find my footing, as I have many times since coming to this house and, despite my aching limbs, manage to pull myself up the great tree, high above the stench and the raging knots of gorged flies. Here, lodged into the v-shape formed by two great boughs, I can feel safe, calm – at least for a little while. This is where I go to think. Not when Moussa is around, or if Doodi is awake, of course. But when the time is right. I settle into my place, my buttocks wedged un-comfortably between the branches. One long, thick bough stretches above the roof of the little house which Moussa has had built for Yola. Carefully avoiding the jagged thorns, I reach out to stroke the small white and yellow flowers, their honeyed perfume enveloping me, making my head dizzy. I shuffle to make myself more comfortable and feel my *pagne* stick to the gummy sap at my back. From here I can look out over both Moussa's compound and Doctor Kwao-Sarbah's. Across the rooftops I can see the glittering dome of the Mosque du Gao. In the mornings, when I wake up in my little storehouse, I can hear the call of the Imam's devotions. Soon after I arrived in Niamey Yola helped me clear the garbage from this building where Moussa had left me amongst the oilcans and bicycle parts and plastic bags the night before I learned about the death of my mother. We swept the floor and stacked Moussa's tools and clutter on a bench at one end of the little structure. I found a place to keep my thin bedroll and an empty Solani container in which to keep my few belongings: my beads, a bracelet given to me by Madame Kantao, my plastic comb. My treasures I used to keep with me at my hip, safely bundled together. My letters, postcards, photographs. My life. Gone now, but for fragments and a single image of Abdel and my mother, with Momi and Efrance, which I keep hidden in my storehouse. These, then, are my physical refuges: my storehouse, my Whistling Mgunga tree, occasional visits to and glimpses of Candice Kwao-Sarbah's world. My spiritual refuges have been my treasures, my memories and God Himself (I have long ago discarded my amulet). Doodi has taken away my treasures. God has abandoned me. Now, only my memories remain, and these I must cling to.

I pull a heavily-laden offshoot towards me, drink in the thick scent of its flowers, then let it spring away from me again. I think about the baobabs at Wadata – 'the upside down trees' we called them: about climbing them, getting leg-ups to their gnarled boughs and reaching out to pull the next person up too; jeering boys spitting on us from above; warning each other never ever to pick the flowers. Bunchie said that to do so invited bad luck, evil spirits, into one's home. She said that, in Goteye, a niece of Madame Fatake had done so and that was why Madame Fatake had given birth to twins whose backs were stuck together. I picture Bunchie's tired, sad, crumpled face, telling me that the babies had died and that we should not talk any more about such things. But sometimes, when our crops were poor or attacked by locusts, or the rains failed, or someone in our family took the sleeping sickness or *nagana* or was bitten by a tse-tse, or it seemed that the harmattan storm would never end, she reminded us that her own mother had also picked flowers from the upside down trees.

I picture Abdelkrim, handsome in his uniform. I shake my head as the image of him with a bullet in his skull tries to fight its way into my mind. I picture my mother, slowly disappearing into herself. I try to imagine her two dead babies

– my brothers – but no faces will come. I try to imagine Bunchie's mother plucking flowers from the upside down trees and wonder why the old gods have sent such sorrows our way.

I think about Fatima. I wonder if my father has already promised her to another cousin, or uncle, or friend. I hope that she will instead have an education and be saved from a future like mine. I wonder if she will make friends with *anasara* children from the other side of the world. I think about Katie and Hope and their father's father's father who lived such a long life. I wonder if they miss my letters, as I miss theirs.

I think about Monsieur Boubacar, the surprised look on his broad, kind face as he recoiled from my father's snarling features. *She could be a doctor, or a teacher, or a great writer*, he had said. *A great writer*. I had hoped to read many books. I had hoped to travel to the places he showed me on his maps. To go far beyond L'arbre du Ténéré and gaze upon the ocean. I watch little pieces of Mgunga blossom fall away like my dreams.

I think about Adamou and pray that he will not follow the ways of our father. I wonder if he is now attending Koranic school. Again I try to imagine what it might have been like living here in Niamey with my sister and brothers. Being cared for by Abdelkrim. Perhaps becoming friends with Efrance and Momi. I think about Miriam. See her in the classroom, eagerly raising her hand to answer a question. And about her mother on the evening before my marriage, trying to reassure me that I would, most likely, be eased into life with Moussa's family. That he would leave me alone. Let me settle. Before. . . that. It did not happen. He took me on the first night. Yanked me by the wrist from the sanctuary of half-sleep, dragged me from my bedroll, my storehouse, across the compound and into his bedroom. Doodi in the next room. Hurt me. Bloodied me. Left me shivering on the floor, afraid to cry out loud, while he retired to his raised sprung bed; grunting, snoring, farting.

I think about Mademoiselle Sushie. I see her bright smile. Hear her warm, cheeky voice taunting the elders, causing the womenfolk to double up with laughter. I wonder where she is now: if she has left Wadata, perhaps Niger itself; if VCI and the other agencies will ever return. I think about Moussa Boureima. My husband. I have watched him in the dim light after he has fallen asleep, beside or on top of me. Watched the drool ooze from the corner of his slippery lips. Listened to the whistle of the wind through his nostrils. His gurgling, bloated stomach fanfaring the night. I think about his great weight. His thick, heavy limbs thrown across my torso like the rubbery roots of the baobab tree. Feared his wrath, if I disturbed his slumber, as I kicked away the cascading mosquito net and heaved my squashed, near breathless body away from his bulk. Feared his cruel tongue, the flat of his hands, the wooden paddle that he keeps on the shelf.

It was said on my wedding day that love would grow, but I know that it will not. Though I know that it is wrong, I hate this man. I will never love him. I am shocked to realise that I no longer have feelings for my father also. Now, after everything, there is only numbness. Here and now I decide that, if I become an adult, I will one day find my father and I will say to him: *This is me, Haoua Boureima, who was your daughter. I am disgusted by you. I feel nothing else for you. I will not treat you as my father.*

I realise too that deep within me there is a burning sensation. An ache, a fire. Not in my belly, like that caused by hunger or fouled water, but deeper still. From within my soul perhaps. Deeper than the hatred I feel for my husband or the numbness I feel towards my father.

It is anger. Rage. And panic, driven by fear and loneliness. And now, high above the compound, safely wedged between the branches of my Whistling Mgunga tree, where I have retreated many times before, closer to the spirits of Bunchie, Mother, Abdelkrim and all the *Shadow People* who have gone before them, and closer to God too, I realise that it is God Himself with Whom I am angry.

This is the moment that I lose my faith. The moment I truly realise and accept that I have been abandoned, not only by my flesh father but by my spiritual one. I have not prayed for days. I did not fast properly for Ramadan. Stealing crusts from the kitchen through the day. Guzzling water at the faucet when no one else was around to see.

As if to confirm this revelation, the constant pounding of Yola's pestle ceases. I look down and watch her lean the wooden club, worn smooth by years of pounding millet, against the gable end of the house. I recall her – before *Eid ul-Fitr* – stooping to pick up a little clay spittoon, summoning a loud, raw, rasping, animal-like growl to clear her throat then, pointing her lips into a fine spout, to deposit a stringy residue expertly into the tiny clay pot.

All day she kept it by her side. She did not swallow so much as a morsel of food or a drop of water. Not even her own saliva. She did not do so between sunrise and sunset throughout Ramadan. She took her spittoon, overflowing like a foul little pot of slimy glue, and flung its contents into the latrine and only when the sun went down did she replenish her body. But it is now *Eid al-Adha*, and tonight when the sun goes down, especially tonight, she will feast – with Doodi and the womenfolk of our neighbours' compounds, all dressed in their finest clothes.

She will finish this work, then she will return to the house and help to prepare the food. There will be laughter and music and singing and dancing, all in the name of the God who has forsaken me.

This is our way. But I will not do it any more. I think again of Abdelkrim. Of his lack of belief. His alcohol drinking, failure to pray. The concern these things caused my mother, and how her fears were passed then to me.

Around my face, the scent of the Mgunga flowers mingles with the rising diesel fumes from the traffic thundering by our compound. I feel nauseous, dizzy. For a moment I think that I may vomit. I imagine emptying the contents of my rumbling belly in a vile cascade down the bark of the great tree, then quickly banish the thought. I take deep breaths of the heavy, tainted air and put my head in my hands.

Below me, to my left, lies Doctor Kwao-Sarbah's compound. Today there is no sign of Candice, his daughter, who has become my only true friend here in Niamey's Yantala district. Candice is fourteen – two years older than me. This morning she and her shy, handsome brother, Etienne, will have stepped outside the Kwao-Sarbah family's fine home in their clean-smelling, freshly pressed, red and grey school uniforms. Candice will have skipped across the neat yard, scattering the chickens as they picked through the cracked earth, and waved to her kindly Egyptian mother. She and Etienne will have placed their fine satchels and lunch pails on the rear seat of their father's car and climbed inside – just as I have seen them do many times before. Khalaf, their family's Fulani guardian, will have swung back the great metal gates and Doctor Kwao-Sarbah's clean, white Land Cruiser will have swept on to Rue de Kongou and roared off towards the heart of the city. Candice will have glanced back and up at my tree to see if I have been able to steal away from my duties, but she will not have seen me this morning.

I think of Doodi, ridiculing me for calling myself a friend of Candice's. Chiding me for protesting when she tells me that I cannot visit the Kwao-Sarbah's compound this evening.

'Remember your place, girl,' she had said, before she had set upon me, teeth bared. 'That child is the daughter of a rich man!'

Momentarily, I had risked looking the old witch in the eye. 'And I am the wife of a successful merchant, am I not?'

That was when she had begun to flail all around her. 'You are nothing but a little whore and an errand girl!' she had screamed at me.

I scan the compound again, searching for a glimpse of Khalaf. He is nowhere to be seen. A fly lights on my lower lip, hooking a thin, tickling leg over its upper curve, so that its spindly foot lightly touches the moist, inner part of my mouth. I spit, violently, shaking my head with irritation.

Yola rubs her eyes and peers up into the branches. 'You'd better come down now, child,' she says, staggering a little, steadying herself with her pestle. 'He will be back soon!' She waggles her drained head towards the entrance of the compound as she speaks.

I peer down at her tiny figure. Sweat drips from her brow. Her eyes look wrung dry. Suddenly I feel defiant, powerful. I do not answer. I peer down, through the thin branches and foliage and scent. I hold my hand out so that it masks Yola's gently bulging figure entirely. I bear no malice towards this woman yet, for a brief, terrifying moment I imagine what it would feel like to crush her in my hand, like a helpless insect. I think, What if God simply allows these things because He is not, in fact, a just God, as the Holy Koran teaches? What if He is malicious, or jealous or bored? And although the thought chills me, it stays with me, just the same.

I am on my knees, sifting pounded millet, when the clanking of bicycle parts announces Moussa's arrival home. Yola gathers up her utensils and walks towards the house as he enters the compound.

'Bring the grain to me as soon as you are finished,' she says. Her eyes flit momentarily towards Moussa, then back to me.

In that brief exchange, I read a signal and venture a glance in Moussa's direction. We both know that he has consumed alcohol.

He scowls at us and then lets go of the bicycle. It falls to the ground and lies twisted, useless, spent in the settling dust like a felled gazelle.

As Moussa follows Yola, I resist the urge to get to my feet and go to the bicycle. Lift it up. Dust it down. Soothe it. Lean it against the wall of my storehouse.

To do so would be to invite Moussa's wrath. I have little doubt that part of the reason he treats the machine with such carelessness is to aggravate me, but mainly he does it because he can – and because he is a pig. Several times I have asked him for the use of a bicycle. He has many: gleaming new ones in his shop; tatty old ones in pieces, both in the shop and lying in a jumbled heap in and behind my storehouse. A bicycle would make my life so much easier; carrying goods from the market would be so much quicker, so much less exhausting. But each time, Moussa snorts and laughs at my requests.

'Do you think that I am made of money?' he says, shaking his head. He has forbidden me to waste his money on taxi fares also. Every centime must be accounted for.

I think of Djibo, a boy back in Wadata, whose father had brought a fine, black bicycle back after a trip to the city. For a moment I wonder if he might have purchased it from Moussa. With this machine, Djibo was able to ride to the river, draw two buckets of water and return to our village before we were even half way there on foot. Perhaps he spilled more than we did, our buckets and jars balanced expertly on our heads – his swinging precariously on the handlebars – but it hardly mattered because he could make another trip so easily.

'You're not in Wadata now, girl!' Moussa snaps, when I tell him about Djibo. 'We live a civilised life in Niamey. How many other households do you know with running water?'

'But the walk from the market!' I say. 'The purchases are so very heavy! If I could. . .' Sometimes the look in his eye is enough to stop my protestations. At other times, when I am feeling more reckless, it takes the flat of his hand.

On occasion, I have even heard Doodi chastise Moussa for the misuse of his machine. 'A man in your position ought to take care of such things; show others that you are a dignified businessman!' Though he might grumble, he never lays a hand on his senior wife.

Later, I am scrubbing clothes, head down, lost in thought, sweat dripping from my brow, when I see his gnarled, yellowed toenails before me. I look up at his face, shield my eyes from the afternoon sun. 'Husband?' I say.

'Come with me,' he says, without explanation. He turns his back and walks towards the storehouse. Cautiously, I look around the compound. Yola and Doodi are indoors, preparing food for this evening's celebrations. I dust down my *pagne* and stretch my aching neck from side to side. As I follow Moussa, the pain in my side catches me unawares and I let out a slight gasp. Moussa stops and turns towards me. He removes a chew stick from his mouth and sucks his teeth irritably. 'Get a move on, girl,' he says. 'We haven't got all day!'

A shiver passes through my body as I try to prepare myself, once again, to be defiled. For a brief moment, a wave of anger washes over me as I consider the injustice of my situation, the ordeal that I have already endured today at the hands of that witch Doodi. Then, as I trudge across the compound behind my husband, the futility of protest as clear as daylight, I seem to move outside my own body, as I have learned to do – watch this slight, dead-eyed girl move in step with the man towards the inevitable act of brutality – and fear leaves me to be replaced with the familiar and welcome mantle of numbed resignation.

But Moussa passes the open doorway to my storehouse and walks instead towards the corral, where our small herd of goats and *moutons*, seeking shade, has pressed itself against the compound wall.

I shake myself alert, suddenly aware that Moussa has turned to speak to me again.

'Be sure none of the beasts get by you,' he says. He pauses, noticing my swollen lip and bloodshot eye, perhaps, but does not comment. Then he enters the corral and grabs a young ram by the horns. The rest of the wide-eyed herd circle the enclosure, aware that the selected beast's time has come. A young hogget stops and squares up to me, considering its chances, then bleats forlornly and scuttles along behind the rest of the herd. A ewe darts back towards the gate, stops in its tracks and shits, before moving off again. 'Get ready to open the gate!' Moussa calls, as he drags the terrified ram towards me. The animal twists and lurches as I close the gate behind it, its back hooves digging into the gritty sand and leaving deep trenches as Moussa bears his weight down on its shoulders. 'Grab the haunches! Grab the haunches!' he calls, as he loses his grip with one hand. I throw myself at the animal's rear, grabbing fistfuls of its coarse hair, while Moussa regains purchase on its horns before wrestling it finally to the ground. 'Hold it!' he calls. He brings his knee up and lays his shin across the ram's windpipe. The helpless creature's eyes are full of fear. It struggles once again and I grip all the harder. Moussa draws a cord from a pocket and, catching the animal's front legs in the crook of his arm, binds them together just above the hock. The ram makes a deep, forlorn bleat and then kicks violently with its back legs, catching me in my already tender ribcage. Before I know it, I have released my grip and the beast has twisted its haunches around so that its rear sticks up towards the sky, despite Moussa grappling with its shoulders. He pushes me aside and kicks the animal's feet from under it. 'You stupid girl!' he snarls at me. He falls squarely onto the animal's flank and digs an elbow into the side of its head. 'Pin it down while I tie the back legs!' Moussa shouts. 'And don't let go this time!' The animal grunts as Moussa shifts his weight. I do as I am bid, falling upon the creature so that my face is close to its head and I am looking directly into its staring, pleading eye and breathing its hot breath and the stench of terror. In a moment, Moussa has bound the back legs and the animal is helpless.

Moussa stands up and dusts himself down. He scowls at me again, and for a moment I think that he may beat me. But there is still work to be done, as always. Moussa gives the animal a kick and then crosses to the fence where a skinning knife is hanging in its sheath. He draws the blade out and runs his finger along its ancient dark grey edge to check that it is sharp. He looks up and catches my eye, bares his bad teeth at me and says, 'We'll feast tonight.' He laughs and I stand back as he moves again towards the hobbled animal. Standing before the beast for a few moments, he seems to hesitate. He looks at me again. Cold eyes. Then he drops to his knees, lays the knife down close to the creature's head and begins a hurried prayer over the still bleating ram.

When he has finished praying, he gets to his feet again, lifting the knife as he rises. He turns again to look at me. 'You like to watch this part, *Little One?*' he says, his voice full of sarcasm, the blade dipping and thrusting in my direction.

Don't call me that! I think. *It is not your right to call me that!* I move back to the fence, aware that what he has said is true: I am unable to take my eyes off the blade; I have watched my father perform this task many, many times, yet I am still fascinated by the moment when a simple act, a slight movement, removes life from a living, breathing creature. The ram's final, protesting bleat is stifled as Moussa forces its chin upwards and pierces its throat with the point of the knife. A deep, red arc cascades upwards and outwards before spilling on to the dust and, as the animal's body stiffens and shudders, Moussa draws the blade expertly across its windpipe and calls for a bowl. I stand frozen as I watch the life ebb away from the animal, a dull greyness replacing the former brightness of its eyes. Then the sound of Moussa's impatient voice brings me again to my senses.

'The bowl! The bowl!' he shouts, reaching a bloodied hand towards me. I hand him the battered metal bowl.

He snatches it away from me, shakes his head and says, '*Walayi!*' Then he tells me to find him a good straight stick.

I cross the compound and begin to scratch through the dust and debris in the shadow of the Whistling Mgunga tree until I find a suitable stick. It takes no time at all but, when I return to the corral, Moussa is squatting beside the limp carcass with his elbows resting on his knees, waiting for me, his chew stick clamped between his teeth and a foul look on his face. As I offer him the stick, he jumps to his feet and lunges towards me. The sudden movement alarms me and I step backwards, my eyes wide with anticipation and fear.

'You are such a stupid girl, aren't you?' he says, catching my forearm and yanking me forwards. 'What kept you? Why do you dawdle so?' The tip of his chew stick almost touches my cheek.

'I am sorry, Monsieur. . .' As I speak, my hand opens involuntarily and the stick drops to the ground.

For a moment he stares deep into my eyes, and though I know I ought to lower my gaze, I cannot. His breath – hot, metallic, tinged with alcohol – wafts around my face, and I feel my gut tighten. His dirty, bloody fingernails dig into my skin so hard that I wince and peer at my arm. The fingers of my left hand are curled towards the sky, palm upwards, Moussa's grip rendering it limp, lifeless, as if it too has recently been slaughtered. I gaze at the skinning knife in his fist. For a moment I think there may be a part of him that might wish to use it on me. At last, he releases his grip, leaving a bloodied impression of fat fingers on my forearm. He shakes his head, stoops to pick up the stick and, turning his back on me, squats down before his kill. Then I hear him suck his teeth as he begins to whittle the stick into a sharp point.

'Should I return to my chores, Monsieur?' I ask, my voice shaky.

'You stay nearby,' he says, without looking at me. 'I may need you again.' He inspects the point of his stick, tests it against his palm, then, with a grunt, leans forward and, hooking a finger into the loop of cord, drags the dead animal's rear legs onto his lap. Its head lolls to one side, the tongue protruding now, giving the creature an almost comical expression. Its rear legs jerk apart as Moussa inserts the bloody blade between the hooves and cuts the cord. Then, seizing one of the hooves, he inserts the point of the stick into the animal's flesh, just above the hock. I can just make out the sound of tearing, skin separating from muscle, as Moussa levers and heaves the stick forwards, upwards and from side to side until he is satisfied that it has penetrated far enough. He withdraws the stick and throws it down, wipes his palm across the torn flesh and, inhaling deeply, leans forward to put his mouth to the aperture. I recall how – as tiny children, crowded around the elders in Wadata as they prepared for *Eid al-Adha* – we used to laugh at this part of the process. Cupping his hands around his mouth, Moussa empties his lungs, breathing deeply into the ragged wound, then clamps a hand over the laceration while he inhales once again. It is always a strange sight, in spite of the fact that I have seen this ritual carried out countless times before; this man blowing air into the leg of a dead beast. When he is done he ties off the cord above the matted gore, spits, and drags the back of his hand across his mouth. The now bloated carcass is laid on its back, legs jutting outwards. The skin on the underside of the animal's belly is stretched taut as a *djembe*, as if one could beat a fine rhythm on it. Instead, Moussa picks up the knife and runs the steel blade from loin to throat in one effortless, sweeping movement. The skin parts like a soft new coat which has suddenly popped its buttons. Moussa flings the knife to one side, then, digging his fingers into the tissue and fatty layers of the creature's belly, he grips hard and begins to peel hide from muscle; tearing, pulling, wrestling a final struggle from this lifeless beast. Minutes later it is done; the creature lies in the bloodied dust, its leering, lidless eyes staring wildly at its own twisted pelt. Moussa stands up. Turns towards me. I can tell that he is pleased with himself. Indeed, he has made the task look easy. His shirt and trousers are saturated with blood, which is already beginning to congeal in the late afternoon heat, and a crust has formed on the contents of the bowl as it bakes in the glaring sun. Moussa stretches, then gently prods the flayed carcass with his toes. He pulls back his lips to expose his bad teeth. It takes a moment before I realise that he is smiling at me – if his expression could be called a smile. I avert my eyes for a second and, when I look again, I see him take the knife and hook it under the saggy flap of what was the ram's jowl. Then, silhouetted against the now softening light, he lifts the whole hide on the tip of the knife and, with his arm outstretched, holds it above his head in a triumphal, frozen gesture before flinging it towards me. It lands a short distance from my feet – buckled, twisted, spiritless.

I look up at the sound of Moussa's cackle. 'There's a new pair of sandals for you, *Little One!*' he says, and I know that not one part of this poor beast will be wasted. He removes the creature's innards, tying up the stomach and intestines with scraps of oily cord, and places them in two large plastic basins on the ground.

'Fetch me some water,' he tells me, cleaning off his knife against the shaggy coat of the *mouton*.

When I return, laden with two full pails, water sloshing over my shins and feet, Moussa has skewered the butchered beast to a cross made of rough timber in preparation for cooking later this evening. He props the timber cross upright and makes certain that it is secure. He dips his hands into one of the buckets, then tips the contents of both over the carcass, splashes of stained and muddied dust splattering over my feet and his. He laughs as I wipe the bridge of my right foot against the calf of my left leg. 'You ought to be well used to blood by now,' he sneers. He has a filthy look on his face.

He moves towards me. Holds a hand close to my face. I can see traces of gore and sinew and grit beneath his long fingernails.

I take a step backwards, but he catches me by the ear;

pulls me towards the slaughtered beast. Without letting go of
me, he stoops down so that I am bent almost double as he
dips a finger into the bowl and brings it towards my cheek.
I tug frantically, but he is strong and simply twists my ear
harder. My head is already full of echoes and bad music from
Doodi's beating. I reach out instinctively and clutch his
wrists but he twists at my ear again and yells – something
indecipherable – into the other. I drop my arms and gaze
wide-eyed at the wagging finger, lingering like a bloody-
headed snake before me and all the while the sound of my
tormentor's voice echoes inside my head and my belly is full
of rage and fear.

I close my eyes and spit as Moussa draws his finger across
my lips. In an instant he has released me, but only so that he
may swing the flat of his palm hard against my cheek. I let
out a cry, bring my hands up to cover my face, then spin
around on the balls of my feet in preparation for my escape.
I tilt my weight forward, only to realise that I have twisted
my left foot out of my sandal and, before I can run, Moussa
has grabbed hold of my *pagne* and yanked me back towards
him. He grips my chin hard, his cruel fingers sticky and steely
with the scent of blood. Now he brings his sweating face
close to mine again and for a moment I hope that he will see
not only fear and panic in my eyes, but my rage too.

'Monsieur! Monsieur!' I say.

'Monsieur! Monsieur!' he mimics.

'Monsieur, please. . .'

Locked in his grasp and unable to move my head, I roll my
eyes from side to side in a vain attempt to search for help.
For a moment, Moussa appears to read my mind, appears to
consider the possibility that someone, anyone, may indeed
come to my aid; he looks over my head, toward the compound gates, then, reassured once again that he is safe within
this compound, he digs his fingernails into my chin and
shakes my head vigorously.

'You spit at me? You spit at me, huh? You little bitch! I

take you into my home. Save you from a life of scratching around in the bush. Feed you. Clothe you. Give you shelter. And you spit at me? I take you from the squalor of your stinking little hole. . . pay mightily for the privilege, give you a proper home and you disrespect me like this?'

I see him through a curtain of tears, his loathsome, wavering face bearing down on me, his hot breath filling my nostrils and lungs. Again I try to speak, but only a pathetic mewling emerges from my lips.

'Don't stand there sobbing, you stupid girl!' he barks. 'You are a disgrace to your family! You are nothing!' He sucks his teeth. Curls his top lip up towards his nose. Says, 'It is little wonder that my wife beats you!' Then he pushes me away. Looks at his hand. Wipes it on his trousers. Tells me that he will deal with me later. That I should return to my chores.

I do not return to my chores. As I run past Yola emerging from the house, she calls out to me but, although through my tears I see her mouth form words, I do not actually hear her voice. Nor do I stop. For a brief moment, I consider running through the compound gates, following the traffic mustering beyond. Then, having considered the consequences of leaving the compound without permission, I bolt instead in the direction of the latrine house.

Before I know it, I find myself back in the branches of the Mgunga tree. My chest is heaving uncontrollably and mucus drips from my nose. I press down first on one nostril, then the other, and so clear the filth from my face. I wipe the tears from my burning cheeks with the palm of my hand, noticing again the bloody impression of Mousssa's hand on my forearm.

From beyond the storehouse (the closest thing to a home which my husband has provided for me) I can hear Moussa re-sharpening his knife on a stone. The stinging pain on my cheek and the raked furrows on my jaw are nothing to the pain I feel inside my head. And his words are seared into my brain. Filthy, brutal lies. I picture the humble yet neat home that my mother kept, and Bunchie before her, and my eyes well up once again.

Down below, out on Rue de Kongou, the traffic thunders by: cars and camels and *camions*, taxis and trucks, bicycles and carts all threading their way through the sultry early evening haze. Heavy-laden pedestrians, tatty refugees, and office workers in crisp white shirts scurry past our compound gates like termites, heading for Plateau, Gao or the shanties at Pays-Bas. Mixed with the diesel fumes and dust and stench of piss, there is a frenzy in the air this evening: a feeling of celebration and excitement as people prepare for *Eid al-Adha*. I steady myself on the curve of a great bough, with my knees drawn close to my face, and wonder how it is possible to feel so alone in such a busy place as Niamey, home to so many people.

At last, my breathing becomes more steady and my vision less blurred and I hear someone calling to me from Doctor Kwao-Sarbah's compound. When I look down through the branches, I see Khalaf, Doctor Kwao-Sarbah's guardian, peering up at me, his narrow face beautiful like a girl's, his skin the colour of sweetened coffee. Across his shoulders lies a long, ancient stick, rubbed smooth by toil and handling, over which he has hooked both elbows so that, in the ebbing light and shadow of the great tree, he seems as if skewered like Moussa's *mouton*.

'Mademoiselle! Mademoiselle! Why are you crying? What has happened?' he says, in his strange, syrupy accent.

'Nothing, Monsieur Khalaf,' I say. 'I am fine.'

He mutters – Tamashek words at first, which I do not recognise – and shakes his head. 'You are fine, yes. You are fine. And yet you weep. Why do you weep if you are fine, Mademoiselle?'

'I am thinking about my mother. I am sad about my brother Abdelkrim. I am missing my brother Adamou and my sister Fatima, that is all.' I claw at my eyes and feign a smile at the guardian.

Khalaf unhooks an elbow and uses his free hand to shield his eyes from the light behind me. He stares up at me with his mysterious, cat-like eyes and I feel myself bathed in his desire to be protective. At last he shrugs. Hooks his arm over the stick again and turns away to tend his animals or water his vegetables or do whatever he does.

I have not yet had time to settle back into my misery, when I hear the deep rumble of Doctor Kwao-Sarbah's vehicle pausing on the road. I look towards the Kwao-Sarbahs compound gates in time to see the vehicle enter in a flurry of metal and glass and rubber and dust, the engine giving a final roar before dying completely.

The rear door closest to the boundary wall is the first to be flung open and, to my delight, Candice wriggles out, dragging her school satchel behind her. I force myself to drive away my jealousy as I peruse her neat uniform and beautiful shoes. She spies me instantly and bounds across the compound towards the wall, a great smile on her face.

'Hey, Haoua!' she calls. 'You'll come to watch television at my house again later, won't you?'

'*Oui*,' I say, suddenly overcome with defiance and the desire to do so.

'Good! Well, we'll talk later. I must go and help now. We had to go shopping and it's getting late. My mother has prepared many lovely things to eat and my father has arranged for some musician friends of his from Zinder to come too. We will have a great time, Haoua!' Candice beams at me again before charging off towards her father's fine, white house, prancing like a young gazelle who has just found her feet.

There is to be no reprieve for me. No rest. No hiding place. When the stone hits my foot, I look down, expecting to see Doodi or Moussa. Instead, I note with surprise that Yola is my assailant.

362

'Haoua! Haoua! Come down here now!' She is hissing my name in an urgent whisper.

Without a word and ignoring the pain in my ribs, I swing down through the branches before, with a final lurch, dropping to the ground beside her.

'Didn't you hear the old witch calling you?' she says, reaching out with a licked thumb to daub at my dirty, tear-stained face.

I shake my head vigorously.

'Do you really want another flogging?'

I spare her the details of my most recent encounter with our husband.

She tugs at my pagne, straightens me up, before nudging me gently towards the house. 'You are to finish preparing the soup and couscous while Doodi and I go to greet Madame Kwao-Sarbah and offer her galettes and lady's fingers this evening.'

I stop and turn to face her, noticing only now that she has changed into her blue and cerise *pagne*, a great swirl of petals perfectly central and taut on her bulging belly. 'Can't I come too?' I whisper. 'Candice has already invited me, and we. . .'

She cuts me short. 'It is not up to me, Haoua. I'm only going with Doodi because she insists that I accompany her. I'd just as soon be seen dead as with her!'

She leans in towards me, glances over her shoulder and then says, in a conspiratorial voice, 'She's such an old whore, that one! Wheedling her way around these rich neighbours of ours. Pretending to be gracious.' There is a wicked glint in her eye as these words tumble from her mouth, like jagged rocks in a landslide.

I smile as she prods me gently in the small of my back, and continue trudging towards the entrance of the house.

Inside, Doodi is wearing her finest *pagne* and matching head wrap. Her wrists are heavy with finely carved bracelets and she wears a beautiful silver Agadez Cross around her throat.

With some reluctance I have to admit to myself that, even with her hard and wizened face, she looks quite elegant. For a moment I consider how she might have looked as a young bride, as new to this household – and to Moussa – as me. I remind myself that she at least was already familiar with Niamey. I wonder if she too was frightened and if she willingly endured Moussa's attentions or suffered them in silence. Then her cold eye falls upon me and I cease to care about the child that she once was, intent instead on my own preservation. She looks as if she is about to scold or lift her hand to me again, but then appears to change her mind. Instead, she speaks to Yola – indicates that she is impatient to leave. Then she tells me that I must be sure to have finished preparing the rest of the food before darkness falls; that she will send Yola back over to fetch it. She moves towards the doorway, Yola close behind her carrying a tray. She pauses to remind me that Moussa has forbidden me to visit the Kwao-Sarbahs' house at all this evening – as a punishment.

Despite Madame Yola's warning look, I cannot stop myself from asking the question. 'Punishment for what exactly, Madame?'

She moves towards me, her eyes squeezed thin, her voice full of venom. 'You are an insolent girl! You'd do well to learn some respect!' To my surprise, she does not strike me. After they have gone, I stand for some time in the centre of the cool, dark room, aware only of the relentless thrum of traffic on the road outside and the soothing stillness of the moment.

At last, I sneak a look out through the doorway to check that Moussa is not around. I am relieved to see that his bicycle has gone. When I am certain that it is safe, I make my way outside to the faucet. I turn the brass wheel and, miraculous as ever, the plumbing emits an initial belch followed by a gush of cool, clean water. I stoop down and let it cascade over my head, my neck and my aching shoulders.

Standing in the damp, darkened dust, I wash myself thoroughly; rub at my forearms, my feet, scrub at my neck and ears, scrape and poke at my encrusted nostrils, dab at my stinging face and work the cloth inside my *pagne*, under my arms and over my tender, swelling breasts. When I have finished, I stand upright, tilt my head first to one side, then to the other, and slap the remaining moisture out of my ears with the palm of my hand – just as my mother showed me when I was little. It occurs to me then that, although I have had my twelfth birthday and I am married and living in a busy, important city like Niamey, I do not really feel as a woman should, and still yearn to be held in my mother's arms.

I cross the compound to the storehouse, dry myself thoroughly and do my best to tidy up my hair and face. I check my reflection in my little cracked mirror, tilting it this way and that. I try to convince myself that I look fine. I peel off my soiled, damp and dirty *pagne* and take my old clean one from the nail on the back of the storehouse door. As I wrap it around my body I am startled by the peering eyes of a praying mantis which has fixed itself to my *pagne* and is now perched upon my thigh. Even though I know that the creature will not harm me, I gasp and pull the wrapper hastily from my body and shake the insect out of the door. When I have retied my *pagne* I cast an eye over Moussa's tools and bicycle parts and the cluttered, oily shelves. On the underside of one of the lower shelves I have pinned the photograph of my mother and brother with Efrance and Momi in the shanties. At night, when I lie awake on my bedroll, I gaze at this picture until the light fades completely or until sleep or exhaustion overtakes me. I bend down now and run my hand along the hidden surface, to check that the photograph is still there. To check that Moussa or Doodi have not discovered it yet and robbed me of this treasure also.

I straighten up and look around the storehouse once again. Candice has asked me to show her my 'room' several times, but always I have made excuses.

Now that I am clean again, I re-enter the house. I lift the lid off a large pot of Yola's *o jo jo* meatballs, the smell making my mouth water. Also on the table, covered in little scraps of cloth, are basins full of okra fritters, platters of roasted cassava, bananas, chunks of fresh pineapple and mango salad; food which I had rarely seen or tasted in Wadata. When I have finished preparing the couscous, I spoon it carefully from the pan into three smaller basins and place these on a plastic tray. I cover these too with cloth, then wipe my hands and step back from the table. Back outside, I wash cabbage heads, cauliflower, carrots, celery, tomatoes, peppers, onions, leeks. I return to the kitchen and chop the vegetables, wondering if I will even get to taste my spicy cabbage soup. I add ginger, laurel leaves, chillies and garlic, then fill the large pot with water and leave it to simmer.

Beautiful music drifts across from the Kwao-Sarbahs' compound: the plucked notes of a *gurumi* and the rhythmic beat of a *djembe*. I look out through the little window, as if to search for them, as if they might be there, floating in the air outside. Then I stack the dirty utensils carefully into a pail and go outside to the faucet again. As I am washing the pots and ladles, the music ends and, after a brief pause, the rich, deep tones of a man's singing voice begins. I look up into the branches of my Mgunga tree and the words, beautiful, tender, honourable, and with a hint of sadness, fall gently around me, like ripened fruits.

She is beautiful to the eyes, oh my Lord, and God gave her
    Gave her a breast new and green appearing like two balanced weights
    Gave her a waist lined with stripes
    Gave her a thigh with stretch marks reaching from her stomach to her knee
    Gave her calves beautiful and soft, you have never seen such creations

Gave her a heel like none a son of Adam ever walked on

The song gives way to sounds of laughter.

It is now that I decide to defy my husband: to pretend to be stupid; to pretend that I have misunderstood; to play deceit as ignorance. I decide not to wait for Yola to collect the food that I have prepared. I decide that I will take it to Candice's house myself. I persuade myself that, when darkness falls and the whole neighbourhood is immersed in the celebrations, my indiscretion may go unnoticed.

Candice is delighted to see me. I am waiting, tray in hand, outside the Kwao-Sarbahs' iron-framed mesh door when I see her coming down the tiled hallway accompanied by Feisha, the family's cook, a stern-looking woman with heavy scarification marks – like a meat griddle – on her face. Feisha looks me up and down, just as she does every time I visit Candice. My friend has changed out of her smart school uniform and into the most beautiful dress that I have ever laid my eyes on. Her smile reminds me a little of Miriam back home in Wadata, and for a moment I think about the journey we made together in search of Monsieur Longeur and his magic camera. Now, it is like thinking about a movie of someone else's life.

Candice holds the pleats of her dress out wide for me. 'It's from America,' she says, beaming, as Feisha swings open the heavy door to let me enter. 'Papa brought it back for me.' She bunches up the blue-green chiffon and invites me to touch it. I am almost afraid to do so, so delicate seems the fabric, like the wing of a butterfly, coated in magical dust, which, if touched, may spoil and thus lose the power of flight. I stroke the hem gently with the backs of my fingers. Then both of us giggle.

Feisha takes the tray from me and I realise that she is still staring at me – but in a different way now.

'You look nice too, Haoua,' Candice says.

I hang my head. Shrug. There is an old stain on the front of my *pagne*. I do not feel nice. Her words are just a kindness.

'*Walayi!* What have you done to your face, child?' Feisha says, balancing the tray on one arm and clutching my jaw with her free hand.

I do not answer. There is nothing for me to say.

Feisha sucks her teeth, then walks off with the tray towards the kitchen, mumbling under her breath as she goes.

I think that Candice might ask me about the marks on my face too, so before she can do so, I say, 'Can we watch television now?'

She nods. 'Of course,' she says. Hooking her arm through mine, she leads me down the wide hallway towards her bedroom. We have taken only a few steps when I hear the sound of conversation and I stop dead.

'What is it?' Candice says.

I grab at her forearm and whisper urgently, 'That old witch, Doodi. . . she must not find out that I am here!'

Candice shakes her head and pats my arm in reassurance. 'The women and babies are out in the rear garden.' She leads me through another entrance and down some steps into a large, bright room where Doctor Kwao-Sarbah and a group of men – including several musicians – are drinking tea and discussing politics.

'I tell you we're no better off than we were with Mainassara,' one of the guests says, as he tunes his *gurumi*.

'There's nothing democratic about slaughter!' Doctor Kwao-Sarbah says. He looks up as we cross the room and the conversation stops, leaving only the sounds of the ceiling fans swiping overhead and the padding of our feet on the cool, tiled floor.

'*Ça va*, Candice? Haoua?'

'*Ça va bien*, Monsieur,' I say, lowering my gaze.

'*Ça va*, Papa. Messieurs,' Candice says. 'Excuse us, please. We are going to my room to watch television.'

Doctor Kwao-Sarbah nods, smiles warmly at us, then turns back to his friends and to the discussion.

As we enter another, smaller hallway, Candice turns to me and whispers. 'Do you know who that was?'

'Who are you talking about?' I say, distracted, overwhelmed by these surroundings.

'The one with the *gurumi*. The old one.'

'I wasn't really looking.'

'That was Monsieur Boukia!' Candice says, her eyes wide with pride and amazement. She sees that her words mean nothing to me. 'The great poet from Tchin Talaradin! You must have heard of him, Haoua?'

I shrug.

'He is my father's most honoured guest this evening.'

I nod; a response which seems to frustrate Candice.

'I'd have thought that your wonderful Monsieur Boubacar would have talked to you about Boukia!' she says, a little sulkily.

My friend's room is a wonder to me. She has a proper, raised bed, softer than any I have ever seen or sat on before, and a whole wall of shelves lined with books and fine dolls and brightly coloured plastic toys. Posters of French and Malian musicians line the walls and in one corner is a huge silver radio with black speakers. Across the room sits a beautiful polished wooden dressing table, with drawers and a large mirror and Candice's very own television set. Through the window grille, we can see Madame Kwao-Sarbah entertaining her guests around the flickering fire of a clay oven in the garden. There is a lot of laughter. I can just make out the forms of Doodi and Yola in the rapidly fading light. I pick up a book which has been lying on Candice's bed. It is an atlas, a lot like the one which Monsieur Boubacar used in my school in Wadata. As I flick through the pages, I am startled both by the familiarity and the strangeness of the object I hold in my hands, and I am reminded once again of my home village. Already it seems as if it only ever existed in a dream.

'This is where Papa bought my dress,' Candice says, pointing to a city called Boston in the United States of America.

I nod. 'My brother wanted me to go there, to learn how to become a teacher.'

Candice looks at me in a curious way and for a moment again I think she is going to ask me about my bruises. We have been friends for only a short time but she seems to sense that I do not feel like talking much today. 'You will be a fine teacher, Haoua,' she says. 'Papa wants me to be a doctor, like him, but I don't know. . .' She takes the book from me and sets it on the little table beside her bed. She gives me one of her great smiles, then says, 'Shall we watch television now?' Without waiting for a reply, she moves over to the set, presses a button and the screen flickers into life. Then she turns, crosses the room and bounces on to the bed beside me. We giggle again and then settle down to watch. I don't mind what is on, ever. I am simply fascinated by the images and by what I can learn from them. Sometimes I think that television is better even than books.

At first the image pitches and rolls, but Candice jumps up and fiddles with the set until the picture settles. An *anasara* man is working on the engine of a motorcycle, by the side of an asphalt road. As he does so, he talks to himself. *Would you believe it?* he says, and *Of all the stupid. . .* He shakes his head and throws down his wrench. The words, in French, do not really fit the shapes that his mouth forms.

Candice and I look at each other and laugh, while from within the television we hear a great many other people laugh too.

It is dark and the man stretches and yawns. He has shiny black hair and a strong, square jaw-line. He is wearing blue jeans and a white shirt, which is covered in stains. He looks at his watch and then says, *Well, Ralphie, I guess you really did it this time!* He looks up and down the road and then towards the camera. He is obviously very disheartened. He crosses to a tree and unhooks a black hide jacket from a branch. Then he walks into a forest and begins looking around. He pushes through heavy foliage and comes into a clearing. He looks around again, nods, then sits down on the ground with his back resting against a broad tree trunk. He puts his hands behind his head and closes his eyes. As soon as he closes his eyes, we hear the hooting of night birds, a great cacophony of crickets and bullfrogs and all manner of howling beasts. After a while the man opens his eyes and stares wearily. He now looks very irritated.

Candice looks at me, rolls her eyes and gives me a great smile and I put my hand to my mouth and snigger. Just as I do so, the invisible audience gives a little snigger too.

The animal noises intensify and the man now looks angrier still. He sits forward, stretches his neck muscles and moves his head from side to side, then puts his hands in front of his chest and quickly draws them outwards, in a cutting action. His arms now form a cross shape. He says, *Hhhhhey!* loudly, and all at once the animal sounds stop and there is complete silence in the forest. The man nods, leans back against the tree and then closes his eyes again, and almost immediately the silence is broken again by the chorus of laughter from the invisible audience.

Candice and I are rolling around on her bed, giggling and slapping each other playfully, when I suddenly become aware of another sound. I turn my head and realise that Feisha has been calling to us over the clamour of the television set. Her face is like a storm and she points to the set and indicates that it should be turned off.

Candice bounds from the bed in an instant and I stand up too, sensing that something is wrong.

'It is that man!' Feisha says. She looks at me. 'Your *husband*! And he is not happy!'

Immediately, my heart is seized by fear. I am on my feet in an instant and spare only a fleeting moment to glance towards Candice. I see the concern on her face, notice how quickly the happiness we were sharing just a few moments earlier has been snatched away from us both. Then, with my heart racing, I put my head down and follow the billowing blur of Feisha's *pagne*: back along the tiled hallway and into the large living room where Dr Kwao-Sarbah's guests are still enjoying his hospitality. As we pass through and Feisha excuses us, I can feel a dozen pairs of eyes boring into me, but I am determined not to look up. I am almost as mortified as I am scared. The floor passes beneath me like the never-ending desert. To help me cross it, I try to concentrate on the slap of Feisha's sandals on the hard tiles. All at once, I become aware of a gentler padding behind me, a lighter step. Without turning around, I guess that Candice is following us.

At last we reach the steps rising from the living room to the outer hallway. As we climb to the top and turn right into the brightly lit corridor, I become aware of the silhouetted figure of a man – an elegant man, not the mean, scruffy form of my husband – lingering just inside the screened doors.

Doctor Kwao-Sarbah looks at me and, while attempting something close to a smile, rolls his eyes. 'Ah, Madame Haoua,' he says, 'Monsieur Moussa is here to escort you home.'

His words sound awkward, full of unease. He has never addressed me as 'Madame' before.

For my part, I feel frightened, deeply embarrassed, and perhaps I even dare to be a little angry.

My husband stands on the veranda with a chew stick in his mouth.

I can tell immediately that he is irritated by the way he rolls it from side to side in his teeth. His clothing is still covered in gore and blood. He is babbling something, fawning before Candice's father but, I am certain, determined that he will not be shown up by me.

'I'm sure she simply misunderstood, Monsieur Boureima,' Doctor Kwao-Sarbah says.

I steal a glance towards Candice, perhaps in some vain attempt to seek help, but the look on her face confirms that she too feels helpless and fearful of my situation.

As I shuffle along towards the doorway, I keep my head down, not daring to look Moussa in the eye. Doctor Kwao-Sarbah puts his big, clean hand on my shoulder and gently guides me on to the veranda. Before me, I see Moussa's ugly feet, his long, yellow toenails still splattered with the fine spray of the *mouton*'s blood. I hear him suck his teeth and hiss the word, *Walayi!* Then, as Doctor Kwao-Sarbah takes his hand off my shoulder, Moussa reaches out and clutches my arm tightly. He is clever enough not to apply too much pressure with his fingers – not yet – but I am instantly aware of a certain amount of discomfort. He draws me firmly towards him and then steers me down the steps of the Kwao-Sarbahs' veranda. My head is reeling. I am frantically trying to think of excuses.

'I apologise for this intrusion, Doctor.'

'Really, as I have said, it is no intrusion,' Doctor Kwao-Sarbah says. 'Candice has grown very fond of your dau. . .' He checks himself. Gives a little cough. 'Perhaps you'll come back with your young wife later on, Monsieur? And join Mesdames Doodi and Yola?' But, like seeds sown on barren ground, his words fall, lost behind us as Moussa marches me towards the gates.

No sooner have we rounded the corner of the Kwao-Sarbahs' compound than I feel a sharp pain in the muscles of my upper arm. Moussa has gouged his filthy fingers into my flesh, and now proceeds to fling me towards our own compound. He catapults me through the entrance and I stumble and fall awkwardly to my knees as he releases his grip momentarily. On the street there are few passers-by now, and those who do notice us choose to ignore us. For a moment I dare to hope that Khalaf, the Kwao-Sarbahs' guardian, whose eyes have just bored through my husband as we passed him, will follow us. But we are alone.

I am trying to get up from the ground when I feel the fabric of my *pagne* tighten around my throat and shoulders.

'Get your lazy hide off the ground, you little whore!' Moussa spits, wrenching me upwards with one hand.

Before I can even put a foot forward, he shakes me, like a dog with a rat, and pushes me again, jabbing at my shoulder blades with his rough fingers. My blood is racing. For a moment I consider protesting. Offering some reason, some excuse, as to why I have disobeyed his word. As he swings me around the gatepost, and slams me against the block wall, I decide that it is pointless to protest, and resign myself to my fate. What will happen will happen.

'I'll teach you to embarrass me! I'll show you who is master of this house!' He repeats such phrases over and over again, between slaps and punches and kicks, his spittle peppering my face each time he opens his mouth. He grabs my jaw. Shakes my head from side to side. Breathes his foul breath right into my nostrils and squeezed open mouth. His eyes are slits of fire and rage. He is a demon, a devil, from whom there is no escape for me. 'You pathetic little insect!' he hisses. 'Do you really think the doctor's daughter gives a damn about the likes of a stupid little bush girl like you? An ungrateful, ignorant, worthless little nobody who does nothing to justify the food I struggle to provide for her?' He grabs at my chest again. Pinches my left breast with his sharp fingernails. Then he takes hold of the neckline of my *pagne* and shakes me again from side to side. He lowers his head and summons a hideous, animal-like growl from deep within his gullet before discharging a sickening lump of phlegm at my feet.

I yank myself away from his grip and take a step into the air, my foot failing to propel me at all as I am wrenched back by Moussa once again. I see the flat of his silhouetted hand like a raggedly black crow as it moves towards the side of my head. I make a poor attempt to avoid the blow and barely feel it as it connects; Doodi has covered my body in a mantle of pain already, so that Moussa's frenzied attack renders only bruise upon bruise and little in the way of new shock to my flesh. Bent over now, with my hands above my head and my knees ground into the dust, I feel somehow that I am witnessing this beating, rather than enduring it – from the vantage point of my Whistling Mgunga tree, or from the kitchen window, or on television. And what I see is a small, frightened girl being slapped and kicked and shaken mercilessly by a screaming bully whose words have become a formless rant; just another assault on already ringing ears. The vision makes me angry. Reminds me of watching Souley and her awful friends as they picked on smaller children, me and my classmates powerless to help, having already been warned that we would face a similar fate if we breathed so much as a word to Monsieur Boubacar or the other teachers at Wadata.

Perhaps it is really this image that now causes me to throw my head back, look defiantly into the eyes of my attacker and smile through bloodied teeth.

This is not happening to me.

This girl is dragged across the compound, her kicking heels ploughing deep, broken furrows in the cooling sand.

Her assailant has buried his fingers in the bedraggled cornrows of her hair. His jaw is set; his brow creased with fury. Without looking back, he trails his victim towards the storehouse. He kicks open the door – swears as it bounces back and strikes his elbow.

The girl has taken hold of the door frame and is gripping it tightly with both hands.

The attacker barks something at her; then, still clutching her hair, boxes her ears with his free hand.

She grits her teeth and grips the frame still harder, until a series of kicks to the ribs forces her to let go with one hand. With the other she clutches frantically at the rough timber, the look of desperation on her face suddenly replaced by one of anguish as her fingers are crushed against the doorframe by the sole of her assailant's sandaled foot.

As the girl finally releases her grip, her attacker grabs her wrist and flings her into the storehouse. She stumbles forwards, trips over her neatly-rolled bedding and crashes into a stack of oil drums and a wheel-less bicycle frame. She fights back tears, coughs, quickly wipes the back of her hand under her dripping nose and then scrambles to her knees. She puts a hand flat against the oil-stained floor and tries to push herself to her feet but, feeling the weight of a body much larger than her own bearing down on her and realising that she cannot break away, she succumbs at last to her assailant, who once again has a fistful of her hair.

He pushes her forward. Presses her face into the dust. Pins her down. Grapples with her *pagne*; wrenching and tearing at the fabric until he has exposed her.

Then – as the girl sobs and reaches back with one small, broken hand in a futile attempt to thwart him – he forces her legs apart and ruts her like an animal.

When Moussa leaves the storehouse, I remain on the filthy floor for quite some time, oblivious at first to the surge of pain building up within me. Then, as my head begins to clear a little, it strikes: burning my gut; searing behind my eyes, between my legs; stabbing at my knuckles and the oddly crooked fingers of my left hand.

I realise now that I was wrong not to fear this man more. That Doodi's wrath is just a gentle breeze compared to the rage that Moussa has just unleashed on me. This is not the first time. But it is the most vicious. He has hurt me more than ever before. I know that this time I am really damaged.

I am lying on the ground with my knees drawn up to my chest, my torn *pagne* clamped tightly between my calves. I taste my own blood, mingled with dust and grit, and smell the stench of the slaughtered beast, transferred from Moussa's loathsome body to my own. Outside, the light has all but faded, yet I can still make out the shapes of bicycle parts and tools strewn all around me; knocked from their shelves or from a nail on the wall in the recent struggle. I recall the morning, soon after I was brought to live in Niamey, when Yola came to me and helped me arrange the space; reorganised Moussa's clutter, so that I could at least sleep here in relative comfort. I wonder if Yola is aware that Moussa has retrieved me from the Kwao-Sarbah house – if she even knew that I was there. I try to raise my head a little to listen for her but, in truth, I know that neither she nor anyone else will come to help me.

With my good hand, I brush some of the dirt from my cheek. I push myself up, so that I am in a crouching position. I lean forward and attempt to bear some weight on my left hand but an intense pain, like none I have ever experienced before, tells me that I cannot. I bring the grazed, misshapen form close to my face, then, gritting my teeth to fight back the tears, I wedge it into my right armpit. With great effort I roll myself on to my bottom and lean back against the cool wall. Each breath I take is punctuated by a fresh wave of pain in my side. I remember my father telling me the story of how once, as a boy, he had climbed one of the great upside-down trees near our village and fallen, awkwardly, cracking several ribs. For weeks afterwards he endured great pain, with every step he took, every movement he made, even when he laughed. I am certain that I too have damaged ribs. I wonder if I shall ever laugh again.

With my eyes closed, my mind again starts to wander back to Wadata. I see my mother's face. Bunchie's. I see little Fatima, Adamou, Abdelkrim, Miriam. Then, as another surge of pain catches me, I let the images go and, attempting to control the discomfort, concentrate instead on trying to breathe calmly and steadily.

The door creaks open and the light from a kerosene lamp swings across the floor of the storehouse. I open my eyes and see Moussa before me once again.

'You must draw me a bath, girl,' he says.

I bury my head into my chest and do not answer. 'Do you hear me, girl?'

I shake my head without looking up.

'Hey!' he says. 'Get up and do as I tell you. I can't go back over to the good doctor's house looking like this.'

Although I still do not look at his face, I can tell from the tone of his voice that he is smirking. I put my right hand on the back of my head and ignore him until his fingers jab me on the shoulder. 'Hey!'

I throw my head back so suddenly that Moussa takes a step backwards, much to my satisfaction. 'I won't do it!' I shout, angry with myself for allowing great tears to well up in my eyes again, but hopeful that I have warned him off.

But instead of relenting, he bends down, leans his face in close to mine again and says, calmly, slowly, and with great menace, 'I don't mind doing that all over again, you know. It's your choice, Little One.' The light from the lamp flickers and reflects in the whites of Moussa's bulging eyes. He sucks his teeth. Stands upright. Shrugs. Gives a little laugh and then turns and leaves, taking the lamp with him and leaving me in the darkness with my pain and blubbering rage.

Seized by cramp deep within my belly, I wince again, my nose bubbling and leaving a filthy trail of slime on the shoulder of my already sullied *pagne*. I peer at it in disgust, through raw eyes, and realise that I feel sullied inside too. I put my good hand between my legs; feel Moussa's ooze, cold, on my flesh and hair. I contemplate the task that Moussa has set for me: the lugging of numerous pails of water from the faucet outside to the tin bath inside the house, followed by several more to the big pot on the gas burner in Doodi's kitchen to take the edge off the cold. I long to cleanse myself. To scrub and scrub at my skin. To peel it off, smooth it flat against the stones of the great river; scrub it clean with soap and rhythmic fervour, while the songs of my mother and grandmother swoop and dip around my head like swallows, heady with living.

I know that Moussa will return soon if he does not hear or see me going about my work. When I finally manage to get to my feet, I stumble, and have to catch hold of the edge of a workbench in order to reach the door of the storehouse.

The weight of the slopping bucket causes me great discomfort, jarring my ribcage and under my arms, and bouncing off my knees and shins. Usually I can carry two at once but, when I attempt to lift a second with my left hand, the pain takes me by surprise, shoots all the way up my arm and causes me to cry out. The pail falls to the ground, bending oddly, collapsing under its own weight and reminding me of the recently slaughtered beast. As its contents seep into the dust, my mouth fills with the foul taste of bile. I barely make it to the latrine house before I retch.

When there is nothing left inside me and my belly feels like a rag wrung dry, I return to the faucet, splash water over my face, retrieve the pail and wait for it to be refilled, my head lolling with fatigue and pounding with the rhythmic certainty of the pestle.

When I enter the house, Moussa has already dragged the bathtub over the bare concrete floor into the centre of the living room. He sits in near darkness, with only a small towel to hide his nakedness, listening to the radio and smoking a cigarette.

I shuffle to the kitchen, take the large pan from the shelf and place it on the burner. I fill the pan from the bucket, the strain of lifting it above my waist causing me great discomfort. I turn on the gas, take the matches and attempt to strike one with hands that will not stop trembling. After several attempts, the match ignites and I leave the water to heat. As I make my way through the living room, Moussa rises from his chair and steps out in front of me, the towel sliding to the ground. I sidestep him quickly, without looking at either his manhood or his loathsome face and the smirk that I know it will be wearing. He laughs as he moves towards the door. I make another journey to the faucet. And another. And another. When I am satisfied that the bath is full enough, I begin to add the hot water. As I carry pan after steaming pan from kitchen to living room, I find myself thinking sinful thoughts; of vengeance, retribution, but push them quickly to the back of my mind. I pour the scalding water into the tub and dip my hand in to mix it. I am in no doubt that Moussa will complain: it is not warm enough, not full enough, or there has been grit in the bucket, but I am too exhausted to do more.

I kneel beside the bath, submerge my broken hand in the water and draw the other slowly backwards and forwards across the surface. For a moment, I consider submerging my head too; imagine sucking the water deep into my lungs and escaping this place forever.

The sound of the bedroom door banging shut brings me to my senses and I gather up the empty buckets and pans as Moussa enters the living room again. He does not thank me and I do not wait to see if my preparation is to his satisfaction. I return the buckets to their place outside by the faucet and then, having rinsed the cooking pans, take them back inside to Doodi's kitchen. When I have stacked the utensils neatly, I pass quietly towards the main entrance once more, eager to return to the storehouse and my stained bedroll; to embrace sleep and so, hopefully, begin the long process of healing.

I stop at the main door, aware of the sound of snoring. I look back over my shoulder and, through the gloomy light of the kerosene lamp, see that my husband has fallen asleep in the now filthy water, his head tilted back against the lip of the bathtub, his mouth open, his jaw slack, his scrubbed skin strained taut around his windpipe. For a moment, I think that I may vomit again.

My head reels as I trudge across the compound. My bare feet are as heavy as tablets of salt. I drag them through the moon-cooled sand, past Moussa's carelessly strewn skinning tools, and across the cold, blood-soaked patch near the corral. It is a short distance to the door of the storehouse, but I might just as well be travelling to Zinder or Agadez.

The sounds of music and laughter drift across the wall from the Kwao-Sarbah compound, mingling with a chorus of crickets, subdued motor traffic and other peoples' parties, and I stop; stand still in the damp sand, to listen or not listen. The smell of roasting meat tugs at my gut, catching me unawares, and I steady myself, tilt my head back to gulp at the cool night air, and gaze up at a raggedy canopy of stars, dulled by the city's electric lights; a poor imitation of the sky above Wadata.

Mademoiselle Sushie Varrelmann	Haoua Boureima
Vision Corps International	Niamey Civil Prison
Tera Area Development Programme	Avenue de Seyni
C/O BP 11504	Kountche
Niamey	Niamey
Republic of Niger	Republic of Niger

19th September, 2000

Dear Mademoiselle Sushie,

With God's grace this letter will find you in good health. My friend, Gisele, says that it will be a miracle if it reaches you at all, and that if it does so, it will be heavily censored, but I pray that if such a miracle is necessary then God will provide it; though I have tested Him and angered Him greatly.

Please do not be alarmed by the things I am about to tell you, because my main purpose in writing is to ask you to send me news of my brother Adamou and my sister Fatima. I have been here now for eight months and have had no news from my village. I want you to know how I came to be in this place, because you helped me and my family in so many ways.

As you may have heard, Mademoiselle, they say that I murdered my husband. What I tell you now is the truth as I remember it, as God is my witness. I can remember deep despair, and that this man hurt me badly, and it is true that on the evening of his death I had witnessed him slaughtering a beast to celebrate *Eid al-Adha* and so I would have known exactly where to find the knife and how to use it. But as to actually cutting my husband's throat, I have no recollection of this whatsoever. There seems to be no doubt that I committed this sin, but I can assure you, Mademoiselle Sushie, this was never my intention, and if I could alter events I certainly would. My lawyer, Monsieur Hubert Soglo, who was sent here shortly after my detention and who has visited only once since, briefly, says that this is a clear case of provocation, but days turn into

weeks and months and still my case has not been heard. To me
he seemed disinterested from the beginning.

During the time that I was living with Doodi and Moussa,
I have to confess that I sometimes felt great anger towards
them, but if I had planned to kill anyone I could have
poisoned their food, or put a snake in Doodi's cooking pot, or
a scorpion in Moussa's pocket. But, apart from the fact that
such thoughts occurred to me only in passing moments of
rage and humiliation, I would not have put Madame Yola and
her unborn child at risk, since during my darkest hours she
showed me some kindness. I am happy to say that my ribs
and fingers have mended fairly well, although my hand is
now a little twisted and gives me some discomfort. Most of
the time I try to pretend that that part of my life never
happened.

One of the chief guards here, Kwame, a vile man who is
not much liked by the inmates, has promised that my letter
will reach you if I treat him 'favourably', but I intend to find
some other means of getting it to you, because I will not allow
anyone to defile me ever again.

Gisele hates all of the guards fiercely and makes no secret
of the fact. She particularly dislikes Kwame. In fact I think
she would gladly take his life if she could get away with it. In
some ways we have a lot in common. The first time I met
Gisele, she stroked my face and said, 'Someone has been
cruel to you, child, eh?' and when I told her that it was me
who had been cruel and that I had killed my husband, she
laughed and told me that she had killed three of her tormentors with their own guns. They were Touaregs who had kept
her as a slave in the mountains for many years. Gisele can
get away with a good deal more than most of the inmates
here, because Kwame has a particular dislike for Touaregs
(there are many of them in the male wing). He is quite in awe
of Gisele in fact. I might still be in leg irons were it not for
her. After I arrived here my shackles were left on for several
days, (I am considered a 'dangerous detainee', due to the

nature of my crime) but Gisele demanded that Kwame remove them. And he did. Even behind bars, Madame Gisele is a formidable woman, and Heaven help anyone who makes an enemy of her. Of course, Kwame did not miss an opportunity to assault me as he was removing my leg-irons – running his scaly fingers underneath my ragged *pagne* – but I thank God that both He and Gisele were watching over me, and that she barked at Kwame like a hyena and spat in his face. This earned her several jabs in the ribs with a baton from one of the other guards, but Kwame looked more shaken by the incident than she did.

There are two other women sharing my cell: Veronique and a Hausa woman known as Desire. They have been quite kind to me too, although they seem to be wary of Gisele. Veronique has experienced a great deal of discomfort due to an infected cut above her eye. Gisele says it happened in a fight in the shower block a couple of weeks ago. Veronique is an angry woman. She says that the police were looking for her boyfriend, and when they could not find him, they arrested her. She has been in custody here for three years.

She goes back and forward to the court, just to sign papers, but she is never tried. There is a kind young doctor, who calls to dress her wound now. He was visiting our wing one day to treat a woman who had given birth (the baby was stillborn) and Gisele had prevailed on Kwame to bring Veronique's eye to his attention. The first time he came to our cell I was sitting on the floor on a slab of cardboard, examining a scrap of old newspaper that one of the guards had discarded. As he carefully bathed and dressed Veronique's wound, he smiled at me and asked me if I could read, and then ordered the guards to unlock the cell door so that I could visit the prison's tiny library and take some air outside in the compound. Later, Desire and Veronique teased me about this man, but I ignored their silly talk.

The next time the doctor came, he brought us a little parcel of guavas and a bundle of books tied together with string, but when we were queuing at the shower block the guards stole the fruit from the plastic bags in which we keep our few belongings hung on nails in the crumbling walls. I knew that he had intended the books for me because none of my cell-mates can read, but I felt guilty about looking at them at first because each time I brought them out we were all reminded of the sumptuous fruit that we did not get to eat. The doctor also gave me a prescription for some medicine for my injured hand, but, of course I have no money to pay for it. If you come from a poor family, life can be hard here. If you have no friends or family, it is worse still. A woman who works in the kitchen with Gisele told me that a boy died in the male wing a few weeks ago because he did not have any money for medicine. He had been sick for three months but received no medical attention.

The guards have to put up with a great many complaints from the inmates, as the director of the prison never makes himself available for discussion. In fact, the guards are suffering too, because although their food is better than ours, and their quarters less squalid, they nevertheless are prone to the same skin diseases as we inmates, not to mention infestations of lice and other parasites. There are two pails supplied to each cell: one for use as a toilet and the other for drinking water. Ventilation is not good and there is a permanent stench that cannot be escaped. We have limited access to proper toilet blocks, but these are shared with the male wing and we have to clean them with our bare hands. We are each supposed to receive a cake of soap every second week but, in reality, it is far less often. Gisele sometimes returns from the kitchen with extra supplies that she gets from the male prisoners and shares with us. I do not ask her how she gets them, but such goods are a form of currency here and some people resort to any means to get them. The food here is very poor, so when Gisele brings an extra potato or some fish paste back to our cell, it is almost like a celebration. We receive one meal a day, usually rice or millet paste or gari or beans. Extra food can be supplied to those whose families live locally. Desire's sister occasionally brings her flat breads, which she shares with us, thankfully. Drinking water is not a great problem, although we have to share a single cup and washing properly after cleaning the toilets is very difficult.

Many of the prisoners here have been on remand for many months. Some for years. So, you will understand, Mademoiselle, how fearful I am that my case might be forgotten too.

It was a great joy for me to learn of the little library housed in the male wing of the prison but it is difficult for me to gain access. We have electric light in the cells, but this is switched on only between six and seven each evening. The women's wing has been supplied with two sewing machines, but one of these has broken recently and there are no technicians here to repair it. We are supposed to get outside for exercise each day, but sometimes the guards keep our cells locked for several days at a time – especially if Kwame is off duty. Thankfully, this does not happen often, as most guards work six or seven days a week. On the two occasions that it happened since I arrived here, Kwame received such a barrage of abuse from Gisele's vicious tongue that he took it out on the two younger guards who had been on duty during his absence. He lashed out at them with his baton, making sure that Gisele was watching. Of course this did not help anyone in the long run because the two guards in question then took it out on us in turn. In fact, late one night last week, a young woman, two cells up from ours, was molested. She is too frightened to issue a complaint. This incident has worried me a great deal, as you can imagine, (I still have nightmares about Moussa) but I have some comfort in that Gisele is usually not far away. Without her protection, I would fear for my sanity, if not my life.

My grandmother, Bunchie, used to say, 'You think the sun sets on your compound alone? Stand up and see how it falls on the entire village!' How my heart aches when I pass the old people's cells, on the way to the shower block. There are, perhaps, eight or nine very old women and approximately half as many old men. There is even a married couple. Mademoiselle, I tell you, I thank God that my grandmother never ended up in such a place as this, for these poor souls are truly standing on the shores of Hell. It is not easy for any of us to survive here, but some of these old ones have been here for a very long time – one for over thirty-five years! Most have been on remand for so long that they have given up on their cases ever being heard. Some cannot even remember how they came to be here. Their clothing is little more than rags, and one poor old man (who claims to be one hundred and twenty years old) has a terrible lump at the base of his belly. Another, who is unable to walk, lies on his mat all day long. Gisele says that a group of lawyers from the city have approached the director and urged him to form an amnesty committee in order to help such prisoners. They seem to have been abandoned by their families, or perhaps they have simply outlived them. They have only death to wait for. At home, in Wadata, such people would be treated with great respect but, locked away in their offensive-smelling cells, they are a sorry sight. I try not to think of them, at night when I am alone with my thoughts, otherwise I might picture myself still here as an old woman, wizened as a walnut, and drive myself mad.

Contact with prisoners from the male wing is very limited, but Gisele's position in the kitchen means that she hears a great deal about what goes on there. Currently, the director is asking questions about a recently arrested inmate from Nigeria who claims that a wound on his chest was inflicted by the gendarmerie during his arrest. He says that he came to Niamey to visit his family, and was minding his own business, looking for his brother in the market, when he was arrested. We also heard that just yesterday another inmate, said to be mentally incapacitated, tried to kill his cellmate.

We women do what we can for each other when we are sick,

but the men here are helpless: their cells are overcrowded and barely big enough for them to lie down at night, and tuberculosis, pneumonia and anaemia bother many of them. Many of the inmates are HIV positive too. A good deal of these illnesses go untreated, so that at night it is difficult to rest, what with the constant coughing and moaning and the frequent cries of prisoners jolting themselves awake from their terrifying dreams. Until recently the prison had a sick bay room, but several prisoners managed to escape from this area, so the facility is now used only for storing bodies until they can be taken to the mortuary.

A few days ago we were disturbed by a great deal of noise coming from the male wing, and discovered that some of the men were rioting because their clothes had been taken from them before detention, while a European had been allowed to keep his clothes on. The trouble was dealt with quite quickly, but the sounds of men being flogged outside in the main compound was more frightening still. The following day, the *anasara*'s lawyer returned with his country's ambassador to collect the prisoner. As they passed through our wing, the lawyer spied me in my cell, curled up in a ball on Gisele's mat, and spoke to me kindly through the bars. He asked me my name and age and what my crime had been, and told me to be strong and that he would make some enquiries with the director and notify the Nigerien Women's Defence Association of my presence here. As yet I have heard no news. But I live in hope and imagine myself one day reunited with my brother and sister.

One of my few pleasures here is to be able to read to the other inmates. Very few of the women can read, so, what with my ability and Gisele's friendship, I find that I am treated quite fairly by most people, especially now that the television set is broken. (Once again, Kwame has said that if I am 'nice' to him, he will ensure that it is repaired.) But the library has very few books and I am not permitted to visit it often. However, I was much in demand recently when a prisoner, who had been transferred back to Niamey from Cotonou in Benin, paid dearly for posting a flyer on the library door. It read:

'On the eve of the third millennium, at a time when humanitarian organisations have even recognised the rights of animals, there still exist cells of torture in this country, an example of what is Democracy in Africa.

There are limits that dignity imposes on the submission of the most patient spirits.

There are limits to the human state that marks the difference with the animal state...'

He went on to complain about lack of food, poor hygiene and corrupt staff and when a group of Kwame's colleagues attacked him with batons, he continued to curse and protest and called one of the guards a 'son of a whore', at which point the guard shot him dead. Gisele says that the case has been brought to the attention of the authorities, but that the dead man's family have decided not to pursue the matter in court, presumably because they are too poor to do so.

I seize any opportunity I can to get out of the cell, if only for a short while. The stench is deeply unpleasant, what with the plastic pail that serves as a latrine for all four of us and the overflowing dustbin in the corner that cries out to be emptied. In all, there are ten proper toilets and two shower blocks serving the entire prison. I have counted fifty-seven of us in the female unit (this includes minors, such as myself, and babies born in the prison). Gisele says that there are over eight hundred males here too. When the guards are carrying out their duties as they are meant to, we are allowed out of our cells before the men. But despite the fact that our numbers are much fewer there is always a great rush to be first in the queue. And even when they are working, the showers have to be cleared of fat black cockroaches in the morning. When we step onto the concrete floors we have to be careful not to tread on these creatures, and the sound of them scuttling away into the corners, to escape the cold water, is very unsettling.

We are plagued by lice and mosquitoes. The lucky few possess – and manage to hold onto – mosquito nets but, for the rest of us, night time is a time of irritation. Veronique managed to bribe one of the guards for the loan of some scissors, and has been busy cutting our hair short, to combat the lice.

Sometimes I stand on an upturned Sprite crate to look through a small, barred window, high up in the wall of our cell, and watch the male prisoners exercising, or praying in the courtyard, but this occurs perhaps only once or twice a week; like us, the men are kept locked in their cells most of the day.

Still, I find my existence here preferable to living as a slave to Moussa and Doodi. I have asked God for His forgiveness for my questioning His wisdom, and for my weakness and desperation which led me to take another's life. But perhaps He will only help me if I first forgive my earthly father for the misery he has brought upon our family. And yet I cannot.

Mademoiselle Sushie, I ask you, as a true friend: if you can help me in any way, please do so. I remember and cling to your words of encouragement as I hold on to life itself. Of course, I long for freedom, but even news about my brother and sister (or Miriam, or a few words from you or our friends in Ireland) would give me strength. I fear no one even knows or cares that I am here. I had hoped that Madame Yola might have visited me, but most probably she has not been allowed to do so by Doodi. My neighbours in Yantala, the Kwao-Sarbahs, had a letter delivered here, but it was so censored when I received it that it might just as well have been only the envelope!

My thoughts are with you often, Mademoiselle. I pray for you and your family. I pray too that you have not already returned to America and that this letter will reach you soon. I apologise for the length of my letter and for the untidiness of my writing. It has been quite a while since I have had the opportunity to hold a pencil at all.

I would like to thank you for all you have done for my

family and me. Sometimes, still, I dare to dream that one
day, just like Monsieur Boubacar I will stand proudly in front
of a classroom full of children, and teach them many things,
and that the spirits of my mother, my grandmother and my
brother will draw near me and smile.

God bless you. Affectionately yours,
Haoua Boureima

Mr Noel Boyd   Vision Corps International
Member No. 515820   443 Ashley Old Road
Ballygowrie   Manchester
Co. Down   M10 4NB
N. Ireland   United Kingdom
BT22 1AW

12th May, 2001
Dear Mr Boyd,
Thank you for your letter regarding the
marriage of Haoua Boureima, and also for
your willingness to continue to support VCI's
child sponsorship scheme. I have enclosed
details of a boy from Niger, as requested in
your letter.
   I appreciate your feelings concerning this
matter and want to assure you that we are
endeavouring to change the thinking of the
people in these cultures by stressing the
importance of education for girls in our
projects. However, this will take time and
perseverance, but hopefully the children in
our care will start to think differently and
eventually be instrumental in changing

cultural attitudes.

Unfortunately the girls who marry cannot continue their education because a girl at school is not allowed to get married; therefore reluctantly we have to release them from the project. It might be helpful for you and your daughters to know that the initial stage of marriage is just a celebration and although the child will live with the in-laws, there is sometimes a waiting time for her to mature before being given to the husband.

I hope you find this information helpful. Once again, many thanks for your continued support.

Yours sincerely
Winifred Quinn
Supporter Services

ACKNOWLEDGEMENTS

This is a story that I first suggested my daughter try to write for a school project. I am thankful that she found such a life unimaginable. The story, however, would not go away. Such stories – featuring real individuals rather than fictional characters – continue to unfold every day, not just in Africa but all over the world.

I would like to thank the following people for their support, expertise, encouragement and enthusiasm in helping ensure that this particular story has been told:

Eilish Bergin, Dr Joseph Boyle, Viv Burnside, Craig Campbell, Dr Drew Cannavan, Alan Cargo, Cate Conway, Rosemary Crawford, Panos Dalakas, Beverley Green, Ed Handyside, Kerry Hiatt, Ian Lewis, Anne McReynolds, Jim Maginn, Steve Mallaghan, Stafford Mawhinney, Ciara May, Clare May, Kate Nash, Amuda Oko-Osi, Nuray Onoglu, Jan Orr, Naana Otoo-Oyortey, Mona de Pracontal, Naomi Reid, Catherine Smith, Hope Smith, Katie Smith, Adam Weston, Hazel Weston, Holly Weston, Dr Paul Young.

The following texts were immensely useful and I am indebted to their authors:
Africa on a Shoestring by Geoff Crowther
Le Niger Aujourd'hui by Jean-Claude Klotchkoff
The Samaka Guide to Homesite Farming by Colin M. Hoskins
Marriage in Maradi by Barbara M. Cooper

West African Lilies and Orchids by J. K. Morton
Myths and Legends of the World by Geraldine McCaughrean/Bee Willey
When Sheep Cannot Sleep by Satoshi Kitamura
Africa: Traveller's Literary Companion by Oona Strathern

I am also grateful for the support of Ards Arts, The Arts Council of Northern Ireland, The Tyrone Guthrie Centre and staff at The Africa Centre, London.

F⇒RWARD
Safeguarding rights & dignity

The Foundation for Women's Health, Research and Development is an African Diaspora women's campaign and support charity that campaigns against child marriage and seeks to advance sexual and reproductive health and rights as central to the wellbeing of African women and girls. If you would like to know more about the work of FORWARD please visit www.forwarduk.org.uk.

GW

ABOUT THE AUTHOR

Gavin Weston is a visual artist and writer who lives in his native Ireland and is a former aid worker in West Africa. *Harmattan* is based both on first-hand experiences of Niger and its people and his continued involvement as an aid sponsor.

MORE BESTSELLING INTERNATIONAL FICTION FROM MYRMIDON

Mrs Lincoln
Janis Cooke

(May 20th)
Mrs Mary Lincoln admitted today – from Chicago – Age 56 – Widow of ex-President Lincoln – declared insane by the Cook County Court May 19th – 1875.
Patient Progress Reports for Bellevue Place Sanatorium.

Incarcerated in an insane asylum after committal proceedings instigated by her own son, Mary Lincoln resolves to tell her own story in order to preserve and prove her own sanity and secure her release. But can she succeed?

"...this epic drama exerts an exceptional pull... an impressive, engrossing and moving piece of historical imagining and characterisation." Holly Kyte, *The Sunday Telegraph*

"...a tender and thoughtful portrait of a 19th century woman severely misunderstood... *Mrs Lincoln* unfolds with plenty to inspire and is all the more poignant for a timely arrival." Sarah Emily Miano, *The Times*

"As I read it, I wept. I cannot recommend a book more... a very powerful novel." Pat Schroeder, President of the Association of American Publishers

"...one of those rare books that turns the reader into an admiring fan of both the author and her subject. You feel a compulsion to urge others to read it." *USA Today*

"...a gripping tale of scandal, war, intrigue, and séances...for sheer page-turning fun, Mary is perfect." *San Francisco Magazine*

"...thoughtful and thoroughly enjoyable...Mary is not only a fascinating read, but also a touching love story." *Chicago Sun-Times*

"Moving and with an almost palpable compassion for its subject, yet clear-eyed and even humorous at times, this is a book I will be re-reading." *Historical Novels Review*

"Mary is a daring novel about the inner life of Mary Todd Lincoln; an intelligent, sympathetic, well-written work of speculative fiction." Kevin Baker, author of *Paradise Alley* and *Strivers Row*

ISBN: 978-1-905802-21-0

SUMPTIOUS AND CAPTIVATING TALE
OF 12TH-CENTURY CHINA

Taming Poison Dragons
Tim Murgatroyd

"A riveting story."   John Green, *The Morning Star*

Western China, 1196:
Yun Cai, a handsome and adored poet in his youth, is now an old man,
exiled to his family estates. All that is left to him are regrets of a growing sense of futility and helplessness and the irritations of his feckless
son and shrewish daughter-in-law. But the 'poison dragons' of misfor-
tune shatter his orderly existence.

First, Yun Cai's village is threatened with destruction by a vicious civil
war. His wayward second son, a brutal rebel officer, seems determined
to ruin his entire family. Meanwhile, Yun Cai struggles to free an old
friend, P'ei Ti, from a hellish prison – no easy task when P'ei Ti is the
rebels' most valuable hostage and Yun Cai considers himself merely a
spent and increasingly frightened old man.

Throughout these ordeals, Yun Cai draws from the glittering memories
of his youth, when he journeyed to the capital to study poetry and join
the upper ranks of the civil service: how he contended with rivalry and
enmity among his fellow students and secured the friendship of P'ei Ti.
Above all, he reflects on a great love he won and lost: his love for the
beautiful singing girl, Su Lin, for which he paid with his freedom and
almost his life.

Yun Cai is forced to reconsider all that he is and all that he has ever
been in order to determine how to preserve his honour and all that he
finds he still cherishes. Only then can he summon the wit and courage
to confront the warlord General An-Shu and his beautiful but cruel
consort, the Lady Ta-Chi.

ISBN: 978-1-905802-37-1

E BOOK AVAILABLE

Breaking Bamboo
Tim Murgatroyd

I, the great Khan Khubilai, order my armies to advance by sea, river, land and mountain. Those who serve us by persuading the treasonous to submit to our just rule shall be rewarded. . . those who persist in foolish opposition shall endure every woe imaginable. . .

Central China, 1264. . .

When Mongol armies storm into the Middle Kingdom, the descendents of Yun Cai (*Taming Poison Dragons*) are trapped in a desperate siege that will determine the fate of the Empire. Guang and Shih are identical twins, one a heroic soldier idolised by the city he defends, the other a humble doctor. In the midst of war, jealous conflicts over Shih's wife and concubine threaten to tear the brothers apart. Enemies close in on every side – some disturbingly close to home. Can the Yun family survive imprisonment, ruthless treachery and Kublai Khan's bloody hordes? Or will their own reckless passions destroy them first?

Breaking Bamboo is the second instalment of a trilogy set in Song and Yuan Dynasty China, exploring love, war and poetry and charting the trials and adventures of the Yun clan. The third instalment, *The Mandate of Heaven*, will be published in hardback in September 2013.

RELEASED IN PAPERBACK JUNE 2013

ISBN 978-1-905802-42-5

E BOOK AVAILABLE

The Gift of Rain
Tan Twan Eng

Penang, 1939:
Sixteen-year-old Philip Hutton is a loner. Half English, half Chinese and feeling neither, he discovers a sense of belonging in an unexpected friendship with Hayato Endo, a Japanese diplomat. Philip shows his new friend around his adored island of Penang, and in return Endo trains him in the art and discipline of aikido.

But such knowledge comes at a terrible price. The enigmatic Endo is bound by disciplines of his own and when the Japanese invade Malaya, threatening to destroy Philip's family and everything he loves, he realises that his trusted sensei – to whom he owes absolute loyalty – has been harbouring a devastating secret. Philip must risk everything in an attempt to save those he has placed in mortal danger and discover who and what he really is.

"A powerful first novel about a tumultuous and almost forgotten period of history." *Times Literary Supplement*

"A remarkable book. . . about war, friendship, memory and discipline." Ian McMillan, BBC Radio 3

". . .a stunning debut which heralds the author's arrival as a major literary talent." *The Southern Reporter*

"A rich, absorbing epic." *The Times*

"Anyone who thinks the novel is in decline should read this one." *The Philadelphia Enquirer*

"Haunting and highly evocative. . . a deeply moving tale." *Cape Times*

"Tan Twan Eng spins out his complex, nuanced story with skill and grace. His style is assured and clear, his imagery powerful, often beautiful." Rick Sullivan, *Adelaide Advertiser*

". . .a remarkable debut saga. . . measured, believable and enthralling." *Publishers Weekly*

"A masterful achievement." *The Age*, Melbourne

ISBN: 978-1-905802-14-2
AVAILABLE AS AN E BOOK

The Garden of Evening Mists
Tan Twan Eng

On a mountain above the clouds in the central highlands of Malaya lived the man who had been the gardener of the Emperor of Japan. . .

Teaoh Yun Ling was seventeen years old when she first heard about him, but a war would come and a decade would pass before she would journey to see him. A survivor of a brutal Japanese camp, she has spent the last few years helping to prosecute Japanese war criminals.

Despite her hatred of the Japanese, she asks the gardener, Nakamura Aritomo, to create a memorial garden for her sister who died in the camp. He refuses, but agrees to accept Yun Ling as his apprentice 'until the monsoon' so that she can design a garden herself.

As Yun Ling begins working in the Garden of Evening Mists, another war is raging in the hills and jungles beyond. The Malayan Emergency is entering its darkest days: communist guerrillas are murdering planters, miners and their families, seeking to take over the country by any means, while the Malayan nationalists are fighting for independence from centuries of British colonial rule.

But who is Nakamura Aritomo, and how did he come to be exiled from his homeland? And is Yun Ling's survival of the Japanese camp somehow connected to Aritomo and the Garden of Evening Mists?

"Elegant and atmospheric." Kate Saunders, *The Times*

"Tan writes with breath-catching poise and grace." Boyd Tonkin, *The Independent*

"Complex and powerful . . . a sophisticated and satisfying novel that explores the ways time reconfigures memory." *Sunday Times*

"A strong, quiet novel." *New York Times*

"Grace and empathy infuse this melancholy landscape of complex loyalties enfolded by brutal history, creating a novel of peculiar, mysterious, tragic beauty." *Kirkus Reviews*

"Readers in search of spectacular writing will not be disappointed." *Book Dragon*

HARDBACK 978-1-905802-49-4
Limited Edition Signed, Slip Case HARDBACK: 978-1-905802-73-9
TRADE PAPERBACK: 978-1-905802-62-3
AVAILABLE AS AN E BOOK.